ALLEN COUNTY PUBLIC LIBRARY

3 1833 04162 3122

Cynthia Harrod-Eagles won the Young Writers'
Award with her first novel, THE WAITING GAME,
and in 1992 won the Romantic Novel of the Year
Award. She has written over fifty books, including
twenty-two volumes of the Morland Dynasty – a
series she will be taking up to the present day. She is
also creator of the acclaimed mystery series featuring
Inspector Bill Slider.

She and her husband live in London and have
three children. Apart from writing her passions are
music, wine, horses, architecture and the English
countryside.

Visit the author's website on
http://www.twbooks.co.uk/authors/cheagles.html

D1021677

MAR 2 1 2002

Also in the *Dynasty* series:

DYNASTY

9

The Flood-Tide

Cynthia Harrod-Eagles

WARNER BOOKS

A *Warner* Book

Copyright © Cynthia Harrod-Eagles 1986

The moral right of the author has been asserted.

First published in Great Britain in 1986
by Macdonald & Co (Publishers) Ltd
First Futura edition published in 1986
Reprinted in 1988
Published by Warner Books in 1993
This edition published by Warner Books in 1994
Reprinted in 2000

All rights reserved.
No part of this publication may be reproduced,
stored in a retrieval system, or transmitted, in any
form or by any means without the prior
permission in writing of the publisher, nor be
otherwise circulated in any form of binding or
cover other than that in which it is published and
without a similar condition including this
condition being imposed on the subsequent purchaser.

All characters in this publication, save those clearly in the
public domain, are fictitious and any resemblance to real persons,
living or dead, is purely coincidental.

ISBN 0 7515 0646 X

Printed in England by Clays Ltd, St Ives plc

Warner Books
A Division of
Little, Brown and Company (UK)
Brettenham House
Lancaster Place
London WC2E 7EN

SELECT BIBLIOGRAPHY

J. R. Alden   *The American Revolution 1775/1783*
T. S. Ashton   *An Economic History of England*
Asa Briggs   *The Age of Improvement*
H. Butterfield   *George III, Lord North, and the People*
Dorothy George   *London Life in the Eighteenth Century*
Herbert Heaton   *The Yorkshire Woollen and Worsted Industry*
William James   *The Naval History of Great Britain*
Stanley Loomis   *Paris in the Terror*
Dorothy Marshall   *English People in the Eighteenth Century*
J. C. Miller   *Origins of the American Revolution*
David Ogg   *Europe of the Ancien Regime*
R. E. Prothero   *English Farming Past and Present*
M. J. Sydenham   *The French Revolution*
S. Watson   *The Reign of George III*
P. Wells   *The American War of Independence*
Basil Willey   *The Eighteenth Century Background*

·THE MORLANDS OF MORLAND PLACE·

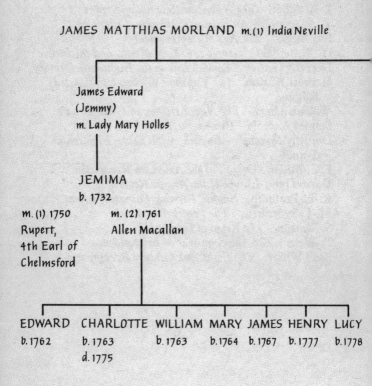

JAMES MATTHIAS MORLAND m.(1) India Neville

James Edward
(Jemmy)
m. Lady Mary Holles

JEMIMA
b. 1732

m. (1) 1750   m. (2) 1761
Rupert,   Allen Macallan
4th Earl of
Chelmsford

EDWARD   CHARLOTTE   WILLIAM   MARY   JAMES   HENRY   LUCY
b. 1762   b. 1763   b. 1763   b. 1764 b. 1767   b. 1777   b. 1778
          d. 1775

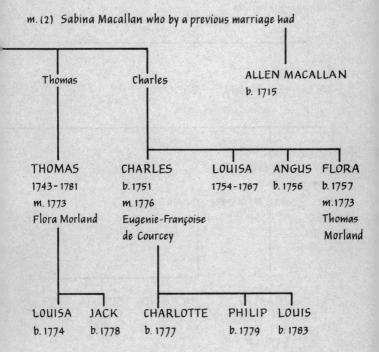

m. (2) Sabina Macallan who by a previous marriage had

Thomas   Charles   ALLEN MACALLAN
b. 1715

THOMAS
1743–1781
m. 1773
Flora Morland

CHARLES
b. 1751
m. 1776
Eugenie-Françoise
de Courcey

LOUISA
1754–1767

ANGUS
b. 1756

FLORA
b. 1757
m. 1773
Thomas
Morland

LOUISA
b. 1774

JACK
b. 1778

CHARLOTTE
b. 1777

PHILIP
b. 1779

LOUIS
b. 1783

·THE CHELMSFORD FAMILY·

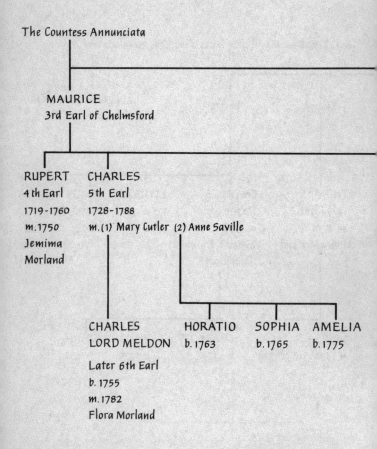

The Countess Annunciata

MAURICE
3rd Earl of Chelmsford

RUPERT
4th Earl
1719-1760
m.1750
Jemima
Morland

CHARLES
5th Earl
1728-1788
m.(1) Mary Cutler (2) Anne Saville

CHARLES
LORD MELDON
Later 6th Earl
b.1755
m.1782
Flora Morland

HORATIO
b.1763

SOPHIA
b.1765

AMELIA
b.1775

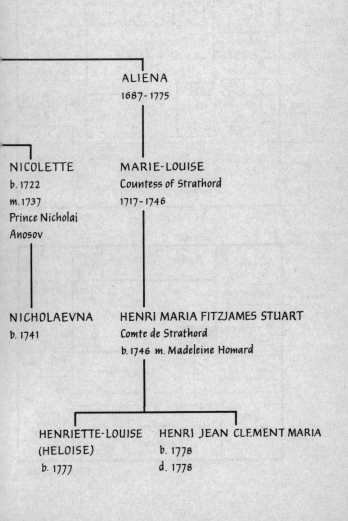

ALIENA
1687–1775

NICOLETTE
b. 1722
m. 1737
Prince Nicholai
Anosov

MARIE-LOUISE
Countess of Strathord
1717–1746

NICHOLAEVNA
b. 1741

HENRI MARIA FITZJAMES STUART
Comte de Strathord
b. 1746 m. Madeleine Homard

HENRIETTE-LOUISE
(HELOISE)
b. 1777

HENRI JEAN CLEMENT MARIA
b. 1778
d. 1778

Morland Place in 1789

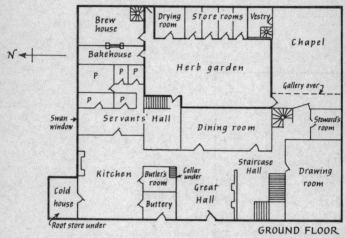

GROUND FLOOR

N ←

Brew house

Drying room

Store rooms

Vestry

Bakehouse

Chapel

Herb garden

P P P P P P

Gallery over

Swan window

Servants' Hall

Dining room

Steward's room

Kitchen

Butler's room

Cellar under

Great Hall

Staircase Hall

Drawing room

Cold house

Buttery

Root store under

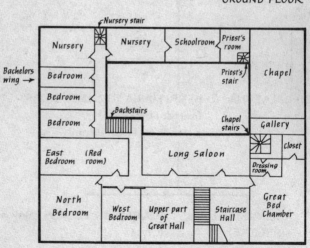

FIRST FLOOR

Nursery stair

Nursery

Nursery

Schoolroom

Priest's room

Bachelors wing →

Bedroom

Priest's stair

Chapel

Bedroom

Bedroom

Backstairs

Chapel stairs

Gallery

East Bedroom (Red room)

Long Saloon

Closet

Dressing room

North Bedroom

West Bedroom

Upper part of Great Hall

Staircase Hall

Great Bed Chamber

To S. E. H.:
Quod spiro et placeo, si placeo, tuum est.

3 1833 04162 3122

BOOK ONE

The Lily

This, sure, is Beauty's happiest part;
This gives the most unbounded sway;
This shall enchant the subject heart
When rose and lily fade away;
And she be still, in spite of time,
Sweet Amoret in all her prime.

Mark Akenside: *Amoret*

CHAPTER ONE

The kitchen at Morland Place was dim and full of shadows, even on a bright September day, for it was built when a northern gentleman's house had also to be his stronghold, and its windows were few and small and high up. In the great arch of the chimney the fire glowed fiercely under the household's biggest pots, making the heat almost intolerable, and the crouching scullery maid worked the bellows with a kind of despairing energy, as the sweat dripped off the end of her nose and onto the stone flags.

It was the very peak of the plum harvest. Jemima Morland, mistress of the house, found herself remembering the time the moat had risen and flooded the kitchen, as the plums advanced on all sides in a yellow, crimson and purple tide. The children brought them in heaped in baskets like rubies for an Egyptian queen. They lay piled on tables and dressers and on the floor; odd escaped ones winked tauntingly from corners; and every available hand cut and stoned them, jammed, preserved, pickled and dried them, set them to ferment into wine or linger into brandy.

The air was full of the smell of their ripeness, mingled with hot sugar, and delinquent wasps, frantic with greed, gorged themselves on the fruit until, drunk with plum juice, they fell soddenly to the floor on their backs. The household's youngest boy, aged three, was under orders to scoop them up into a jar and take them outside – Jemima could not like to see them killed when they were drunk, and therefore possessed of as much happiness as a wasp can hope for. The youngest boy evidently thought this a piece of womanish folly by his air of lofty amusement as he passed her each time with a full jar. She did not like to inquire what he did with them outside.

The sweat was beading her upper lip, and she raised a bare forearm to dab it, for her hands were red with plum juice. Her hair was escaping in maddening wisps, and under her calico skirt her feet were gratefully bare on the cool flags. She thought how horrified her mother would have been to see her now! Lady Mary had been half-sister to the great Duke of Newcastle, and had never let anyone forget it. As far as Jemima knew, she had never once set foot in her kitchen. As for going barefoot, rolling up her sleeves, and helping, Lady Mary would probably sooner have been hanged at Tyburn.

'Mother! It's not fair!' A familiar, strident voice upraised in fierce complaint preceded Jemima's ten-year-old daughter Charlotte into the kitchen. Charlotte was big for her age, with long, strong bones, a glow of health in her freckled face, and curly hair that defied discipline. She had all the restless energy of a colt, and a head that seethed with plans, usually for forbidden activities. She was quick-tempered, clever, untidy, and passionately devoted to her twin, who held the other side of the loaded basket she was bringing in.

Poor little William presented a very different aspect. Jemima often thought that Charlotte must have absorbed all the strength when they were together in the womb, for William was small, pale, thin, and meek-tempered. Jemima was agreeably surprised to have kept him to the age of ten for he was frail, troubled with coughs and headaches, and likely to take any illness that was around. The smallest knock bruised his delicate skin; if cut, he bled frighteningly; his digestion was uncertain. And yet he adored Charlotte, and followed her like her shadow, climbing trees to fall out of them, swimming in rivers to catch cold of them, eating wild sloes and crab apples because she recommended them, having herself a digestion that could have thrived on horseshoe nails. He got himself cut and gashed and bitten and stung in her wake, and wept far more when she was punished for leading him into danger than he ever did for his own pains.

'My dear Charlotte,' Jemima said with amused exasperation, 'you look as though you had been doing battle.' Charlotte's dusty face was drawn into a frown, her head was like a gorse bush, her mouth, hands, clothes and even her hair were stained with plum juice.

'It isn't fair. William and I are doing *everything*, and the others aren't helping at all. James has hardly carried three pounds, and now he's swimming in the moat and won't do any more, and you never let me swim in the moat.'

'He's only six, dearest, and he's probably tired. He has worked hard for a little one,' Jemima said, avoiding the more delicate question of swimming. It did seem hard to her that a girl should not be allowed to do some of the more pleasant things that boys did, but it was the way of the world. 'And surely Edward is helping.' Edward, her oldest son, aged eleven, was immensely conscientious.

'Well, he *was*,' Charlotte said, reluctant to concede any point. 'But now that silly Anstey boy has come, and he says he is his guest and he has to take care of him.' John Anstey was the son of a neighbouring merchant, and Edward's best friend, and they were to go to school together next year, something to which Edward looked forward with great excitement, since he had always been educated at home before by Father Ramsay. 'And all John Anstey wants to do is moon over Mary. Imagine, over Mary!' Charlotte's voice took on a tone of horror. Mary, a year younger than Charlotte, was in every way different from her, and had an almost squeamish horror of dirtying her clothes or hands. 'Mary isn't any use at anything. She can't ride properly, or climb a tree, and all she's done all day is sit on a seat in the orchard primping and primming, and then the Anstey boy comes and takes her basket from her and says she shouldn't be getting herself hot and dirty. It's awful.'

Jemima couldn't help laughing at Charlotte's outrage, but as her frown grew ferocious, she added hastily, 'Mary's ways are very different from yours, my love.'

'But you let her off tasks that you make me do, Mama, and never rate her as you do me. It isn't fair!'

The eternal cry of childhood, Jemima thought, though in her own childhood it could never be uttered aloud. There were many in the household who thought she allowed Charlotte to speak too freely to her, but she had been so oppressed and miserable herself at Charlotte's age that she could not be so strict with her.

'You and Mary are made of different clay, my love,' she said mildly. 'It will not serve to try to make the same vessel of you both. We shall all stop in a little while for some dinner, in any case. Would you like to help carry it out to the orchard?'

Charlotte allowed herself to be pacified. 'May I ring the bell, too, Mama!'

'Yes, if you like. William, you're looking pale. Do you have the headache?' She stretched her hand out for him, and he came to her side and leaned briefly against her.

'Not really,' he said. 'Not very much.'

Jemima ruffled his pale hair and laid the back of her hand against his hot forehead. 'No more picking for you after dinner. Poor little William. I wish you had some of Charlotte's strength.'

Because her hand was in the way, and perhaps also because her mind was on other things, she missed the expression of anguish that crossed her son's face.

It was not an elegant feast, such as her mother might have consented to preside over; and certainly Lady Mary would never have so far forgot her dignity as to sit on the grass in the orchard, even had her silken clothes and rigid hoops and stays allowed it. Jemima had been one of the first ladies in the neighbourhood to adopt the new calico and cotton fabrics for common wear, and in the summer especially they were a boon, not only being cooler and allowing more freedom of movement, but being infinitely easier to wash than woollen. In the country, except on formal occasions,

Jemima wore no hoops and only the mildest of stiffening, and she was able to settle herself in the place of honour on the grass before the spread cloth, under the old medlar tree.

Father Ramsay came through the trees to join her, looking cheerful and relaxed after his morning's picking. 'It is a good thing to change one's labour from time to time,' he said, rolling down his sleeves. He had bits of broken twig in his hair, and smuts on his face, and his breeches were tied at the knee with string. Jemima smiled at him affectionately. 'It makes one appreciate the advantages of one's normal pursuits. I have enjoyed the fresh air and sunshine, but my hands!' He turned them over and back and shook his head sadly.

'Come and sit down, Father. Here, you shall have this bucket for a seat,' Jemima offered. 'I must make you comfortable, or you will leave me for an easier position. When I think of all the tasks I force you to undertake, I tremble. How should I ever manage wtihout you?'

Father Ramsay upended the bucket, examined it, and lowered himself, grimacing, onto it. 'My dear Jemima, if I had thought the post of chaplain here meant only saying Mass and tutoring the boys, I should not have taken it. What is in the jug?'

'Buttermilk. Will you have some?'

Father Ramsay smiled his sphingine smile. 'You know my opinion of buttermilk,' he said. 'I'll wait for the ale.'

Charlotte and William brought it a few moments later, in two large jugs, and from the other direction Edward and his friend John Anstey joined them, escorting Mary, who managed to make it seem that the picnic spread under the trees had been arranged entirely for her benefit. At nine years old there was already nothing left of the child in Mary, and looking at the perfect little woman, Jemima could not remember that she ever had been a child. She was very pretty, with perfectly regular features, even teeth, black curling hair and blue eyes with dark lashes; she wore her clothes with an air, was neat and particular, and had a great conceit of herself. Jemima regarded her with something like wonder, that she could have borne a creature so unlike herself. It was Nature taking her revenge, she thought sometimes: Mary was a daughter such as Lady Mary would have liked Jemima to be.

'Ah, there you are, boys. Sit down. Come, Mary, it's only a dead leaf. Don't make such a fuss, child. Father Ramsay, will you cut the pie?' Her family gathered round and helped themselves from the laden cloth. Though not elegant, the food was ample and good: one of Abram's pork-and-liver pies, if not quite the size of a cartwheel, at least the size of a cartwheel hat; and venison pasties, and the morning's bake of bread with slices of brawn and cheese and cold beef; and sticky brown bricks of gingerbread, and, since plums would have been almost an insult, baked apples, the first of the year's harvest. 'Now, do you all have what you like? But where is Flora?'

'Here I am, Cousin Jemima – and my little Jamesie,' Flora said, coming from the direction of the kitchen garden. James was looking pale and thoughtful, besides grubby about the mouth.

'Oh dear, what has he been doing now?' Jemima said, gathering her youngest son to her side. He had lost all his infant chubbiness and was growing wiry, though he was small for his age. He would be like his father, she thought, small and compact; like him in character, too, from what she remembered of Allen in his young days: reserved and curiously self-sufficient. James could happily spend a whole morning alone playing with two twigs and a beetle, utterly absorbed in some inner world of his own.

'He was eating radishes,' Flora said.

'Oh dear. How many?' Jemima asked.

'There were an awful lot missing from the row. I think they're mostly up now though,' Flora said delicately.

'Oh dear. Well, come and sit down, Flora, and have some dinner,' Jemima said apologetically. James settled unconcernedly under her flank and reached for a venison pasty, and Flora, declining the offer of the bucket from

Father Ramsay, took her other side. She was the daughter of Jemima's youngest uncle, Charles, the botanist who in the intervals of his 'herborizing' expeditions abroad had married the daughter of a Glasgow shipowner. There had been four children: young Charles, who was following in his father's footsteps and already making a name for himself, Louisa, who had died young, Angus, and Flora. Aunt Mary had died when Angus and Flora were very young, and since Uncle Charles was so much abroad, Jemima had offered the two youngest children a home at Morland Place. Angus, who was seventeen, was at university in Edinburgh. Flora was sixteen, and ravishingly pretty, and now that Uncle Charles was also dead, having succumbed to the bite of some lethal insect in the South American jungle, she regarded Morland Place as her permanent home. She had been a great help and comfort to Jemima, and in the past few years had provided her with a much-needed female companion. The life of the mistress of Morland Place was often a lonely one.

'Baked apples! How lovely,' Flora said as she surveyed the feast. 'I'm glad it's not plums. I don't feel as if I should ever be able to look at one again.'

Jemima laughed. 'And to think only a fortnight ago we were so delighted with the first pies and junkets.'

'It is rather all or nothing with plums,' Father Ramsay said. 'Flora, will you take ale or buttermilk?'

'It's a pity the cider isn't ready yet,' Jemima said, 'but it will be another week at least.'

'We must be sure to put a cask aside for Cousin Thomas to take back with him,' Flora said eagerly. Jemima smiled inwardly. It the past few weeks Flora had managed to bring his name into a surprising number of conversations. 'It is quite dreadful to think of him drinking green water, thick with living things. The privations our sailors endure are enough to break one's heart.'

'I dare say Thomas manages to get something else to drink from time to time,' Father Ramsay said drily. 'And as to privations – remember last time he was home on

21

leave, he was but a lieutenant. I imagine the hardships of even a junior captain are far less. But doubtless he will know how to value your concern for him, Flora.'

Flora blushed painfully, and Jemima came to her rescue.

'We are all very proud of him, to be made "post" at such a young age. He is evidently well thought of at the Admiralty.'

'He evidently has friends in high places,' Father Ramsay amended. 'For almost the most junior captain on the List to be given command of a new-built ship, not even out of dry dock yet, argues something more effective than virtue. He is rising more swiftly even than his father.'

Thomas's father, Jemima's Uncle Thomas, had had a spectacular career in the navy, rising to be the youngest Rear Admiral in the fleet, before yellow fever carried him off on the West India station. Since Thomas's mother was also dead, he, like Flora, now regarded Morland Place as his home. Seeing Flora about to defend her cousin, Jemima interposed again.

'It is wonderful that he is to have such a long leave with us this time. Though I daresay sailors and sailors' families are always at odds about the desirability of time spent on shore. If the winds serve he should be here by next week. I dare say he will write from Portsmouth to tell us when he arrives. He will have things to do there before he comes north.'

'Sailors can always find things to do in Portsmouth,' Father Ramsay said. 'Perhaps he may never come north at all.'

'Of course he will,' Jemima said hastily. 'The old *Hydra* is to be broken up, and his new ship is not finished yet, so he will have plenty of time to spend with us. Father, have one of the pasties. They are excellent.'

Jemima's dinner was interrupted by one of the grooms from Twelvetrees, where the stud horses were kept.

'Mester 'Umby says 'at one of th' visitin' mares is lookin' proper dowly, mistress, an' could you come?' he chanted breathlessly, rosy with embarrassment at having to speak

22

before the entire assembled family. Jemima sighed inwardly, but Humby, the head man, could be relied upon not to send for her on a trifle.

'Which mare is it?' she asked.

'Her that come in from Wetherby this mornin',' the boy said, and grew more confident. 'Mester 'Umby were right put-about, and sent her straight to the isolation box. She's proper poorly lookin'. Mester 'Umby says—'

'Yes, very well, I'll come,' Jemima said. There were six visiting mares at Twelvetrees, sent to be covered by the Morland stallion, Artembares, besides valuable stock of their own, and an infectious disease could wreak havoc there. 'Go up to the house, boy, and tell them to saddle my horse, and then go straight back and tell Master Humby I'm on my way.' The boy scuttled off, and Jemima got to her feet. 'I must go up and change. One failing of calico is that one cannot ride in it. Flora, will you take my place here?'

'Oh Mother, Mother,' Charlotte cried in an agony, having been alerted by the word 'mare' to a conversation about horses, her ruling passion. 'Please can William and I come? You said he must not work any more this afternoon, and a ride will be the very thing for him, to cure his headache.'

'And have you the headache too, Charlotte?' Father Ramsay asked, amused. Jemima looked at him, wondering why he should even consider trying to separate the twins.

'I think the harvest is well enough advanced to be able to spare the little ones, don't you, Father?' she said. 'We shall finish all today in any case.'

'Without a doubt,' he said obligingly. 'They have worked well this morning.'

'Run up to the house, then, and change. And be quick – I will not wait for you.'

The stables at Morland Place were almost empty now, sad contrast to their heyday when Jemima was young. Her own mare, a handsome Morland chestnut named Poppy, three rough ponies on which the children had been taught to ride, and two stout cobs for common use, were all that were kept in. When Allen comes home, she often said to herself, things will be different. She tried not to think about it too much, for she missed her husband so much that if she dwelt on his absence she would unfit herself for all her numerous tasks.

Charlotte was strangely silent as she and William, on Mouse and Dove, followed Poppy out of the yard. She sat well on the pony, making it walk out in a way that no one else could manage. She must have a proper horse soon, Jemima thought, and remembered her own excitement when her father had given her her first horse, the beautiful black gelding Jewel, long since gone to the Elysian fields.

'Mother,' Charlotte said at last, in a voice unusually subdued. 'Mother, why do you want to be rid of me?'

'Rid of you? Whatever can you mean by that?' Jemima checked Poppy, who was eager to gallop, to let the ponies come alongside her.

'Well, when Alison was brushing my hair just now she said to Rachel that you'd have a hard job to get rid of me when the time came.' Her voice was small, and she looked up at her mother with something like fright. 'Are you going to send me away? Me and not William?' Jemima's heart melted.

'Oh, my dear, it's only servants' talk. It doesn't mean anything.'

'But she meant *something*,' Charlotte persisted with perfect truth.

'She meant that I should have a hard job to find you a husband, because you are not like Mary,' Jemima said, deciding honesty was the best response.

'But I don't want a husband. And I don't want to be like Mary. You don't want me to be like Mary, do you?'

'I want you to lead a happy and useful life, my love. You must be married one day, and I'm afraid husbands like

24

their wives to be like Mary – at least, to have some of her qualities.'

'But why must I be married? I don't want a husband. I've got William. Do I have to get married, even if I don't want to?'

'I would not force you to marry someone you disliked. To be married to a man you disliked would not make you useful or respectable,' Jemima said feelingly, remembering her own first marriage to her Cousin Rupert, Earl of Chelmsford, who before he had drunk himself to death had all but ruined them, and brought the Morland estate to the brink of bankruptcy. 'But you must marry someone. Boys can have a career, but there is nothing else for girls to do.'

'It's not fair,' Charlotte cried.

'It's the way the world is,' Jemima said. 'Even for me – I was my father's heir when my brothers died, and he taught me business, but still my mother arranged a match for me.'

'The wicked Earl,' Charlotte said. It was something of a cautionary tale in the schoolroom.

'I was fortunate that he died when he did, and I was able to marry your Papa,' Jemima finished. It deflected Charlotte for a moment.

'Is Papa *ever* going to come back?' she asked. It was only a childish emphasis, but it made Jemima shiver: her unspoken dread was that she would never see him again. 'He has been gone so long.'

'Almost three years, but it seems longer. James does not even remember him,' Jemima said sadly. 'Father Ramsay says it cannot last much longer.'

'But Papa does not even write like Cousin Thomas.'

'Father Ramsay says one must not expect letters from someone on a diplomatic mission. His business is for the King, and secret, and it may not be possible for Papa to write to us without giving a secret away.'

'I wish the King had never sent him,' Charlotte said crossly. Jemima nodded. She wished, even as she had wished at the time, that her brother-in-law, the new Earl of Chelmsford, had never presented Allen at Court, where his talents could come to the King's notice. Chelmsford did it to be kind, just as he had sold Morland Place to Allen at less than its true value, as a kindness to Jemima, who had been left destitute on Rupert's death. But so often the Morlands had been involved in a king's business, and it had rarely brought them anything but grief. Her father had met his death as a result of the '45 rebellion, and Allen had spent fifteen years in exile in France because of it. It was that exile which had given him the special experience which made him so useful to King George, and taken him from her for three long years.

'I wish it too,' she said. 'It is a fine thing to serve the King, and no doubt the King will reward him. But I had sooner he stayed at home with us.'

'You miss him, don't you, Mother?' William said, watching her face.

'He is the best man in the world,' she managed to reply.

'Perhaps Charlotte could marry someone like him,' William said. 'If she learns to keep her hair tidy.'

'But I don't want to marry anyone,' Charlotte scowled, and the conversation had turned full circle.

When they left Twelvetrees, Poppy was still pulling and fretting, for she had not been out much in the past few days, and since Charlotte was in the same condition, Jemima took pity on them and said, 'We shall ride a long way back, and have a canter across Hob Moor, and go down to the Hare and Heather and see if there are any letters.' It was a convenient excuse, and Charlotte, who opened her mouth to say that the footman had been down for letters only that morning, had wit enough to close it again. They skirted Morland Place through the fields, galloped as fast as the ponies could go across the moor, where the common herdsman was tending the village cattle, jumped the Holgate Beck in fine style, and pulled up just in time to avoid running down a little girl who was herding geese back from High Moor. They were just above the South Road, opposite the new racecourse, which Jemima's father had helped to build. Below them was St Edward's School, and across the road from it St Edward's Church and the Hare and Heather Inn.

'There's the London coach!' Charlotte cried excitedly. 'Stopped outside the inn.'

'It must be putting someone down,' Jemima said. 'Sometimes it is easier to set down here than to go right into the city, if a person is travelling on by another coach.'

'There's Jack taking down the boxes,' William said. 'And Abel holding the horses.' The children knew most of the inn servants, who often came up to the house to bring messages or parcels or casks of ale. 'Shall we go down, Mother?'

'No, we'll wait until the coach moves on. There will be enough bustle, without our adding to it.'

The children watched, enough interested in the sight not to mind being kept at a distance, until the coach drew away again and lurched up the road towards the city. Then they saw that the alighted traveller, instead of going inside the inn, was standing outside, giving directions about his boxes to Jack and Abel.

'Why, Mama,' William cried, 'it's—'

'Yes,' said Jemima, who had recognized the traveller at the same instant. 'It's Cousin Thomas.'

'But why did you not let us know you were coming?' Jemima asked. She had dismounted to embrace her cousin, and Poppy, poking her mistress in the back with a hard, impatient muzzle, made her voice jerky.

'Oh, the mail is so slow, and I knew I could be here by the stagecoach sooner than a letter, so I did not bother,' Thomas said. In his brown face his eyes were a brilliant blue, and his teeth startlingly white as an irrepressible grin revealed his delight to be home. 'Did I do wrong?'

27

'My dear Thomas, of course not! We are so glad to see you. Only this morning—'

'We were all talking about you in the orchard,' Charlotte broke in, trying to edge Mouse nearer to the exciting newcomer. 'Flora was saying—'

'But what were you doing on the London coach?' Jemima asked hastily. 'I thought you were to come in to Portsmouth.'

'I was, until I came up with the Channel Fleet off Flushing. When I made my number the Admiral diverted me with dispatches to London Pool, and the Admiralty have decided to give the poor old *Hydra* one last run up the coast before she's laid up for good. So I have an extra week or so of leave, since the *Ariadne* is not ready yet.'

'Well, I am entirely delighted, though I'm afraid we have been plum harvesting today, so it will be poor feasting for you tonight. Abram will be most put out, not to have a special dinner ready for you. You know he never feels we keep enough state even on common occasions.'

'Poor Abram! Well, I should not like to upset him. Suppose Charlotte and William ride on ahead and warn him, while you and I walk back together?' He gave her a significant look, and so Jemima agreed and the twins, delighted to be the ones to bring the great news, turned their ponies and dashed away homewards. Thomas took Poppy's reins from Jemima politely, and looked directly into her inquiring eyes. 'I have news for you, which I thought you would like to have first alone.'

Jemima tried to ask a question, but her mouth had dried, and she could only move her lips soundlessly. Thomas smiled and took her hands.

'Yes,' he said. 'He is home, he is back, safe and sound. He is in London this very moment, and another week should bring him to you. He bid me bring you all the proper messages, and would have written but he has not an instant's leisure from making his reports to the King. But his greetings he bade me bring you, and his love he will bring himself in a week more.'

28

Jemima had no words, no words at all; she only gripped Thomas's hands so hard that there were tears in his eyes, to match those in hers.

'His lordship is waiting for you in the drawing room, Sir Allen,' said the butler, stepping behind him to lift off his wet cloak. 'Her ladyship has retired.'

Allen gave a grimace, not at the news, but at the appellation. He had been born Allen Macallan of Braco; in recent years he had been known as Allen Morland, since he had decreed that his children should bear that name so that Morland Place should not pass out of Morland hands; he had gone incognito by various names while on his recent mission; but he had been knighted only at this morning's levée, and was not at all sure he liked it. It was typical of the butler at Chelmsford House that he should not make a mistake even about so new a title.

'Thank you,' he said, handing over his soaking hat. Drops of dirty water fell onto the black and white tiles of the elegant Wren mansion's great hall, and a piece of mud the size of a walnut had dropped from the heel of his shoe, but the butler gave no sign of having noticed these things.

'Shall I have some refreshment sent in to you, sir? His lordship was not sure whether you would have supped.'

'Yes, please, a little supper would be welcome,' Allen said, and made his escape. He had felt at home embraced by the fantastic etiquette of Versailles, had navigated the dangerous shoals and narrows of St Petersburg and a dozen minor foreign courts, but Chelmsford's butler made him nervous.

The Earl himself, Jemima's brother-in-law, was waiting for him in the drawing room, and jumped up to greet him. 'My dear Allen, come to the fire, you must be drowned. I haven't had a chance to congratulate you yet. It is the least that you deserve, and I am sure that further honours will come your way.'

'Thank you, Charles. The King has told me I am to be

the next Justice of the Peace when I get home, and when I think what that will cost me in terms of work and worry, I'm not sure I can afford any more honours. My knighthood will mean five shillings on every innkeeper's reckoning on my way home.'

'But my dear friend, the honour, the increase of influence! If you do not value it for yourself, think of your wife, your children. Ann said just now that your daughters must be presented at Court when they are old enough. You must let us present them.'

'You and Ann are very kind,' Allen said, easing himself into the grateful embrace of the sofa corner. 'I dare say the girls will like that, though Jemima, I know, would be happy never to see St James's again.'

'She saw it in unhappy circumstances,' Charles said. 'With you beside her, and her daughters being honoured, she will see it differently.'

Allen smiled and let him have his way. There existed a great affection between the two men, despite their differences of character and opinion. They were distantly related – Allen's mother had been a Morland – and Allen had spent some years of his childhood in the household of Charles's grandmother, Annunciata. They had met for the first time in the exiled Court of James III in Rome, where Charles had served for many years until his brother's death had called him home to assume the title. Allen, serving the King of France, had sometimes been sent there as an envoy.

The servants came in, bringing Allen's supper, and Charles talked idly of this and that while Allen assuaged the first pangs of hunger. Then he said, 'I wonder what you would think to serving the King again in some diplomatic capacity? This American business, you know, will need some clever talkers. You met Franklin this morning, I believe?'

'I did, and needed all my wits to conceal that I understood but one word in three of what was being said. What on earth is the Tea Act, and what has it to do with the East India Company? I have been abroad for three years, remember.'

'Oh, it's a very good notion,' Charles said, looking as pleased as if he had thought of it. 'You remember how the Americans made such a fuss about import duties that North was forced to take them all off, except the tax on tea?'

'Which he maintained as a symbol of our right to tax the colonies?'

'Exactly. Lord knows, it's only a token tax – threepence in the pound, much less than *we* pay – and the late wars cost us dear in the defence of America. Why shouldn't they pay something towards their own defence?'

'Because, my dear Charles,' Allen said drily, 'no-one likes to pay tax. It's against human nature.'

'At all events, they don't pay it. There's so much Dutch tea smuggled in, that not one cup in a thousand drunk over there is made from taxed tea. And as for stopping the smuggling – as well try to nail the north wind to a tree. But to hear the colonists cry, you would think they were being thoroughly abused, robbed and enslaved. Hence the Tea Act.'

'Yes?' Allen said encouragingly. Charles frowned, marshalling his thoughts. He was not a quick man, and found it hard to tell a story in order.

'The East India Company – you know that it has been near bankruptcy?'

'Yes, and there would be the Dark Gentleman to pay if it went under.'

'So the Government has paid its debts, and the Tea Act allows the Company to ship tea directly to America, without passing it through London. That means no London duties, and no middleman's profit. Which means that even after paying the import tax in America, it will still cost about half the price of the smuggled tea. So the Company will make a profit, the colonists will have plenty of cheap tea, and they will pay the tax without complaint so we

31

won't lose face by removing it. And the smuggling will stop for lack of business.'

'It sounds like a wonderful scheme,' Allen said. 'I hope it works.'

'But it must work,' Charles said indignantly. 'It is so reasonable.'

'Yes, my dear Charles, but men aren't,' said Allen from the depths of experience.

There was silence for a while, while Allen finished his supper, then Charles said, 'So you will go home tomorrow? I shall miss you, but I suppose you must be eager to see your family.'

'Do you only suppose it? Think how you would long to see your Ann and your little Horatio and Sophia.' The death of Charles's first wife, from whom his fortune derived, had left him so well placed that he had been able to marry an entirely portionless woman for love, by whom he had had two children. His son by his first marriage was away at Oxford.

'Yes, but I should never go away from them in the first place. There are penalties, you see, to being clever. I stay safe at home, and have all the credit of being your brother-in-law. Family is a wonderful thing.'

'Indeed. And talking of family,' Allen said, stretching his feet to the fire, 'I had meant to tell you that I visited your Aunt Aliena while I was in Paris. She sends her duty to you, and keeps remarkably well, considering her age, though her eyesight is worse. She cannot read now.'

'She must be – oh, eighty-five or -six by now,' Charles said. 'Astonishing that she has lived so long. Do you realize that when she was born, King James II was still on the throne? How the world has changed in her lifetime!'

'But you are a long-lived family. Your grandmother was nearing ninety when she died, and your father lived well into his seventies.'

'Yes. Still, I don't suppose she can last much longer.'

'I think she feels that herself. She wanted to know

whether you will continue the pension after she is gone,' Allen said. Charles looked blank.

'Should I? I don't know. I inherited the pension from my father and brother, and never much thought about it.'

'Your father began it so as to support your aunt while she brought up the child!'

'Yes, the mysterious child! He must be well grown by now,' Charles smiled.

'He is twenty-seven,' Allen said. 'You could consider him independent. On the other hand, he has no other form of income, and family, as you have said, is a wonderful thing.'

'Well, the amount is not much, and I have no wish to inflict hardship on him. Does his grandmother leave him anything?'

'Aliena will leave him the house, which was bought outright for her in the beginning. They have moved, you know, from Clichy to the Rue de St Rustique, on the slopes of Montmartre, within sight and sound of the convent at the summit. She can hear their bells, and makes her devotions by their divisions. It comforts her a little, I think. It was hard for her to give up her orders. She goes up to the convent for Mass, and is a great favourite with the nuns. But she was always loved.' Charles looked at him curiously.

'I know a little of the story, of course, that Aunt Aliena's daughter produced this child and died doing so, and that the child was carried away to be concealed in France, and Aunt Aliena left her convent to bring him up. But you were a party to it all, you must know a great deal more. Won't you satisfy my curiosity?'

Allen shook his head. 'It would do no one any good for the secret to be known. The arrangement was made so that young Henri could be brought up in obscurity and though I acknowledge that you have the best right to ask questions, I beg you will not.'

'I knew you would refuse me,' Charles sighed. 'But I love you for it. Well, as to the pension, do you recommend

33

that I continue it? You have seen him – what sort of a man has he made?'

'He is very handsome, very charming, and popular. He is well liked at Court, speaks sensibly, has the entrée everywhere.' That was the truth; but Allen hesitated, wondering whether to add the rest, that he was a rake, and a gambler, and that the move to the smaller house had been made by Aliena in order to pay off his debts; and the further, unspoken truth, that he was breaking his grandmother's heart. In the end he said cautiously, 'It would ease your aunt's anxiety greatly to know that you would continue the pension to him after her death.'

That was enough for the good-hearted Charles. 'Then I shall do it. Will you write and tell her so? I should wish her to be happy, and after all, the young man is of our blood. One does what one can.'

'Bless you, Charles,' Allen said.

CHAPTER TWO

In the days of the first King Charles, an ambitious master of Morland Place sent one of his younger sons to the New World, to settle some land along the banks of the Chesapeake in Maryland. Enthusiasm was high in those days, and hopes higher, but the settlers knew too little about conditions in the New World, and as an investment it did not answer. No golden fortune came back across the Atlantic to enrich the master and extend his influence. The son and his wife almost perished from famine and hardship, and though they did survive, communication between York Plantation and Morland Place was thereafter slight.

Charles Morland found his way to York almost by accident. He had been 'botanizing' in the West Indian islands, but as the summer drew to a close he began to think about getting home. He inquired about boats going northwards to New York, and was directed to the master of a Dutch privateer who was calling at Yorktown.

'It's on the Chesapeake Bay,' he told Charles, 'and there's plenty of trade between there and New York. You'll get a ship easily.'

At Yorktown Charles grew interested in the new place and decided to stay for a week or so, and in conversation with the landlady of his lodging house he learned of the near proximity of York Plantation.

'Charles Morland,' she said musingly. 'There was a Charles Morland visited there some years back.'

'That would have been my father. I remember he wrote once to say he had stayed there.'

'Well, you'll know all about the family, then,' she said disappointedly. Charles smiled and shook his head.

'My father was so little at home that I can remember only two conversations with him in the whole of my life.'

The goodwife settled herself in gossiping mode, arms folded and feet spread.

'Of course, it isn't Morland now, it's de Courcey, on account the Morlands only had daughters, and married into a French family – French and Papist, but you'll likely not mind that?'

Not knowing how *she* felt about such things, Charles confined his reply to a noncommittal grunt, which seemed to satisfy her.

'Well, I don't mind it, for I'm broadminded. I get all sorts staying here, you wouldn't believe, and what I say is if they keep themselves to themselves and pay their bills, they can worship a block of wood if they like. The good Lord will sort them all out when the Great Day comes. But they're not well thought of in general, aren't Papists, even in Maryland, though Mr de Courcey is quite a gentleman, and to look at him, when he comes in to Yorktown every month, you'd never know any different.'

Charles wondered whether Papists were supposed to bear some brand or hideous deformity that marked them out as less than human. He made another encouraging murmur, and his landlady said, 'I suppose you'll be wanting to pay your respects, now you're here?'

'Well, I think I ought,' Charles said deprecatingly. 'Family is family, you know, even if the connection is far back.'

'Oh, they talk about the Morland connection; all the old families talk about England and where they came from. We know the whole story here. I can send a boy up the river with a letter if you want.'

Charles wrote, and the reply came inviting him most cordially to go and stay at York; and so having done a little shopping and attended to some business, Charles boarded the sailing boat that was sent for him, well primed by his hostess in the history of the family in its more sensational aspects.

Philippe de Courcey met the boat at the landing stage, from which well-tended green lawns ran up to the house.

36

The house was a pleasant surprise to Charles, for though not large, it was distinguished from its neighbours by being built of brick instead of wood. It presented a pleasant, symmetrical aspect, a long building of two storeys, with a white porch and stone chimneys at either end. White jasmine was scrambling energetically over the porch, and in beds all around the house were white rose bushes in full bloom.

'Welcome, welcome, my dear Cousin Charles Morland,' de Courcey said, seizing Charles's hand in a friendly grip. Philippe was a tall, dark man, appearing taller by virtue of his great slenderness, and darker by his brown skin and blue beard-shadow, but his smile was open and friendly. 'I hope you will not mind my calling you cousin. We think of ourselves as Morlands, you know, though we have lost the name.'

'I am honoured, sir,' Charles said, following him along the broad path, while two Negro servants attended to the bags. 'And delighted to exchange my lodgings for this beautiful house. You must be very proud of it.'

'It is my second greatest joy,' he said. 'My grandfather, the first de Courcey to live here, built it. Brick, as you can imagine, was very expensive, stone even more so, and there was a great deal of jealousy amongst his neighbours, and some ill-natured inquiry as to where he got the money to afford it.' He smiled, a sudden white flashing in his dark face. 'We in the family think we know where, but even we do not talk of it. These roses are our particular pride, sir. They are all descendants of the one bush that our ancestor Ambrose Morland brought with him from England in 1642.'

The lawns were as fine as any Charles had seen in England, and he said so, to gratify his host. The setting, too, was beautiful in the sort of artfully natural way that English lords paid Capability Brown large sums of money to achieve. But it was evident that Nature had provided it here for nothing: pretty little creeks, spanned by rustic bridges, knolls and gentle slopes, clumps of tall graceful trees here and there. The less attractive parts of the estate were set at a good distance from the house – the scrawny cattle, the farm buildings, the long-legged fowls and the tough little black pigs, the acres and acres of corn and tobacco, and the wooden dwellings of the slaves that tended them.

Philippe de Courcey was anxious to show Charles the house, of which he was justly proud, though the furnishing presented to Charles the curious appearance of having been assembled almost at random. Many of the pieces were useful but plain local work; others the massive, heavily-carved treasures of earlier ages; and here and there throughout them were scattered what might have been the remains of a pirate's hoard: delicate little French chairs, an English table with intricate inlay, Italian statuary and hangings, Spanish mirrors and boxes. In the chapel, de Courcey displayed the other great treasure of the house, an ivory and rosewood crucifix which had also been brought from England by the first Morland planter.

'The chapel caused a great deal of hostility of first,' he told Charles. 'My grandfather built it at the time when England was busy ejecting James II from the throne, and there were several anti-Catholic riots. The chapel windows were broken again and again, and "No Popery" was daubed on the walls with pitch. But these things die away, given time. Catholicism is frowned upon, but we are left alone, and no one suspects us of drinking the blood of murdered infants any more.'

Again the flashing white smile, and then de Courcey said, 'But my dear cousin, here I am boring you with a display of my meagre treasures and you are probably fatigued from your journey and longing for some refreshment. We shall dine in—' he drew a beautiful little gold watch from his pocket and studied it, 'in an hour, but perhaps you would like to take some wine in the meantime?'

Charles, though not in the least fatigued, consented, and was soon established in the drawing room with a passable claret in a fine Italian cup, his eye roving round the strange collection of worthless and valuable. De Courcey, having seen him comfortable, settled himself on the sofa opposite and raised an inquiring eyebrow.

'I was wondering how you managed to acquire pieces from so many different parts of the world,' Charles said. 'You must have very good trade here on the Chesapeake.'

'We do, as good as anywhere in America, but in fact most of these pieces were brought here by my grandfather. I had better tell you the story. Our common ancestors, who came here from England, left behind them only one daughter, who inherited the original York Plantation. Before they died, they arranged her marriage to a neighbouring planter, Noel Chanter, and the addition of his land made York one of the best properties on the bay.

'But the Chanters had no son, only three daughters, Maria, Louisa, and Philippa. Philippa was much younger than her sisters, and was only a child when her parents died, so it was left to the elder girls to bring her up. This they did, and between caring for her and running the plantation, they never had time to marry. Then one day my grandfather, Gaston de Courcey, arrived. He was the younger son of a rich sugar planter from Martinique, and, being the younger son and having no inheritance to look forward to, he had to make his own way in the world. He had become quite an adventurer. He had a ship of his own, and traded in this and that, and was known to be very rich – rich, moreover, in gold, which was then, and is still, a rare commodity in America. I'm afraid,' the white smile was apologetic, 'that many people said he was no better than a pirate.

'At all events, he heard about the beautiful – and unguarded – Chanter sisters, and managed somehow to make their acquaintance, broke the hearts of the elder two, and ran away with the youngest. I believe he truly loved her. At all events, he would not be parted from her. For ten years she sailed with him, living on shipboard and sharing all hazards, until finally ill health drove him to seek reconciliation with the sisters. They returned to York with an infant son – my father – and a hoard of gold and furniture and other valuables, made their peace and settled down. My grandfather built this house for my grandmother, and died very soon after it was finished. I fear, you see, that it may have been pirate's gold that bought the bricks.'

'It's a wonderful story,' said Charles, not at all minding that he had heard it already from his landlady, though in a spicier form. 'And the house is a wonderful monument to it.'

'Thank you. I wish its future did not hang by so slender a thread, however. I have but one daughter to leave everything to, my wife being dead. That's her picture, over the fireplace. Beside her is my sister Eugenie. Both died of the swamp fever thirteen years ago.'

'Your sister was very beautiful,' Charles said. De Courcey nodded.

'She was only twenty-five, poor child. She was much younger than me, all the children born between us having died; York has not been a lucky house. I named my daughter after her.' He smiled, and added, 'She is my *first* greatest treasure, you see. Or rather, you will see. She is resting upstairs but she will be down for dinner very soon.'

Only moments later the door opened, and Eugenie-Françoise de Courcey came in. The two men stood, and Charles was introduced, bowed over her hand, looked into her eyes, and was lost. She was all in white – white lace over white silk, and white roses in her hair – a fit setting for her ephemeral beauty. She seemed to move as though drifting a little above the ground, her face as serene as an angel's, her gestures languid, as though she moved in an element apart from the common air. Her skin was transparently white, her glossy curls black, her features perfect, her eyes grey as rain, fringed with dark lashes.

Charles was no fool. He was twenty-two, he had travelled the world and known women in many different countries. He could guess how much artifice went into the creation of an appearance of such simplicity, how much practice was needed before a woman could move with that natural grace, but it made no difference. She looked up at him gravely as he took her hand, and her lips moved a little, as if she was not sure whether it would be proper to smile, and his senses were ravished, his heart taken as neatly as a snared bird.

At Morland Place, that October of 1773 was unexpectedly warm and sunny, and the family were enjoying it by taking a long, leisurely Sunday walk about the gardens. Jemima, her hand tucked through Allen's arm, was savouring the bliss of having him back again. He was talking about Paris and Versailles, mostly for the benefit of Charlotte, who hopped about at his side asking questions; for Jemima it was enough that he was there, and while she felt the sound of his voice on her skin, she cared little what he talked about. William had drooped in the sunshine, and had been sent to sit in the shade, where Mary, with unexpected kindness, had joined him in exile and was telling him a long, involved story that required a great deal of gesticulation. Behind her, Jemima could hear Edward telling little James about school; ahead Flora walked on Cousin Thomas's arm, her enchanting little face tilted up to his in rapt attention, like a bird drinking from a flower. Jemima strained her attention for a moment to hear what Thomas was telling her that was so enthralling.

'They're doing away with the old beakhead now, and *Ariadne's* to have a hull all in one piece. You can't conceive how it's been argued about, but to my mind there's no question that the new design is better, and in a few years they won't build ships any other way.' Flora nodded agreement, as if she had come to the same conclusion herself. Encouraged, Thomas went on. 'She can carry more sails on her bowsprit this way, and with headsails and staysails, and with her bottom coppered, there won't be a ship of her class she can't outrun – and she'll hold the wind better, and come round in half the time, which is most important.'

'Most important,' Flora echoed, having only the vaguest idea of what he was talking about, but loving every word of it. 'But can you be comfortable in your ship? Do you have your own room? And how does your cook dress your food? I suppose you must eat your meat cold when you are away from the shore?'

Faced with such enchanting ignorance, Thomas drew her closer and set to with a will to tackle it, and their steps soon took them out of earshot. Charlotte had just dashed off to tell William what Father had been saying, and Jemima took the chance to say to Allen, 'What do you think of a match between those two? I think Flora is determined upon it. She makes herself a little obvious. I do hope he will be kind to her.'

'Yes, I saw that he was under fire,' Allen said. 'But don't worry. He is an open-hearted young man, and just back from two years at sea with no female company. That will do his business for him, if her sweet face and pretty ways do not. I suspect he will propose to her before the *Ariadne* sails.'

'You would approve, then?' Jemima asked.

'I think it quite suitable. He is an energetic young officer, and doing well in his career. She will have a little money from her father's estate, and they are equal as far as rank is concerned. And though he is some years older than her – well,' with a smile, 'you and I have not minded the discrepancy.'

The young couple turned at the end of the walk and came back towards them.

'From the expression of Flora's face, you would think he was proposing to her this very minute,' Jemima said. A moment later Thomas's voice became audible again.

'And I must tell you,' he was saying to his eager audience, 'what an interesting thing they are doing with the lateen on the mizzenmast.'

*

William seemed definitely ailing that evening, low and uncomfortable and admitting to a headache, and Alison, the nursery maid, called Jemima up to the nursery for a conference, shook her head and sucked her teeth and finally pronounced that she thought he was sickening for something.

'You don't think it's just the heat?' Jemima said anxiously. 'He was walking in the sunshine for almost an hour today.'

'I don't like the look of him, mistress. I think he should have a dose.'

Alison's doses were uniformly repellant, and William having such a delicate stomach, Jemima thought it would likely do him no good. 'I think he should have some rosemary water and honey. I'll order it to be sent up when I go downstairs,' she said firmly, in the voice that the servants as well as the children had learnt not to argue with. She went to say goodnight to her son, felt his damp forehead, smiled into his anxious eyes, and said, 'I shall send up something for you. It won't taste bad, I promise.'

'Thank you, Mama. I shall be better in the morning,' William promised anxiously. 'I'm sorry—' His voice trailed off. Jemima, who had straightened to leave him, stooped again.

'What for?'

'I'm sorry I'm such a disappointment to you,' he said very low. Jemima was arrested by the sadness in his voice, too adult a sadness for one only ten years old, and she suddenly realized how little she knew about her children. There had never been time to spend with them, in the frantic years of work and worry. She had supervised their bringing up from a distance, and though they had never been forced to observe the formality with their parents that she had with hers, she had seen very little more of them. The King, a great family-lover, was making it fashionable for parents to have their children around them, to go for outings with them, even play with them, but it was too late for Jemima's family.

She touched his cheek with a forefinger, and tried to smile at him.

'Not a disappointment, William. Naturally I worry about you, and wish you were stronger, but I'm not disappointed in you. You mustn't think it. Settle down and go to sleep now. Sleep is the best thing for you.'

He gave her a pale smile, and she left him, aware that she had done nothing to reach him, that she had had too little practice for her words to sound natural or reassuring.

She left the nursery and walked back along the passage through what had come to be called the Bachelor's Wing, because it contained the three small dark bedrooms that the young men of the family occupied until they married. As she turned the corner by the Red Room, she came face to face with Flora, scurrying in the other direction. They both stopped short, and there was a moment of wildly-waving candle-shadows.

'Oh, you surprised me,' Flora exclaimed. 'I was just going to see how William was.'

'Not well. Alison thinks he is sickening for something. I am going to send him up some rosemary water.'

'I thought he looked as though— poor little man,' Flora said tenderly. Jemima looked at her with dissatisfaction.

'Yes, it seems you are more of a mother to my children than I am,' she said. 'Certainly Jamie loves you far better than me.'

Flora reddened. 'Why, ma'am, it's only because I have the time to play with them. They love you very much, and respect you, but you are too busy to—'

'Exactly,' Jemima said. 'I am not blaming you, Flora, or criticizing. It is only natural, and I am grateful that they should have had your love and guidance.'

'You mustn't blame yourself either,' Flora said shyly. It was a great thing for her to offer comfort to her elder, the head of the house. 'You do so much. No one could do more.'

'When the mare was sick at Twelvetrees I went at once, and stood and petted her, and though there were no

44

symptoms, I knew by her preoccupied look that she was ailing. When Artembares sprained his fetlock, I was there every day, and Humby had to oblige me not to change his bandages myself.'

'But Artembares is so valuable,' Flora protested, and then stopped, seeing where that led. 'You can only do so much,' she finished instead. Jemima was silent, sunk in thought, and Flora thought it best to change the subject. 'I did want to speak to you, as well, if you have a moment?'

'Of course,' Jemima roused herself. 'Shall we go to your room?'

Flora had the West Bedroom, the smallest of the principal bedrooms, but Jemima thought the prettiest and most comfortable. Annunciata, the Countess of Chelmsford, had always used it when she lived at Morland Place, in preference to the great bedchamber itself. The walls of the West Bedroom were panelled in a warm, honey-coloured wood, and its drapes were blue, matching a pale blue Chinese carpet on the floor. Flora slept in Eleanor's Bed, older by half a century than the Butts Bed in the great bedchamber, but smaller and more delicate, with slender fluted posts and fine carving at the head and foot; and the basin and ewer were of chased silver, fine Elizabethan work, the gift of a past Thomas Morland when he married his cousin Douglass two hundred years ago. They were amongst the very few pieces of old plate that Jemima had managed to save from her first husband's depredations.

'Well, now, you wanted to talk to me?' Jemima said, closing the door behind her. 'Is it about Thomas?'

'How did you guess?' Flora said innocently. Jemima smiled.

'Shall I guess some more? You are in love with him, and he with you. You want to be married. I take it he asked you after dinner, when you went slipping off together into the gardens?'

'You really do know everything,' Flora said. 'Then – you don't mind it?'

'Mind it? I think it is the best thing possible. You are

exactly suited to each other. I knew how it would be when he came home. So, is that all you wanted to tell me?'

'Not quite,' Flora said, frowning a little. 'It is true that Thomas asked me, and I said yes, but I don't know whether I should have. You see, I don't know what to do, who to ask. Now Papa is dead, I suppose that my brother Charles is the head of the house, but he is in America, no-one knows quite where; and Angus is only a year older than me. Who gives permission? Can Thomas ask Cousin Allen? After all, I have lived here in your care for a long time. What should we do?'

'Your brother is the proper person to ask,' Jemima said. 'You are under age, and his permission will be necessary. It will be for him to approve and to release the money your father left you. Allen and I can make our recommendation on your behalf, but I cannot think that Charles will object in any case.'

'But we don't know where he is,' Flora said with some agitation. 'And even if we had a direction for him, a letter would take too long going and coming.'

'Too long for what? I am sure you may become engaged to Thomas while you wait for Charles's official approval. I think Allen and I could go so far as to license an engagement.'

'You don't understand,' Flora cried. 'Thomas and I want to be married at once, before he has to sail, and *Ariadne* will be ready after Christmas at the latest. Once he sails, he may be away for years. He may—' She stopped herself abruptly, but Jemima knew what she was thinking, having thought the same things herself about Allen. Life was such a hazard, and the life of a traveller at even greater risk. Suppose Thomas never came back? Flora wanted to grasp her happiness while it was within reach, and Jemima could not blame her.

'My dear,' she said gently, 'I do know how you feel. But the best we can do is to write to your brother at the direction on his most recent letter, and wait for his reply.

In any case, he is bound to be returning to England soon – he never stays away more than two years.'

'But—'

'I know, I know. It is hard. But we are all in God's hand. What He wants for us will happen. We can only do our best, and keep faith.'

Twice in the course of half an hour Jemima had felt how useless she was. Leaving Flora, she met a servant on the stair and sent her for the rosemary water for William, and then, seeking consolation, she went towards the chapel, thinking Father Ramsay might be there. But passing the steward's room and seeing a light in there, she turned towards another consolation. Allen was at the table, bent over a heap of paperwork. She went quietly up to him, and he reached out for her hand without looking up, and drew it fondly against his cheek.

'I did my best not to leave things for you,' Jemima said, 'but there were always some matters—'

'You worked miracles,' Allen replied. 'I'm not complaining. If you were away for nearly three years, there would be more than this awaiting you on your return. I am quite sure you do three-fourths of the work of the estate.'

'But there is always something I neglect,' she said discontentedly. He looked up at her, saw her mood, and put down his pen. 'I was thinking that I was as little use to my children as my parents were to me. It is Flora and Father Ramsay who have brought them up and shaped them.'

Allen kissed her hand, and put it back against his cheek. 'We can all of us only do our best,' he said, unconsciously giving her back her own words. 'What have I been to them or to you?'

'Everything to me,' Jemima said quickly. He stood up, pushing the papers away and extinguishing the reading-candle, and then drawing her to him with an arm about her waist, moved towards the door.

'And now that I am to be Justice of the Peace, I will have even more to do. So, if we are to have any time together at all, we must have more hirelings. A housekeeper to take the work of the house from you, a steward to run the estate – whatever it takes, Jemima, I am determined upon it.'

'But can we—'

'Afford it? Yes, I think so. And besides, we must – I am Sir Allen now, and you are Lady Morland. We have a position to keep up.'

Jemima laughed, the tension leaving her body quite abruptly. 'Well, call it what you like, if it means that I shall have leisure to be with you, and touch you, and talk to you.' They walked out into the passage and turned towards the stairs. 'By the way, I have been talking to Flora. Thomas has spoken at last.'

Charles and Eugenie were taking their walk in the driest part of the day. He had been astonished, used as he was to the busy, active women of his own family, at how little Eugenie did, but he was beginning to fit himself to the languid pace of her days, and to find it less strange as each day passed. She rose at nine, and took an hour to dress for her daily devotions at ten in the chapel. At eleven she took her breakfast, then from twelve to four she performed her daily tasks: she sewed a little, read a little, wrote a letter sometimes, and took her walk. At four they dined; at six they took tea. Then came the evening's occupation, more sewing, conversation, or cards, or sometimes music, Eugenie playing upon the harpsichord and singing. Supper came in at nine, and at half past ten she retired for the night.

Even the walk, the most active part of a day spent otherwise mostly upon the sofa, was performed slowly, and with some ceremony. The weather must be fine, the paths dry. Eugenie would have her hat and her parasol and her black and white spaniel, and her Negro maid would trot along behind carrying a cushion, in case 'mis' wanted to sit down somewhere, and a handkerchief and lavender water and a book and whatever other toys and nonsenses Eugenie thought she might need during the expedition. Mrs Craven, Charles's landlady in Yorktown, had said with peculiar emphasis that Eugenie was 'a proper young Creole lady', and from what he observed and what he gathered from the servants, he learnt that Creole ladies were famous for their ignorance and indolence, perfected and polished to a fine art.

Eugenie had told him about her education during their walks. He loved to listen to her light, sweet voice with its faint and lilting drawl, so different from any other Maryland voices he had heard. This, and her divine indolence, were the product of the four years she had spent 'back home' in Martinique.

'I have lots of cousins there,' she said, 'and Papa did not want me quite to forget our origins. So he sent me to the convent of Les Dames de la Providence, where all the best familes send their girls. I went when I was ten, and stayed for four years.' At the convent she was taught to read, write, embroider, sing, play the harpsichord, and to dance the Court dances. She also learnt what to Charles was her only real academic attainment – to speak and write perfect French. But she had acquired there also this divine and languid grace, her enchanting Creole drawl, and her charming, polished social manner, all the things that made her, for him, unlike any other living creature he had ever encountered.

'It is so beautiful on Martinique,' she told him, and in speaking of 'home' she grew almost animated. 'It is hot there, and green, and rich in colours – the orchids such as you have never seen, and amaryllis of such brilliant colours, like Turkish headdresses. And the scarlet flambeau trees, and the hibiscus, and the bougainvillaea climbing all other the porch, and the jasmine and honeysuckle – the scent of it, Charles! When I came back, I brought a piece of jasmine in a pot, to remind me. That is what you see climbing on our porch here. It seemed to like the transition. I should have broke my heart if it died.'

She told him about the forest of tall palms and banana

trees, tangled with creepers and filled with birds of brilliant plumage, which darted and swung in the green shade, vivid as jewels. She told him about the fabulous insects, as big as birds and as gaudy, and the pink lizards who would sit all day on the ceiling of her bedroom, whom it was bad luck to harm. And she told of the terrors of the tropical land, the ants who marched in columns like soldiers, devouring all in their path, of the poisonous snakes and spiders and little black scorpions, of the earthquakes and the fear of hurricanes and of the island's volcano. It had been for her a time of wonder and intense life, and he listened with sympathy as well as interest, not telling her that he knew about tropical islands, for in her words his memories took on a new significance.

'Today I shall show you my favourite walk,' Eugenie said that morning as they strolled along the path in front of the house, beside the white roses, coming to the end of their season now. Bendy, the little black and white dog, trotted ahead, sniffing here and there and looking back every few moments to see Eugenie was still following. 'It is up to the knoll, you see over there?' Her voice took on animation, as if it was a great expedition they were undertaking, but the knoll was only two hundred yards from the house, a perfect little hill shaped like an upturned cup, with a path winding up to the crest, topped with a clump of beautiful trees, whose foliage, not yet turning, looked blue in its shadows.

Charles assented, and they walked in silence for a while. Then she said, gazing into the distance as if she were making the most casual conversation, 'So you leave us the day after tomorrow? Do you really have to go?'

'I think I must,' Charles replied, feeling his heart bump at the second question. 'You see, I have sent a number of plants on ahead, but I must be home to attend to them before they die, which they will if they are left in a warehouse. And the weather for the crossing will be so much worse if I leave it too late.'

She said no more until they had reached the summit of

the little hill and were standing in the shade of the trees, looking at the view.

'Now you can see the Patuxent River properly,' she said. 'And the extent of our land – from that line of trees, over there, all the way to the shore of the Bay. Our ancestors were amongst the first settlers, so they got the best land.' She turned her head to look at him, and her grey, clear eyes seemed to hold some question, to be searching for something in his face. 'We are cousins, of a sort, you and I?'

'Cousins, I suppose, though very distant ones,' he said, not sure whether she wanted them to be related or not.

'It is very pleasant here at Christmas,' she said, and though the statement seemed a random one, he knew there was a connection somewhere. 'Many of our neigbours visit us, because on the whole Americans do not keep Christmas so much as we do, and they like to see how we do it. When you came, I hoped – Papa hoped that you would stay for Christmas.'

'If I stayed for Christmas, I probably would not be able to leave until spring,' Charles said, and Eugenie smiled – he was sure she smiled, fleetingly, before she turned her face away again to contemplate the view.

'Yes,' she said. 'That seems probable.' A pause. 'So you will go. A pity.' And at once she changed the subject by pointing out to him a blue crane, flying over the river.

Dinner that day was evidently a special one, though no special occasion had been announced. There was fried chicken, a local speciality, with a pungent sauce, and oysters, and a boiled lobster, and cold roast teal, and a dish of fish done in some kind of sauce that burned the tongue and made Charles's eyes water.

'A West Indian speciality,' Philippe told him, not without amusement. 'We call it pepper-pot.'

'It's very good,' Charles gasped, 'once you get used to it.'

'You are determined to leave us, after so short a visit?' Philippe asked next. Charles glanced across at Eugenie, but she was busy with her glass, and did not look up. The lace of her sleeve fell back as she lifted it, showing the white and tender curve of her forearm.

'I'm afraid I must,' Charles said, wondering how he found the courage. 'The journey—'

'I understand. I should like to ask you if you would do us the honour of visiting again – for a longer time perhaps. Have you plans to come back to America?'

'I have not yet planned – but I shall certainly return. Next year, perhaps—'

'You will think me importunate, but I should like to engage you for a visit, perhaps next summer. You could stay all summer, and we could show you something of the country. There are few places we cannot reach by boat.'

Philippe's eyes held his, and they, too, contained some message.

'We have so little company here, so few visitors. We should be honoured if you would return.'

Charles left early in the morning, when the mist still lay like milk over the river and the strange cries of water birds echoed hollowly in the fluky half-light. The servants were ready with the sailing pinnace to take him to the trader, anchored in the Bay, which had promised him passage to New York. It was too early for Eugenie to be up, but he felt her presence everywhere, as if he could know she was thinking about him. The white mist and the dark shadows, and the slow sound of water slapping the unseen piles of the jetty, were somehow full of her. Philippe came down to wave him off, but the morning was too cold for long farewells. They clasped hands once, and the boat was shoved off, and in seconds the landing stage and the master had been swallowed in the white murk.

Passage up the coast was slow, and in New York Charles found it so difficult to get a passage to England that it was December before he was on board a merchant ship bound for Liverpool. The boxes he had sent on ahead were in the hold, for he had found them held up in New York harbour because of a shipping-clerk's error. Angry though he was at their delay, he was not sorry to have the precious things under his own eye again.

The merchantman was old, slow and unwieldy, and made no speed when the wind was not astern, and Charles was not surprised one day in the middle of December to see that they were being rapidly overhauled by a small cutter, which clung to the wind like a limpet. She came up alongside, and trimmed her sails to keep pace with the merchantman for a while, while her captain, a young, dark, active man, wearing gold earrings like a gypsy, came aboard to talk to the master of the bigger ship. Charles watched with interest from the taffrail, until the young captain reappeared upon his own deck and the graceful little cutter shook herself loose from restraint, leaned again to the wind and sped away.

Within minutes the talk was all over the ship, and a seaman found Charles with the express desire of having someone to whom to tell the amazing news. The cutter had come out of Boston, where there had been trouble over the East India Company's tea, and serious violence barely avoided. Three Company ships loaded with tea had come into Boston at the end of November, ready to undersell the smugglers and provide cheap drink for the colonists. But some radicals feared that the Company was being given a monopoly in order to destroy trade and subjugate the colonists. The Town Committee had refused to allow the tea to land, while the Governor of Boston had refused to allow the ships to depart.

'You see, sir,' the sailor said, 'the duty has to be paid within twenty days of arrival in port, or the goods must be seized. Now if the Governor was to seize the goods, he'd have to land them, which the Town wasn't going to allow, nohow. The Governor had troops, not far off at Castle William, and the townsfolk had arms, all ready for the militia, and there looked like to be a terrible bloodshed over it. Then on the nineteenth day, a great party of men, dressed up as Indians, to disguise them, like, boarded the ships, and broke open the holds, and tipped the tea over the side. The captain of that cutter, sir, he's on his way to England to tell about it. There'll be a terrible to-do, you mark my words. Worth twenty thousand pound, he reckons, that tea was.'

By the time the slow old ship had made her journey to Liverpool, the news of the Boston 'tea party', as it was being called, was all over England, and was a matter of wonder and outrage. Other news had already reached England, too, of similar incidents up and down the coast, where tea was refused landing, and sometimes destroyed. From the dock hands Charles learnt of tea being tipped into the harbour at New York, into the river at Charleston, and burnt in Maryland to the strains of a rebel song called the 'Tea Deum'. He thought, anxiously, of York Plantation.

'There'll be trouble over this,' everyone said. 'This won't be the last of it. Those colonists will have to be taught a lesson.'

The words 'trouble' and 'Eugenie' attained an unpleasant proximity in his mind as he travelled, just before Christmas, across England to Morland Place, and he wished, more than once, that he had not so stubbornly refused to stay in Maryland.

CHAPTER THREE

November had been a miserable month at Morland Place, for Thomas was recalled to London, throwing Flora into despair, and William came down with the measles. Allen did his best to comfort Jemima who, though she had nursed more sick horses than she could remember, was completely unnerved by the illness of her children. He told her that it was certainly *not* smallpox, of which he had had enough experience both at home and abroad to be sure; that the measles were rarely fatal, that strong and healthy children shook them off with no ill effects.

'But William is not strong, he has never been strong,' she cried. Allen took her hands.

'He may look frail, my darling, but just think – he has lived to be ten, through every illness known to childhood, so there must be some kind of inner strength to him.'

As an attempt at lightness it failed, for whatever Allen might say, he was deeply worried himself. William was very sick, and for three days the household moved about on tiptoe and spoke in hushed voices while his temperature climbed and climbed. Father Ramsay made a special intention for him, and the chapel was haunted at all hours of the day by members of the family and servants slipping in to pray for the 'poor little boy'. Only Alison remained robustly unmoved by fears, declaring that if it did not get to his ears or lungs, and did not make him blind, she dared say he would be none the worse for it in a month's time. But even she was seen to dab her eyes with the corner of her apron when his fever finally broke.

Though cross and crotchety in her ways, Alison was a fine doctor, having been brought up amongst sheep people, and having a great deal of common sense. She rubbed William's chest with goose grease, and bound it with raw sheep's wool, to protect his lungs, and gave him marsh-mallow tea and heather honey to ease the cough which was the most wearying thing about the disease. Jemima's favourite rosemary water she discarded with a sniff for a nauseous brew of willow bark for the headache, cinchona bark and hyssop for the fever, and camomile and straw-berry for the rash. When the fever went down and he was able to eat again, she fed him on barley bread seethed in ewe's milk, which she considered more wholesome than cow's milk.

'She said,' Allen reported with a smile to Jemima, who had been forbidden the sickroom, 'that though she could not stop us drinking cow's milk, she was perfectly sure no child in her nursery was going to drink it.'

'How is it she lets you in so readily?' Jemima complained, and Allen looked smug.

'Oh, she thinks I have a "deal of sense" and that if God had fashioned me on a more rational plan, I'd have made an excellent mother. But William is so much better she will let you in to see him tomorrow, if you promise not to excite him. Thank God ideas have changed since my childhood. Truly terrible things used to be done to the sick, in the ignorant belief they were cures.'

No sooner was William pronounced out of danger than Charlotte and Mary both became sick. Mary had it so lightly that she did not even feel ill, but she made a bad patient, fretting all the time that she would be marred for life, and demanding that Charlotte should be nursed separately from her. Charlotte's attack went to her ears, and though she bore the pain with astonishing stoicism, barely whimpering, she cried dreadfully at being parted from William.

But December brought better things. Sickness left the house, and Thomas returned, with the news that there were delays in the building of *Ariadne*, and that he was not wanted in London again until January. Even then, he said, she would have to be fitted out and manned, and then there would be trial sailings. He should be able to be in

London tolerably often, and probably would not receive his orders until mid-February.

Flora's brother Angus arrived at Morland Place from Edinburgh for Christmas, and on the same day a footman brought a note over from Shawes, which was at that time let to Sir John Fussell, his wife Marjorie, and their five children.

'Well, here's something that will add to our pleasure this Christmas,' Allen said as he read the note. The family was gathered around him in the drawing room, where they had been listening to Angus's tales of undergraduate life in Edinburgh, and all looked at him expectantly. 'Mary, here will be excitement enough even for you. My dear,' to Jemima, 'it seems your brother and his family are all come to stay at Shawes for the Christmas period.'

'I did not know they were so intimate,' Jemima said. Allen shrugged.

'I dare say they are not. But all the great families go into the country at Christmas, and since Charles has still not bought himself a country estate to replace this one, he must either stay in London – which would be intolerable – or depend upon an invitation. They have arrived today.'

'Well, it was very courteous of them to let us know,' Jemima said.

'Ah, but that is not all – the exciting part is still to come,' Allen said, smiling round at his family. 'They are to give a grand ball on St Stephen's Day to which we are all invited, in return for allowing them to join our hunting parties.'

'I am sure he could not have said anything so improper,' Jemima smiled.

'Oh no – from what little I know of Sir John Fussell, he is incapable of impropriety. It is very properly worded, but the meaning is clear enough. He speaks regretfully of the fact that Shawes has no estate attached, and therefore no hunting, and of the splendid hunting to be had on our estate, and then goes on quite innocently to mention the ball. We could not be so indelicate as to ignore such a *cri de coeur*, could we, my darling?'

'But Papa, Papa—' Mary was almost jumping up and down in her anxiety. Allen took pity on her.

'Yes, little one, you are invited to take tea with the Fussell children, and to watch the opening of the ball from the gallery. That, I imagine, is to remind us that the little Fussells will want to hunt as well,' he added to Jemima. 'Well now, how shall I reply to this? Do you think I ought to refuse their kind invitation? To be sure, we hardly know them.'

There was a chorus of agonized pleas from the younger ones, and Jemima, joining gravely in the fun, said that the presence of the Chelmsfords would naturally increase their intimacy, and advised him solemnly to accept.

The sudden return of Flora's brother Charles on the day before Christmas Eve brought more excitement, and great joy to Flora, for, once he had unpacked his specimens, mourned over those damaged beyond hope, and satisfied himself that the others were being properly cared for, he readily granted her permission to marry their cousin Thomas. And when pressed a little further, he even saw the necessity for an immediate marriage, so that Flora could be with Thomas in London for the last six weeks before he went to sea.

'But won't you mind not having the grand wedding you must always have dreamed of?' he asked her. 'There will be too little time for anything but a quiet ceremony and private dinner.'

'I don't care,' Flora said rapturously. 'I want to marry Thomas – I don't care about the wedding.'

So Christmas passed in its accustomed way, but with the added happiness of Flora's approaching wedding, and the added interest of the families from Shawes. On Christmas Eve, Allen and Jemima gave a dinner party for the adult members of the families: Flora and Thomas, Charles and

Angus, Sir John and Lady Marjorie, Lord and Lady Chelmsford, and Chelmsford's son from his first marriage, Lord Meldon, back from his first term at Oxford. Jemima was sorry to see a certain amount of uneasiness, even hostility, between her brother-in-law and his son, and during the course of the evening traced it to its source – Meldon resented the second wife and the new family, felt he was being neglected by his father. And indeed, judging by how often Chelmsford mentioned his wife and their children, who were, it seemed, more clever and handsome than any other two children who ever lived, Jemima could hardly blame him. She placed him opposite Angus at dinner, as they were more or less of an age and both in their first year at university, and made a point of talking to him herself during the evening, to make sure he knew he was welcome.

Christmas Day was always busy at Morland Place, being not only a day of Holy Obligation, but quarter-day too. They rose early for first Mass, then, having broken their fast, rode or drove into the city for the morning service at the Minster. Then they came back to Morland Place to receive the tenants, collect the rents, pay the servants' wages, and hand out spiced wine and cake to all. Then came dinner, featuring the Christmas goose, well stuffed with apples, sage and onions. Dinner lasted from four until six, when it was time to repair to the chapel again for sung Mass, which many of the tenants and villagers traditionally attended. By the time they had been wished well and sent on their way, there were but two hours left of the day in which to gather round the fire or the harpsichord and sing the traditional Christmas songs.

On St Stephen's Day, first Mass was even earlier, for there had to be time enough to eat and dress before the traditional hunt. The whole party from Shawes came over, and everyone at Morland Place was hunting – even Mary, who preferred her horses as near stationary as possible, was going out rather than miss the illustrious company. There was such a crowd, and so many of them on doubtful-looking hirelings, that Jemima was afraid Poppy would get kicked in the crush in the courtyard, and decreed that the meet should take place outside, and ordered the food and drink be carried across the drawbridge and set up on trestles. There was mulled wine and plum brandy for the hunting folk, and jugs of mulled ale for those who had come to watch or follow on foot, and Abram's irresistible mincemeat pies for all.

Jemima, walking Poppy about, for she was too excited to stand still, watched the scene with interest – it was always the best part of Christmas for her. Best of all, there was Allen on his black mare, looking a well-schooled rather than a natural horseman, but master of his own hunt again after so many years. His eye met hers whenever she looked at him, however many people were between them, and they exchanged smiles of perfect accord. There was Flora, looking exquisite, talking to young Lord Meldon, who rode one of his two hunters, brought with him from Oxford, a wicked-looking chestnut with a dangerous eye. The other he had lent to Angus, which seemed a kind gesture, had Jemima not suspected he did it mostly to avoid having to lend it to his father. It was a bay of equally uncompromising aspect, and Angus, who was no horseman, looked as if he wished he was mounted on one of the cobs, like his brother Charles.

Lord and Lady Chelmsford were both mounted on hirelings, and Jemima got her first sight of their younger children. Eight-year-old Sophia, plump and pale with surprising yellow ringlets, was on a fat grey pony which slept determinedly through all the excitement, its leading rein in the hands of a groom, who grasped it as though it were likely to take off at full gallop at any moment. Her brother, Horatio, who was ten, was on a hireling horse too big for him, which he had been cantering about so continuously that it was already sweating and rolling its eyes. This, Jemima guessed, was mainly for the benefit of Mary, who, demure and dainty on her pony, was already surrounded by a group of swains, including John Anstey and Edward, all vying to bring her refreshments and offering to show her the best line when hounds ran.

A movement beside her made her turn her head, and there was Charlotte, with William just behind, looking neat and horsemanlike on her pony.

'Such a lot of nonsense,' Charlotte snorted, watching the crowd round Mary. 'If they hang around her, they'll miss the hunt, for Mary never went out of a trot in her life. I know exactly what she'll do. She'll ride to the first covert, follow at the back of the field until we come to the first jump, and then call for a groom to take her home.' It was so perfect a picture that Jemima could only smile. 'And look at the stupid Horatio person,' Charlotte went on. 'His horse is nearly knocked up already, and we haven't even moved off. He doesn't deserve to have a horse at all. Look at it frothing! Mother, why do we have to have people like that at our hunt?'

It was not a question, as Jemima knew quite well. 'You and William had better try and stay at the front,' she said instead of answering. 'There are some strange horses out today, and I'm afraid you may be kicked. And stay together, won't you?'

'Yes, Mother, I'll take care of William,' Charlotte said, answering the thought rather than the words.

It was a wonderful hunt, with one of the longest gallops Jemima remembered, so long indeed that all but the best horses got left well behind. Jemima found herself at the front, for there were few horses who could outrun Poppy over her own country, with no one but the huntsmen in front of her and only a handful of hard riders nearby. A few yards to her left was Lord Meldon on his wicked-looking chestnut, and as she turned her head, he gave her a challenging smile and tried to urge an extra ounce of speed from his mount. Jemima smiled back, glad to see him so cheerful. Angus was not far behind, more from the determination of his bay to keep up than any desire of his own, and a little way behind them were Thomas, Flora and Allen, comfortably together. Half a dozen well-mounted neighbours made up the rest of their company, and the rest of the field was out of sight.

Thus Jemima was in at the kill, but missed all the drama. Horatio's mount, brought to a pitch of near-hysteria before the first covert, took off like a catapult shot as soon as the first run started. Charlotte and William had at first thought this all of a piece with his previous behaviour, but when the animal passed them with its head up, its eyes white, and froth spraying from its rigid jaw, they realized that young Horatio was out of control. They were coming up to a stout but jumpable hedge. The horse swerved violently sideways and galloped off into the wood, and under Charlotte's leadership they swung away in pursuit.

A wild pursuit it was too, through a tangled wood at full-pelt, but where the tall horse could go, their shorter ponies could follow. The path led to a thick thorn hedge, its top smashed through in a welter of broken twigs. Charlotte in the lead pressed her pony on; it jumped boldly. On the other side the hireling lay thrashing, tangled in its reins, with the boy half under it, caught by his foot in the stirrup. All this Charlotte saw in mid-air; she wrenched at the reins and her pony twisted its body sideways in a desperate attempt to avoid the fallen horse. They landed awkwardly, her pony fell, and she was thrown clear.

William was in time to avoid the jump, hearing the cries from the other side. A little further along was a lower place in the hedge, and he jumped there in safety, to find that Charlotte, unperturbed by her fall, had flung herself onto the hireling's head and was struggling to free its feet from the reins.

'William, William, come and hold a leg,' she panted.

By the time help arrived, they had got the hireling to its feet, stiff and trembling, and freed young Horatio who, though very shocked and bruised, was not seriously hurt by his escapade. It was only then that Charlotte saw her pony, standing beside William's, holding off the ground a foreleg that dangled horribly and uselessly.

*

The Honourable Horatio Morland was whisked off to be examined by the best surgeon in York, while plain Miss Charlotte Morland was taken to her home to be bathed, annointed, and put to bed by Alison. While everyone was dressing, a message came from Shawes to say that Horatio was not considered to be in danger, and that the ball would therefore take place as planned, but that the children's part of the entertainment was cancelled. William would not in any case have gone without Charlotte, and Edward and Jamie had never much cared about it, so they were not too disappointed, but Mary was furious, and by a fine piece of illogic, blamed Charlotte for the whole thing.

'Naturally they cancelled it because they heard Charlotte is sulking in bed. It isn't *fair*. Why is everyone against me? I shall never forgive her for this, never!' she cried through tears of rage.

Rachel, the under-nursery-maid, threatened her with a whipping, and Abram sent up a special batch of cakes for consolation, but as Edward said unconcernedly as he set off to find a book for the evening, 'When Mary sulks, she likes to do it for a good, long time.'

When Jemima emerged from the closet, where the powdering was always done, dressed except for her gown, Allen, preparing resignedly to take her place, said, 'I don't wish to be vindictive, but I rather resent that the boy didn't hurt himself more seriously. If he was going to cause so much trouble, he might at least have got the ball cancelled, and saved *me* the trouble of flouring my head. Darling, must I really powder?'

'You really must,' Jemima said, not without sympathy, for her own hair was tortured up over a horsehair 'piece', stuffed full of pins, larded, and powdered according to fashion. 'It would be quite an insult to your hosts – and besides, you are Sir Allen now, and must keep up appearances.'

'Well, I suppose we must suffer to be beautiful,' he said with a whimsical smile, and Jemima stepped closer and laid a hand on his shoulder.

63

'Besides again, you look *so* handsome in powder, I am almost in sympathy with the fashion. It makes you look so young, and so dashing – what are you doing? Darling, you'll get it all over you! Allen!'

'For two pins,' he murmured, kissing her again, 'I'd send word that we're both ill.'

'No pins!' she cried, extricating herself laughingly. 'What, sir, would you shock the whole world by proclaiming that you are in love with your wife? Your *wife*, sir? No, no, go and powder. I must go and see my poor Charlotte before we leave.'

Charlotte was lying hunched face down in her bed, one hand clutching a wet handkerchief beside her towelled head on the pillow. Jemima thought she was asleep, and was about to tiptoe away, when Charlotte said in a dull voice, 'Mother?'

Jemima sat down on the edge of the bed and stroked the rough hair, and after a while Charlotte rolled over and looked up at her with red-rimmed eyes.

'It isn't fair,' she said after a while, not passionately this time, but in a low, tired voice that affected Jemima much more.

'So many things in life seem unfair,' she said.

'But why did Mouse have to die?'

'Because we can't set horses' legs, darling, you know that. I wish we could.'

'I know that, but I mean *why*? It wasn't fair. He didn't do anything wrong. Why would God make him die like that?'

'Oh Charlotte, I don't know,' Jemima said, sighing. 'Animals' deaths always seem so hard, much harder than humans'. I suppose because they don't understand. But God knows even when a sparrow falls, and He has His reasons for everything.'

There was a silence. Charlotte stared past her mother at the flickering candle flame, bowing in the draught from the doorframe. At last she asked, 'What happens to animals, after they die?'

'What do you mean, after they die?' Jemima asked, puzzled. Horses were always cut up for dog food, but she had already promised Charlotte that Mouse would be buried honourably, though she had not had time yet to consider where such a grave could be dug.

'Father Ramsay says that horses have no souls. So that means they can't go to Heaven, doesn't it?'

Here was the heart of her trouble. Her eyes came reluctantly back to her mother's and she swallowed, trying to look grown-up and unconcerned.

'I don't know, darling. Father Ramsay ought to know best – but then, he has never known horses, the way we do. And I don't think God would let anything true and brave and faithful perish, do you?'

Charlotte did not answer, and in a moment Jemima pushed the damp hair from her forehead, kissed her, and stood up. The eyes followed her up, and Charlotte said in a voice shy with unaccustomedness, 'You look very pretty, Mama.' Jemima smiled down at her, and turned away. As she reached the door, she heard her say, almost too low to heard, 'I don't think I'd want to go to Heaven, if there were no horses there.'

Jemima enjoyed the ball. Though she was past forty, she was still pretty, and had a lively eye and a neat figure, and was evidently considered young enough to be asked to dance every dance, though some she refused for decency, in case there should be not partners enough for the young women. When she sat out, she enjoyed looking round the great ballroom, with its magnificent chandeliers and its mirrored wall, modelled, it was said, on Versailles, and its little gilt chairs and sconces. It had all once, for a little while, been hers, but she had never felt ownership of it, of the graceful house called 'Vanbrugh's Little Gem'. To her it always seemed to belong to the woman for whom it was built, the Countess Annunciata, whose portrait by Wissing hung over the fireplace at the end of the ballroom.

65

Jemima had met her only once, just before her death, when she was an old, old woman, but she remembered that interview vividly. Annunciata had given her, in her will, the magnificent diamond collar, gift of King Charles II, much to the annoyance of her granddaughter who had expected to have it herself. Jemima had thought then, 'I am her real heir,' though she had not entirely understood the thought. But it had turned out to be true. She had become, in her turn, Countess of Chelmsford, and mistress of Shawes, though she had not kept it long. But she saw now that it was in being mistress of Morland Place, and guardian of the family as Annunciata had been before her, that she was truly Annunciata's heir.

'If you would not think it improper to dance with a married man, would you come to the set with me?' Allen's voice broke her reverie. Jemima shook herself and smiled.

'A fig for convention. Let us shock them all,' she said, putting her hand in his.

'You were very pensive, my love,' he said as they stepped to the bottom of the set.

'I was thinking about the old Countess,' she said.

'Annunciata? Yes, she does seem particularly present here,' Allen said, smiling round as if she stood behind him.

'I don't think she would like the Fussells much, do you?' Jemima said, behind her fan.

'Nor the Chelmsfords,' Allen grinned. 'She was an exceedingly particular old lady. But I must say I find them very good sort of people. Lady Ann has been overwhelming me with her gratitude on behalf of her son, which has extended beyond poor Charlotte to a sort of generic virtue. We are all heroes by contamination. She is determined to show her gratitude, as is your brother.'

'And what form is this gratitude to take?' Jemima asked, amused.

'They beg leave to honour Flora's wedding with their presence, to offer Shawes for the wedding party, if we want it, and to have Flora and Thomas stay at Chelmsford

House when they are in London. Lady Ann offers to chaperone Flora, and to introduce her at Court, and to have her to stay for as long as she likes when Thomas is gone to sea.'

'All very well for Flora and Thomas, but what of Charlotte?' Jemima asked.

'Charlotte was mentioned at the very beginning of the conversation, but was soon swallowed in the general flood of gratitude. Now here is the part that needs a decision, my love: young Horatio is to go to Eton in January, and Chelmsford offers to do all the right things in order to send William there as well.'

'William!' Jemima said, aghast. Allen nodded.

'Yes, my own reaction was the same. But, you know, it may be that we protect the boy too much. One would not like to make him soft, through over-indulgence.'

'But I have heard how the boys live at public schools. William would not survive a week there. Besides, how could we part him from Charlotte? He would grieve terribly.'

Allen nodded. 'Well, on the whole, I think you are right. My notion was to suggest that Edward takes William's place in the scheme. He was to go to school in any case, and Eton will be so much more of an advantage to the boy than St Edward's. It doesn't matter so much what he learns, it's who he will meet. Your brother has remained friends all his life with the boys he knew at St George's.'

'Yes, Edward would take it in his stride. I don't think that boy ever notices anything. Do you think Charles would agree?'

'I think so, if I speak while the plan is still hot in his mind. I'll do it after this dance.'

'We are only half-way up the set. Do it now, if you like. I will sit down again,' Jemima said, and then saw the couple at the top turning to dance down. 'I must say, I am surprised to see Flora dance a third time with Lord Meldon. I sometimes think Thomas takes good nature a

67

little too far. But they look happy enough. Lord Meldon
has quite lost his sulky look.'

'I should think he would,' Allen said. 'He is dancing
with the second prettiest woman in the room. And since I
am dancing with the prettiest of all, the scheme must wait.
I would not have you sit down for the world.'

Flora's wedding took place on 30 December, in the chapel
at Morland Place. The Chelmsford family came to the
service, and the Fussells to the wedding breakfast, which
was held at Morland Place, Jemima refusing the more
elegant surroundings of Shawes on the grounds that it
would break Abram's heart, but really because she wanted
it to be a simple family wedding, as her own to Allen had
been.

There had not been time for a grand wedding dress, but
Jemima and Alison and the two sewing maids had got
together over Jemima's best blue silk, and Jemima had
lent the wonderful Brussels lace from her first wedding,
and the pearl half-hoop headdress which was one of the
family heirlooms, and everyone agreed that Flora could
not have looked lovelier if there had been six months and
twelve London dressmakers to prepare for it.

The young couple set off for London in the Chelmsford
coach, accompanied by Lord Meldon and Lord Chelmsford, who left Ann and the children to finish their holiday
at Shawes and who, Jemima thought, looked secretly
pleased to be going back to civilization. The families parted
on the best of terms, with the promise of a great deal more
intercourse in the future.

'I feel as though nothing exciting will ever happen again,'
Charlotte said mournfully when the coach had gone.
Jemima put an arm round her shoulder.

'Here's something exciting already for you – I have
decided that you and William are to have proper horses. So
you can help me choose, and school them. It was time you

were properly mounted – I thought so even before the accident.'

It was successful in cheering Charlotte, though William took it as quietly as if it was nothing to him. Jemima noticed from time to time that he was out of sorts, but between all her usual tasks, and trying to guide Charlotte away from unsuitable horses, and trying to find out what Edward would need for Eton, she had little enough time for observing children's moods. She did, however, witness the goodbye between William and Edward when the coach was ready to take the latter away to the south.

'I'm sorry it's me instead of you,' Edward said gravely as the brothers shook hands.

'Yes, I am too,' William said. 'But – well, you know.'

'Yes, I know. I'm sorry.'

Jemima went indoors thoughtfully as the coach passed out of sight, wondering why William should be sorry not to be going. She would have liked to ask Allen about it, but he had gone with Edward, to take him on the first part of his journey, and by the time he came back, she had forgotten the incident in the busy press of her days.

Edward was miserable from his first day at Eton. He and Horatio lodged with a sour, hard-mouthed woman called Dame Weston, whose parsimony meant privations for the boys in the way of food and coals which came hard to growing youngsters. Edward was a quiet, hard-working, obliging boy, who made no particular enemies amongst his fellows, but by the same token made no particular friends. Horatio made it clear from the beginning that he resented sharing a name with a farmer's son, and had no intention of being friendly with him: indeed, he took the lead in deriding Edward's peculiar habits, such as washing, and saying his prayers night and morning, and writing home, and reading books. Like all boys, Edward wanted to be inconspicuous amongst his peers, so he soon modified those aspects of strangeness, and once Horatio tired of baiting him, the other boys let him alone.

In his lessons Edward did well, for he had been well taught by Father Ramsay. Being by nature obedient and willing to please, he avoided the most savage beatings by the masters, though flogging and birching were so much part of education at Eton that it was impossible to remain entirely unscathed. Eton was only the width of the river from Windsor, where King George liked to spend much of his time. King George had a great interest in education. When he rode across the river to Eton, he would cry cheerfully to any boy he met, 'Well, well, my boy, when were you last flogged, eh?' If there happened to be a master about, the King would enjoin him to put the boy's name on the list for the next round of punishments. It was no comfort to the boys that the young princes were flogged as savagely, or that it was all done for their own good.

Lessons consisted mostly of Latin grammar, construing and composing, with a little writing and arithmetic on alternate days. The many other subjects Edward had been taught at home – French and Italian, astronomy, history, geography, theology – were quite neglected, but he soon learned not to talk of them, for to be highly educated was considered ungentlemanly, suitable only to 'ushers and Jesuits'. With the ill will of Horatio to help rumour along, he might have become unpopular, but he did his best to hide his education, and showed a willingness to help the others with their 'construes', and was soon put down as being 'clever', which was an epithet of pity rather than contempt. A man could no more help being 'clever' than being blind or crippled.

But even if a boy avoided being beaten by the school-masters, he might still be beaten by his fag-master when he returned to his boarding house. Edward was unfortunate in being assigned to fag for one of the worst of the seniors, a boy called Stevens, who was lazy and vicious and brutal, and as arbitrary and whimsical as any tyrant. Edward had no particular wit or charm to defend himself against such a person. Even before he had learnt what his duties were, he was being beaten for failing in them, and if he managed to get something right, Stevens would change the rules and beat him just the same.

Even the other boys, hardened to physical punishment and receiving a good deal of it themselves one way and another, pitied Edward, and were grateful Fate had not assigned *them* to Stevens. Sometimes when he had been beaten for a speck of mud on Stevens' boot, or because his fire smoked when the wind was in the east, they would gather round Edward with a certain rough sympathy to examine his wounds.

'Two of 'em are bleeding, Morland. I will say Stevens knows his stuff.'

'That one's a bit low.'

'His aim is never up to much after the second bottle.'

'Thank God I've got Crosby. Crosby can't flog for anything.'

The toast was Edward's worst trial. It was his duty to toast Stevens' bread and cheese for his supper, and it had to be done perfectly, not undercooked or burnt, and ready fresh and hot at the exact moment that Stevens wanted it. Moreover, Stevens would not allow him to use a toasting fork, and in order to get the toast near enough the flames to brown at all, Edward had to subject his fingertips to severe burning. At night in bed he wept from the pain of them, and when the blisters burst they festered. At times he could barely hold the toast without dropping it – another beatable offence. At first he prayed nightly to the Lady, and St Anthony, patron of the oppressed, to help him; but as time went on he prayed simply and desperately to God to let him die.

It was on a day in spring that Edward first caught the eye of Chetwyn, the House Captain. He had been out picking flowers for Stevens' nosegay, and had passed the senior boy with no more than a scared duck of the head, when Chetwyn called him back.

'Morland – from York, aren't you? Any relation to the Morlands who breed the racehorses?'

'My mother and father, sir,' Edward said, wondering what new derision or imposition was coming. But Chetwyn lounged gracefully against a windowsill, and seemed to be looking at him with kindly interest. 'Well, my mother mostly,' he added, encouraged.

'Your mother, eh? Well, well. Know anything about horses, boy?'

'A bit, sir. Our stallion, Artembares – I helped Mother hand-break him, sir.'

'Artembares – yes, I've seen him run. Know what your mother's sending down to Newmarket this year?'

'Yes, sir, we've a good colt called Persis, by Artembares out of a mare called Dawn. Mother thinks he's bound to do well, sir.'

'Don't call me sir, Morland. Oh, it's all right, don't look so scared, I won't eat you.' He paused thoughtfully, while Edward moved from foot to foot, worried that the flowers would wilt, or that Stevens would be looking for him. Suddenly Chetwyn smiled. 'Listen, Morland, I've got two horses over at Biggs' stable, and they need exercising. My damned groom is laid up with some sickness or other, so I need someone to ride my second horse for me. I'm taking them over to Dorney Common for a run – care to come along and help me?'

Edward stared, torn between his terror of Stevens and the inadvisability of refusing a house captain. In the end he managed to stammer, 'But S-Stevens—'

'Oh, I'll square it with Stevens, don't you worry. All right, Morland, I'll see you at Biggs' in half an hour.'

It was for Edward a blissful day. To be riding a horse again, to be away from the terror and torment of Stevens, would have been enough for him, but in addition there was the completely new experience of the kindly interest of an older boy. Chetwyn was charming to him, praised his handling of the horse, expressed an interest in all Edward's family, and displayed a knowledge of racing and breeding

72

that made Edward feel at home. They took dinner together in Datchet, and continued to chat amicably about the stud at Twelvetrees.

'You write home a lot, so the other fellows tell me,' Chetwyn said, lighting his pipe and leaning back comfortably when they had cleared their plates. Edward looked surprised, and Chetwyn said, 'Oh yes, I hear things. It's my business as House Captain to know who's who in the house. Does your mother write back to you? Does she tell you about the horses?'

'Well, she would if I asked. She only says if something important happens,' Edward said, a little puzzled.

'Ask her, next time you write. She'll be sending something to Ascot, I dare say? I'd be interested to know what. I'd be interested in *anything* she says about horses, understand?'

Edward didn't, quite, but he was too pleased and grateful for the notice to ask. 'Of course, Chetwyn,' he said. 'I'll tell you everything. Do you go to the races?'

'Oh yes,' Chetwyn said. 'I'll take you, if you like.'

'But aren't they out of bounds?'

'Certainly. But the trick is, not to be caught. My chestnut, now, he has a turn of speed. Would you say he was as fast as your mother's horses?'

At the end of a delightful day, they rode back towards Eton, and Edward felt the shadow of the place descending upon him again. They put the horses up at Biggs', and walked back through the darkening streets. As they turned into a dimly lit alley, Chetwyn stopped and put a hand on Edward's shoulder.

'I say, Morland, how would you like to be my fag, instead of Stevens'?'

A soul suffering the torments of Hell, who was offered a free passage to Heaven, could hardly have stared with more surprise, longing and gratitude than Edward stared at Chetwyn. Hardly able to believe it was a true offer, yet ready to adore and serve him to the last drop of his blood if it were, Edward could only nod speechlessly.

'Very well, I'll fix it. Come to my study tonight at supper time. I'll speak to Stevens right away. Don't worry, he'll agree. He'll have to.'

'Thank you, Chetwyn,' Edward breathed, his eyes shining. Chetwyn's hand increased its pressure a little on his shoulder.

'That's all right. I'm sure we'll get on very well, you and I.'

CHAPTER FOUR

Henri Maria Fitzjames Stuart, who used his title of Comte de Strathord when it suited him, was lying very languidly in bed with the plump and pink Madame Brouillard when his servant Duncan gave the alarm from down in the street. The two-note whistle meant that Monsieur Brouillard was coming home, unexpectedly early, and its effect on Henri was electrifying. Electricity had been demonstrated before the late King Louis XV, when a hundred monks, holding hands, had been connected to an electric current, and had all jumped simultaneously, a most amusing sight. Henri jumped out of bed and into his breeches with as much violence, bundled the rest of his clothes in his cloak and threw them out of the window to the waiting Duncan, kissed Madame Brouillard on her soft, sulky lips, and departed by the same exit as his clothes. The projecting stone lintel of the window below made a stepping-stone, and Duncan's arm steadied him as he landed from the six-foot drop.

'This way, sir, down this alley. There's a doorway where you can dress in safety,' Duncan said. He handed Henri his garments imperturbably and knelt on the slimy cobbles to fasten the breeches over the stockings as if it were a first-floor apartment at Versailles, but Henri could feel his disapproval seeping through his fingertips. Duncan did not object to his master having mistresses, and obviously mistresses must be married women, but he did not think it right or dignified that he should debauch the wives of the bourgeois, who objected to such things and necessitated descents from windows. Moreover, Poissonnieres was one of the less pleasant and most odiferous sections of Paris, and traces of rotting fish were extremely difficult to eradicate from silk and velvet clothes.

'Thank you, Duncan,' Henri said, lifting his chin for his cravat to be tied. The sounds of altercation came from the open window through which he had just departed. 'I think we had better put some distance between us and the scene, in case good Brouillard takes it into his head to come searching for us.'

'Very good, sir,' Duncan said, and Henri clapped his shoulder consolingly.

'Comfort yourself, my man, that I do not think I shall be able to go back there again.' Angry voices suddenly sounded in the street around the corner, and Henri grabbed his cloak hastily. 'I shall go to Madame de Murphy's. You had better go and get yourself something to eat. Come for me there at dinner time.'

Madame de Murphy's house was in the Rue St Anne, not far from the Palais Royale, small but handsome, with a courtyard front and rear and lime trees growing around it. Her husband Meurice was a Colonel of the Royal Ecossais, whose forebears had gone into exile in the time of James II, and had added the 'de' to their name long enough ago for Meurice to bear it comfortably. Madame was very rich in her own right, being the daughter of a silk merchant. On arriving at the house, Henri found a clutch of coaches standing in the courtyard and the road outside, and realized at once that Ismène was having one of her tiresome 'salons'. He slipped quietly round to the back courtyard and up the servant's stair where he met Ismène's maid just coming out of her bedroom.

The girl stifled a squeak of alarm, and then laid a hand to her breast.

'Oh m'sieur, how you startled me! I thought you were a robber.'

'Do I look like a robber, Marie?' Henri asked, smiling as he slid an arm round Marie's pliant waist.

'But yes, most like a robber,' she said, yielding with accustomed pleasure. He kissed her mouth, and the curving tops of her breasts.

'Your mistress has company, I see.'

'The usual ones, all come to talk, talk, talk. But I think they will not be long now. Will you not join them, m'sieur?'

'No, Marie, I will not,' he said, allowing the hand at her waist to slip downward to her buttocks. 'I will wait for Madame quietly in her room. That is why I came in the back way. Like you, my censorious little friend, I do not care for their talk, talk, talk.' He gave her one last hearty kiss and sent her away. 'Tell Madame I am here when they have gone.'

When her guests had gone, and Madame de Murphy finally stepped through into her room, Henri was lying on her bed, one arm propped behind his head, peacefully smoking a cigar.

'Faugh! Henri, what have you been doing? You smell dreadful,' she cried.

'That is why I am smoking a cigar, my dear Ismène, to disguise the smell.'

'Well, get off my bed at once. How should I explain such a smell to Meurice?'

'The smell is only on my clothes. If I take them off—'

'Definitely not, Henri. Come into the other room and have some coffee, and be civilized.' She swung on her heel and went back into her drawing room, and Henri smiled and got up and sauntered after her.

'You are loveliest when you scold me, Ismène,' he said.

He came up behind her and kissed the nape of her neck, but she shook him away and asked sharply, 'So why do you smell so abominably of fish?'

'I was in bed with a fishmonger's wife, and had to leave through the window. I threw my clothes out first, and they landed in – something.'

She looked at him scornfully, her eyes spitting anger. 'Why do you do such things? The wives of bourgeois, indeed! Why must you go to bed with women whose husbands object? Are there not enough with complacent husbands?'

'For the same reason that you mix with those dreadful

77

friends of yours who have just left,' he said serenely, 'because it amuses me.'

'They are not dreadful, they are very clever people, who say very clever things.'

'None of them has an original thought, Ismène, and you know it. They quote from books all the time.' He walked to the table and picked up the books that covered it and put them down again contemptuously. 'Look at them! Corneille, Plutarch, Cicero – and this, the worst of all – Rousseau!'

'I forbid you to speak a word about Rousseau,' Ismène snapped, setting down the coffee pot so hastily she almost broke it. 'I will not have his noble works sullied by your wicked tongue.'

Henri crowed with laughter. 'Noble! The bilious outpourings of an impotent adolescent, hovering on the edge of—'

'Henri, be silent!' She stood up, quivering with rage. 'Be silent or I shall strike you.'

'Listen to this, for instance,' he went on, watching her from the corner of his eye as he picked up a book of Rousseau's and opened it at random. ' "Man is born free, and everywhere he is in irons." How stirring! How noble! And how completely untrue! Man is born in the most abject of dependence, unable even to control his own bowels, and is in feoff to anyone who will feed and house him until at least his tenth year. But the untruth of the statement will not deter Rousseau, or his ardent followers, will it?'

He had his wish. She flew at him like a wildcat, and he dropped the book, laughing, and caught her wrists, and wrestled with her until he had her arms pinned behind her back and her body pressed against his.

'You are irresistible when you forget your dignity and show your claws,' he murmured, kissing her lips until they softened and he saw the ferocity in her eyes replaced by that thrilling look of languor. Her body ceased to resist him and began to press against him avidly, and in spite of his exertions with Madame Brouillard, he felt his own reaction rousing in him. 'I do think I had better get out of these clothes, don't you?'

'Damn you, Henri,' Ismène murmured between kisses. He released her arms, and she took his hand and led him into the inner chamber.

Later, when they were lying in each other's arms, happy, flushed, and satisfied, Ismène reproached him again, but affectionately.

'Really, Henri, why do you go with such dreadful people? What possible amusement it can be to you completely escapes me.'

'But I feel just the same way about your salons,' Henri said equably. 'All your earnest young men, with the down barely grown upon their cheeks, swapping a stale mash of undigested, half-chewed, whimsical ideas—'

'But you do not know!' she sat up as she grew animated. 'We talk about so many things – not just the works of those authors you despise, but about important things—'

'What important things?' he said cynically.

'The way the country should be governed, and the nature of Man, and Freedom—' Henri caught her in his arms and pulled her mouth down to his in a kiss that stopped the list.

'*That* is the nature of man. It takes more than good intentions and the conversation of ardent young men to change man's nature for very long. And as for freedom – it is just a word. A very dangerous word, it is true, for it has a thrilling, ringing sound that fires the heart. You expect somehow that at the very sound of it all walls will fall flat and all doors fly open. Beware of thrilling words, my Ismène, like freedom and truth. The first thing they do is kill somebody.'

'Then how would you have us live?' she said crossly, pouting a little. 'Like beasts? We must search for the truth.'

'This is the truth, my darling,' he smiled, 'that my hand fits your naked breast as a nest fits a bird. And that your

79

tongue tastes of honey and apples—' a long silence, 'and that it is time I got up and got dressed, before your husband, my friend, comes home.'

'Oh, Meurice will not dine at home today,' she murmured, the languid look returning to her eyes. 'We have plenty of time.'

The *Ariadne* was somewhere in the Mediterranean in October 1774 when Flora gave birth to a daugher at Morland Place. Her brother Charles was there, however, and he persuaded Flora that Thomas would be pleased if the child were named Louisa after their dead sister. It had not been a difficult birth, and Flora was soon up and about again. The baby was sent to be suckled by the shepherd's wife who had also suckled little James, and was the only wet-nurse Alison would trust.

'She'll look after your little one all right, don't you worry,' she told Flora, dosing her with periwinkle to stop her milk. 'She'll bring her up to the house every day, so you'll see she's well, and as soon as she's got the little lamb weaned onto ewe's milk, we shall have her back here in the nursery.'

Flora, too preoccupied with the pain of her breasts to care much about the baby, only wondered a little whether it might not be better to give her milk to her baby than to try to send it back whence it came with tight bindings. Alison looked shocked.

'And spoil your pretty figure? What an idea! You'll thank me in years to come, when you've still a figure like a lady, instead of like a cottager's wife. I know it frets you now, child,' she added more kindly, 'but the periwinkle will soon stop that. In a week's time you'll have forgotten you ever had a baby.'

And true enough, in a week's time she came down from her chamber to re-enter the world, and was happy to forget her confinement, which seemed like a strange dream, and interest herself in the affairs of the family.

Charlotte was excited about her new horse, Sorrell, which Allen was afraid was too much for her, though Jemima was sure she'd manage it in the end. Allen was preoccupied with the election, which had given Lord North and the Government a majority, on account of the low level of land tax which had made it popular. Jemima was worried about the price their cloth had fetched last week, and because Allen had to go to London to consult the College of Arms about their coat of arms.

'We have to get special permission, you see, for Edward to display the Morland arms in the first quarter when he inherits,' Allen explained to Flora. 'Normally he would show my arms in the first quarter, and the Morland, Moubray and Neville arms in the other three, in that order. But as the Morland estate is far the most important, and he is taking the Morland name too, it would seem more appropriate—'

'But I just wish you could write, and not have to go yourself,' Jemima said plaintively. 'I've only just got used to having you back.' He smiled indulgently and patted her arm.

'I shall be gone only a fortnight, dearest. I shall have to be back for the assizes in any case.'

William, Flora found, was most interested in a letter from Edward, now in his second half at Eton, which was so much more full of interesting detail than his letters during his first half had been. Charles had been excited that the sweet gum tree he had brought back from America had not only survived its first year in the American Garden, but was displaying the beautiful autumn foliage for which it was prized, and had provided sufficient seeds for him to begin cultivating them for sale. But on the day Flora came downstairs he received a letter from Philippe de Courcey, which was an event to eclipse even a prize tree in his mind.

The situation in America was so little generally discussed in England that it was largely from Philippe that Charles had learnt of the measures taken since the Boston 'tea party' incident, though Allen took a mild interest in it for his sake, and passed on tidbits he gathered from his brother-in-law Chelmsford. The Port Act had closed Boston harbour to all trade, which should have been a severe blow to colonial trade in New England; while the Massachusetts Government Act abolished the locally elected Council of Massachusetts and replaced it by one nominated by the Crown. In June the Quartering Act had allowed the billeting of troops away from barracks, in barns or uninhabited houses, thus allowing them to be spread more effectively. But by far the most unpopular act with the colonists was the Quebec Act. The government had hoped that this Act would 'settle' and 'anglicize' the northern province of Canada, but it had not.

'I believe the act intended to be fair to the settlers in Canada, rather than unfair to the rest of America,' Philippe had written, 'but our neighbours do not see it that way. Most of all they object to the clause that gives religious freedom to Roman Catholics in Canada. Naturally *we* rejoice at that, but the Protestants, particularly in New England, claim that the British Government is a convert to Rome, and that the Act is the first step in crushing their religion and imposing Popery over the whole country. I shall never understand this hysterical fear of Catholicism. We have been in fear of reprisals but apart from some offensive drawings sent to us anonymously there has been nothing. Tempers grow cooler the further south you go.'

That had been written in July, and Charles had been anxious to hear that no harm had come to them. Philippe's October letter spoke of the Continental Congress which had opened in Philadelphia in September.

'Representatives were sent from all the colonies except Georgia, and the meetings so far have been very calm and moderate. They are trying to discover ways of restoring harmony between ourselves and the Government, and the Government seems not to have objected – at least, the Congress has not been banned.'

A little further down in the letter, Philippe broke off an account of local affairs to add, 'I have just heard more of the Continental Congress, which is still sitting. I am afraid it is not good news. It seems a rumour reached the Congress that General Gage had blown up Boston Town, which though proved false was readily believed in Philadelphia. The Congress has resolved to ban all imports from and exports to England. The import ban is to operate from December the first; the export ban, on account of the hardship it would cause the southern colonies, is not to come in until September next year. Whether it will have the effect on England that the Congress hopes for, I cannot guess. But I am sure that it will make relationships more strained than ever between America and England. A war between our countries is unthinkable, and yet our differences seem to be irreconcilable. How I wish you could have visited us this summer, as we hoped – it would have been such a comfort to us both. Write soon, and let us know what is being said in England, and if anything is being planned, give us due notice. I worry more for Eugenie's sake than my own.'

When Charles had read this part aloud, Allen said, 'He is right that war is unthinkable, and you may write and tell him, Charles, that the Government has no more desire for it than he. Chelmsford tells me that one of the reasons Lord North called an election now was so as to be free to deal with the American situation immediately. And the King wishes only that the colonies should acknowledge sovereignty, not that they should be subdued. Chelmsford said that North was talking of a free pardon and amnesty, and a scheme to allow the colonies to conduct their own taxation affairs.'

'I will tell him so,' Charles said, not looking any happier, 'but I am afraid that there are some hotheads amongst the colonists who will be satisfied with nothing less than a complete break with England, and you know yourself, sir, how a few wild men can sway a mass of indifferent people.'

'True. But I do not think even the indifferent people will actually fight, for it would be a civil war, you know, not like fighting a foreign enemy. Most men will stop at killing their own countrymen. I saw it again and again in Scotland, in the '45.'

'Well, I hope you are right, sir. All the same, I wish there was some way I could be there with them, and see for myself.'

From being so miserable at Eton that he wanted to die, Edward had passed to being so happy he never wanted to leave. His work was so good that he had been advanced to a higher class, and with his usual care and attention to lessons he was able to avoid beatings from his masters and even win their praise and approval. But most importantly, he had the protection and friendship of Chetwyn.

Edward had always been a lonely boy, though it was only now, bathed in the roseate glow of his association with the House Captain, that he realized it. From birth he had been enclosed in the solitude and responsibility of being the eldest, the heir, a solitude made more absolute by the fact that the next to him in age were the twins, so utterly wrapped up in each other. He had had no companion to share his thoughts, even amongst the adults: his father was away so much, his mother so busy, and Father Ramsay, though a good teacher and just lawgiver, was not a kindly or affectionate man. It was only a few months before that he had made the acquaintance of John Anstey, towards whom he had been making the first shy approaches of friendship when he was sent away to school.

But he could never have imagined a friendship like this, with an older boy whom he could respect and admire and serve, whose apparent affection for himself was such an honour that Edward knew not how to deserve it. The tasks he had done in fear and loathing for Stevens he did with pride for Chetwyn. He managed to get the best coals from the weekly ration for Chetwyn's fire, and when they ran out, as they always did in the winter half, he roamed far and wide in his free time to pick up firewood. He polished Chetwyn's boots to a glassy gleam, brushed his clothes better than a valet, made his bed and mixed his bath, fetched and carried for him, toasted his supper cheese, and glowed with delight when Chetwyn invited him to stay and share it.

Love brought out the best in him. He was a boy of no outstanding beauty, but he had pleasantly regular features, wavy brown hair, and large pale-blue eyes, which needed only an expression of happiness to be attractive. Chetwyn, on the other hand, was handsome. He was a tall, well-made young man, excellent at all sports and games, a fine horseman, a graceful dancer, and charming enough to get by without being particularly clever at anything. He had a handsome face, high-coloured, with bright green eyes and smooth, shiny hair the colour, Edward always thought, of a bay horse – almost conker-coloured.

Their friendship, extending as it soon did beyond the normal bounds of fag and fag master, attracted attention, but no great curiosity. Chetwyn's father, the Earl of Aylesbury, was a racing man, which gave them enough in common to explain anything that needed explaining, and Chetwyn's rescue of Edward from Stevens was only what everyone expected from a good-natured fellow like him. Once or twice a master, in beating Edward for being out of bounds with Chetwyn at Datchet or Ascot races, might wonder whether to reprove the elder boy for his bad example; and sometimes another senior boy would ask Chetwyn to tell his damned fag not to take more than his share of coals and hot water. But no wonder could outlast seven days in such a community.

One bitter-cold evening in December, Edward was kneeling pensively in the hearth preparing supper, while Chetwyn, with a great deal of splashing and half-finished songs, was bathing in the next room. The latter had been out hunting with a couple of his peers, and Edward guessed that they had been in an alehouse for some time before Chetwyn had finally come home for his bath. He wondered whether Chetwyn had met a girl there, for he seemed more than usually cheerful. He knew some of the seniors had girls, and only last week Stevens had been flogged savagely for attempting to seduce the headmaster's daughter. He was still wondering about it when Chetwyn came through from the next room, flushed and damp and wrapped only in his towel, and scurried to the fire saying, 'Make room there, Morland. It's so damned cold, the water's turning to ice on my back. Here, take an end and rub me down, will you?'

Edward laid down the toasting fork – no blistered fingers in Chetwyn's service – and took the end of the towel and rubbed briskly at the smooth-skinned back, while his master leaned forward to the glow and dried his face and neck with the other end.

'That's better – brrr, I thought I should perish. Rub as hard as you like, Morland, I shan't mind. You know my mother says if two people use the same towel, they will quarrel. She's full of little nonsenses like that. Do you think there's any chance of us quarrelling?' He laughed, not requiring an answer. 'Do you know, MacArthur offered me five guineas for you the other day. You're getting a reputation for assiduousness, old fellow! Well, you can always set up as a valet when you leave here, if you have no other career in mind.'

He realized there was a certain lack of response from the younger boy, and paused to look at him. Edward had his eyes averted, and Chetwyn said kindly, 'What's the matter, Morland? You're very quiet.' No answer. 'Has anyone been upsetting you? Has Stevens been at you again?'

'No – no, Chetwyn. Nothing like that.'

'Well then, what's the matter?' He waited a long time, while Edward turned the end of the towel round in his fingers, his eyes on the flickering flames.

At last the boy said, 'I was thinking of Christmas, and going home.'

'Yes?' Chetwyn said encouragingly.

'And then I thought – well, you won't be here much longer will you?' It came out in a rush, and Edward's eyes

86

came up and round to him, with all sorts of unaskable questions in them.

'Only one more half,' Chetwyn said gently. 'If I weren't so stupid, I should have been gone by now. You might never have known me,' he added, trying to make a joke of it. Edward's eyes were dangerously bright. Chetwyn leaned a little towards him. 'I say, Morland,' he said, 'would you like to come home to Wolvercote with me, to my people, for Christmas? I'm sure my parents would like it, if yours would give permission.'

Edward glowed. 'Really? Do you really mean it?'

Chetwyn nodded. Edward stared at him, filled with a strange and indescribable delight. Chetwyn's smooth side was rosy where the fire-glow warmed it, and two tiny images of the flames danced in his eyes, which seemed dark by contrast. A lock of his straight, silky hair had fallen forward in a smooth curve, like a wing, and Edward suddenly wanted to reach up and push it back, though he did not dare. The towel lay forgotten on the floor between them, the bread was abandoned untoasted in the hearth, and there was no sound but the snap and hiss of the wood burning in the grate. It was Chetwyn who finally put up a hand to brush away the brown hair, Chetwyn, too, who reached forward to place his hands on Edward's trembling shoulders.

On a dark and showery, windy day in April 1775, large ragged clouds were tearing across the sky, dark grey against the flat grey of the cloud blanket above them. Rain fell in soaking hatfuls, thrown by the wind against the ramparts of Portsmouth and the oilskins of the few hardy souls who walked there. The sea was grey and tossing, flecked all over with white horses, and with the larger white patches that were the sails of ships.

The coach put William down at the dockyard gates, and he huddled into his collar as a cold squall dashed around him, and felt completely lost. Beyond the gates and the grey buildings, he could see a forest of masts and spars, like naked winter trees against the low sky. The wind smelled of salt and fish and dead weed and tar, smells so alien to a nose accustomed to earth and grass and sheep that they made him feel dizzy. The coachman let down his box, and the second coachman thumped it to the cobbles beside William. Accustomed as he was to delivering young boys to the gates of their naval careers, he yet felt sorry for William.

'By God, you're a little 'un, though,' he shouted. 'I wonder they thought of the sea for you. How old are you, boy?'

'Twelve,' William said, trying to keep his lip from quivering. The second coachman shook his head.

'You look no more than eight. There's the dockyard gates. Go through to the office, and tell 'em your business. They'll see to you.'

'Thank you, sir,' William said, grateful for any guidance in this strange world. He managed to get his box onto his shoulder, and heard the coachman say as he turned away, 'I wouldn't wonder if that one hadn't run away. Well, they'll sort him out in the dockyard. Twelve, my foot!'

There was enough rain on his face for the odd tear not to show, but he had his voice under control by the time he came to the office, and spoke to the one-armed clerk inside.

'The *Ariadne*? What name?' William told him, and he checked with a list. 'Quite right. Well, she went out of harbour this morning, first light.'

William stared in panic. Out of harbour? 'I have missed her?' he said, dry-mouthed. The clerk sucked his teeth impatiently.

'No, no, she's gone up to Spithead. There'll be a boat going out to her at six this evening from the sally-port. You can go in that.'

'Thank you, sir,' William said, and then just stood and stared. He had no idea what to do next, where to go, how to occupy himself until six o'clock. The clerk took pity on him.

'Just come off the coach, have you? I daresay you'll be hungry.'

'Yes, sir.'

'Got any money?'

'Yes, sir.'

'Well, go out of the gates and turn to your left. You'll see a tavern along there, The Ship. Go and get yourself a fourpenny ordinary and sit by the fire until it's time to go. They'll tell you where the sally-port is. And keep your hand on your money, child, and don't show more than fourpence of it to anyone. There are sharks even in these waters, and you look more tender than the usual bait.'

At the corner of the trestle nearest the inn's fire, with his feet safely on his box, and his jacket gently steaming, William felt a great deal more cheerful, and attacked the plateful of food in front of him with childish appetite. Boiled mutton, pease pudding, carrots and winter cabbage, and a large hunk of rather mousey-looking bread at the side to mop up the gravy, made a good fourpenn'orth, and William had proudly ordered two pennyworth of ale to go with it, and felt for the first time in control of his life. It was the first time he had ever eaten in a tavern, or indeed paid for his own food, and as the damp, pale hair dried on his forehead, he felt his spirits rising.

'Make the most of it, young 'un,' the waiter had said jovially as he slapped an extra dab of pease pudding on William's plate. 'Nothing for you now but salt meat and hard bread for God knows how long – maybe for ever, if a cannonball takes your head off before you see home again. Still, your father'll be glad to know you're provided for.'

But William was not deterred by such talk. It had been his idea from the start, ever since he had heard that Cousin Thomas was to spend a week at Morland Place before sailing for the West Indies. General Gage in Boston had asked for more troops, and the Generals Howe, Clinton and Burgoyne were to sail to join him. *Ariadne* was to collect one of them at Portsmouth, and then sail round to Cork to pick up and convoy one of the troopships, the

Norwich. Troopships, being built for the purpose of carrying as many men as possible, were not able to carry also the firepower to defend themselves, so a convoy was necessary.

Uncle Thomas had not been hard to persuade: to him, nothing was more natural than that a boy should want to go to sea.

'I'll take him with me as a volunteer. He can be my servant, and run messages, and as soon as he learns his way around, I'll give him a warrant as midshipman,' he had said. The reaction of the family, however, was exactly as William had feared.

'William go to sea? Nonsense!' Jemima had cried. 'Why, he would not last a week on a ship.'

'Once we are out of harbour, it is a very healthy life, you know,' Thomas had said mildly. 'Plenty of fresh air, no infectious diseases—'

'But the hardship,' Jemima cried. Allen agreed with her.

'The food and accommodation, Thomas,' he protested. 'I know you make nothing of them, but William is delicate. I doubt whether—'

'And the damp, always to be damp and cold. His lungs, Thomas, consider!' Jemima broke in. 'He would die for sure.'

'I do not think,' Father Ramsay said, 'that the boy has the strength or constitution for such an active life.'

It was the beginning of a week of hard work and frustration for William, a week of arguing and persuading, and finally of passionate pleas.

'You sent Edward to school instead of me! You never let me do anything. I am strong, really I am, if you'll only give me a chance. I keep up with Charlotte, in everything she does. How can I ever make anything of myself if you keep me at home here like a baby? I might as well be dead as stay here like that, to be an invalid all my life.'

'William, be quiet,' Jemima said. 'No one wants you to be treated like an invalid all your life. But there are other careers open to you that do not need so much physical stamina – the Church, for instance, or the law. What sense is there in taxing yourself beyond your powers?'

But in the end, it was his father who came to his rescue. 'He really seems to care deeply that we sent Edward to school instead of him,' he said to Jemima when they were alone. 'He feels that we slighted him, that we are ashamed of him. I think, whatever we fear, we ought to let him do this, if it is what he wants. He is probably much stronger than we think.'

'Than *I* think, you mean,' Jemima said, and sighed. 'It is my fault, I know. I try to keep him safe. I didn't know he was so unhappy. I remember you once said you thought we protected him too much. You understood him better than I.'

Allen kissed her. 'We cannot keep them from every danger, whatever we do. And as Thomas says, it is a healthy life.'

Jemima smiled. 'Oh no, you cannot persuade me I am wrong about the hazards involved. I consent to let him take them, that is all. I don't suppose I shall ever see him again—' The smile quivered and broke, and he took her in his arms, and held her tightly.

The worst thing for William was quarrelling with Charlotte for the first time in their lives. Charlotte was always quick-tempered, and that they had not quarrelled before was probably largely due to William's habit of agreeing with her. But that week she was more than usually irritable, and when it was all agreed, and Thomas had departed, having left instructions as to how William should join him and what he would need in his box, she entirely lost her temper. William was still not clear what it had been about.

'So, you are going off and leaving me!' she had cried. 'I might have known it. Boys have all the luck, and girls have none, but I might have expected you to stand by me, my own twin! Why should you go to sea, and not me! You know it's what I've always wanted, more than anything.'

'But I thought it was to be with horses you wanted

most,' William had said, bewildered. 'You couldn't have horses at sea.'

'You're jealous because Sorrell's a better horse than yours. But then I'm a better horseman than you – I suppose you were jealous of that, too. So you thought you'd show me. Well, I don't care. Go to sea, and leave me behind, and I wish you luck of it! You'll be drowned first minute, and I shan't care. I'd have made a better sailor than you ever could. It isn't fair. You ought to be the girl, and me the boy. Why should you have everything?'

And she burst into tears of rage, and rushed away. William was sure she had not been making sense, but though temper was nothing out of the way, it was strange to him to be the victim of it, and stranger still not to understand what was going on in her mind. It grieved him terribly not to be close to her. It had only been his determination to prove to his parents that they need not be ashamed of him which had given him the courage even to think of parting from his twin. It had not occurred to him to explain his feelings to her, for he had always thought she understood them better than himself. It had not entered his mind that he needed to say to her, 'It will tear my heart to leave you, but it is a thing I must do.' He had assumed she knew all that.

Their estrangement had lasted until the day he left, and had almost persuaded him to change his mind. But on the last morning, she had come to him before he was up, and slipped under the cover with him, as she had used to do when they were much younger, and hugged him. No words had passed, of explanation or forgiveness, but William felt easier at once. Then she slipped something into his hand – a lock of tough, grey hair, tied into a circle with red thread.

'It's a piece of Mouse's mane. Josh cut it off for me, before he buried him. Promise you'll keep it with you all the time?'

'I promise. It will be my talisman, like in the stories,' William had said. Now, by the fire in The Ship tavern, he felt for it in his breast pocket, for reassurance. He might be gone two years, or three. He might not see Charlotte again until she was a young lady, and dressing her hair up. The West India station was the best of all to serve on, everyone said that. He thought of the things he would bring back for her, when he came home again, whenever that would be – shawls, and tortoiseshell combs, and mother-of-pearl brooches, and coral earrings. He might have made a fortune by then. As the flickering fire dried his wet stockings, he dreamed of telling her his adventures, and imagined her gazing at him, open-mouthed but silent with admiration.

CHAPTER FIVE

With the April wind blowing from a gentler and more springlike quarter, the weather had turned mild, and in a matter of days everything seemed to have burst simultaneously into bud and blossom. A restlessness came over Flora, driving her from room to room in search of company or occupation, but she was out of luck. Allen was away in London again, on some undisclosed business; Jemima was over at Twelvetrees, where five mares had come simultaneously on heat, and two entire colts had fought each other in more than mere play. Father Ramsay, of course, was teaching the children, except for Mary, who had been whisked away by Alison. Mary had grown rapidly and Alison wanted to go over her frocks with her, to see what she needed new. Father Ramsay allowed her to go without regret. Mary was an undistinguished scholar, and had a particularly penetrating sigh which was driving the priest to distraction.

Flora picked up a book and laid it down again, played a few notes on the harpsichord, looked with disfavour at her embroidery frame, and was kneeling on the windowseat in the drawing room, dangling her arms out of the window in a most ungraceful manner, when Rachel, the younger nursery maid, found her.

'Oh, there you are, miss,' Rachel said, advancing on her with a large white bundle in her arms. Flora wriggled round on the seat and held out her arms.

'How is she today, Rachel?' Little Louisa, six months old now, was growing heavy, Flora noticed, as she jiggled her in her arms and stared into her face. It was odd how much her features altered, she thought. When she was newborn, she was the image of Thomas; in a few weeks she

94

had begun to favour Flora much more; now, at six months, Flora thought she looked most like her brother Charles.

'Oh, she's a little nuisance today, miss, and won't settle for anything. I think maybe she's starting a tooth. I was for taking her out in the fresh air for a while, and I thought you might like to see her first.'

'I'll take her out,' Flora said, glad for something to do, and when Rachel looked doubtful, she added, 'only you must come with me, to make sure I don't harm her.'

'You won't harm her, I'm sure, miss,' Rachel said out of politeness. 'But come with us by all means, if you like.' She took the baby back from Flora firmly, having been brought up to the opinion that parents should not take too much notice of their children, for everyone's sake. It was quite proper for a mother or father to hold the bairn for a minute or two each day and say how handsome it was growing, but that was all. 'Best let me carry her, miss, in case you rumple your dress.'

Flora, reduced to her proper status again, yielded the baby up and walked meekly in the wake of the nursery maid. Outside, the air smelled so fresh and sweet it roused her restlessness to a new pitch of agony.

'Oh, how I long for something to do!' she cried aloud, unable to restrain herself. 'Don't you ever get bored, Rachel? So bored you could scream?'

'I don't have time to get bored, miss,' Rachel said severely, and then, realizing she had spoken out of turn, seeing as Miss Flora was a married lady now, and no more in the province of the nursery, she added kindly, 'You'll be missing Captain Thomas, miss, that's only natural. It is a shame when a man's work takes him away from his home and family. The poor master, for instance, up and down to London, and into York and Leeds and I don't know where-all-else. A man should work in his own house and his own field, that's what my father always said. He had a cousin that went to work in a finishing shed near Leeds, a factory when all's said and done, and he always said it was unnatural. But I suppose a man can't be in the navy without being away from home. I suppose it's all right for a young man that's not married – though I cannot remember being so surprised as when the mistress agreed to let little William go. It'll be a wonder if that child lives to his next birthday – and here's Miss Charlotte pining for him so badly, she'll make herself sick with grief.'

'Yes, she does seem rather quiet since William went,' Flora said, 'but I suppose that's because she has no one else to talk to. Like me.' A neat twist brought the thread back to its beginning. 'With the mistress out all day, I've no one to talk to and nothing to do. I wish now I'd accepted Lord and Lady Chelmsford's invitation to go to London. At least I'd have had some company there. But it seemed wrong, somehow, with Thomas only just gone away.'

Rachel paused under a blossoming apple tree – they had walked into the orchard – and gauging Flora's mood, said, 'Well, miss, it doesn't seem to me that it matters whether Captain Thomas went yesterday or two months ago. Gone is gone, and there's no reason for you to stay here and be fretful if you'd sooner be elsewhere.'

'It's not as if I'm any use to anyone here,' Flora agreed readily. 'Not even to little Louisa, since you won't let me near her.' She pulled the shawl back from the baby's small face and looked down at her. Louisa's dark blue eyes stared past her with a kind of imperial disregard, and her lips pursed as if in disapproval. A white petal, bruised brown at the edges, drifted down and landed on the baby's cheek, and Flora brushed it away with a finger. 'Will she be pretty?' she asked Rachel.

'Pretty enough,' Rachel granted. Her praise was always meted out as if there were only so much to go round. 'I'll be taking her in in a minute – I know the master thinks fresh air is a cure-all, but it's only April when all's said. Why don't you walk on for a bit, miss? I think your brother's in his garden somewhere.'

'I see – you want to be rid of me. You doubt my influence on the child. Well, perhaps you are right. Take her away,

Rachel. I shall go and find Charles, and try to corrupt him instead.'

'Nay, miss, you shouldn't talk so light,' Rachel shook her head, and hurried the baby away as a mild puff of wind ruffled her wrappings. Flora went on to the American Garden, which was taking shape very nicely now, and found Charles sitting under a tree, smoking a pipe of tobacco.

'Well, I see I am too late,' Flora called out as she came upon him. 'I meant to come and corrupt you from hard work into idleness, but here you are courting rheumatism by sitting on the wet grass, and doing nothing after all.'

'I have a sack under me,' Charles said, not offering to rise, and Flora saw in a moment that he was not dreaming happily.

'What is it, Charles? You seem too melancholy for such a fine day.' He did not reply, and she said impatiently, 'If I cannot sit down, I do think you might at least stand up.'

'Oh, I'm sorry,' he said, pulling himself to his feet. Even the lassitude of his movements proclaimed him unhappy. 'One of my orchids has died, and those roots I was storing through the winter have rotted. I shall lose the half of them. It's enough to make one give up altogether.'

Flora eyed him without sympathy. '*That* isn't why you are gloomy. You've lost plants before – hundreds of them. You're thinking about those Americans again, aren't you?' He did not answer. 'Really, Charles, what's the use of thinking about them all the time if it makes you so miserable?'

'Can't you understand that I'm worried about them?' Charles said. 'They may be in danger, and they are all alone—'

'Don't be silly,' Flora interrupted. 'Rich people are never alone. And besides, why should *you* worry about them? They are nothing to you – hardly even cousins.'

'Philippe was very kind to me,' Charles began weakly, and Flora scoffed.

'Oh, Philippe was kind to you, was he? Come, Charles,

you must think me a simpleton. It is the daughter you are thinking about, not the father.' His silence was confession enough. 'Well, it's you who are the simpleton, and I'm sorry a brother of mine should be such a fool. You only met her once, Charles, you don't know her well enough to be carrying on in this way.'

'Oh Flora, how can you talk like that? How long do you have to know someone to fall in love with them?'

'You think yourself in love with her? Well then, there's no more to be said. You had better make an offer for her hand, and then you'll carry her off and leave that kind father all alone.'

'Of course I wouldn't,' he said unguardedly. 'She's her father's heir, so she couldn't come to England. I would have to—'

'You would have to go and live over there?' Flora shook her head. 'Give up everything, leave your own land, and go and live in a strange country amongst foreigners for the rest of your life, all for a girl you've seen only once?'

'You go too fast, Flora. He would probably never agree, anyway.'

'Oh Charles!' She stared at him ruefully, and many things went through her mind, none of which she could say. For her own selfish reasons, she wanted to shake him out of this notion, for she had lost too many of those near to her to relish the prospect of losing him too. But deeper and darker than that was the growing doubt about her own marriage to Thomas. She did not want, though she could not admit it even to herself, to think of Charles marrying as she did, on a whim, someone he did not in the least know, only to discover afterwards that it did not answer. Charles could have refused permission when she had asked to marry Thomas. If only the positions could now be reversed, and she could refuse him permission to marry the Creole!

She left him to his brooding, and walked about the moat for a while before going in, and when she reached the barbican she saw Jemima approaching it from another direction, riding Poppy, with little James up on the saddle in front of her. Not so little James now: he was nearly eight, and his hard, wiry body was almost as big as William's at twelve.

'Look what I found paddling in the brook,' Jemima called to Flora as she rode up. 'This naughty truant, barelegged as an eel! I cannot find out if he has lost his shoes and stockings, or if he never had 'em on.'

'Eels don't have legs,' Flora objected.

'Some eels do – Cousin Charles said so,' James offered unwisely.

'You hush, you wicked thing,' Jemima said, pinching him. 'What your father will say I can't think.'

'Papa isn't here,' James said with some complacency.

'He'll be back tonight,' Jemima said sternly, tossing him down to Flora and dismounting.

'Why is it wicked?' James changed position quickly. 'Papa says fresh air is good for you.' He leaned back familiarly against Flora, his accustomed prop.

'It's wicked because you were disobedient. I sent you to your lessons this morning. You hadn't permission to leave them.'

'You didn't exactly *say* I had to go to lessons this morning. And you didn't exactly *say* I wasn't to leave them,' James said wheedlingly. Jemima led Poppy across the drawbridge, and James and Flora followed hand in hand. Jemima swung round and levelled a finger at him.

'Not another word, you sea-lawyer! I'm taking you straight to Father Ramsay. Flora, will you give Poppy to Josh to rub down?'

'Of course. What time is Allen coming back?'

'He'll be back for supper, perhaps earlier. Come, truant, to your doom.'

Jemima could not be angry with James, for she had played truant when she could in her childhood, but she had at least to pretend to be strict with him, for he was too inclined to go his own way, thinking that a charming smile, or even, in an emergency, an apology, was enough to get him out of trouble. 'They'll hang you for a highwayman,' she warned him sometimes, and dreaded the day when he would be old enough to notice the opposite sex. He would be exactly the sort of charming rogue that women could not resist.

She found the schoolroom deserted, and had to seek out Father Ramsay in his room.

'I've found one of your strayed sheep, father, but where's the rest of the flock?'

'Mary was fetched away by the nurse,' he told her, 'and as her wardrobe is evidently going to be of more use to her in her future than her brain, I let her go.'

'And Charlotte?'

'A headache. She went to find Rachel.'

'Really a headache?' Jemima asked suspiciously. 'She was never a sickly child, but she complained of the headache twice last week.'

'I think she was speaking the truth. She was very pale, looked quite sick with it,' Father Ramsay said.

His kind words worried her more than anything, and she dropped James's hand and left him to his fate while she went to find Rachel. William had suffered from headaches, but never Charlotte, until just recently, since William had gone to sea. Was she pining for her twin, or pretending sickness to gain sympathy? Or was it some mysterious transference of strength between her and William? She smiled at herself at the last idea, and wondered what Father Ramsay would say at such pagan thoughts. Rachel was out with the baby, but she found Alison unpicking the seams of an old dress of Flora's, to be made over for Mary.

'She was really bad,' she told Jemima. 'Poor mite. I made her lie down for a while, and then it went away, and I sent her out to walk in the herb garden, where the scents will do her good. I sent Mary with her.'

'But she's never sick – until this last week or so,' Jemima said. Alison nodded.

'I thought maybe she was grieving over William – that's what Rachel thinks – but now I'm not sure. I think perhaps all the studying is too much for her. It's well enough for the boys, mistress—'

But Jemima wasn't going to be trapped into that old argument. 'It's traditional in this family to educate the girls,' she said firmly, and Alison had nothing more to say. She revered tradition, as only a shepherd's daughter could.

It was still cold enough in the evenings for a fire, and Flora, Charles, Jemima and Father Ramsay were sitting round it in the drawing room when Allen arrived home. Jemima leapt up at the first sound of hooves in the yard and rushed out to greet him, and the other three waited, smiling, through all the sounds of dogs and boots and voices in the hall, until the drawing room door opened again and Allen came in with Jemima attached to his side like a third limb.

'Well, Charles, it is all fixed, all settled,' he cried cheerfully by way of greeting. Charles looked startled, but Flora had an inkling of what he was going to say, and felt a sinking.

'What is?' Charles asked. 'You are looking very pleased with yourself, sir, I must say.'

'And so I should,' Allen said, sitting down in his own chair by the fire and rubbing his hands briskly. 'I have done a good piece of work, pleased myself, advanced you, and served science, all in one.'

'Congratulations,' Father Ramsay said drily. 'And how many times will we have to ask before you tell us what you have done?'

Allen grinned. 'I have found a way for Charles to go to America, that's all. Potatoes! Potatoes, my dear cousin! You know – or at least you should know by now – that I have a very deep interest in potatoes. I think they will be as important as turnips – more important, in fact, for there's no denying that turnips are not fit for anything but animal feed, whereas potatoes, I am sure, can be made into a very seemly dish indeed, fit for anyone's table.'

'Really, Allen!' Jemima protested, and he took her hand and kissed it.

'Yes, really, dearest. It will only need time for enough people to be eating them for a host of new ways of dressing them to be discovered. And I am persuaded that they are as good for the land as turnips are. I have been reading a pamphlet upon the subject, and it recommends—'

'Yes, I'm sure, but what of Charles and America?' Father Ramsay said hastily, nipping the effusion in the bud.

'I think I begin to guess,' Charles said.

Allen, still holding his wife's hand against his cheek, said, 'My brother Chelmsford and I have been dining with various people – members of the Royal Society, and men with large estates and advanced ideas – and we have got together a group of six, all interested in potatoes. And we, with the Society's help, of course, have put up a sum of money to send a man to America to investigate potatoes – what different sorts there are, what conditions they grow best in, what diseases they are prone to, how they may be improved, and so on – with the object, of course, of breeding a better potato, suited to our climate and soil. Now, of course, we need only find the right man to send.'

There was a burst of exclamation, congratulation, and thanks, in which Flora's lack of enthusiasm went unnoticed. Charles shook Allen's hand heartily before restoring it to Jemima's. The conversation revolved around the planning of Charles's trip and the validity of Allen's ideas about potatoes, and the time passed rapidly until supper. And then Alison came in to tell Jemima, quietly and aside, that Charlotte had been sick.

'Which doesn't seem natural to me, madam,' she went on, 'because as to the other end, there's been nothing for two days, and I was going to give her a dose tomorrow if she didn't mend her ways. And now being sick – it doesn't seem natural. I think perhaps we ought to get the 'pothecary to her tomorrow.'

'I'll come and have a look at her,' Jemima said. She couldn't quite shake off the idea that Charlotte was somehow doing these things deliberately, to punish them for taking William away from her.

The next morning, while Jemima was dressing, Alison came in to say that Charlotte would not get up.

'She just lies there, mistress, huddled up, with her face in the pillow. I thought she was being naughty, but now I'm not so sure.'

'I'll come,' Jemima said. 'Has she a headache, or a pain?'

'I asked, but she wouldn't answer me,' Alison said. Jemima finished dressing in a hurry and went along to the night nursery, which Charlotte shared with Mary. It was as Alison said – Charlotte was hunched up in her bed, with her face in the pillow, which she seemed to be trying to pull round her head.

'Come now, Charlotte, you must get up,' Jemima said, trying to sound normally cheerful. There was no reply, no movement even. 'What is the matter, chick? Have you a pain?' Still no reply. Jemima tried sternness. 'Charlotte, enough of this silliness. Get up this minute, or I shall be angry.' Charlotte only burrowed deeper into the pillow. Jemima bent over her and pulled her ungently by the shoulders, turning her face upwards for a moment; but Charlotte gave a strange little moan, and with astonishing strength freed herself, pressing her face back into the pillow with a violent movement, as if the light hurt her. Jemima and Alison exchanged doubtful glances, and Jemima cautiously felt Charlotte's brow.

'She does seem a little hot,' Jemima said hesitantly. Alison spoke quietly, so that Charlotte would not hear.

'I don't think she's pretending, mistress. Did you see? She was sort of squinting. Maybe the headache has come back.'

Jemima was still hesitating when Charlotte gave again that strange, muted moan. It was a sound of pain and fear, such as an animal might make, and it convinced her.

'Let her stay in bed, and send for the apothecary,' she said.

Charlotte was sick again before the apothecary arrived, and her temperature was certainly up. The apothecary examined her, and shook his head. He could not say what was wrong. Certainly her head hurt her, and the light hurt her eyes, but he did not know what was the cause of either. He prescribed aperient medicine and a febrifuge, and when he had gone, Alison snorted her derision and made up her own doses, though it was hard to get Charlotte to take them, for she was unwilling to uncurl herself, or to speak, or open her eyes.

By the following day it was clear that she was in pain. She twitched and moaned with it, her hands plucking at the covers, her legs moving restlessly, drawing up and then straightening with a spasmodic jerk. The pain seemed to come and go, sometimes making her grimace with a sudden stab. The light hurt her, and loud noses made her jump and cry out. Alison's face looked suddenly old, as she advised sending for the surgeon from York.

'You think it's serious then?' Jemima asked, and Alison nodded.

'Aye, mistress. I'm afraid.'

The surgeon was with the child for a long time, and when he came out, Jemima knew from his face that it was bad. But Charlotte had always been strong, she thought; whatever it was, she'd get over it, big, strong, healthy Charlotte.

'I think,' said the surgeon, 'that it is brain fever.'

Jemima stared blankly at him. It meant nothing to her. Then she grasped at the word fever. There were all sorts of fevers, and most of them were easily shaken off.

'What should we do? How could she have caught it?' she asked.

'Your nurse says that she had inflammation of the ears

after the measles,' the surgeon said. 'It has been my experience that the fever enters the brain most often through the ears or the nose. This sort of fever attacks children, hardly ever adults. I'm afraid it is usually fatal.'

Jemima's brain did not take in the words. 'But what should we do? Can you give her anything? Should we bathe her head? She's a strong child, she has always been healthy. She'll make nothing of a fever.'

The surgeon reached out and took her hand, and she flinched at his touch, as it ushered in understanding.

'Lady Morland, you have not apprehended me. There is nothing I can do for her. I would be failing in my duty to you if I did not tell you that I have never known a child recover from this particular malady.'

Jemima pulled her hand away, staring at him, and then shook her head. 'Not Charlotte. Charlotte won't die. It's William we were always afraid for. William's gone to sea – he's too young, and too frail for it, but he would go. Charlotte should have been the boy. She was always the strong one of the two.'

The surgeon looked at her for a moment with pity, and then turned to Alison, to speak to her in a low voice, giving her what instructions there were. When he had gone, Alison came and took her mistress's arm comfortingly.

'Surgeons don't know everything,' she said. 'We'll nurse our little miss, and she'll get better. That old black crow of a surgeon – well, I didn't like to be rude to him, but I nearly told him what I thought of him.'

The next day, the pain continued to come and go, but instead of whimpering, Charlotte began to scream – a terrible, shrill, high cry, like that of a rabbit caught in a trap, repeated over and over with an almost machine-like regularity, while the pain lasted. In between she lay in silence, broken only by her rapid feverish breathing, her hands clutching the covers, her eyes tightly shut. Those who nursed her spoke only in whispers, for even a normal speaking voice made her jerk and moan, as if any sound were pain. Straw muffled the floor in the passage outside, and no noise was permitted anywhere near. Alison tried to feed her, broth or ewe's milk, but she would take nothing, and it seemed to distress her too much to make it worth persisting. Then the pain would return, and her head would arch back rigidly, her face distort, and the terrible crying begin again.

Jemima begged the surgeon for something to give her, Allen demanded it, but he only shook his head.

'Something for the pain, at least – poppy, or mandrake – or – or something! You can't let her suffer like that,' Jemima cried.

'There is nothing that will be effective for the pain,' he tried to explain. 'The pain is inside her head. Even poppy would have no effect.'

No matter how anyone told her, or even if she told herself, Jemima could not go on with her normal occupations, even though she knew there was nothing she could do to help Charlotte. She could only wander about the house, walk up and down outside the sickroom, look in during the quiet phases, bite her knuckles when the screaming came. She could not even pray. Father Ramsay exhorted her to place her burden in the hands of One who was stronger, but she was numbed with anxiety, and could not make her mind frame the words. Allen made at least a pretence of being busy, but he never went far from the house, or for very long, and often as she stood helplessly at the sickroom door she would find him behind her, and reach for his hand. At night they lay sleepless, holding each other, waiting through the silences for whatever would happen next.

After two days of the crying, she became quiet. Jemima came to look at her, and found her lying utterly immobile, as if in a stupor.

'Is she better?' she whispered. Alison looked at her with a kind of agony.

'Oh mistress, I hope so. But I don't – I wish I could think—' She swallowed. 'You know how noises troubled her? Well this morning the maid dropped a spoon and it hit the table and – she didn't seem to hear. She doesn't seem to hear our voices. Oh mistress, I don't think she hears us at all.'

Jemima turned her head slowly to look at her. Alison looked grey and old and tired. Did she look like that herself? 'Deaf?' she said. She looked back at Charlotte. The child's face was visibly thinner, shrunken almost; even the gorse-bush hair looked thin and limp. It hardly seemed like Charlotte at all. Jemima no longer thought she might suddenly open her eyes and smile and say she had been pretending all along. She could no longer imagine her getting up at all. It was as if Charlotte had gone away somewhere, leaving this shrunken stranger-child in her place, a changeling.

Then as she looked, Charlotte slowly opened her eyes, and Jemima saw that the pupils were so hugely dilated that there was hardly any of the iris visible, just empty blackness, as expressionless as two gaping holes. It was horrible, and she moaned and then stuffed her knuckles in her mouth to stifle it. But Charlotte made no sign of having heard or seen. Slowly the lids lowered over the empty stare; the shallow breathing continued unchecked.

She lay in a stupor all day, and then in the evening a convulsion took her, leaving the left side of her face twisted, as if drawn up into a ghastly wink and sneer. Under half-closed lids the left eye had rolled away upwards and inwards, so that only the white showed; the right eye was still wide and black and unseeing.

'Better she should die,' Alison whispered now. 'If Our Lord would take her, without making her suffer more—' But Jemima could not wish it, though she could find no strength to pray for recovery either. In a stupor of her own, she could only wait for the outcome, clinging to Allen for wordless comfort. He did not leave the house now, though he still managed to conduct some of his business.

The next day the pain returned, and Charlotte began to scream again, arching her head back so fiercely that her body came up off the bed in an impossible bow. The paralysed side of her face wasted almost visibly, as if the flesh were wax and melting away, the left eye drawn up in a diabolical squint, the right open, black, staring and blind. Alison broke down, and wept, and prayed for her child's deliverance, called upon Our Lord and Our Lady not to torture the poor child any more, but to take her, take her quickly. Jemima gestured to Rachel to take her away and make her eat, and give her brandy. 'She has borne it all herself,' she said. 'Make her rest a little. There is nothing to be done here.' When Alison was gone, weeping and protesting, Jemima found herself stronger, in some strange way, through the nurse's weakness. She sat by Charlotte's bed and bore her share of the watching and suffering, until the child lapsed again into a merciful stupor.

Towards evening, Allen came to her there, sat beside her silently, and took her hand. Jemima turned and stroked his hand between hers, not looking at it, but knowing and remembering the shape of his fingers and palm, the strength and gentleness of it, the pleasure it had given her, the number of times she had held onto it for comfort.

'She won't recover,' she said quietly. The hand moved in hers in reply. 'She was always my favourite – not to love best, perhaps, but to understand. I always thought she was the one most like me, and in some odd way most like you too. I can't think of this poor wreck as Charlotte. I can only think of her as she was – rough and untidy and happy, galloping on Sorrell with mud on her face. Just as if she was like that still, somewhere – somewhere out of reach. But not changed.'

'It's a good way to think,' Allen said. 'Hold on to that.' She turned to look at him, her love for him flowing peacefully beneath her sorrow like a great tide that is not troubled or turned by the wrecked ship on the surface.

'You don't think she will recover?'

'No,' he said after a long while. They sat in silence, watching the shallow breathing of the stranger-child in the bed, waiting for time to release her. The candle burned lower, and at nine in the evening the breathing stopped.

'No need now to send for more candles,' Jemima said in a voice so unlike her own that she wondered if she had said it. Allen took her in his arms, and she pressed her mouth against his neck, because her throat hurt her so much. 'I hope there will be horses in Heaven for her,' she said.

At the end of July the *Ariadne* sailed into New York harbour with her newest volunteer, William Morland, almost hanging off the bowsprit in his eagerness to see. After convoying the troopship to Boston, the *Ariadne*, being the fastest vessel in the West India fleet, had been taking messages from one outpost to another, and William, who until April had never been more than ten miles from home, had now been to Boston, New York, Savannah and Kingston, Jamaica. Yet though he had already seen New York and it was his watch below, he was on deck gawping like a yokel.

A shouted order to shorten sail and a clatter of bare horny feet on the deck planking made him crouch further out of the way as the foretop men rushed for the rigging, and he felt his hands and feet twitch in sympathy, for the foretop was his station on watch. His four months at sea, when he tried to look back on them, were a crowded blur. They had sailed from Spithead on the day after he had come on board, when he was still unable to tell which direction he was facing when below decks. This ship had seemed huge and maze-like to him, at once vast and crowded, stuffed to bursting with strange and strong-smelling men who spoke an incomprehensible language, and threw orders at him that he could not understand but must obey instantly.

To add to his feelings of dislocation, he became violently seasick as soon as they cleared the shelter of the Isle of Wight, and remained so for three days. As a volunteer seaman, he swung his hammock with the rest of his watch.

Twenty-four inches a man was allowed, and the hammocks swung in three tiers, so that William in the middle tier was nose to back with the man above him and the man below him. Lying tortured with sickness in almost complete darkness, his lungs stifled with the thick air, smelling of unwashed bodies and bilge, he struggled to come to terms with the continuous noise. At home there was always silence between and underneath the immediate sounds; here, there was ever and for ever the creaking and groaning of the timbers, and the shrill singing of the wind in the rigging, transmitted through the fabric of the ship, so that even on the lowest deck, below the water line, the all-important wind was a presence.

The confusion, the perpetual noise, and the large number of strangers at too-close quarters compounded with his seasickness to make those first days seem like a long and terrible nightmare from which he had the impression of waking one day to discover that he knew where he was, that he could stand upright, and that his stomach was promising to deal justly with whatever he next put into it. From that day he did not look back. It seemed, in the foreshortening of his memory, that he had woken that first clear day knowing everything. He no longer had to pause and think to know port from starboard; he could patter his way with confidence from foretop royals to cable tier, and could make his way along the lower gun deck in darkness without stumbling. His mind adjusted quite naturally to taking night and day in four-hour bites, and his body to living on salt meat, hard bread, pease pudding, and musty water. The cacophony of ship noise sank into the background so that he no longer heard it, until it stopped, when he would miss it like a loved voice.

Sailing into New York harbour, he thought back to their first visit there, and his first trip on shore, when he had attended Captain Thomas on his official business. He remembered his astonishment and confusion as he stepped on solid ground and found himself unable to walk, how the ungrateful cobbles had thrown him about and refused to bear him, how Captain Thomas had stood hands on hips and roared with laughter.

'Now you're a real seaman, my boy!' he had crowed, and William had begun to grin unwillingly. Later, when they had gone back on board, he remembered those words and was proud. For one thing emerged clearly to him: that he loved the life. With all its privations and discomforts and its thousand perils, it was for him. He remembered the day that they had been thrashing along with the trade wind, making for Jamaica, a day of high, pellucid sky veined with silver mare's-tails. The sea was a deep, impossible blue, the foam breaking under *Ariadne*'s bows dazzling white. The snowy deck beneath his feet was warm from the sun, and above him piled tower on tower of canvas, and he smelled the clean wind and heard consciously for the first time the symphony of wind and water. Then the knowledge had come over him with a rapturous certainty, like the moment of falling in love: he was a sailor; it was in his blood and he would never again be happy away from the sea.

There were other vessels in the harbour, amongst them the flagship, but the sight of them did not thrill William so much as the fact that Captain Thomas had promised him his warrant as soon as they made New York: he was to be Mr Midshipman Morland. The *Ariadne* made her number and dropped anchor; the chain went rattling and thudding out from under her bows; she turned, snubbed, tugged a little like a horse finding herself tethered, and then was still. Almost simultaneously came the sound of the ship's boat hitting the water, going off to the flagship, and the cry from the lookout that a boat was coming off to them from the shore with a visitor. Ten minutes later Captain Thomas was in his cabin giving a hearty embrace to his brother-in-law Charles.

'My dear Charles! How wonderful to see you. I did not expect to see anyone from home for many more months yet.'

'I'm waiting for a passage to Yorktown,' Charles said.

'I could hardly believe my luck when I heard the docksiders singing out that it was *Ariadne* coming in. It amazes me how those men can tell one ship from another, just from a glimpse of its sails on the horizon.'

'In the same way that a shepherd can tell his sheep, or you, my dear Charles, can tell one orchid from another,' Thomas smiled. 'Practice. So you are on your way to Maryland, to our cousins?'

Charles explained Allen's scheme. 'It is like his kindness to find me a way to come back here. He knew how worried I was.'

Thomas shook his head gravely. 'Things don't look too good,' he agreed. 'I wish more of those back home understood the dangers.'

'Yes, it was a bad thing when Parliament rejected the conciliatory Bill.'

'I don't think the Bill would have changed things much. It might have delayed the troubles, but there are certain elements over here, hotheads and troublemakers, who would never settle for any terms. They want war.'

They talked over the situation, for Charles, having only recently arrived in America, had news to catch up on. The second Continental Congress had met and had determined on rebellion. There had been an incident at Concord near Boston in April, when General Gage had sent men to seize a store of powder being held by 'Patriots', as the rebels called themselves, and shots had been fired and the first blood shed. The Continental Congress regarded this incident as a declaration of war, and had proclaimed the need to defend the colonies against the British army, demanded a Patriot army of twenty thousand men, and appointed as their commander-in-chief a man called Washington, a wealthy landowner from Virginia who had been a major in the Virginia Militia.

'They've already taken some of our forts,' Thomas told Charles, 'and talked about establishing a navy. The trouble is that our generals are hampered by their orders. The King and Parliament don't want bloodshed because of the bad feeling it would create once the rebels are subdued. They want order restored, but without the use of force. The whole business has completely unnerved General Gage. You heard about the incident at Breed's Hill? The Patriots established themselves on a hill overlooking Boston Harbour, which would have given Gage enormous trouble if they were allowed to fortify it. So he sent a force to take it – two or three thousand men I believe – and lost half of them. Trained soldiers against ordinary citizens! You can imagine how the rest of the army feels.'

'But surely if the Patriots are only an unruly element the loyal citizens will resist them?' Charles said.

'The trouble is that the unruly element is drawn from the influential section. Those who are debarred from government in the colonies – religious minorities, those without property qualifications and so on – seem to have remained loyal, I suppose thinking they have more chance of protection under British rule. But they have no power or influence. The rich landowners and merchants are the ones who matter, and they are the very ones who make up the Patriot Party.'

There was a moment or two of gloomy silence, and then Thomas said, 'But tell me news of home! Have you any letters for me? How is Flora, and the baby?'

'Well, both well. Flora misses you, of course, but the bairn flourishes. She will tell you all in her letter. But we have had sadness at home. William, where is William? He should be told as soon as possible.'

'I can send for him in a moment. But what is it? Is someone ill?' He went to the door of his cabin and said to the sentry, 'Pass the word for William Morland.' By the time he had closed the door and turned to face Charles again, he had deduced the nature of the bad news. 'Charlotte? Ill?'

'She is dead,' Charles said quietly. Thomas shook his head slowly.

'Poor little girl. I can hardly believe it. She was well and strong when I saw her last.' Charles told him briefly what had happened.

'He will feel it terribly, I'm afraid,' Charles said. 'He was devoted to her.'

'I will see he has a little time to himself. His watch will be called in half an hour, but I'll excuse him. He'll want to be alone, I expect.'

William's impulse to flight sent him up to the foretop, his second home, and, when the men were not at quarters, a place of solitude – a rare commodity in the *Ariadne*. Above him the fore topmast described slow and erratic circles against the blue sky as the ship rolled a little at anchor; beside him the topmast shrouds hummed delicately in the light wind that brushed his face and ruffled his hair. Far below him the life of the ship went on, and beyond the wooden walls of his little world the life of the harbour went on, but he turned his eyes away from both, and looked outward, towards the open sea.

Charlotte, dead. He tried to think about it, but his mind baulked like an overfaced horse, refused to grasp the notion. She had always been there, commanding and protecting him, from the first moment she had stood upright on her strong legs, and pulled him up, weak and tottering, beside her. As the steady swing of the foretop lulled and mesmerized him, he imagined that he could remember her even before that, when they sucked at the same breast, when they lay curled together in the same womb. He remembered when he had seen her last, that last morning, when she had forgiven him for breaking away from her, and given him her most prized possession, the lock of Mouse's mane, in token of it.

And now he would never see her again. He would not bring her gifts from the West Indies. The letters he had written to her, telling of his progress and feelings, would not be read. She would not grow handsome and turn up her hair and marry and produce little nephews and nieces for him. She would never again be scolded for being rough or untidy or disobedient. All her rebellion was at an end. She was dead. He stared out at the endless blue sea, fading mistily into the paler blue sky, and forced himself to think about, drove his mind to tackle the thought of his beloved twin's death.

I'm free, he thought. All my life I have lived in her shadow, been measured against her and found wanting. All my life I have been 'poor William', who should have been a girl, because Charlotte would have made the better boy. Now I can be myself, and be judged only as myself, not as the lesser, the worse half of a pair. He folded his arms tightly around himself, and rocked in an agony of grief for her, because he had loved her, and she ought not to die unmourned, betrayed by the one closest to her, whom she had needed most. He grieved because part of him could not grieve; because his freedom gladdened him; because what he had felt that first moment in the captain's cabin when he heard the news had not been sorrow, but relief.

CHAPTER SIX

The Rue de St Rustique was hardly more than a narrow cobbled alley, running up the shoulder of the hill Montmartre to debouch under the walls of the convent, and made dark and damp by the high walls of the houses on either side. No. 7 was a small, square house, with a tiny courtyard, too dark to grow even the hardiest of flowers, hemmed in by a high wall pierced only by one forbidding iron gate. The walls had been painted rust-red, but the paint was flaking off in patches. Inside the house was dark too, only the second-floor windows being high enough to receive light.

It was by one of these windows that Aliena customarily sat. She had never minded the darkness of the house, the single gate, the high walls, the sense of being shut in, for a great part of her life had been spent in a convent, and it was to be near the convent that she had chosen this house from amongst those she could afford. But she missed the flowers and gardens and woods of Chaillot. There had been gillyflowers outside the window of the Mother Superior's parlour, which in the summer had filled the room with their scent. Aliena had always loved flowers, and birds. Her comfort here was the sparrow which had built its nest under the roof above the window where she sat. The cheerful, noisy life of the little birds was a background to her thoughts.

She had little to do now but think, for her eyesight had dimmed to a point where she could not work or read, and her strength was such that she could only with difficulty go downstairs. The priest who said Mass at the convent came to her three times a week to give her the Sacrament; otherwise, she had no visitors. She listened to the sparrows, and the bells, and dozed a little, and thought her thoughts.

On 8 September 1775, the birth feast of Our Lady, she had had her eighty-eighth birthday. Patiently as she had endured her life, she hoped it would be her last.

In the pretty house in Clichy, which Allen Macallan had bought for her and the baby so many years ago, she had thought often of Chaillot and St Germain; but since coming here to the Rue de St Rustique she had found her thoughts returning to England and Yorkshire, and the years she had spent there with her mother, Annunciata, and her daughter Marie-Louise. So much wrong, and so much sorrow, the one, she felt, following on naturally in consequence of the other; and the baby, Henri Maria, a baby no longer but a full-grown, full-blooded man of nearly thirty, going on with the wrong, and perpetuating the sorrow.

He was at Versailles today; last night he had been at the opera in the party of the new little Austrian Queen, Marie-Antoinette, who loved pleasure and dressing-up and gaiety as the lark loves the air; afterwards to a private party at the Palais-Royale for drinking and card-playing amongst the fashionable set who surrounded the Duc de Chartres. Henri always came and told her about his activities, and she enjoyed hearing about them, about the Court world she had once known so well and was not so far from; but she listened always with the strained attention of one who awaits a secret message of bad news. The vice was in him; he did wrong; and though he loved her, she believed, as much as was in him to love, it was not enough to persuade him to virtue. It was her fault – it must be her fault; she had brought him up from babyhood. How had she failed? She sometimes thought she had not loved him enough, half her mind being always on the life she had had to leave behind. How could she warn him for the future? What would happen to him when she was gone?

She had left word for him to come up to her room when he returned home, but the evening passed without him. Her maid came to change her candles before going to bed, and Aliena sat on, waiting; night and day were all one to her now. The sky was paling, the birds beginning their morning racket, when he finally came in, homing at dawn like a roving tomcat, she thought. But she must greet him before scolding, or lose his confidence.

'Well, Grandmama, have you not been to bed? You are as big a reprobate as I,' he said cheerfully, coming to kiss her cheek and bringing the reek of stale tobacco and wine and women's scent with him. Smelling of his iniquity, she thought, but she did not speak it, nor reprove him for his loose talk.

'What need have I of going to bed?' she said instead.

'True,' Henri said, sitting down on the stool beside her couch. 'You do not need it for either of the things I use it for. Now, don't scold! I come home in good spirits today, and in a position to swear I have not increased your debts by one sou. In fact, I am weighted with ill-gotten gold. The cards were with me last night, and you shall have it all – all but the price of a new suit for me, that is; and one or two trifles that I have been in need of; and – in short, you shall have most of it.'

'Some of it,' Aliena corrected, and was not so blind that she could not see the smile that broke across his face like the rising sun. If he had such charm as that, he could not be past redemption, could he?

'Some of it,' he agreed. 'How well you know me, Grandmama. You have spoilt me for other women, you know. Where could I ever find a wife to match you for loyalty and understanding, or for beauty and intelligence, if it comes to that?'

'Henri, please don't speak in such a way. You know it distresses me,' she said.

'Ah, I sense a reprimand on its way. This is the moment, Grandmama, at which I claim to be overwhelmingly tired, and in grave need of sleep—'

'Sit down, Henri. I must and will talk to you,' Aliena said, and Henri hesitated in the act of rising, and then sat again, stretching out his legs and trying to look nonchalant. 'Who is it you have been with tonight?' she asked him, by way of opening. He didn't answer, but she had known he would not. 'A new perfume, I detect,' she said. 'My eyes may be failing, but my nose is good. Another, different woman, Henri – and how many does that make?'

'Really, Grandmama, how can I possibly—'

'No, I don't mean in your life, child. Even I would not expect you to have kept such a tally. But in a week? In a month? This year alone? There was the fishmonger's wife—'

'How the Devil—!' Henri cried explosively, and controlled himself as quickly. 'I beg your pardon,' he said smoothly. 'Honour where honour is due. I suppose the odour of Poissonnieres *is* rather clinging.'

'He came here, Henri,' Aliena said. 'The fishmonger himself came here, angry and grieved, looking for you. I managed to calm him and send him away.'

Henri looked pained, genuinely sorry that she had been forced to engage in such a scene. 'I'm sorry that you should have been troubled. Not for the world would I have had you face—' He hesitated.

'Face what? Your cuckold. Or rather, one of your cuckolds?' The use of such a word by her shocked him. 'But his sorrow, Henri, was as strong as his grief. Can't you understand that? What you do is not a sin because it is forbidden, but because of the harm it does.'

He felt a little ashamed, remembering how Madame de Murphy had chided him with taking the wives of men who minded when there were so many complacent men that he might cuckold; and shame made him surly.

'I assure you, madam, that the fishmonger was an aberration. The vast generality do not mind in the least, and if they do not mind, who is harmed?'

'You are,' she said. There was a moment of silence, in which she heard the sparrow outside the window chipping away at the dawn with its territorial call. 'You harm yourself, not only with your adulteries, but with your gambling and drinking. You harm your soul, Henri.' She saw him turn his head away with an exasperated movement at the word, and sadness welled up in her. 'You are not entirely to blame,' she said. 'You are the child of sorrow and sin, and it is in your blood. Perhaps I have been in error in not telling you more about yourself. I hoped to keep you isolated from the infection, but I should rather have alerted you to it.'

He looked at her with dawning interest. 'You are going to tell me now?' She was silent a moment more, marshalling her thoughts.

'My mother,' she said, 'was an Englishwoman of gentle birth, a Countess—'

'The Countess of Strathord,' Henri supplied, nodding. She shook her head.

'No, that title was given to your mother, created for her by King James III. My mother was Countess of Chelmsford by marriage. She was royally descended, but illegitimately. *That* was the first snag in the thread, and from that one, followed all the others. She had—' where was a long pause, for it was hard to say the words, 'she had an incestuous relationship with her stepson. I was the child of that union. The second snag. I produced your mother, Marie-Louise—'

'The King's daughter,' Henri said.

'The King's bastard. She produced you. From an honourable stock – the Morlands of Morland Place in the County of Yorkshire – there came forth this rogue shoot, and like many a rogue shoot, it proved almost stronger than the parent plant. With a rose bush, the gardener cuts out the sucker, so that it does not drain the true stock of strength; but the family did not cut out this shoot. They honoured it, and it has gone on growing, stronger and stronger, carrying the evil with it, keeping it alive. Don't you see, Henri, what you are? Unlawfully got, as was your mother, and her mother, and her mother before her. And how many more bastards have you fathered to carry on the line?'

'None that I know of,' Henri muttered sullenly. Aliena heard the tone of his voice, and controlled herself. She folded her hands in her lap, and drew on her reserves of strength.

'Don't sulk,' she said sharply. 'Sit up straight, and attend to me. I must be practical. I cannot turn you out of your own nature. I cannot persuade you to chastity—' She could not see the small smile of irony at the word, but she sensed it. '—and therefore another way must be found. Henri, you must marry, get your children lawfully.'

'Grandmother, how can I marry? I could not afford to, even if I wanted to, and I am sure I do not want to. What nobleman is going to bestow his daughter on a man whose wealth consists in this dreary house and a handful of debts?'

'I did not say you were to marry a noblewoman.'

'What? Marry a commoner? I am the Comte de Strathord.'

'That worthless title! I wish I had never told you about it. In my folly, I thought it would help you, but it has only betrayed you into error. Forget it, Henri, remember what your mother was.'

'And my father?' Henri said silkily. 'What was he?' She was silent. 'You never will tell me.'

'To what purpose? I say again, marry some good, sensible, pretty girl and use your energies to keep her and your family.'

He shook his head. 'It's too late, Grandmother,' he said, but gently. 'I have lived for too long as the Comte de Strathord, however worthless you deem the title, to become plain Monsieur Morland. You don't understand society, living outside it as you do. The two worlds are separate, and cannot intermingle. Nothing can change that.'

'You are too high,' she said, clenching her fist in her anger and frustration. 'You think too well of yourself. I tell you you must marry, give up this life of dissipation before it is too late.'

'We shall quarrel if I stay longer,' Henri said, standing up. 'I am going to my bed now. Shall I wake your maid? No? Then goodnight, Grandmother,' he said coldly. 'I am sure you mean for the best, but you don't understand how things are.'

His footsteaps went to the door, the door opened and shut, and Aliena was left alone with her thoughts again.

Henri slept soundly through the morning, and woke in the afternoon hungry and cheerful. The conversation with his grandmother seemed far away, and had acquired in his mind the unreality of the hour before dawn. He dismissed it easily as an old woman's fancy. Talk of retribution and sin indeed! And inherited taints? Foolish nonsense! Like all good Catholics, like all his friends, he intended to be virtuous, to repent and be forgiven and live a pure life – when the time came. Virtue was for old men, who could do no better and had the grave before them for a warning. He dressed himself, dismissed Duncan, and slipped out of the house in search of amusement and dinner.

Paris was spread below him as he came to the precipitous edge of the hill, where a long flight of steps would take him down between the crowded crooked dwellings to the plain below. His heart lifted as he looked out over the smudged and rosy city, lifting a thousand church spires above its chimney smoke, hedged in by dark green woods and bisected by the silver snake of the Seine. It was the place to be, the only place to live! He trotted down the steps, eager and unconcerned as a ranging dog, sniffing at the smells from the houses he passed – here was bread baking, here a brief rapture of coffee, there the heartbreaking smell of frying onions. At an upstairs window, a pot of scarlet geraniums flamed in a patch of sunshine; from inside a dark and odorous house, a canary sang as though pleading for release; an old woman, dressed all in black, sat at her door on a broken chair and called out to him as he passed; a young girl came toiling up the steps with a basket on her arm, filled with onions and giant radishes and a scrawny-necked boiling fowl, and blushed deeply as she incautiously caught Henri's eye.

The whole city, the whole of life was his, he felt, that sunny autumn afternoon. He wondered where to go. He thought of Madame de Murphy, his good friend, but suddenly could not bear the thought of intelligent conversation. He wanted something as uncomplicated as that shiny-faced girl going home from market with her radishes. He wandered on, simply enjoying the day and the city, until he came to the river, where the Pont Neuf crossed it. Suddenly he was too close to his usual life. There was the Old Palace on one side of him, the Palais de Justice in front of him, the homes of the rich all around. He hastened across the river and dived for shelter into the maze of alleys and courts and tenements that crowded the left bank.

The awareness that he was very hungry impinged upon his senses at the same moment as the delicious smell of roast mutton, and he realized that he was standing outside a café called the Cheval Bleu. Not the sort of place he would normally patronize: a common café, frequented by lawyers' clerks and students and working men of the craftsman class. But it looked clean and decent, and the memory of the girl with her basket was fresh in his mind. It was an adventure. He looked down at himself, removed the obvious marks of his rank, and decided that he would not be too badly out of place, unbathed and unshaven as he was. He went in.

The silence that fell over the place told him that he had been too optimistic about his appearance. But the proprietor came hurrying forward, beaming a smile, his old-fashioned wig and blue coat immaculate, his white napkin over his arm like a badge of rank.

'Well, well, sir – my lord – welcome to Le Cheval Bleu. Let me show you to a table – the best table of course, for m'sieur – milord—'

'Just plain Monsieur Ecosse,' Henri said hastily. 'That table over there will do very well.'

'But of course, m'sieur. We have not had the pleasure of seeing you here before. I am M'sieur Homard, the proprietor. Lobster by name and lobster by nature, that is what they say of me, for I furnish a man with an excellent meal! Such is my fame, and my pride, M'sieur Ecosse. This table? And what can I get you, dear sir?'

'I am hungry enough to eat anything, even you, Homard, so beware,' Henri said, beginning to enjoy his adventure very much. 'What is your ordinary?'

'Today there is a choice of roast mutton, roast veal, or beef à la mode d'ici, m'sieur, but—'

'And what comes with it?' Henri overrode him.

'Lentils and bacon, sir, with a salad and cheese to follow, and bread, naturally, and a carafe of red wine – but if I may suggest—'

'Suggest nothing, I beg you. Your ordinary, please, and at once. The beef, I think.'

'But of course, sir,' Homard said unhappily, bowed, and went away. Henri looked around him, saw the eyes of other customers hastily withdrawn as his met theirs, heard the conversation gradually start up again as they became used to his presence. I like this place very much, he thought. Why have I wasted my time amongst people I care not a jot for? I doubt whether this ordinary will cost me more than ten sous, and that will make it the cheapest day's entertainment I have ever had. Grandmother would be so pleased!

Soon a thin and terrified slavey came and brought his bread and wine, his napkin and knife, and a moment later another woman, whom he took to be Madame Lobster, scuttled shyly out from the kitchen with a flower in a small blue vase for his table. Then came Homard himself with the tray, from which issued wonderful smells. The beef à la mode turned out to be a stew redolent of onions and herbs with delectable little dumplings swimming in it. Henry ate with more appetite than he had felt for months, mopped up the gravy with his bread, savoured the crisp contrast of the salad and the sharp tang of the cheese – goat's cheese, but what else could one expect in such a place – and washed it all down with the harsh and vigorous wine. Delicious, he concluded, clean, uncomplicated tastes, plain surroundings, the cheerful hum of good fellowship all around! In the back of his mind he was perfectly well aware that it was only a passing mood, that tomorrow he would see the shabby place and unsophisticated food in quite another light – but what of that? Tomorrow was another day.

And as he sat back and enjoyed the feeling of fullness and warmth, he noticed the young woman. She sat upon a high stool behind the *caisse* near the door, a pen in her hand, working away at some ledger or other in the intervals between receiving payment from the customers for their meals. The afternoon sunlight came in through the narrow windows in thin bars, one of which just brushed the top of her head, making her brown hair gleam red-gold like an autumn leaf. She would be a tall girl, he thought, buxom and strongly made, from what he could see of her, but not without some refinement. Her hair was neatly, almost elegantly dressed, and on the nape of her long neck, as she bent her head over her books, the sunlight kissed a fringe of tiny curls into dazzle.

Suddenly she looked up, and straight at Henri, as if she had felt his eyes upon her. She had a broad, high-cheekboned face, wide blue eyes, a small straight nose and the most beautiful mouth Henri had ever seen. For a moment she returned his look, and then a faint blush coloured her cheeks and she dropped her eyes to her book again. Yet it was done entirely without coquetry, that was what fascinated Henri. Her first impulse had been to look at him with the frank curiosity of a child, simply wondering what he was like; only the second impulse had reminded her of conventional manners, and her blush as she looked away, Henri felt, was more evidence of annoyance with herself for having been caught out than of maiden modesty.

He kept on looking at her, but she did not look up again. He found Homard hovering nearby, and said, 'Thank you, my friend, I have dined excellently. Now, must I pay the young lady there—?'

'My daughter, sir, Madeleine,' Homard said with simple

125

pride, and at the sound of her name the girl looked up again, and the faintest shadow of a smile touched the lovely mouth. 'She keeps the books, sir, better than I can myself.'

'You are a fortunate man, M'sieur Homard,' Henri said gravely. Homard beamed.

'Thank you, M'sieur Ecosse. I hope that you will come again, and honour us with your custom. And that you will bring your friends, too. Thank you, m'sieur. *Thank* you, m'sieu,' he added warmly, when Henri waved the change away. The old man bowed Henri out with every courtesy, but the daughter would not look up again, and Henri went on his way with the memory of the long white neck bent over the books, the golden curls at the nape of it, and the one, faint smile he had won. Yes, he thought, I will go back some time, but no, Mr Lobster, I will not, assuredly not, be bringing my friends.

The afternoon was now pink and gold, like the dress Queen Marie Antoinette had worn to the Opera the night before last. The imagery turned his mind and feet naturally towards his other life. He could go and see Madame de Murphy, and tell her of his little adventure; maybe also, as if it were an amusing anecdote, of his grandmother's censure. Ismène would make him feel all right about it. She was intelligent, sensitive, his good friend. His brief passion for the simple life was over, and he trotted eagerly northward, across the river, and towards the Rue St Anne. Ismène might also have the samples of fabric by now, from which he was to help her choose new furnishings. He had a great talent for that sort of thing, and many of his friends asked his advice when they decorated their rooms.

There were no coaches outside the house, so he went in by the front door, walking through a carpet of dead yellow lime leaves. The liveried footman who opened to him gave a start at the sight of him, and when he inquired for Madame, said, 'Oh, Monsieur le Comte – Madame – that is – I am instructed to bring you to Monsieur immediately you arrive. Would you please come this way?'

Now, what the Devil? Henri thought as he followed the liveried back up the stairs. Diverted from Madame to Monsieur – surely Meurice was not going to become another Brouillard and demand satisfaction for the seduction of Ismène? Thinking rapidly, Henri played over the possible scene, working out what he might say. But it was ridiculous for Meurice to object after all this time. Besides, Henri liked Meurice better than any other man he knew, and Henri was not a man for men on the whole. He would refuse to fight, he decided, and rely on his wit to make Meurice see it all as a joke.

He was shown into the master's drawing room, and Meurice came forward at once to meet him, tall, good-natured, elegant as always, but now wearing a worried frown. Henri was suddenly nervous, reconsidered his approach, thought of reminding Meurice that he himself kept a plump little mistress in lodgings in the Rue Boudreau, behind the Opera.

'Henri, my friend, they have been looking for you everywhere. Your servant was here twice, and left a message. My dear, prepare yourself. Your grand-mother—'

'What!' Henri cried, startled. Meurice took both his hands and pressed them.

'A seizure,' he said gravely. 'You must go to her at once. In view of her great age – my friend, will you take a horse of mine? My servant can go with you and fetch it back. Henri, dear friend, I am so sorry.'

The horse was saddled and ready, and Henri took it, and hurried homewards. All he could think was that he had left her in anger, went to bed without kissing her, left that day without saying goodbye to her. For the first time in many, many months he prayed – give me another chance. Let her recover this time. Duncan let him in when he reached the house, Meurice's servant took the reins of the horse, and Henri ran up the stairs to the bare little room, like a nun's cell, where Aliena slept. A surgeon was there, and the priest from the convent.

'Thank God you have come,' the priest said, but Henri did not even hear him, thrust past him to the bed.

'Grandmama!'

'She sleeps. She does not hear you,' the surgeon said. Henri knelt beside the narrow bed. Aliena lay composed, her hands folded upon her breast. Her face was like white marble, her hair in two long white plaits upon the white pillow, so that she might have been a statue upon a tomb, and though he wanted to take her hand, or kiss her, he found suddenly that he could not touch her, or disturb that quiet integrity. The fine structure of her features showed how beautiful she once had been; in the relaxation of human care, she was beautiful again.

'Grandmama,' he said again, but quietly. 'Will she recover?' he asked, and it was the priest who answered.

'She has had the last rites. She had a second seizure a little while afterwards. She is very old, my son, and very tired. One should not wish her to remain for one's own selfish reasons.'

'I need her,' he cried out in agony. 'I love her.'

'Many people loved her,' said the surgeon. 'She was a very great lady.'

Henri looked up, and then started with surprise.

'I know you,' he said. 'I have seen you at Versailles.'

'I am one of the royal surgeons. I attended the late Queen and the princesses. I was at the Palais Royale when your servant came looking for you, and came at once to see if there was anything I could do.'

Henri could only nod a thanks. He had grown so used to thinking of Aliena as his property; he had forgotten she had lived at Court, had been the mistress of a King, and had danced many a time with King Louis XV.

'I knew her many years ago,' the surgeon went on, 'when she was at St Germain.' He looked around the room. 'It seems strange to find her here, in these surroundings.'

Then there was silence, until a while later the surgeon

went to the bedside and quietly placed his fingers against her throat, and said, 'She is at peace now.'

The priest knelt and began to pray. Henri thought, I should not wish her back, when she must have been so glad to go. But he could not help it. He understood now, for the first time, what it was to be alone.

Jemima was as much surprised as pleased when they were asked to join a large party to spend Christmas at Castle Howard, at the invitation of Frederick Howard, fifth Earl of Carlisle.

'I did not even know you knew him,' she said to Allen, who was trying not to show how pleased he was with the honour, but betrayed it by a quirk of the lips. 'It proves how highly thought of you are.'

'Oh, one cannot help knowing people when one is involved with Court matters,' he said. 'His father the fourth Earl lived a great deal in Rome, and I met him there when I was at the Court of King James. The present Earl has held a number of minor posts in the Government, and he's something of a protégé of Chelmsford's, so of course I've met him in London.'

'I thought he lived in great retirement,' Jemima said. 'I had heard that the Earl of Carlisle lived at Castle Howard because he could not afford to live anywhere else.'

'Yes, that *was* the case,' Allen said. 'He was a great friend of Fox's, and lost a deal of money gambling, and by backing Fox's bills, but I believe he has straightened out his finances now. At any rate, he has become very interested in politics in the past few years, and is aching for some real Government post. I would not be surprised if that was behind this invitation. Having seen me arrive for private consultations with the King, he may have overestimated my influence.'

'Well, never mind if he has. I am so excited at the thought of seeing the house. I have heard it talked of for ever. Have you ever seen it?' Jemima asked.

'Never. But you know that Vanbrugh built Castle Howard at the same time as Shawes, and I remember the Countess saying that there were many features similar, though of course Shawes is tiny in comparison. So you think we should accept the invitation?' he asked innocently. Jemima squeezed his arm.

'Fool!' she laughed. 'And how very kind to invite Flora too.'

'Why not?' Allen said easily. 'In a place of that size, one more or less cannot signify. Besides, she is sure to be wanted. The Earl writes plays, you know, so we shall certainly have some theatricals, and Flora, being such a handsome young woman, will be wanted for the heroine, who is duped, abducted, and all but murdered, before being rescued at the last moment by the hero.'

'Oh, I see. *That* sort of play,' Jemima said, smiling. 'But what am I about, standing talking to you? I shall need a new gown, two new gowns, and Flora will too. And we will have to powder, and what shall I do about a lady's maid? Allen, talk to me, reassure me! I am so nervous, I cannot think. We shan't know anyone – I shall feel so out of place.'

'My darling, how can you be made nervous by an invitation from an Earl?' Allen said, amused. 'You were a Countess yourself, don't you remember?'

She stepped up close to him, and put her arms round his neck. 'I remember that I am Lady Morland. That is pride enough for me.' And he put his arms round her, and they wasted some pleasant minutes in blissful silence, before she sped away to tell Flora the news.

Jemima, while underestimating her husband's fame in the world of London society, had been in complete ignorance of her own. Ever since Queen Anne had made horse racing popular, it had been the passion and province of the nobility, and from the moment she arrived at Castle Howard, she found people flatteringly eager to be introduced to her, and almost as well-informed as to the names and condition of her horses as she was. She found also that she was not entirely without acquaintance in the company, for besides a number of people to whom she had sold horses, there was her brother-in-law Chelmsford and his wife, and their son Lord Meldon.

'Now I need only to know that my dress is right,' she said to Allen as they dressed for the first night's dinner, 'to feel quite at home.'

'You look beautiful whatever you wear,' Allen said soothingly.

'That,' remarked Jemima, 'is the most annoying thing a man ever says to his wife, and entirely beside the point.' The servant problem had been overcome by promoting one of the maids, Esther, to lady's maid for Jemima, and bringing Rachel to attend Flora and help Esther with the hair. Allen had the butler, Oxhey, to attend him, and guided him so carefully and subtly through the problems of his new position as valet that Oxhey eventually returned to Morland Place believing he had managed everything through his own natural talent.

When eventually they went down together, Jemima had her nervousness well under control. Flora, behind them, was still young enough, despite her matronly status, to be dressed all in white, which was always finery enough in itself. Jemima had lent her the pearl half-hoop, and Rachel had used it to great effect in the piled-up and powdered hair, along with some white feathers and silk roses. Jemima's gown was of a very dark green, almost sea-green, silk, with silver rosettes and lace, and she wore around her throat the diamond collar, which was enough to give any woman courage. Allen saw as much in her eyes when she turned her head to smile at him, and he pressed her hand against his ribs and murmured, 'What a pity it is that this is the last time we shall be together this evening. I am sure there cannot be another woman present to rival you.'

'*Now* you may call me beautiful,' she answered the

thought rather than the words. 'And you look wonderful too. Most distinguished.'

'My head feels like an uncooked pudding, and these breeches are so tight I shall lose all feeling below the knee in half an hour,' he said with a comical grimace, 'but if you approve me, it is enough.'

'I hope they give you someone amusing at dinner,' she said as they passed into the state room, to be absorbed into the glittering crowd and separated.

Jemima was given into the charge of a very handsome young man, who was introduced to her as Lord Calder but who at once claimed a right of acquaintance with an eager and endearing smile.

'I am James Chetwyn, madam. I knew your son Edward at Eton.'

'But of course,' Jemima said, returning his handshake heartily. 'Edward has spoken so often of you, and in such glowing terms, that I feel I know you already.'

'And how is my young friend?' he asked.

'Very well, progressing with his studies.'

'Ah yes, he always was a scholar – unlike me, I'm afraid. If I ever had the misfortune to learn anything, I was careful to forget it again by the next day.' Jemima shook her head in mock reproval, but she could see why Edward had been so devoted to this young man. He was charming.

'You are at Oxford now, I believe, at Baliol?' she asked him as they walked in to dinner. 'The young men of my family go to Christ Church. Are you doing well?'

'I am doing what one does at Oxford, madam,' he said. 'I am making friends with the right people. Amongst them a young kinsman of yours – Lord Meldon?' He nodded his head to where, on the other side of the immensely long table, Meldon was helping Flora into her seat. Jemima frowned slightly at his attentiveness; she rather wished Flora had not been partnered with young Meldon, though she was not sure why it made her uneasy. She shivered slightly, and Chetwyn was instantly aware of it.

'You feel the cold, madam? May I send for a shawl for you?'

'Certainly not,' she said, rousing herself to smile at him. 'I am not yet so old that I need a shawl.'

'Certainly not, I protest! And I must say that Castle Howard is the warmest large house I ever was in.' He helped her into her seat, and when the company was all assembled sat down himself and surveyed the innumerable dishes with interest. 'Now you must tell me at once what you like, and I will see you have it. These ducks are nearest – may I carve you a little? The really intolerable thing about parties in large houses is that the food is always cold. My father – the Earl of Aylesbury, madam, as I believe you know – was a great man for society in his youth, and he swears that it is by eating cold food he has kept his health. He never had a hot dish during the Season for fifteen years, he said, and never had a moment's indigestion either. But my father is a great talker. My own belief is that he talked so much he never had time to eat anything, and *that* is what saved his constitution. What do you think of that, madam?'

'I think that you talk a great deal yourself,' Jemima said, amused by his chatter. 'And my understanding has always been that those who talk a lot do it to prevent people from finding out something about them. Now what could it be about you?'

'Your penetration, madam, is devastating. I can see where young Edward got his wit. I owe him a great deal – and you too, Lady Morland. What do you think of my suit?'

It was a very odd question, and abrupt, but Jemima was enjoying him, and pretended to examine it. It was very gay and very elaborate, with as much silver lace as her own gown had, and a great many more ribbons. 'I like it very much,' she said gravely.

'I am glad,' Chetwyn said swiftly, 'for, you see, it is really your suit. I won a hundred guineas on your wonderful colt Persis, on the advice of your son. So all my good fortune and good looks are entirely due to you.'

Jemima could only laugh. 'I have not heard nonsense spoken so engagingly for a long time,' she said.

'If it amuses you, I shall continue to do it,' he said. By the end of the meal they were like old friends, and Jemima had invited him to come to Morland Place and ride her horses whenever he found himself in Yorkshire.

After dinner there was musical entertainment, which was really an opportunity for a talk and flirting – Jemima felt quite sorry at one point for a performer to whom no one, not even her host and hostess, were listening. But she was having such a pleasant time, sometimes talking nonsense with young Chetwyn, at others talking horses with a number of other guests, that she barely heard the music herself. Allen, meanwhile, had been annexed by Lord Carlisle and Lord Chelmsford, and the three of them were discussing 'this American business', in which Lord Carlisle had a growing interest.

'We cannot doubt any longer that the colony has rebelled,' he was saying. 'The King himself, in his proclamation, has referred to "rebellious war". We must move to settle it as soon as possible.'

'Measures are being taken,' Chelmsford said vaguely, and Lord Carlisle snapped his fingers.

'The whole thing has been shamefully mismanaged. What is needed is a series of definite – and liberal – offers of reconciliation to the Americans, but backed with decisive military action. Gage is hopelessly inadequate. Spirited attack, swift action, that is what is needed.'

'Yes, my lord,' Allen said, trying to be tactful, 'but I believe it is very difficult for us to understand the conditions over there. The size of the country alone, for instance—'

'Then someone should be sent,' Carlisle retorted, 'who could report back to the Government, someone with real powers. I myself would be willing to go, if I were asked. You have family over there, I believe, Sir Allen?' he added.

'A cousin and a son in the West India squadron,' he

said. 'And another cousin, Charles Morland, the botanist, is living in Maryland at present. He is forwarding a project of my own there, in the matter of potatoes—'

But Lord Carlisle was not interested in potatoes. 'They must write to you, of course? You have news of conditions over there tolerably often?' Allen nodded, seeing where he was being led. 'I should be most interested to hear about it from you. We must have a talk. Tomorrow morning, perhaps, in my sitting room? If it would not fatigue you?'

A few moments later, when the Earl had left them to speak to other guests, Chelmsford said to Allen, 'Well, there you have a reason, if you wanted one.'

'Yes. Charles, is it really to be war? It seems shocking—'

'He is right about one thing – decisive military action. They *must* acknowledge our authority, then a liberal settlement can be made. The father punishes the rebellious child first, then placates him.'

Allen nodded. He was thinking of William, and the hazards of naval action. So young, little William, to be exposed to such things! Chelmsford's thoughts had gone in another directions. 'By the way,' he said, 'I had meant to tell you – I have heard from Paris that my Aunt Aliena is dead. She died of a seizure in September.' There was a moment's silence, and then Chelmsford continued, 'She was buried at the convent at Chaillot. It was her wish. She left everything to the grandson, though it was little enough.'

'The last of her generation,' Allen said. 'I feel as if an age has ended.'

'Yes,' said Chelmsford. 'She mentioned you in her will,' he added after a moment.

'Did she?'

'Yes – she spoke of your kindness, but she had nothing to leave you.'

'What will become of the young man, I wonder,' Allen mused.

'I will continue the pension, for his lifetime. He is all

Parisian, I am told, so we shall not be troubled with his presence here. He will live in France, and when he dies there will be an end of our dealings with that branch of the family. Oh look, they have asked Flora to play! I am glad – she performs very prettily. Oh, and my son is going to sing with her. Shall we approach? I should like to hear them together.'

'By all means,' said Allen.

CHAPTER SEVEN

'There now, Meurice,' said Madame de Murphy, throwing open the door of her newly-decorated drawing room, 'does it not look a vast deal better?'

Meurice dutifully stepped into the space left him between his wife and his friend Henri, looked around, and nodded gravely.

'Indeed, my love, I congratulate you.'

'You see, Ismène, you should have trusted me from the beginning,' Henri said, gratified. 'All these weeks we have wasted wrangling, and I knew from the beginning that it must be the green, and not the coquelicot.' He did not in the least think the wrangling had been a waste of time: generally, arguments with Ismène ended in bed. But he could hardly admit so much in front of Meurice. All relationships have their etiquette.

'I still do not believe that the coquelicot would not have done,' Ismène said stubbornly. 'If you had only changed the walls – but however, as it is, I am very pleased with it. It remains to see how my guests like it.'

'Since your guests all ask Henri's advice on their own decor, they are sure to like it, my dear,' Meurice observed. 'I wonder you do not start charging for your services, Henri – you could be the richest man in Paris in a year.'

'Instead of the poorest,' Henri laughed. 'Well, I must be poorer yet before I begin working for a living. Ah, do I see a new publication on your table of iniquity, Madame?' This was what Henri called the low round table upon which the 'controversial' books were laid out for her salons.

'Oh, do not pick it up,' Madame de Murphy cried. 'I do not wish to hear what *you* have to say about it. You will laugh and make some cutting remark. I did not intend you to see it.'

'Then you should not have displayed it so prominently,' Henri smiled. 'How could I resist its virgin charms?' He picked up the pamphlet and examined it. 'What is this? *Commonsense*? What a title! When was anything found upon this table either sensible or common? And no author named upon the title page. It is, then, something to be ashamed of?'

'Everyone knows who wrote it,' Ismène said furiously. 'It is no secret.'

'Then why not own it?'

'It is out of America,' Meurice said abruptly. 'It is supposed to be written by the Adams brothers, and Benjamin Franklin, the leaders of the Congress.'

'You know of it?' Henri said in surprise.

'I know of it,' Meurice said quietly. 'Ismène, you should not have this about the house. It is dangerous nonsense. It is an attack upon the monarchy, and as the wife of a King's officer, you should not countenance such things.'

'But not our monarchy, Meurice,' Ismène protested earnestly. 'These men attack the King of England, our enemy of old, and say that though there have been a few good kings in England, there have been a far greater number of bad ones.'

'You have not read it properly, if you think that is all it says. It claims that monarchy itself is evil, and contrary to the laws of nature and the scriptures, and that a republic is the only natural, good and sensible kind of government for mankind.'

'Well, my friend, you cannot be ignorant of the fact that Madame's salons talk of little else,' Henri said, trying for lightness. 'All their reading of the Latin classics, their adulation of Rome, this Rousseau of theirs—'

'I know, I know, and I have thought it no harm. They do not really mean it, it is their way of passing the time,' Meurice said. 'But this pamphlet,' he flicked the corner of it with a nail, 'this is a direct incitement to republicanism. Give it to me, Ismène. I must see it destroyed.'

Madame de Murphy pouted, but she did not resist.

Meurice let her go her own way, but if ever he did put his foot down, she knew it was useless to resist him. She nodded to Henri, who handed the pamphlet to Meurice.

'And now I have business to attend to. I congratulate you both on this room – it is charming. Do we expect you for dinner, Henri? I shall be dining at home today.' Meurice added the last as much to Ismène as to Henri, and Henri suddenly felt guilty and sorry that he and Ismène deceived this good man. But of course, he shook away the unwelcome sentiment, they did not deceive him. Meurice knew perfectly well what was going on. Still, just at the moment, that did not make it any better.

'Then I shall certainly dine, if I am welcome,' he said.

'Always welcome,' Meurice replied, kissed his wife, and left them.

When he had gone, Madame de Murphy walked about the room for a while, expostulating on the cruelty of having her American pamphlet taken away from her, and the rightness of republicanism, but finding that Henri did not attend her she gradually ceased, and took her seat on the chaise longue before the brightly burning fire, and looked invitingly towards him until he came and sat on a low stool beside her, where she could lean on him and stroke his cheek and give him little kisses. Even this did not rouse him, and he received her caresses absentmindedly, staring into the red heart of the fire. At last he gave a deep sigh, and she said gently, 'You are very much changed, Henri, since your grandmother died. It is six months now—'

'Five,' he corrected her automatically.

'Very well, five months, and still you mourn her.'

'I will mourn her all my life,' Henri said seriously.

'That is quite proper,' she said, 'but you are grown so quiet, my friend. I used to scold you for your wickedness, but now I am half inclined to wish you less virtuous, for the sake of seeing you more like yourself.'

'To tell the truth,' Henri said, 'I do not find so much pleasure in my sins, since I have no grandmother to care about my soul.'

'How that poor, good woman would grieve, if she knew that you were wicked only to vex her. She would not have clung so long to life if she knew that by leaving it she could mend your ways.'

'Do not jest, Ismène,' Henri said sullenly. 'I am learning that pleasure and pain are the same, when one has no one with whom to share them.'

'Have you not me?' she reproved him gently. He patted her hand.

'You are my good friend – but you are not mine alone. Grandmother cared for me and no one else. I have no one person who is all mine, to please and care for and plague and wound.'

'You need a wife,' Ismène said wisely. 'I have said so before.'

'So did my grandmother – but who would have me?'

'Hmm,' Ismène said tactfully. 'Then you need something to occupy you. Why do you not oblige the Prince Ferdinand de Rohan after all, and help him decorate his palace? He has asked so many times.'

'Because it would mean going to Bordeaux, and I wish to stay in Paris.'

'But you are not happy in Paris. Perhaps the change would do you good.'

'I would be even less happy in Bordeaux,' Henri said stubbornly. Ismène pushed him away.

'Oh, you are impossible. The truth is you are bored, and you will not do anything to shake yourself out of your boredom. You should have something new to think about. Why don't you—'

'No, I will not interest myself in your nonsensical philosophies. I had sooner die of boredom in Bordeaux than listen to your puny, effeminate friends whining about freedom and equality, when all they want is for their fathers to give them a bigger allowance.'

'If you insult my friends, we will surely quarrel,' Ismène said angrily, and Henri considered for a moment provoking her until she flew at him, and then taking her to bed. But even the thought of that palled. He stood up.

'Then I shall not risk annoying you. I shall leave at once.'

'But you were to stay to dinner,' Ismène said, taken aback. He had never before refused a quarrel. Henri bowed.

'Make my excuses to Meurice, I beg you. Your servant, Madame.'

Outside, he dismissed Duncan, saying that he wanted to walk alone, and Duncan, as he always did, accepted his dismissal, and turned for home; but this time he went only round the corner, and followed Henri at a discreet distance. His master was accustomed from time to time to wander about the city, but Duncan did not think it either fitting or safe, and especially now, when he was so obviously not himself.

It was only when he found himself at the mouth of the bridge that Henri suddenly thought of the Cheval Bleu café, and the young lady, Mademoiselle Lobster, he had so admired. He had not been back there, for his wanderings took him rarely across the river, and besides, he had not been in a mood to think of such things since Grandmother died. But now his restlessness and his anger with Ismène made him remember the pleasures of simplicity with nostalgia. His step quickened to a brisk and purposeful tread. In an alley near the café he took off his wig and cravat, and made other small adjustments to his appearance, and felt all the thrill of play-acting as he adopted his role of Monsieur Ecosse, and entered the little café.

His welcome was flatteringly warm. Monsieur Homard came rushing forward as though to greet and old friend.

'Monsieur Ecosse! What a pleasure, sir, what a great pleasure. We have not seen you in such a long while that I said to Madame Homard we had lost you to the Parnasse or the Mauvais Garçons, and we racked our brains to find what we had done amiss. Come in, come in, m'sieur, and have your old table.'

The café was almost empty – it was early for dinner – and Henri gave a small private smile at the thought of his 'old' table, when he had only been there once, and wondered if he would even have been recognized if the place had been full. But his heart was warming despite his thoughts, and his eyes went at once to the *caisse*, and there was the beautiful Madeleine, with what was almost a smile upon her lips. Homard's quick eye did not miss the look, but he said nothing, ushering Henri into his seat and brushing the crumbs off the table with his napkin.

'So tell us why we have not seen you this long while?' he asked. 'You have not, I hope, found anywhere with a better ordinary for eight sous?'

'No indeed,' Henri said genially, quite prepared to play the game. The table was close to the *caisse*, and Madeleine, he could see by the tilt of her head as she bent over her books again, was listening to the conversation. 'I was sorry to have been unable to come again, but the fact is that I left Paris the very next day – for Bordeaux,' he said in a burst of inspiration. 'My business takes me all over France.'

'And may one inquire what is your business, m'sieur?' Homard asked with a perfect politeness.

The sleeping devil in Henri was waking up at last, and he answered smoothly, 'The decoration of great houses, Monsieur Homard. I advise the aristocracy on how to decorate and furnish their rooms.' Madeliene's head was up again, and he could feel her eyes fixed on him. 'In Bordeaux I was advising Prince Ferdinand upon his new palace.'

It was amusing to see the surprise and respect dawning in Homard's eyes, and to realize also that he would regard the man who could perform such a special and lucrative service to the nobility far higher than the nobility itself. One could almost see him calculating what a man might charge a prince of the blood for advice of that sort.

'Indeed, Monsieur Ecosse, that must be a fascinating business,' Homard said. 'You must know the Prince tolerably well, then?'

142

'We have talked many times,' Henri said. 'But I am very hungry, my friend, and food interests me at the moment far more than princes.'

'Of course, of course, forgive me. What would you like, m'sieur?'

'What do you recommend?' Henri asked equably.

'The pork, m'sieur, is very good – pork and beans, a speciality of the house, done to my own secret recipe.'

'Pork and beans it shall be,' Henri said, thinking with amusement of what Ismène would think of being offered such a dish.

He looked again at the young woman at the *caisse*, and Homard, seeing the glance, said, 'Madeleine, help me to serve Monsieur Ecosse. Fetch the bread and napkin, child.'

'Yes, Papa,' said the girl. Her voice was musical and low, just what Henri would have expected from a girl with such a long neck and such firm and classical features. How could the Lobsters have produced such a child, he wondered. All the same, it seemed that Homard was willing to throw the girl to him, in the way of business, for once he had scuttled back into his kitchen, it was Madeleine alone who served Henri's table. She did it with all modesty, not raising her eyes to him, and yet he was sure that she was very aware of his eyes upon her. As for him, he had rarely seen a young woman who interested him more, and all the time he talked pleasantly to the girl he was planning how to use his *persona* of Monsieur Ecosse to the end of possessing her.

In July 1776 the new general in command of the Royal army, General Howe, arrived on Staten Island in the mouth of the New York Harbour with his troops. Long Island and Manhattan Island were both in the hands of Patriots, and it was Howe's intention to dislodge them and make a base in New York. From there he intended to press on up the Hudson, while Carleton in Canada moved southwards to meet him. This move would hearten the loyalists in the upper part of New York colony, cut the Patriot army in two, and isolate New England, where the revolutionary fervour was greatest.

Howe had not supplies or men enough, however, to begin the attack at once, and messages were despatched to Clinton in Charleston and the general's brother, Admiral Howe, now in charge of the fleet, to bring up reinforcements. The delay was unfortunate as it allowed the rebel generals, Washington and Lee, to prepare their defences, but it was necessary. While he waited for the reinforcements, Howe despatched the *Ariadne* to look into Chesapeake Bay to report on any signs of fortification or fleet building there. Thomas's orders were to anchor there for a day or two, as a show of strength to the Virginians and Marylanders, to remind them that the seas were Britannia's still. Thomas was delighted with his orders as it would give him a chance to see Charles and offer him his congratulations on his marriage in February.

All was quiet in the Bay, and Thomas took the chance to revictual and rewater from Yorktown, while his gig rowed up the Bay to the plantation with an invitation to Charles and his lady to dine on board. He was not quite so sure of his position as to dare to dine off the ship. The invitation was accepted, but on behalf of Charles alone, and Thomas was a little disappointed, for he had never yet seen the famous Miss de Courcey. But he was delighted to see his cousin, whom he embraced heartily, and took him straight to his cabin for a glass of Madeira before dinner was served.

'You are looking famously well, Thomas,' Charles said. 'This damned war seems to suit you. I wish I could say the same for myself.'

Thomas thought that Charles was looking less happy than he would have expected, for a man who had newly married his heart's desire. 'I trust you are in good health yourself?' he probed delicately. 'And your lady? Her absence is not through any indisposition, I trust?'

'Oh no,' Charles said with a curious roughness. 'She is

144

well, but would not come. Eugenie likes her comfort. I bring her excuses and apologies.'

Thomas hardly knew what to say, and there was a brief silence until Charles said, 'You have read the Declaration of Independence, I suppose?'

'We had copies within two days,' Thomas said. 'It must be a widely distributed document. Well, it was no shock, after *Commonsense*, and I cannot see that it changes anything.'

'A formal declaration always changes things,' Charles said. 'What men say is more irrevocable than what they do. All that talk of republicanism and equality – "We hold these truths to be self-evident, that all men are created equal" – that is contrary to everything we have always believed, everything that has made it possible for men to live together in harmony.'

'But my dear Charles, you don't suppose anyone really means it?' Thomas said. 'I see no signs that the Patriots intend to establish equality in their new States. The property qualification, and the religious qualification – yes, even the literacy rule – will prevent a good deal more than half the people having the vote. When they talk of all men being equal, they only mean that they, the upper orders, must not be deemed inferior to the King and the aristocracy, not that the lower orders are not inferior to *them*. And what about the slaves? There is no mention of equality for them.'

'The first draft of the document contained a condemnation of the slave trade, but it was deleted from the second draft,' Charles told him. 'You are right, of course. They do not mean to include the slaves, or the poor, in their new order – but the fact remains that it has been said, and it cannot be unsaid. When you kick a pebble down a mountainside, it falls slowly at first, bouncing and rolling, and a child could stop it with one hand. But it gathers speed, and at the bottom of the mountain it may smash a man's skull. So it is with ideas. So it will be with this one.'

'Oh, I think you exaggerate the importance,' Thomas

said soothingly. 'These ideas spring up and die down again, and things go on much as before.'

Charles shook his head. 'I don't know. There is a tide in the thoughts of men, and the tide is making. I am afraid of the flood.'

Dinner was brought in, and changed the subject, and Thomas told Charles of the progress of events in New York and Canada as they consumed such delicacies as the ship could provide – pea soup, and fried chicken, and oysters, and corn bread, which Thomas was just beginning to get used to. It was at least better than ship's biscuit, now his own flour was finished. By way of dessert they had a dish Thomas had learned about in Boston, which the Indians had invented, made of cornmeal and sugar and molasses, very rich and sweet.

When they had eaten, and the table was cleared, and the port brought out, Thomas said genially, 'So, dear cousin, you have joined the ranks of the married men. I have not yet congratulated you, or wished you joy, which I do with all my heart. How did you manage to persuade her father to give you her hand? I remember you were sure he would not be willing.'

'I did not need to persuade him – he was as eager for the match as I could ever have been,' Charles said, and he sounded dark and bitter, and Thomas looked at him with surprise and concern.

'Surely it was a compliment to you, that he wanted you for his daughter,' he said.

'I thought so at first, but now I see that what he wanted was to get his daughter married at all costs. I happened to be convenient, that's all.'

'What can you mean? A beautiful heiress cannot be hard to match.'

'A Creole, and a Papist. If she had not been hard to match, she would have been married long before, for her father was desperate for an heir. Well, I can't blame him – he wanted to ensure the survival of his line, and he must do what he considered best for his daughter. No, I blame myself for being such a fool.'

'But, my dear, what can be the matter? You were so in love with the lady—'

'Oh God!' Charles cried, suddenly burying his face in his hands. 'This is all so horribly disloyal. I am ashamed to speak so, but I can't help it. There is no one else in the world to whom I can own it.'

'Own what, Charles?' Thomas asked gently. 'Come, you can tell me. It will go no further, whatever it is, you know that.'

'I know, but you will blame me.'

'I won't, I promise. I only care that you should be happy. You are my best friend, and my wife's brother.'

'Oh, Flora – you must not tell Flora, promise me!' Charles cried. 'She was against it from the beginning. She told me so – she asked how I could know I was in love when I hardly knew the woman – and she was right.'

Thomas was now thoroughly alarmed, but he said nothing, waiting for Charles to tell him in his own way.

'She was so beautiful – she *is* so beautiful,' Charles corrected himself, 'and her beauty still moves me. But, oh Thomas, there is nothing underneath. How was it that I did not see the truth before? How could I be blinded to the emptiness inside her. We have nothing to say to each other, nothing. She is not, cannot be, a companion to me.'

'But you used to talk to her – I remember you saying so.'

'It was a trick she was taught in that wretched convent, of how to behave in conversation with a man. Look directly at him, they told her, and nod and agree, and now and then repeat something he has said. That way he will think you very wise. And I was duped and flattered like any other lovesick fool. But now she is married she does not need to go on doing it. All she ever talks of is her clothes and her silly little dog. If I talk to her of my work, or the war, or – or anything, she simply does not attend.'

To Charles's great indignation, Thomas burst out laugh-

147

ing. 'I'm sorry, cousin, but this is not so very strange a thing after all! You will not be the first man to discover that he has married a very foolish woman. Indeed, the majority of women have nothing in their heads at all, and in my experience, the majority of men prefer it so.'

'Is that how you think of Flora?' Charles asked angrily. Thomas sobered himself and shook his head.

'I was spoiled, I grew used to Morland women, and wanted more than a pretty picture to look at. That's why we Morlands so often marry our cousins. You should have waited for a cousin, Charles, indeed you should. But you must make up your mind to love your lady for beauty, which is what you married her for after all. She has not deceived you – you deceived yourself.'

'I know,' Charles groaned, 'and I feel guilty about speaking of it at all. But you cannot imagine how isolated I am. I have no one to talk to, no one at all. In the evenings, even my father-in-law goes to his own room, and I am left alone with Eugenie – talking of Paris fashions.'

'Well, there is the root of your trouble,' Thomas said. 'Other men with silly wives have the society of each other. Why do you not go and live somewhere else?'

'Don't be a fool, how could I leave?'

'Sell York, and buy an estate somewhere else,' Thomas said simply.

'You talk like a sailor,' Charles retorted. 'Land is not so easy to come by; and besides, even if York was mine to sell, I could not do it. It is their home, and I was permitted to marry Eugenie solely to preserve it and provide an heir. That was the bargain, and I cannot go back on it.'

'Then the only other advice I can give you is to start a family. Once you have your children growing up around you, you will find enough to occupy you to keep you happy.'

Charles said nothing, but his gloom did not lift. Though he longed to tell Thomas the rest of the story, it was a thing too private to be mentioned, even to his cousin and best friend. The fact was that he had been virgin when he married, and like most young men he had thought physical rapture, as well as spiritual, would follow naturally from his union with his heart's desire.

But the one had proved as disappointing as the other. The beautiful Eugenie lay passively in his bed, neither encouraging nor discouraging, and indeed, how could he expect her to behave otherwise? But it was as though she was not there at all, and the idea of perpetrating such outrages in her absence, as it were, daunted him. On the occasions when he did pluck up courage to disturb her exquisitely-frilled lace night attire, and touch her remote and flawless body, he gained no pleasure from it: it made him feel obscurely as though he had insulted her.

That was not how it was meant to be, he was sure. He had heard so much about the great joy and pleasure of it, which apparently other men had, and he longed to ask Thomas, with his greater experience of life, to explain it to him, and perhaps tell him where he was going wrong. He was sure that Flora and Thomas had passed together through those hidden gates – but it was simply not something he could ask.

During that summer of 1776, when General Howe assaulted and finally took New York, Monsieur Henri Ecosse was laying long and careful seige to Mademoiselle Homard. It was a project to absorb and intrigue him, but unlike many a man before him, he discovered that he liked and admired the object of his desires more, the more he knew of her.

Madeleine, he discovered, was a cheerful, sensible and, to his surprise, well-educated girl. She had spent her four years at school in a convent learning to read, write and sew; her father had taught her arithmetic, so that she could keep the books; and she had been further fortunate in a godfather, the Curé Fontenoy, who not only had an extensive library at his house near St Sulpice, but encouraged his goddaughter to use it to continue her education.

But added to that were the attributes of her own character. She had the shrewd common sense and level-headedness that he would have expected from a prosperous Parisian bourgeoise, and was an excellent judge of character – except, Henri thought, that she seemed to like him. But there was nothing coarse about her. She had a natural good taste, and distinguished with one glance of her clear grey eyes between the genuinely excellent and the meretricious. She, he was persuaded, would not have been taken in by Rousseau. He enjoyed arguing with her more than with any man he had ever met, for she would cut through the bone of the matter, and never allowed him to obfuscate by claiming greater experience of the world, or greater age.

'If you cannot match sense with sense,' she would say, 'you have nothing to claim from your years.'

He had established his alter ego as the decorator of the homes of the rich, and had enjoyed the business of setting up his double life almost as much as Madeleine's company. Duncan had helped him, having revealed to his master that he knew about the Cheval Bleu from having followed him there. Henri rented rooms in a shabby old house in the Rue des Ursulines, just off the Rue St Jacques, in what had become over the years the Scottish Quarter of Paris. It fitted his false background of being the descendant of a Jacobite exile, and explained the name he had taken at such random. There he kept the clothes Monsieur Ecosse wore, and the books he read, and devised his character and history. It was a wonderful release to him when he grew tired of his own life, when Versailles and the Tuilleries and the Palais Royale palled, to trot away over the bridge to his other life, and he could not disguise from himself that the seduction of Madeleine had ceased to be his only motive for doing so.

He was surprised that the seduction was taking so long, for when she first consented to meet him secretly he had thought the battle half over. A girl who would deceive her father by meeting a man secretly, was, in his experience, unlikely to resist very long the greater sin. But Madeleine was unlike any woman he had met before, and even more to his surprise, he took as much pleasure from walking and talking with her as he anticipated from making love to her.

She was accustomed to walk to her godfather's house and spend some hours there reading, and her father, who admired her cleverness, let her off as often as he could to do so, so it was not difficult for her to meet Henri in the Jardins de Luxembourg. At first Henri had been at pains to establish his false identity, and to tell her of imagined commissions and conversations, but she seemed remarkably incurious about it all, and soon he ceased to trouble and discussed other matters with her. She was as interested as Ismène in the new philosophies, and it amused him to compare her opinions with his mistress's.

Madeleine, for instance, like Ismène, rejected the notion of original sin, but did not from that conclude that man was essentially good, and that there was no need for religion or the Church. 'There is good and base material in all of us, and it depends upon how we are brought up which flourishes. We need all the help we can find for the good to triumph – we cannot reject our greatest helper.'

Ismène's friends were very interested in the ideas of Darwin, and concluded that as there was an essential order in the universe, so man too must be subject to natural laws, and that if it could be discovered what those laws were, a perfect form of government could be established.

'But nothing that man devises can be perfect,' Madeleine argued one day as they walked in the gardens, 'because man is not perfect.'

'So you do not think there is any point in changing the form of government?' Henri asked her. 'For instance, do you not think a republic would be better than a monarchy?'

'In theory it might be,' she said, 'but in practice I think the chance of improvement would be small. For surely anyone seizing power must be more hungry for it than someone who has it already?'

Henri laughed, delighted. 'Oh, it is so refreshing to hear common sense spoken. If only – some other friends of mine could hear you.' He stopped himself in time from mentioning Ismène.

'There is a story, you know, told in the classics, of a wounded soldier waiting on a battlefield for the surgeons to come,' Madeleine said. 'There was a second soldier nearby, worse wounded than himself, his wounds black with flies. The first soldier was about to drive them away, when the second soldier cried, "Oh, do not do so! For these flies are almost sated with my blood, and they are not hurting me nearly so much as at first. If you drive them away, their place will be taken at once by new and hungry flies." '

'What a cynic you are!' Henri said. 'Better one lion than a whole pack of jackals, that's your philosophy!' And he stopped under a tree and turned her to face him, taking both her hands. She smiled up at him, and his heart turned over. How can this be? he asked himself. Have I come to love her? He gazed at her strong, clear face, her beautiful mouth, the tawny-gold hair dappled with leaf shadows, the proud easy carriage of her head upon her graceful neck. She was as innocent and strong and wild as a roe deer, and he wanted her desperately, more than he had ever wanted anything. He pressed her hands, and she returned his gaze levelly, looking into his eyes with a directness that made his bowels melt.

'Oh Madeleine—' he began helplessly.

'Yes, Henri? What is it you want of me?'

'I want you,' he said, drawing her closer. She came without reluctance or coquetry, and he felt the warmth of her body, smelt the sweet, female scent of her, and trembled. 'I want to possess you entirely, to have you near all the time, day and night, to know you are mine only.' She nodded, not a nod of consent, but of attention, like a good student listening to the professor. 'Will you come to my rooms?' he asked her, feeling, even as the words took the air, how paltry they were, how unfitting.

'You know I cannot,' she said evenly.

152

'It is only a few minutes walk from here. We can be alone, private—'

'Henri, you know you cannot ask that of me. I am a child of the Church. I cannot give you what you want without marriage. Even though,' she added in a different voice, low and unwilling, 'even though I want it myself.'

'Oh, my darling!' he said, and pressed her against him. But she pushed him gently away.

'I am wrong to deceive my parents in meeting you like this. I cannot do more.'

'But – I cannot marry you,' Henri faltered, wondering what reason he could give for his unwillingness that did not betray his secret; but to his relief she assented to the propositon.

'No,' she said. 'My father would not agree.'

Henri raised his eyebrows in surprise. He had not thought of Homard as anything but approving. Madeleine smiled kindly.

'Papa likes me to encourage you as a customer by serving your table when you eat at our café. But he would not wish me to marry a man about whom he knows nothing, whose living is uncertain and depends upon the whim of the rich and famous. On your own admission, your customers are very capricious about settling their bills.'

He had told Homard this to explain why he was so apparently poor, when the kind of service he offered ought to have commanded high fees. Inwardly he gave a rueful smile. This deception business had more pitfalls than he had anticipated. In desperation he made one attempt to persuade her to become his mistress, promising his love and fidelity always, as every man had promised every mistress throughout history. Any other honest woman would have been mortally offended by the request, but Madeleine only smiled, a smile of perfect understanding and perfect strength that made him feel weak and confused but somehow safe, as though she had taken charge of his soul and would lead it safely.

'No, Henri, I cannot do that. I love you, and I believe

you love me, and that our love would be happy and successful. Why else did God direct you to the Cheval Bleu, of all the cafés in Paris? But we could not be happy and good without God's blessing. I would marry you with the greatest joy, but I could never consent to be your mistress.'

'It's the old ploy, sir, the oldest in the book,' Duncan said one night as he helped his master to remove his breeches. 'They all use it, from the highest downwards.'

'Guard your tongue, Duncan, if you don't want to win my displeasure,' Henri snapped. Duncan rolled an eye at him expressively. The summer had passed in increasing frustration for Henri, who felt that if he did not have Madeleine soon, he would do something desperate. It had made his temper uncertain, and Duncan, who was not a man to tread warily, had been cursed and cuffed more than once.

'I speak as I find, sir,' he said, easing the tight silk over Henri's calves. 'She's a fine young woman, but there are plenty of others, and once you had her, I dare say you'd find her not much different after all.'

Henri only grunted, not really attending. 'If only she were just a little higher, I believe I would marry her,' he said. 'But a café-owner's daughter! If he were a lawyer, even—' Duncan did not answer. 'Strange as it may seem, I think grandmother would have approved of her. She advised me, you know, just before she died, to marry, even if I had to marry out of my rank.'

'Yes, sir, I know,' Duncan said. Henri found it damned mysterious how Duncan always did know things.

'I believe you must listen at doors,' he said sourly.

'Well, even your grandmother wouldn't have wanted you to sink as low as this,' Duncan said, ignoring the insult. 'A gentleman's daughter, she meant, if you could not get a nobleman's.'

'You insult Madeleine at your peril,' Henri growled.

'I would not insult the lady, sir. She is as beautiful as an angel, and as good a young lady as ever lived. But she is what she is, and that's a fact.'

'I know, I know,' Henri sighed. 'And yet she has filled my life again, when I thought it must remain empty for ever.'

Duncan regarded his master narrowly. He was certain that it was Madeleine's unavailability that was making her so attractive and that her influence would not outlast the conquering of her. 'Now, sir, let's think this out. The lady will not yield without marriage, and you cannot marry her because of her condition. Well then, since you cannot change her condition, you must change the nature of marriage.'

'What do you mean?' Henri asked, with dawning interest. 'You have a scheme, you sly dog!'

'You must persuade her to a secret marriage, an elopement. Once presented with a *fait accompli*, Homard would accept matters, I am sure.'

'But, you dolt, I would then be married to her!'

'No, sir, Monsieur Ecosse would be married to her. And he does not exist. And no one would know.'

'The priest would know,' Henri said, staring. Duncan smiled.

'The young lady has never seen me, sir. The black frock and white neckbands would rather suit me, I think. My mother always wanted me to enter the Church, and I fancy I would have made rather a good priest – don't you think so, sir?'

BOOK TWO

The Ship

Ye mariners of England,
That guard our native seas!
Whose flag had braved a thousand years
The battle and the breeze!
Your glorious standard launch again
To match another foe;
And sweep through the deep,
While the stormy winds do blow!

Thomas Campbell: *Ye Mariners of*
England

CHAPTER EIGHT

Allen and Jemima were strolling arm in arm through the gardens, making a wide and leisurely circuit of the moat. It was a beautiful autumn day, and the blue sky was reflected in the still water, along with the quiet grey walls of the house and the white breasts of the drifting swans, followed by their half-grown young.

'They are like fallen clouds,' Jemima said. The cob turned his head at the sound of her voice and drifted a little towards the bank, but the pen, always more reserved, moved on with her children, and seeing Jemima had nothing to give them, he soon followed her. 'It seems so quiet now, without the children. Edward at school, William in the navy, and my poor little Charlotte gone.'

'The boys are doing so well, you cannot want them back?' Allen said. 'I thought Edward had improved greatly when he came home this summer.'

'Yes – almost a man, and much more – I don't know – confident, I suppose, though he was as quiet as always.'

'I think he has found himself at school,' Allen said. 'I asked him how he was doing there, and though he said very little, he sounded content. He is making friends who will stand him in good stead all his life.'

Jemima smiled at that. 'I cannot see our Edward moving much in society once Morland Place is his. He will be a stay-at-home, if I know him at all.'

'Nevertheless, he will be able to use his influence for his brothers and sister, and his own children, when he has them.'

'Oh don't!' Jemima shook her head. 'I can't think of him married and a father! James, now – James is different.'

'Father Ramsay says he is improving,' Allen said. 'I

think that boy may well amount to something. He has a great many good qualities.'

'And a great many bad ones,' Jemima said.

'We must think what to do with him. The army perhaps, or the law. Not the Church, I think—' Allen mused.

'My darling, he is only ten years old. Leave me some chick to brood over,' Jemima laughed.

'You have Mary,' Allen pointed out.

'Oh, Mary! I cannot take Mary seriously. Did you see her on Sunday, outside the Minster? She was positively flirting with young Tom Loveday, simply to make the Anstey boy miserable.'

'She is as pretty a little jilt as ever broke hearts,' Allen said.

'Where she gets it from I don't know,' Jemima said. 'I'm sure I never gave her such an example. I cannot think about Mary – she is a changeling, not my child at all.'

'All young women like to flirt,' Allen said serenely. 'It is their only pleasure, poor things, before they are married off, and spend the rest of their lives breeding and talking of ailments and clothes.'

'What a startling picture you paint. I don't recognize it at all. My life has not been like that.'

'Yours was not the common lot. Nor the common character.'

'No,' Jemima said. 'I was a most unnatural child, like my poor Charlotte. I never could do what was seemly. I nearly broke my mother's heart with my wicked ways.'

'Do you remember when you ran away and fell off the orchard wall, and landed at my feet?' Allen said, drawing her closer.

'And you bathed my cuts and gave me ginger cakes. I think I loved you from that moment.'

'And I loved you too.'

'Nonsense, I was only eight years old. You were in love with Marie-Louise, then and after,' Jemima retorted. It was a game they often played.

'That was not love – that was fascination, like the rabbit

with the snake. It was you I loved, but it took me fifteen years in exile to realize it. Oh, how I suffered when I learnt you had married.'

'A pleasing fiction, sir,' Jemima said, smiling. 'But I am glad, so glad, that we have had some time together this year. It has been wonderful, having you to myself at last. We've been so much apart, one way and another, since we married.'

'Yes – so busy with the estate in the early years, and then my missions for the King. It was time things changed. You haven't missed Flora, then?'

'Not at all. I thought I should. More than that, I was worried about her going off to London, though she was so restless after her taste of society at Castle Howard there was no point in her staying here.'

'It was kind of the Chelmsfords to invite her. She will enjoy the Season, and her being presented will help Thomas in his career. Your brother-in-law will make sure no harm comes to her.'

'I just wish Rachel could have gone with her, as lady's maid. We know nothing at all about that girl she hired from York. She ought to have someone with her who will look after her.'

'We have talked all this out before,' Allen said firmly. 'Rachel is your servant, and even if she had been willing to go, and had not preferred staying with Flora's baby, you have to accept that Flora is a grown woman now, married, and in charge of her own life. She must hire her own servants, and beyond advising her there is nothing we can do.'

'I know, but I suppose I have got used to treating her as my own daughter. The fact is, I haven't enough to worry about.'

'You could worry about me,' he suggested. Jemima looked up at him with loving eyes.

'I can't worry about you. I can only rejoice in having you near. I've hardly got used to it yet. Are you sure you shouldn't be off somewhere, attending to your duties as

Justice of the Peace, or squire of the manor, or envoy of His Majesty? Is your time really your own?'

'Really my own, to concentrate on you – and my potatoes.'

'Oh, your potatoes!' Jemima cried indignantly at his teasing. 'Don't talk to me of them. Every time we begin a conversation, it comes round to potatoes.'

'The first batch is encouraging,' Allen said, unperturbed. 'Charles is doing his job well, in spite of the troubles over there. And he has sent me such clear instructions on how to cross-pollinate the flowers that I think I shall do a little experimenting myself with the new roots he has sent me.'

Jemima stopped and withdrew her arm, and turned to face him. 'The price of cloth is falling and the price of corn rising because of this American business. Our best pasture is worm sick, and we can't even take a crop of hay off it. We lost one of our best mares foaling, *and* the foal into the bargain, and the summer mastitis cut down our milk yield so far that we haven't enough cheese to last us until Christmas, let alone through the winter. We are so short of servants that the silver hasn't been cleaned for weeks and Abram is threatening to go and work for the Fussells – and you talk to me of potatoes?'

Allen regarded her steadily, the beginning of a smile turning up the corners of his lips. 'I have two things to say to you.'

'Well?'

'The first is that I love you.'

Jemima moved a little closer, and he put his arms round her waist.

'And the second?' she asked suspiciously.

'The second is that I have thought of a new way of dressing potatoes, and I have given Abram the receipt. We are having the dish for dinner today.'

Entirely against her will, Jemima began to smile, and then to laugh. 'You are an impossible man. There isn't an ounce of romance in you.'

He pulled her against him and kissed her brow, and

after a moment she put her arms round his neck and said, 'This is shameful behaviour in broad daylight for a married woman, but love makes me bold. And I will forgive you your potatoes, if you pay proper recompense. You must give me something, by way of a fine.'

'What shall I give you? Name it, and it is yours,' he said, smiling broadly. She looked up at him with shining eyes.

'Give me another baby,' she said.

Flora did not in the least regret her decision to accept the invitation of Lord and Lady Chelmsford, and could only wonder that she had been such a simpleton as to refuse before. When she looked back on her quiet days at Morland Place, with nothing to do but read and sew, or walk about the gardens, with no new sight to be seen and no new acquaintance to be made, she only wondered that she had survived so long without dying of boredom.

In London there was so much to do and see. There was the opera, the plays, the concerts at Ranelagh and Vauxhall; there were the tea gardens at Islington Spa, the wild-beast show at Exeter Exchange, the marionette theatre in St James's Street; there was the wonderful new circus of Philip Astley in the Westminster Bridge Road, where displays of equestrian skills were given, and the delights of Jenny's Whim in Chelsea, where there was a cockpit and a bowling green, and a pond from which mechanical mermaids and fishes arose at intervals to music. And all this quite apart from the balls and assemblies, dinner parties and supper parties and card parties, and the Court functions to which Flora, having been presented, was invited. Besides all the entertainments, there was the park to be walked in, formal calls to be made, shops to be visited, dressmakers to be consulted, and all the world of fashion to be observed, criticized, and imitated.

Flora was happy under the kindly patronage of Lord Chelmsford and the absent-minded chaperonage of Lady

Chelmsford, and, despite the distance of Oxford from London, Lord Meldon was often with them, frequently bringing his young friend James Chetwyn with him. It was entirely proper, Flora decided, that she should notice the young man who had been so kind to her brother at Eton, and she discovered, too, that her married status gave her considerable freedom. She was at first a little wary of being in company with the young gentlemen unless an older woman was also there, but when Meldon begged her to chaperone Chetwyn's sister, she realized that, in social terms, she was an older woman herself.

At Christmas the Court moved to Windsor, and when the Chelmsfords said they were going with the Court Flora made the momentous decision not to go back to Morland Place but to spend Christmas in Windsor too. It was a Christmas she always remembered afterwards as the most pleasant of her life. Even the formal assemblies at Court were made enjoyable by the company of young people, and particularly young men who were flatteringly eager to dance with her or fetch her lemonade or advise her on her hand of cards. There were private parties too, where the pleasures were less formal and where Flora found that she was always the centre of a little group. She learnt to her surprise that she was not only a beauty, which she had become tolerably accustomed to, but a wit; and after the Boxing Day hunt she gained yet another character. Hounds had found in Datchet Woods and had run across Eton Wick and Dorney Common almost as far as Taplow without checking, and Flora, riding a horse lent to her by James Chetwyn, had been in at the kill, rosily flushed by the cold air but quite unruffled.

That afternoon, at dinner given in the house of Lord and Lady Prescott, when it was his turn to propose a toast, Lord Meldon raised his glass to 'Dashing Mrs Thomas Morland, wife of one of our sailor heroes; if he sails his ship as well as she rides her horse, our enemies will be confounded.'

Across the rim of his raised glass, he looked into Flora's

eyes, and she felt herself burning with confusion. Further down the table, Chetwyn took up the toast with enthusiasm.

'Dashing Mrs Tom!' he cheered, and the toast was drunk with applause and laughter, and Flora was 'dashing Mrs Tom' from then onwards.

The winter of 1776/77 found matters in America at a deadlock. The British army had not lost a battle that year, but had failed to take the initiative. Washington had been driven out of New York, but Howe had not followed up the victory and destroyed the army, so that Washington was now wintering comfortably in Morristown with the whole of Delaware and most of New Jersey safely his, while the British troops overwintered in New York and Rhode Island. Carleton had failed to make the breakthrough from Canada down the Hudson, and in the new year 'Gentleman Johnny' Burgoyne was sent out from England to take over; loyalist risings in Carolina had failed; but on the other hand, the Americans were desperately short of supplies, and the British navy was increasing its blockade to a stranglehold.

The war, for Charles, had a curious dual quality of being close up and far off. He knew that he and his new family were regarded with suspicion in Yorktown and St Mary's City, and that his dining on board the *Ariadne* had not gone unnoticed. But the doubts over his standpoint had been balanced by the fact that Philippe was certainly of French origin, and therefore had no cause to love the British. Philippe had been at pains to say nothing provocative on his visits to the cities, and indeed had managed to keep out of arguments altogether, while Charles remained for the most part on the plantation, busying himself with its affairs and his own project. But in such a struggle, neutrality could not be permitted for long. Sooner or later, they all knew, they would be required to state their views.

Early in 1777, Eugenie announced that she was pregnant,

and Charles's viewpoint changed once more. The child would be born in August, and if he had ever entertained thoughts that he might run away – or even, less dramatically, absent himself on some botanical mission – he now had to accept that his life was to be spent here, at York plantation. He was oddly excited at the thought of the child, and often, on his solitary rambles, he would stop at some place that commanded a view, and imagine himself showing his kingdom to his son and heir, as Eugenie had once shown it to him. She, poor soul, was very sick in the early stages of her pregnancy, and for the first time lost that ethereal poise that had so enraptured him. He felt guiltier than ever for his secret infidelity to her, and tried his best to be kind. He would have to spend the rest of his life protecting her and her child, he told himself, so he might as well get used to it.

Philippe was delighted, of course, at the prospect of an heir for the plantation, but more worried than ever about their neutral status. 'At all costs, we must see nothing happens to Eugenie and the baby. If the Patriots demand support, we must give it to them. But then, what if they are defeated? The British will punish us, I suppose. Oh, it is devilish! Thank God you are here, Charles. War is a young man's business.'

The crisis came in spring. Charles was at work in his succession houses, when Sam, one of the house slaves, came running in, filling the hothouse with the smell of his panic.

'A boat's come, master, a sloop filled to the brim wid people from Yorktown. I believe it's trouble, master.'

'What people?' Charles asked, reaching for his coat.

'I seed Master Cluny and Master Hampson and such-like people there, master, and there's an awful lot of strange-lookin' men wid guns. Master Courcey's gone meet them, and sent me to fitch you up to the house, quick as quick.'

'I'm coming,' Charles said tersely. Cluny and Hampson were two of the leading lights of the Patriot Party in

Virginia, known to be passionate orators and averse to any compromise on the war issue. 'Where's my wife?'

'Missus there too,' Sam said, showing his disapproval. 'Master Courcey tried to send her away, but she wouldn't go. You got to be there, master.'

Charles didn't need telling. Outside the porch of his own house were two cold-eyed men carrying shotguns; beyond the green lawns, tied up at the jetty, was a big sailing brig with a gun mounted on her fo'c'sle – a mere popgun, compared with *Ariadne*'s nine-pounders, but enough firepower to threaten an unarmed house. Fear and outrage rose in him, and he thrust them both down, and strode past the sentries with as much confidence as he could display.

Inside the scene was less warlike. In the drawing room the deputation crowded, some seated, some standing, perhaps twenty men in all, but if there were guns they were not in evidence. Philippe was standing at the fireplace, looking somewhat at bay; it was Eugenie who surprised Charles, for she was seated in her usual place on her chaise longue, smiling and chatting to the grey-haired man Charles recognized as Mr Hampson, as if this were a mere social tea visit. Tea was, of course, out of the question. No east coast family had felt completely easy about tea since the Boston tea-party.

'Ah, there you are, Charles,' she said now in her usual languid, lilting tones. 'We have some visitors – I have been telling them how pleasant it is to see new faces. We get so few visitors this far up the bay. Sam, will you go and see what has happened to the wine? I have ordered wine for our guests, Charles. Do come and meet them.'

He walked across to her, thoroughly confused. Was she being immensely brave, or immensely stupid? Did she know that her presence and her condition must hamper any attempt at violence on the part of the visitors, or did she really think they had come for a social visit?

'Gentlemen,' he began, but could think of nothing whatever to say. Philippe gave him a desperate look, and he forced himself to go on. 'Mr Hampson I know, and Mr Cluny I have heard of, by report, but I'm afraid I am not acquainted with the rest of you, and there are rather too many to perform introductions in the normal way. I am Charles Morland. Can I be of service in any way?'

There was an answering growl from the crowd by way of reply, and Hampson, who Charles was glad to see was a little put out by his reception, said, 'We have a matter of business to discuss. Can we see you and de Courcey alone?' He forced himself to bow to Eugenie, as if it were a social call. 'Madam, if we could persuade you to withdraw—'

'Oh, but no,' she said at once, gaily, but quite firmly, 'you cannot be so cruel as to deprive me of the first company I have had since Christmas! Besides, I must perform the duties of hostess, or be shamed for ever. You may discuss business in front of me. I am quite accustomed to it.'

Cluny gave Hampson a savage look, and there was a restless stirring in the rear ranks, where Charles saw two other men carrying guns, but holding them in such a way as to keep them hidden from Eugenie. Hampson said to Charles, 'Then perhaps if you and your father-in-law would step to the other end of the room with Cluny and me, we could speak our piece.'

So it was done, and while Eugenie gently chatted to the bewildered army, the four men walked to the far end of the room, where Hampson began without preamble.

'You know the situation,' he said. 'This war is dragging on, and our men cannot continue without arms and money. General Washington has said that we cannot win without French aid. French aid we must have. That is where you come in.'

'But surely Franklin is in France even now?' Charles said. 'He is a far more able ambassador than—'

'Someone must go – someone with first-hand knowledge of the situation here – but there is the blockade to consider,' Hampson continued as if Charles had not spoken. 'None of our ships can get through it – but your ship, Mr de Courcey, might make it.'

'She's sound and seaworthy,' Cluny took over, 'and the fact that your son-in-law is so friendly with the British navy might give you the edge. Oh yes, I know it isn't a thing you boast of to us, but you might boast of it to any British vessel that stops you. There'll be letters and despatches to carry, and, we hope, guns and supplies to bring back. Just the first consignment of many, if all goes well.'

'And you want me to go?' Philippe said, astonished.

'You speak the language. You're French yourself, you'll know how to put things across. And you're a famed sailor – the crossing will be nothing to you,' Cluny said.

'We don't just want you to go – we're telling you to go,' Hampson said, quietly but with menace.

'And if I refuse?' Philippe asked. Hampson gave a significant look, first at Charles, then at Eugenie.

'Then we'll know where your sympathies lie,' he said. Philippe frowned.

'Are you sure you know where they lie now? How do you know I won't take these despatches of yours straight to Admiral Howe?'

Hampson smiled, not a pleasant smile, and he nodded, acknowledging the courage that would suggest the possibility. 'We know you won't do that. After all, we shall be keeping a close eye on your daughter for you while you're away. You wouldn't want us to remove our protection from her, when she'd be so vulnerable, would you? A house in Virginia was burnt down last month, burnt right to the ground in the middle of the night. We can make sure that sort of thing doesn't happen to your house while you're away. A very pretty house it is too, with its chapel and all.'

Phillipe gave a slight bow, as if acknowledging a compliment. He gave Charles one look and the faintest shadow of a shrug, and then said, 'I am your servant, gentlemen, to command. I pledge myself to your noble cause.'

'*Our* noble cause, sir,' Cluny corrected genially.

Duncan had been both right and wrong in his assessment of the situation: Henri's possession of Madeleine did not end his desire for her, though it did remove the urgency from it. He loved her more and more deeply, but was able to absent himself from her without fret.

The 'secret wedding' took place in the apartment in the Rue des Ursulines at midnight one night towards the end of October. The shutters were tight closed, and only one candle burned, and Henri and Madeleine waited from half past nine for the 'priest' to arrive. This was all part of the plan, so that Madeleine would be sleepy and confused and less likely to notice anything that might go amiss. At midnight there was a smart rap on the door, and Henri opened it to admit a figure muffled in a cloak with an enormous hood. When the cloak was removed, Henri almost applauded, for Duncan's disguise was splendid. He had gone to a young woman who worked backstage at the Opera for advice, and she had certainly helped him to advantage.

The man in clerical garb appeared to be old and immensely fat. He wore a huge white wig of the style of twenty years back; he had bushy white eyebrows, and in the dim and wavering light his face was much lined, and his nose somewhat bottled. A beard or moustache would have been the most effective disguise, Henri reflected, but in a clean-shaven age it would have attracted too much attention.

While the marriage service was spoken over them, Henri glanced from time to time at Madeleine, but could see no evidence of suspicion in her face or bearing. She was very quiet, in fact hardly spoke at all, and her face was grave, and he concluded that the scheme had worked in that she was by now too tired to harbour suspicions of anyone. The service concluded, the priest took a bumper of brandy with them with what Henri considered as too much enthusiasm, and after some hemming from Henri went on his way, leaving Henri alone with his 'bride'.

'Well,' he said at last, 'and now you are mine.' Madeleine gazed at him for what seemed a long time with those level grey eyes, and then gave a small nod and stepped towards him.

'Yes,' she said. 'Now I am yours.'

That had been the beginning of a night of bliss, followed by months of a strange deep contentment for Henri. Making love to Madeleine was unlike anything he had experienced before. She was virgin, of that he was sure, and yet she responded to him in a way so natural and unashamed, that after a few nights he had more physical pleasure with her than with the most experienced of courtesans. But it was not only that: there was another, deeper level to it. He discovered that making love to someone he was in love with was an entirely different experience.

It became inconvenient to have her so far from Montmartre, and he rented an apartement on the first floor of a house in the Rue des Martyrs, a ten-minute walk from the Rue de St Rustique, and there Madeleine settled down. It was better to have her further away from her father, too. He had disowned her for her disobedience, but with such a wistful air that Henri was sure he would forgive her if she once asked him to.

Henri had never kept a woman before, and he enjoyed it so much that he wondered other men did not talk more about the joys, thinking, in his innocence, that it was always like this. Madeleine was an excellent housekeeper. Under her skilled and vigorous hand the little house was soon cosy, neat and shining. The fire was always bright, and there was always a plump chicken bubbling in the pot, and bread and wine in the larder. The house on Montmartre seemed colder and damper and more cheerless as time went on, and more and more Henri came to relish the delights of the hearthside and the good wife. But he enjoyed his double life too much to abandon it entirely.

Besides, there were his Court attendances to perform, for he was still in hopes of gaining a position or a pension from the new King; there was the gambling and the card-playing, from which he derived a good deal of his income; there were his old friends and his old mistresses to keep up with; and however much he liked the simple life, the plain and savoury food, and the warm, tender, wholesome delights of Madeleine's bed, he never forgot that he was the Comte de Strathord, an aristocrat, and with royal blood in his veins. Elaborate clothes, rich food, brilliant rooms, and titled companions were a lure as strong, which kept him balanced in his orbits like a moon between two planets.

Madame de Murphy was amazed and delighted with the difference in him.

'You have become such good company, Henri,' she purred one day as they lay in bed, eating dried figs and drinking wine. Her hair was tangled and her face paint smudged, and she looked most vulnerable, and therefore, to Henri's mind, at her best. 'I never would have thought you would sit all through one of my salons and say not one unkind or cutting thing! You gave the appearance of being most intelligent.'

Henri smiled wryly at the compliment. 'Anyone is intelligent who agrees with you, is that right?'

'But of course,' she said charmingly. 'It would be most indelicate of you to suggest a lady can be wrong. But seriously, my dear, I am so glad to see you looking well. You have positively put on flesh, and you have an air of such—' she hesitated, searching for the word while her eye went over him again, approvingly, 'such contentment, like a man who is at peace with his world.'

'Well, and so I am,' he said, stretching himself luxuriously in her silken bed. 'I am a man in the prime of life, with sufficient to eat, and a lovely woman of my own to please me – what more could any man want?'

Ismène raised an eyebrow at this description of herself, but let it pass.

'But tell me, my dear, why did you come to my salon

today? My heart sank when I saw you – I thought you had come to be rude.'

Henri laughed. 'Yes, I am just such a boor, am I not? I came to meet Monsieur Franklin, and hear what he had to say, of course. I have heard so much about him that I was naturally interested.'

'And what did you think of him?' Ismène asked cautiously.

'A gentlemanly old man, for all his strange clothes and downright air. A man, I think, who would be at home in any company. I can see why he was chosen for the Americans' ambassador – a better choice than one would have thought possible from a nation of uncouth farmers.'

'I trembled when he talked of equality and republicanism,' Ismène confided. 'I was sure you would interrupt him.'

'My dear, you know that talk of equality is all cant and hypocrisy, besides being impious. The lower orders were placed in the position it pleased God to give them, as were the upper orders. If it were not so, if men were all equal at birth as your Monsieur Franklin claims, then it would have to be the case that we had risen by our merits, and that the poor had sunk by their demerits, and you must surely see that that cannot be true? And if the poor are not poor because it pleases God, but because they deserve no better, then instead of helping and protecting them, we should blame and punish them. Is that what you want?'

'Oh Henri, you argue like an eel. It is impossible to talk sensibly with you.'

'That's not what—' he stopped abruptly, having been about to say, that's not what Madeleine says. It had been for her sake that he had attended Ismène's salon, for he knew she would be interested in what Benjamin Franklin had to say, and was looking forward to telling her and discussing him with her. He wished he could bring her to Ismène's salons – she would impress them with her wit, he thought, proudly – but that was impossible, of course. He must keep his two lives separate, or the fragile structure of his life would break.

Ismène was still waiting for him to finish his sentence, so he said, 'Do you think I should volunteer to join the American army, like Lafayette? Meurice would recommend me for a commission, I'm sure. Perhaps he'd like to join me, and command the French volunteers in – what is the name of the place? New something? It would be a new experience for us both.'

'Oh don't be absurd, Henri. If ever a man was *not* born to be a soldier, it is you. And talking of soldiers, I am reminded that the Comte de Vergennes asked Meurice if he thought you would be willing to do something with his house in Paris. It is badly in need of redecoration.'

'I'm surprised he has time to think about such things,' Henri said cynically. 'The Ministry of Foreign Affairs must be better run than ministries usually are. And if he can afford my ideas, better paid too.'

'And that is another thing, Henri. Vergennes spoke most delicately about the question of your services, and whether you would accept a present from him. I do think you ought to accept it, really I do. It would put him so far in your debt, that he might well use his influence for you at Court.'

Yes, Henri thought, it was a delicate point. *His* generosity in allowing Vergennes to 'pay' him for his services would put Vergennes in more obligation to him than if he did the work for nothing. It was interesting that Ismène obviously understood the point, though he doubted that she would have been able to explain it. But there was another consideration here, too. Henri was discovering that it cost money to keep two establishments, and that however thrifty and economical Madeleine was, she was a drain on his income that his income could not well stand. He liked to bring her things, too, bits of furniture and pretty china and new dresses. He stood in need of money – and since he used his 'employment' by the aristocracy as his excuse to be away from the house, it seemed logical to allow it to provide the money too.

'Very well, Ismène,' he said. 'You may tell Meurice that he may indicate to Vergennes that I am willing to be approached, and will not be mortally offended by a present.'

Some time later he went home to tell Madelaine about Franklin and about his new commission from Vergennes. She had news for him, too, news that made him glad he had decided to accept Vergennes' money: she was expecting a baby.

The war had come suddenly close to Charles, bringing the rest of the world with it. With Philippe gone, and not to be expected back for at least three months, the burden of running the estate fell upon his shoulders, and he could no longer lose himself in his familiar and remote world of biology. Instead of dealing with plants and insects, whose behaviour, though sometimes mysterious, was always predictable, he had to deal with people, who were devious and dishonest and violent and corrupt. Philippe had employees, agents and bailiffs and overseers who knew how the business was run and reported to Charles, but he had no doubt that they would cheat him if they could, and was on his guard, sifting their words and checking their work. In having to deal with these white servants, he became very much more appreciative of the Negro slaves, whose motivations were biologically simple, and whose honesty he would far sooner trust.

In addition to the annoyance of business, he had to suffer the intrusion of the Patriot Party. Having commandeered Philippe and his *bâteau*, they seemed to consider his house theirs as well. There were party meetings once a month, sometimes more often, held in the drawing room of York House, because it was 'so convenient'. The house was also used as a secondary headquarters and staging post for the army, for it was a convenient half-way house between Philadelphia and Yorktown. At all hours of the day and night, Charles and Eugenie had to expect the arrival of messengers wanting food and rest, or soldiers wanting a night's billet, or the wounded from skirmishes, being posted home by stages their indisposition could tolerate.

He and Eugenie were hostages for Philippe's good behaviour, he knew, but even had he been able to abandon Eugenie to her fate, he could never have got closer to the British army than a few yards from his door. They were watched all the time. The astonishing thing was that Eugenie did not seem to mind. With the early days of sickness over, she carried her pregnancy easily, and as she grew bigger, she seemed to grow also in grace and in spirits. She was more energetic than he had ever seen her, and whether she was feeding uncouth soldiers, nursing wounded men, or sitting and smiling graciously at the members of the meetings, she seemed to do it all with as much enthusiasm as any daughter of the revolution. He had never been able to discover whether she had managed that first invasion so well through ignorance or design, and he could not discover now what she felt about the situation. He had not been in the habit of talking with her since they married, and could not now begin.

But, forced as he was into the company of the revolutionaries, he began, through hearing more of their ideas, to change his own. Leaving aside their cant about equality and the 'natural justice' of the republic as against the monarchy, he could see that their plain design was to be their own masters, and he could not find that there was anything to be argued against it. They wanted to manage their own affairs, to have their own elective parliament, to decide upon their own taxation and expenditure, to trade freely with the world, and to expand as they would, without reference to any external power. And why shouldn't they? he found himself asking again and again. Loyalty to Britain, the mother-country? But by this stage of the country's development it could only be a political loyalty, and a political loyalty could only ever come poor second to economic necessity.

The Patriots were united in this desire for independence, but Charles discovered through listening and occasionally asking questions that they were united in very little else, and that there were as many internal fears and jealousies and mistrusts as in any group of men. Many doubted the wisdom of calling in the aid of France, for all General Washington's certainty about it. It was likely that Spain would ally with France, and when the British were defeated, many feared that the two Catholic powers would simply carve up America between them, and that the colonists would pass from the comparatively easy slavery to Britain into a slavery to Popish powers ten times as abject.

There was also hostility between the planters of the south and the traders of the north, who felt their interests conflicted and held each other in suspicion. There was fear on the part of the slave-owners that the New Englanders would try to abolish slavery. There was suspicion by the east coast dwellers of the western farmers, who never drank tea and felt the heel of Europe less firmly on their necks. And there was a great fear on the part of the Old Families, the American 'aristocracy', that independence from Britain would unleash the mob, and that a republican government would abolish wealth and privilege.

Despite all this, Charles found himself growing more sympathetic towards the Patriots as time went on, and resenting their presence in his life less. But he was still aware that he was under suspicion, and that if the British navy sailed into Chesapeake Bay, his position would be very delicate indeed.

CHAPTER NINE

The *Ariadne*'s three-year commission ended in March 1777, and she was sent home to Portsmouth; but the navy was desperately undermanned and short of ships, and as soon as she had paid-off she was recommissioned with all her officers, and the men had not one single day on shore to spend their accumulated pay or taste the joys of the Portsmouth grog shops and brothels. It was a delicate time, and there was almost mutiny, and five men had to be flogged before things were quiet again. *Ariadne* delivered despatches, collected letters for the fleet, revictualled, took on a dozen new hands, and sailed without delay.

Even the officers had seen nothing of their families. One of the lieutenants had a wife in Portsmouth, and she had sent a message by a shore boat that she was waiting on the dockside for him, but the most he had been able to do was to borrow a glass and look at her from the taffrail. For Thomas and William it was, of course, doubly impossible, their families being so far away, but there were at least letters. William was better pleased than Thomas, for he had no particular reason to want to go home, and his letters, from his mother and father and Edward, with a line from Father Ramsay, were full of news and more than he expected. His mother, he learnt, was well advanced in pregnancy and had been told not to ride any more until she was delivered, which made her feel frustrated. She was using up her energies on reorganizing the house. Papa had got her a housekeeper, Mrs Mappin, to ease the burden from her shoulders, and the two were at continued loggerheads over the way things should be done.

All this he learnt from his father's letter. From his mother's letter he learnt that his father was doing far too much, and wearing himself out, for as well as all his duties as a Justice of the Peace, he was on the boards of both the Turnpike Trust and the Canal Trust, was a governor of St Edward's School, and overseer of the Workhouse and Hospital, and was now determinedly trying to interest other landowners in growing potatoes. And that Persis was wonderfully fit, and was going to win everything at the York races, and another of Artembares' offspring was going to come second. All in all, he learnt that his father loved his mother, and that his mother loved his father and horses, and thus that all was well in his world, and he was satisfied.

Thomas was less happy. He had hoped, of course, to see Flora; he had longed to see his daughter Louisa, who was now two and a half, and walking and talking and delighting Rachel by promising to have curly hair, and who would not recognize her father if she saw him. That was the greatest sadness in the life of a sailor. But he was not entirely happy with Flora's letters. They were shorter than he would have liked, and never mentioned the child – it was Jemima's correspondence that told him about Louisa's progress – and contained a great deal about London and parties and very little about Flora herself, or her feelings for her husband. He was glad that she was enjoying herself, of course, and that she had been presented at Court, and that she was so friendly with the Countess of Chelmsford; but though he would not go quite as far as admitting he wished her back at Morland Place, he thought she might be sorrier that he was not sharing her pleasures.

However, there was no time for brooding. *Ariadne* sailed again for the West Indies and Thomas had the additional tasks of seeing the new hands settled in, ridding the ship of the vermin they brought aboard, and exercising the crew so hard that they had no time to think of their grievances. They made a quick passage to Kingston, delivered the letters, picked up despatches, and sailed to New York to join General Howe in his new thrust against Washington's army.

Howe had decided against marching the army across

New Jersey, and instead planned to sail the men and horses round the coast to the Delaware River and as far up it as possible towards Philadelphia, General Washington's capital. Embarkation took place on 23 July, 15,000 men, staff officers, baggage and horses, all to be got on board somehow. Conditions below were terrible, even on the three-deckers, and the weather was inimically hot. *Ariadne* had her contingent to carry. William had grown used to conditions on board, enough to consider the available space adequate if not generous, but even he was amazed to see how many more men could be crammed into a wooden ship when necessary. The soldiers regarded the sailors with suspicion, the sailors regarded the soldiers with tolerant amusement. Many of them were seasick, even though the seas were blessedly calm, and exclaimed in amazement at the conditions the sailors accepted as normal. The sailors thought them effete, unused to hardship, unable to think for themselves. Even William, while he was doing his best to offer the hospitality of the gunroom to the colour sergeants, found himself thinking contemptuously that he would like to see *them* run aloft in the dead of night in a storm to reef the tops'ls.

The horses were less of a problem, once they had been swayed aboard and hobbled to the deck-rings. Watering them was a continuous job, for they were always thirsty, and could not, like the men, be expected to put up with it; and the first lieutenant cursed and almost wept at the dinginess of his once white decks, fearing he would never rid them of the stable taint. The horses seemed to adapt to the movement of the ship quite quickly, and there were few accidents. At least they were not seasick; and at least they did not bring vermin on board with them, as did the soldiers. Within hours of the embarkation, William found himself scratching, and it was not long before the men of his watch began reporting to him, with a mixture of shame and pique, that they had got fleas, or lice, or bedbugs. In the heat, and the crowded conditions, the pests bred exponentially, and there was no hope of tackling them until the soldiers were disembarked again.

'It won't be for long,' he tried to comfort the sufferers. 'A week or so and we'll have the soldiers off, and deal with it.'

But it was not a week or so – it turned out to be more than a month. They hove to outside the mouth of the Delaware for some time, while every glass in the squadron was trained on the shores, and then the flagship signalled and they passed on down the coast. Howe had decided that the Delaware was too well-guarded to risk a landing. They were to sail instead up the Chesapeake Bay and land the men at the head of it.

'So we'll be as far from Philadelphia as we were when we started,' a fierce, red-faced colour sergeant said disgustedly when the change of plan filtered through to the midshipmen's berth. 'This is our general's master-stroke then! And how long, boy, will it take, to sail this tub round there?' he demanded of William, who bristled at the idea of his beautiful *Ariadne*'s being called a tub, but forced himself to speak politely.

'That depends on the wind, sir, but I should think two or three weeks.'

The colour sergeant spat contemptuously. 'A fine business it would be if I were to give such an answer when a general asked me how long I'd take to march my men to such-and-such a place! Two or three weeks? A pretty margin of error you sailors allow yourselves! And in two or three weeks – or four or five, for all you seem to know – Washington will have organized his defences and we will have the Devil's job to dislodge him. Pah!'

He had been freely imbibing of his liquor ration, William told himself, keeping his temper with an effort, or he would not be so rude. As soon as he could excuse himself, William ran on deck, and climbed rapidly to the foretop, where at least the stable smell was fainter, to scratch himself in peace and swear away his ill feelings towards the soldiers.

After four weeks on board, the army was finally disembarked at the head of Chesapeake Bay on 25 August, weary and suffering from the heat and confinement. The bulk of the navy was to sail away immediately, but the smaller vessels, and amongst them the *Ariadne*, were ordered to bring up more supplies, and to look into the numerous creeks and inlets in search of American vessels. It was a command to please most captains, for the vessels captured would be prizes of war, which meant prize money. Thomas was less happy. He thought, of course, of York Plantation, and of Charles and his family. He knew that Philippe had an ocean-going vessel, as well as numerous small craft for use in the Bay itself, and it would be his duty to report their existence, even though he knew that Philippe was no friend to the revolution. It was fortunate that the *Ariadne* was too large to penetrate the channels and had been ordered to bring up supplies instead – he would not have personally to give the order to take or destroy the boats. He could at least, he thought, find some way of warning Charles to offer no resistance when the landing party came, for the orders would be to harm no one if they did not resist. Philippe, he thought, might object to losing his boats, even to the British navy, and ought to be forewarned.

However much he wanted to, he could not go ashore himself, but he thought it would be pleasant for William to see his Cousin Charles, even if only for a moment or two. He wrote his letter with great care as the *Ariadne* tacked her way gently down the Bay, and gave it to William, with orders to take the gig and four steady men and deliver it to his cousin. The *Ariadne* hove to at the mouth of the Patuxent River while the boat was lowered away, and then sailed on, to wait for the returning boat a little further down the Bay, where it was wider and safer.

'Don't be longer than you have to,' he told Mr Midshipman Morland. 'Give him the letter, wait while he reads it, answer any questions you can, and then come off. It is not a social visit, remember.'

'Aye aye, sir,' said William, saluted, and dashed away,

thrilled to be sent on his first independent command at the age of fourteen, even if it was such a simple one.

The appearance of the squadron in the Bay had caused panic. Some of the larger privateers would not have been afraid to try and pick off a small vessel of the British navy, if they could have taken her by surprise, but there was nothing on the whole Bay that could have stood up to a single broadside from the smallest vessel in that squadron. Men went into hiding, ships were hastily sailed or towed into the narrowest and most inaccessible creeks, boats were thrust into the reeds or heaved out into boatsheds.

The news that the squadron was carrying an army was soon known, and had to be passed on to Philadelphia as quickly as possible. Messengers on horseback and in small boats hastened up the Bay, and Hampson himself arrived at York House to keep an eye on things even before the ships had gone by for the first time, on their way northwards.

It was lucky for William that he did, luckier still that when *Ariadne* put off a boat the lookout troubled to notice the name of the ship before he ran up to the house with the news.

'It's my cousin's ship,' Charles told Hampson when he heard. 'My Cousin Thomas is her captain. It is probably nothing more than a message for me, a letter from England perhaps, family news.'

'How many men?' Hampson asked the lookout.

'Four men,' he answered tersely, 'and a boy in uniform, midshipman I guess.'

'A midshipman – that could be my Cousin William,' Charles said eagerly. 'You see, it must be family news.'

Hampson and the lookout made no sign of having heard him. 'Four men and a boy,' the lookout said grimly. 'We could take 'em easy. Pick 'em off before they ever landed. Scuttle the boat. The ship's gone on down the bay, there's no one to see.'

Charles paled. 'No, no, I beg you! You must not!'

'Might be reprisals,' Hampson said, still ignoring Charles. The lookout shrugged.

'Who's to say what happened to 'em? A boy in charge—'

'No, please, my cousin – it is family news, depend on it! They mean no threat to you. You must not think of—'

'Must not, sir?' Hampson interrupted him coldly. Charles felt his hands cold and clammy, and a sickness in his stomach.

'I beg you, sir, I beg you,' he said desperately. 'My wife is so near to her time – you must not permit violence here. Let him come and go. I promise there will be no trouble.'

Hampson was deep in thought for a moment or two, perhaps the worst moments of Charles's life. Then he said to the lookout, 'Let 'em come. Keep your men out of sight. I want 'em to think this is their place. He might be bringing information we can use.'

'And afterwards?' the lookout said, licking his lips. Hampson shook his head.

'No, let 'em go – unless I give the word otherwise. I'll be hidden here, I'll know what passes. If the boy doesn't go back, there'll be reprisals all right. I'll be listening, so Mr Morland won't feel inclined to pass him any information to take back.'

'Thank you, thank you,' Charles said. 'I'll say nothing, I promise.'

William had been prepared to have to refuse all kind invitations, to press for his departure against a natural desire for him to stay and chat; but his Cousin Charles seemed as eager for him to leave as his orders could ever have made him. Altogether the atmosphere in the house was strange. Charles received him kindly, but with a strained inattention, as though he were listening all the time for some distant signal. He read Thomas's letter in silence, and when he had finished, looked up at William blankly, as if he had not taken it in.

'I can wait while you write a reply, if you wish, sir,' William said.

'Oh – no – no reply, I thank you. There is nothing to reply to,' Charles said awkwardly. There was a silence.

'Your sister is well, sir, I am empowered to tell you, and enjoying the Season in London. And her daughter flourishes. My mother is expecting an increase to her family at any time. My father—'

'Yes, yes, very good,' Charles said hastily. 'I am glad of it, glad, but should you not be returning to your ship?'

'Very well, sir,' William said, greatly puzzled. 'Have I any message to give the captain?'

'Tell him I thank him for the news. My wife and I are well – she is expecting a child almost daily. I will write when things are more settled. Go along now, and thank you for coming.'

William could do no other than allow himself to be hustled out. Something, he was sure, was painfully wrong, and the first thing that presented itself to his mind was that Cousin Charles had gone over to the other side. That would account for his embarrassment, his unwillingness to exchange news, and his desire to hurry William off the premises. But it would be a difficult thing to get across to his captain, for Charles was his brother-in-law as well as his friend, and he would not want to believe that he could betray his country and family.

When William had gone, Charles stood a moment in silence, clutching the letter and pondering. He was tempted to destroy it, burn it before Hampson came in to read it; but if he did, the men would still come to take the boats, and unwarned, Hampson might fire on them, resist, and provoke the landing party to greater violence. He felt bitter, bitter that he should have been placed in this situation, where his own brother-in-law was his enemy. Philippe and Eugenie had trapped him here, and for a moment he hated them, and longed above all to be able to leave, run away back to England and safety. But Eugenie above in her chamber was great with his child, and that bound him more effectively than any chains.

Soon the news came down the Bay that a great battle had been fought on the banks of Brandywine Creek, and the British, despite their tiredness, had defeated the Americans. Forewarned of the intention of the navy to destroy all small craft on the Bay, Hampson had sent orders for as many craft as could be moved to be sailed far up the creeks, or hidden in the Choptank marshes. The larger vessels were to try to evade capture by dodging about from one inlet to another, keeping ahead of the British ships, until it was possible to slip round behind them to safety. In this way many vessels were saved, although others were captured or burnt. The landing party that called on York Plantation came in an armed cutter, looking for the *bâteau*, and when they could not find her, broke up every small boat in the place. Hampson gave orders for his men to offer no resistance and to keep out of sight, and himself posed as the master of the house, for Charles was otherwise engaged.

'What's that noise?' the British lieutenant asked sharply, as a cry was heard from upstairs just as he was about to leave.

'My wife, sir, in labour of our first child,' Hampson said smoothly.

The lieutenant frowned a moment, and then bowed. 'Your pardon, sir. I won't intrude on you any longer.'

Late that night, after a long and hard labour, Eugenie produced her first child. It was a girl, and they named her Charlotte, after her father. When Charlotte was less than a month old, the news came that the British had taken Philadelphia, thus opening up the Delaware River to British ships, even as the Chesapeake had been opened. And shortly after that came the news that Philippe's boat had been intercepted trying to land arms and ammunition on the Delaware coast. The British ship that intercepted her fired a warning shot, but it was badly aimed, and struck her hull very low. Part of the cargo of ammunition exploded, blowing out the bows of the ship, and she sank in a very few minutes. The British ship had put out boats, but though they had swept the area, there appeared to be no survivors.

The birth of his child, combined with the death of his father-in-law, were sufficient to complete the change of heart that had been slowly taking place in Charles. It was impossible for him to continue to function with divided loyalties, and though he was barely aware of it, it was essential for survival that he should give his whole heart to one side or the other. He had resented the invasion of his home and his private world by the Patriot Party, but he resented even more when his own countrymen came to burn his boats.

The result of the struggle was inevitable from the moment his tiny, helpless daughter was placed in his arms, still damp and red and exhausted from the effort of being born. His adolescent disappointment with Eugenie had been fading all that year, and disappeared entirely the moment she became mother of his child, and a fierce determination filled him to protect and provide for them, at whatever cost. The news of Philippe's death crystallized his resolve. He had liked and admired his father-in-law, and had, in marrying Eugenie, tacitly promised to serve Philippe's ends in protecting the estate and the heritage. Philippe died at the hands of the British, and in doing so made his son-in-law an American. York Plantation would survive, Charles swore by the head of his infant daughter; and Philippe's grandchildren would inherit it, to live upon it as free Americans.

The *Ariadne*, being the mercury of the fleet, was usually the first to receive news, and handled such a volume of it that Thomas did not at first notice the tale of the sinking of a privateer sloop, the *Sainte Jeanne*, running guns from Martinique to Delaware. It was only on second thoughts that he checked the name of her captain, and then sank into deep and gloomy thought.

He had received coldly William's suggestion that Charles might have become sympathetic to the rebels, and found for himself plenty of reasons for Charles's apparent strangeness, though none of them were entirely convincing. But the discovery that Charles's father-in-law had been running guns for the rebels seemed evidence conclusive. Perhaps, he thought, it was not an entirely voluntary betrayal – if his wife were about to give birth he might find himself in a painful position. But even so, it was a betrayal, and Thomas felt it more a betrayal of himself than of England. Added to his disappointment with Flora's letters, and his need of leave after almost three years continuously at sea, it made him morose.

The war news was not encouraging either. Howe had taken Philadelphia, and freed the Delaware River, but had still not crushed Washington's army; and in October grave news came from further north. General Burgoyne had led the Canada troops southwards to free the upper Hudson, but had been trapped at Saratoga. General Clinton who was holding New York had begun to march north with reinforcements, but had been ordered back to help Howe at Philadelphia. Without the reinforcements, Burgoyne had been forced to surrender.

The surrender was made under convention, by which the troops – around four thousand men – were to lay down their arms and were to be allowed to return to England on condition they did not again serve in America. *Ariadne* was sent to New York to collect General Burgoyne and take him and the news of the defeat back to England as rapidly as possible. Other ships would be provided later for the transport of the troops.

It was not a mission to please Thomas, even though it meant returning to England and the possibility of some leave. He had to do the honours of his ship and give up his cabin to Burgoyne – a general ranked far above a mere captain – but a disgraced general and bad news were not the most favoured cargoes. The war was going badly, the rebels were being aided more and more openly by France, and it seemed to him that it was impossible for England ever to win without the use of forces far greater than she could afford to employ.

The passage was a particularly difficult and slow one, and it was December before a weary *Ariadne* sailed up the River Thames to London Pool. Having got rid of his passenger, Thomas made out his reports and, pausing only to change into his best uniform, gathered them and the despatches and passed the word for his gig to take him up to the Admiralty. There, after a considerable wait, he was ushered into the gilded presence of the First Lord himself!

'Ah, Captain, good of you to come,' the First Lord said, as if his word were not law to a lowly captain. 'You know the Comptroller Sir Maurice Suckling and Admiral Sir Peter Parker – and my secretary Johnson – Captain Thomas Morland, Sir Peter, just back from New York with the—' he searched amongst the papers on his desk.

'The *Ariadne*, sir,' Thomas supplied him politely.

'*Ariadne*, 28, yes. Well, Captain, Sir Peter and I would very much like to hear how matters stand out there. We have your reports, of course, but we'd like to hear anything you have to tell us.'

Thomas told all he knew, and the three dignitaries put a number of questions to him, about conditions, and the strength of American seagoing power, and the success of the blockade. He struggled with his fatigue to put his report to them concisely and clearly, for it was not often that a captain had the opportunity of impressing the arbiters of fate. When he had finished, there was a brief silence, before Parker said, 'You have served for some time on the West India station, I believe, Captain?'

'Yes, sir. Three years now in the *Ariadne*, and before that in the old *Hydra*.'

'Hm. And your father, of course, was Admiral Morland, who knew the West Indies well?'

'Yes, sir.'

'Sir Peter is to take over next year as commander-in-chief of the West India station, Captain,' Sir Maurice explained kindly, and Thomas found that Parker was actually smiling at him.

'We shall need all the experienced captains we can get,' he said, 'and I look forward to having you under my command.'

'Thank you, sir,' Thomas said.

'But not yet, I fear,' the First Lord went on. Thomas raised an inquiring eyebrow.

'What is the condition of your ship at present? Is she ready for sea?'

'Once we have revictualled, yes, sir,' Thomas said – there was no other possible answer – but he felt constrained to add, 'The crew are pretty tired, though, sir. We have been at sea continuously since April '75.'

'Hm. Yes,' the First Lord said, frowning a little at the unrequested information. 'Well, Captain, you will not be returning to the West Indies at present. Your services will be needed with the Channel fleet. I see no reason not to tell you that we expect France to enter the war against us very soon.'

'That will at least clarify the situation,' Parker commented.

The First Lord went on, 'Your men are tired, you say?'

'Yes, sir.' No need to add anything more. The First Lord was an experienced sailor, well able to judge the effects of more than two years at sea without a break.

'Very well. I think we can grant you a little leave. I'll make out your orders to that effect. You can have until 6 January, unless anything urgent crops up.'

'Thank you, sir,' Thomas said.

It was late the following day, a cold, wet, dark December day, that Thomas, with William beside him, had himself rowed up the river to Whitehall Steps. There had been too much to do on board to leave any earlier, but though he wanted mostly to get back to Morland Place and see Flora and the child, he felt he could not leave London without paying his respects to Lord and Lady Chelmsford, who had been so kind and hospitable to his wife.

'With a bit of luck, William, we'll be asked to stay the night. I shouldn't mind a hot bath, and a night's sleep in a real bed, before we take the coach.'

'Christmas at Morland Place,' William mused, remembering the great roaring fires and the smell of spiced wine and roast goose and his mother playing the heroine in the *Twelfth Night* masque. Oh, and there would be a new little brother in the nursery now, little Harry, born in August. William was not sure how he would like that idea. He had been too young to remember the birth of James, previously the youngest.

When they arrived, Chelmsford House was ablaze with light and there were a number of carriages in front of it, and Thomas realized belatedly that he ought to have sent word that he was coming.

'Oh well, too late now to worry,' he said. 'If it's not convenient, we can go away again.'

The impassive butler who opened the door did not seem at all put out by the appearance of two rather bedraggled naval officers, though there was a sound of laughter and talk from within, and a piano tinkling, and two elegantly dressed people were just mounting the stairs, as though recently arrived.

'Captain Morland, and Mr Midshipman Morland, to see his lordship,' Thomas said.

'Yes, sir, of course. If you gentlemen would like to wait in the library, I will inform his lordship that you are here.'

'Pray give my apologies if it is inconvenient,' Thomas said. 'We seem to have arrived in the middle of a party.' The butler bowed, but in silence, and left them. Thomas sat down gratefully in the nearest chair, and William wandered across to the bookshelves to examine the books. They were silent for a few minutes, until interrupted by the violent opening of the door to admit a young woman, closely followed by a young man, both of them evidently dressed for the party that was going on above. The young woman was in the middle of speech, her head turned back to her companion.

'I'll prove it to you, and then you shall eat your words, if only I can find the—'

The expression on the face of Charles Morland, Lord Meldon, warned her that something was amiss, and she turned her head and broke off abruptly in mid-sentence, to stare with no less dismay than astonishment at the uniformed naval captain who had risen to his feet a few yards from her. She flushed with confusion, and then grew pale, and her hand fluttered up to her low décolletage in a gesture of defence.

'Flora,' Thomas said, stunned by more different emotions than he could well separate at the moment. 'Flora – I wouldn't have recognized you.'

It was more true than that expression usually was. It was a woman of fashion before him rather than the pretty little cousin he had married four years ago. Her hair was built up into a tower on top of her head, the front a smooth slope, the back a structure of elaborate plaits and curls, the whole powdered white and topped with feathers and ribbons. Beneath it, a little painted face, a long neck, a deep square décolletage, a tight bodice of primrose yellow satin, a much-hooped skirt with wide embroidered robings over a frilled petticoat, and drooping lace and ribbons at the sleeve ends. He told himself that this was his wife, and the mother of his child, but his mind rejected the information. He felt he had never met this woman before.

'Nor I you,' she said at last with an effort. 'You are so—' she waved a small hand vaguely – 'so very weather-beaten. And you have arrived so unexpectedly.'

'I did not know you were in London. I would have thought you would have come down to the ship, or at least sent word.'

She looked indignant. 'How could I know your ship was there?'

Thomas paused before replying. He had always assumed that Flora, like any naval wife, would keep abreast of the news, that she would have been informed the very moment *Ariadne* was sighted in the Channel, and yet, put to him like that, he could see that she might not, indeed, know where to go for intelligence of ships. And yet, 'Surely Lord Chelmsford would have—'

'My father is from home,' Lord Meldon said quickly, with a small bow. 'Otherwise I am sure he would have brought the news.' There was a silence, which Meldon broke by making a graceful escape. 'I am sure my father would wish me to beg you to regard this house as your own for as long as you wish. And now I will leave you alone, as I am sure you must be desiring to be. Pray ring if there is anything you require. Your servant, sir – ma'am.'

When he had left, Flora at last collected herself and presented herself to Thomas, a little stiffly, to be embraced. 'How lovely that you are here!' Her voice lacked conviction, and she hurried on, 'And how long can you stay? Have you leave? Sure the *Ariadne* is not paid off? Did you not tell me in one of your letters that you were commissioned for another three years?'

Thomas told his story briefly. 'Now they tell me I am to be attached to the Channel fleet for a time.'

'Then you will be more often at home?' Flora asked. Thomas shook his head.

'If France enters the war, as they think she will, I doubt if we will have any leave. But of course we will have to put in to revictual, and if you were to come down and take lodgings at Portsmouth, I might see you for an hour or two—'

'Why, Thomas, what do you think I could do with myself in Portsmouth, all alone, month after month?' Flora interrupted him hastily.

'I have cousins there,' he said, 'my Aunt Ann's children, who would be happy to entertain you.'

'But I don't know them, Thomas. No, no it would be impossible. But you have not said how long you will be here.'

'We have leave for Christmas,' he said, making an effort

to rouse himself to cheerfulness. 'We had thought of paying our respects to Lord and Lady Chelmsford and then taking the coach tomorrow for Yorkshire. Can you be ready by tomorrow?'

Flora's expression was dismayed as she looked from Thomas to William and back.

'Of course you will want to go straight away, but it would be very strange for me to rush away so suddenly, without warning. I really don't see how I can go tomorrow.'

'But I am sure they would understand, in the present case—'

'Besides, you see, I was not going to Morland Place for Christmas. I have been invited – we are all going – a large party at Wolvercote. Lord Aylesbury's place, you know.'

'But you must make your excuses, of course,' Thomas said. William, embarrassed by what he was being forced to witness, tried to make himself small, and earnestly studied the pattern on the carpet. Flora looked dismayed.

'Oh Thomas, I couldn't possibly do any such thing. It would look so particular. It has all been arranged these weeks, and not for anything would I offend his lordship. They are not expecting me at Morland Place, you know. But wait, why do you not join me at Wolvercote? Yes, that would be much the best thing. It will be perfectly easy to get you invited too, and Lord Aylesbury, you know, is a great friend of the First Lord, which would be good for your career, would not it? Charles – that is, Lord Meldon – can write and ask to bring you too.'

She beamed with satisfaction at having solved the problem, and Thomas sighed and yielded. It would be a good thing to ingratiate himself with a friend of the First Lord, it was true, but a large house-party was not what he had looked forward to at Christmas.

'Very well,' he said. 'But you will visit Morland Place with me first? There is time before Wolvercote, I am sure.'

'Oh Thomas, I can't. There are ten thousand things to be done here first, and I have already said, I cannot leave the Chelmsfords just like that. I have engagements right up until the moment I leave for Oxford, and it would be too tiresome to break them all. You and William must go, and take my compliments. They do not expect me, you know. If you go post, it will only take two days, and you will have near a week before you need come back to London.'

Thomas could only assent, though with bad grace. 'Very well, if you will not come—'

Flora, now feeling she had command of the situation, smiled prettily and pressed his hand. 'I *cannot* come,' she corrected cheerfully. 'Jemima will understand. But I am so glad you will be with me at Wolvercote. I will enjoy it so much more. And be sure to bring your riding boots. They have wonderful hunting country there, and the Chetwyns keep good horses. I have hunted there a dozen times this year, and had splendid runs, and indeed young Chetwyn says that I am the fastest woman to hounds in all of Oxfordshire! Oh, and I must tell you what Charles – Lord Meldon – said of me. It was so droll!'

She chattered on, and Thomas listened, part with amazement at the change in her, and part with a deepening gloom that he could not quite account for, for she was holding his hand affectionately and smiling at him as she spoke, and surely a loving husband ought to be glad that his wife had found friends to solace her in his absence?

CHAPTER TEN

The defeat at Saratoga had a great many repercussions. Generals Howe and Carleton resigned, General Burgoyne was of course precluded from fighting in America again by the terms of the convention, and Lord North, who before had been anxious to resign the leadership, now became desperate to do so. In December 1777 France recognized the United States of America as an independent country, and in February 1778 signed treaties of commerce and alliance with America, and was thus unofficially at war with Britain.

From the time he came back from Wolvercote to return to his ship, Thomas had been shuttling back and forth from the Channel fleet, under Admiral Keppel, to London and the Admiralty, and so had had considerable time on shore. He was often at Chelmsford House, partly so that he could see something of Flora, and partly because he had struck up a friendship with Lord Chelmsford, who could supply him with the latest information from Court and Cabinet. On the occasions when he would return from the ship to Pall Mall and discover that Flora had gone out to a ball or party or entertainment, he would sit beside the fire with Lord Chelmsford and discuss the international situation, so as not to have to think about the domestic one.

'One good thing about France entering the war – it has finally spurred the First Lord to do something about our naval strength,' Chelmsford said one evening. 'Forty-two new ships of the line for the Channel and Mediterranean fleets, and eight for West India. Well, it is better late than never, I suppose.'

'But why so many for the Channel? Surely more could be sent to America, in view of the situation?' Thomas protested. Chelmsford gave a grim sort of smile.

'And leave the Channel unprotected? My dear young man, do you know how many ships Estaing has, to say nothing of the Spanish fleet? And divided between Brest and Toulon, they cannot even be properly blockaded – they could slip out into the Atlantic at any moment.'

'True,' Thomas said gloomily. 'And where in the world will we get the men to man these new ships? With no more American sailors to be had, and half the West India fleet suffering from either fever or scurvy—'

'Or both,' Chelmsford put in. 'And the army competing for the same men – even a hot press may not round up enough for skeleton crews. But we shall soon have other troubles as severe. Supplies, now – Sandwich was telling me today that the timber for masts comes from America, and where are we to turn to now?'

'The Baltic, perhaps?' Thomas suggested. Chelmsford shook his head.

'Relations are very delicate there. We do not know which way the Russians will turn, and the Swedes have always been difficult, though they call themselves neutral. Well, at least with France in the war the Government's unpopularity has eased somewhat, and the Opposition's guns are spiked. But poor North would give a limb or two to be out of it. He tried again to persuade the King to let Chatham take over, but His Majesty remains adamant. He won't have Chatham at any price. One has to admire him, you know.'

'Chatham?'

'No, the King. He sticks to his guns. And he still believes we shall succeed in America, and won't even think of granting independence. It's a sore subject. You know North sent to treat with this fellow Franklin in Paris? Offered him everything except independence, and Franklin said independence was the only thing he wanted. Most peculiar looking fellow, Franklin. Did you see him when he was in London? Goes about dressed as a farmer. Wears a fur hat with a tail hanging down the back, as if he was going to a masque. Though the way he's fêted in Paris, I daresay his life is one long series of masques.'

There was a silence, in which Thomas, through an inevitable association with the word masque, thought of Flora. It was evident that Chelmsford's mind ran that way too, for he said, almost apologetically, 'It's a pity Mrs Thomas Morland didn't know you were to be in London again today, or I'm sure she wouldn't have gone. It is only a private party at Mrs Montague's, to hear the new soprano. The young people, you know, want always to be doing. They have not yet learnt the joys of sitting by one's own fireside. But my son is with her, and she will be quite safe.'

'Of course,' Thomas said, making an effort to be polite. 'I am glad she has the opportunity to be amused. A sailor's wife is often forced to be solitary.'

'She is very much loved, wherever she goes,' Chelmsford said, smiling. 'My wife and I dote on her, and wish we had the opportunity of seeing more of her. But, dear me, she is always at something or other. She is always in demand.'

'Yes,' said Thomas shortly. He did not need to be told that. Whenever he walked up from Whitehall Steps to Pall Mall, he knew the chances were that Flora would be 'just this minute gone out – but expected back some time or other.'

'By the way,' Chelmsford said after a moment, 'you seem to have made a good impression on Parker – Sir Peter Parker, I mean.'

'Indeed? I am glad to hear it.'

'Yes, Sandwich was telling me after the levee today that Parker said he has a vacancy for a midshipman, and was wondering whether our young cousin William might like to transfer to his ship. I said I thought he would be delighted. Life on a three-decker is not as exciting for a young man, I know, as life on a dashing little frigate or sloop, but—'

'It would be a wonderful thing for his career,' Thomas said, cheering considerably. He was very fond of young

William. 'I have the highest opinion of him,' he added. Chelmsford nodded sagely.

'And it is such a compliment to you, too.'

'I hadn't thought of that,' Thomas said.

'Mind you, I wouldn't be surprised if Aylesbury didn't have something to do with it. You know he thinks the world of Mrs Thomas Morland, and Parker's wife is sister to Aylesbury's wife's cousin, who is a permanent secretary at the Admiralty.'

'I see,' said Thomas. Chelmsford cocked an eye at him.

'It is the way these things are done, my dear,' he said. 'It's the way of the world. You mustn't mind it.'

'No, of course not,' said Thomas.

In April Lord Carlisle at last achieved his desire to be employed as an ambassador by the Government, and was sent to America to treat for peace with the Patriots, though when Thomas heard he was not to be allowed to discuss independence with the rebels, he had little hope the mission would succeed. *Ariadne* was to take his lordship's party to New York, and Thomas welcomed him on board with more than official warmth, as a friend of Allen and Jemima, who, in genuine kindness of heart, had taken the trouble to offer his services to Morland Place in carrying letters to Thomas. From these Thomas, who had not been able to go back to Morland Place since December, learnt that Edward had surprised and somewhat dismayed them all by declaring a desire to read for the Church; that James had frightened them out of their wits by falling from the roof of the kennels, where he had been climbing unlawfully, and breaking his arm; that little Louisa had just completed her first sampler, though the stitches were very large and loose, and was beginning to learn French from Father Ramsay who thought everyone ought to know it; and that Jemima hoped she was pregnant again, but was not yet entirely certain.

For a moment, as he read the letter in the seclusion of

the lee side of the quarterdeck, the grey and choppy Channel and the familiar sights and sounds of a naval vessel faded away, and he saw in his mind's eye with painful clarity the warmth and peace and busy-ness of Morland Place, the children growing up, the work of the estate going on around them, and Allen and Jemima celebrating their love for each other in another child. He smiled at the picture, rejoicing that Flora would be there to share it, safe under the eye of the woman who had been almost a mother to her, far from the glittering temptations of London and society. For Flora, trying hard not to sulk about it, had been sent off home for the rest of the year at least, to be fixed in Yorkshire by maternity. Thomas, during that Christmas at Wolvercote, had managed to make her pregnant again, and was setting sail for New York with far greater peace of mind than he had anticipated.

They made a quick passage to New York, arriving in May, with orders for the British army to evacuate Phila-delphia, and for the soldiers to be dispersed to the West Indies and Florida. The theatre of war was shifting, and with the entry of the French into the conflict it had been decided to concentrate the attack on the French possessions in the West Indies in the hope of diverting their forces and keeping them occupied. Sir Henry Clinton was now commander-in-chief, and he decided to march the men across New Jersey to New York for the embarkation, since large ships would not be able to get up the river as far as Philadelphia. Thomas was ordered to take *Ariadne* up the river to Philadelphia to take off supplies and the three thousand refugees from the Patriot army who had come in during that bitter winter. They had terrible tales to tell of the hardship the Patriot army had suffered at Valley Forge, where lack of supplies had led to disease and famine, and the savage cold and the lack of proper clothes, sometimes even shoes, had led to terrible cases of frostbite, many of them losing feet or limbs.

Thomas took his quota of refugees up to New York where they were to await the main body of the army coming by land, delivered Clinton's reports to Admiral Arbuthnot commanding the squadron at New York, and was immediately sent home to England again by the Admiral with despatches. It was the usual round, the predictable circuit for a small fast ship in time of war, and Thomas was resigned to it. When he made his number at the Admiralty, however, he was summoned before the First Lord and once more found Sir Maurice Suckling with him. Suckling greeted Thomas kindly, despite being evidently unwell – he looked pale and drawn and tired.

'I want your opinion, Captain Morland, of the coppering,' Suckling said, when the preliminary reports had been made. 'How do you find *Ariadne* handles? Would you speak in favour of coppering?'

Thomas said that he would, and a technical discussion ensued, at the end of which the First Lord consulted some papers on the table in front of him and Thomas waited in patient silence on his pleasure.

'You have been a long time on the West India station,' he said at last. It was not a question, and Thomas remained silent. Suckling looked up with a faint smile. 'We are well aware that young captains regard it as a good station. My own nephew has just been sent there, made lieutenant into the *Lowestoft*, and not all the tales of yellow fever could dissuade him from thinking it the best. Prize money is the lure, easier to attain in the West Indies than in Europe.'

'So I understand, sir,' Thomas said neutrally.

'You have been fortunate in your health, Captain? The fever has not claimed you amongst its victims.' It was a statement from the First Lord, rather than a question.

'No, sir.'

'But then, you have not been fortunate in the matter of prize money,' Suckling added. All the information was there in those papers before them.

'No, sir,' Thomas said. It was not necessary to tell Suckling why – a ship used to take despatches back and forth had no chance of single-ship action which might lead to the capture of a prize.

'Well, Captain, a change might be beneficial for you,' the First Lord said, looking up again, and folding his hands before him. 'The *Isabella* has been refitting at Spithead, and while we had her in dry dock we took the opportunity to copper her. You are to proceed with all speed to Portsmouth and take command of her. Here are your orders – you'll be joining the Channel fleet under Admiral Keppel. You had better travel post. We need our ships at sea, not in dock.'

'Aye aye, sir,' Thomas said. He was a little bewildered with the speed of events. 'Thank you, sir.'

'I am sure you will justify our trust in you, Captain. A number of people have your welfare at heart, it seems. *Isabella* is a thirty-six-gun frigate, so you may well have a chance to prove yourself in action. I hope you do. I have a presentiment that the navy is going to need fighting captains before long.'

Thomas, his orders in his hand, hurried back to the waterside, where he took a pair of oars back to the *Ariadne*. He had barely time to pack his dunnage if he was to take a post-coach that night; little time remained for explaining to his officers and saying goodbye to them, after their four years together. He took a last look round the tiny cabin, which had been his home for so long, and felt a foolish constriction in his throat. There was a knock at the door at that moment, and he had to cough before he could say 'Come in'.

It was the midshipman of the watch. 'Mr Blake's compliments, sir, and there's a shore boat coming off, with an officer aboard. Mr Blake thinks it will be our new captain, sir.'

'Very well,' he dismissed the boy, and decided there was just time for one more task, if he was to wait and greet the new captain. He sat down at his desk – his no longer – and scribbled a note.

'Dearest Flora, in great haste, on my way to the coach, I write to tell you that I am going to Portsmouth to take command of the *Isabella*, 36, a great step forward which I know you will rejoice in, though I am sorry to leave my dear *Ariadne* with such short notice. I am to join the Channel fleet, so I hope you will have more frequent news of me than hitherto. Look in the newspapers for mention of me, for I hope to bring glory to the name of Morland. At least, I trust I will never cease to deserve the love and respect of my wife and children, whom I trust think of me and pray for me as often as I for them. Ever your loving husband, Thos. Morland.'

He sealed it and wrote the direction on the outside, and was hastily scattering sand over the wet ink when the bosun's calls shrilled their warning that the new captain had arrived. Thomas hurried on deck.

The new captain was coming through the entry port, his hand at his hat in acknowledgement of the compliment. He was a young man with a swarthy face and black hair in lovelocks, and the lithe walk of a cat.

'Captain Morland?' he inquired, his eyes going straight to Thomas's gold lace.

'Captain Thomas Morland at your service, sir,' Thomas said.

'Captain Hannibal Harvey at yours, sir. I am ordered to take command of the *Ariadne*.' The young man grinned irrepressibly, his teeth looking very white in his pirate's face, and Thomas, from his own memories, guessed how delighted he must be to be appointed to such a new and lovely ship.

Harvey read himself in, and Thomas said, 'Welcome aboard, Captain. You'll find her everything you've hoped, I am sure.'

'Will you do me the honour, sir, of taking dinner with me, and telling me all about her?' Harvey said genially. 'If you don't think it indelicate for the second husband to ask the first husband about the wife's habits.'

Thomas smiled. 'Nothing would please me more, but alas I am ordered to Portsmouth at all speed, and must take your shore boat up the river if I am to get to Charing Cross in time for the coach.'

Harvey bowed his consent. 'I regret that we shall not have the opportunity to become acquainted, then, sir. But time and tide and the Admiralty wait for no man.'

'It is the fortune of war,' Thomas said, equally solemnly, and was glad that he was leaving *Ariadne* in the hands of a captain he felt he could have liked very much.

It was a peaceful summer at Morland Place, and Flora, after an initial tendency to complain of boredom, slowed her pace to that of the burgeoning countryside, and allowed herself to drowse through the days, swelling alongside Jemima and an estimated two months ahead of her. Nothing could ever quite make Jemima rest, but Flora became positively lazy, rising late in the morning, idling away an hour or two dressing and drinking chocolate before joining Jemima for her daily walk in the gardens.

She interested herself in what interested Jemima – Allen's doings, the state of the horses, and the health of the children all taking a higher place than the state of the nation in their talk. Whether Allen should renew the licence for the Bear and Staff, which everybody knew was little better than a brothel, and watered its ale into the bargain; whether Helios's tendon would go down in time for the race at Wetherby; whether James's arm was sound enough for him to be allowed to take part in the cricket match at the midsummer fair; these were the matters of burning interest that summer.

The midsummer fair in itself was topic for endless conversations, for Jemima and Allen had decided that this year they would make it a very grand celebration. There had always been a certain amount of merrymaking at Morland Place at midsummer, both because it was an old traditional fair day, and because it marked the end of shearing. But this year Allen, on account of being Justice of the Peace, and Sir Allen, thought a more public event would be appropriate.

The cricket match was but one part of it, and was to take place on the open ground in front of the house in the morning. Cricket had been vastly improved of late years by the introduction of proper rules, and a third stump to the wicket, and a straight instead of a curved bat, and in some parts of the country it had become as popular as racing, and the subject of as many and as enormous bets. Jemima did not want their cricket match to be compared with anyone else's and found wanting, and so she had persuaded Allen to make it a competition between the village girls and the village boys, all to be under the age of sixteen. They were to be dressed all in white, and there were to be prizes for the winning team, provided by Allen. But nothing in the world could ever stop Yorkshire men betting, and already there was fierce wagering, not only on which team would win, but on how many notches each side would score, and in how many hours and minutes, and many a purse had been promised by way of bribery to improve the performance of the fancied team. The girls had been practising fiercely for weeks on Clifton Ings, while the boys had got together in the field behind St Edward's School, but since the latter team had spent most of their time surreptitiously smoking and boasting of how easily they were going to beat the girls, Jemima was secretly afraid there would be no competition.

The vexed question of whether James should be allowed to risk his newly-healed arm by playing in the match was decided one morning when a deputation of boys came to Allen at Morland Place, just as he was finishing his petty sessions, and begged him to allow it. James, in some way mysterious to Jemima, made himself popular wherever he went, and the boys' team embarrassed Allen in front of his tenants by suggesting that they would refuse to play altogether if James were not allowed to play with them.

'That boy is born to be hanged,' Allen said to Jemima afterwards. 'I can only think he has bribed the team to beg for him.'

'I don't know how he does it,' Jemima sighed. Edward

was home for the summer, but despite his public-school advantages, he had not been asked to play. Jemima felt rather sorry for Edward, who was continually being put in the shade by his younger brother. James, at eleven years old, was ravishingly beautiful, and had the entire staff of Morland Place in slavery to him, and had even bewitched Father Ramsay to the extent that the priest rarely beat him, and then only reluctantly and with the most half-hearted strokes. As it was a known fact that boys only learned through being beaten, it was obvious that James would grow up entirely ignorant, but equally obvious that it wouldn't matter a bit, since he could make his way in the world very well indeed with no discernible talents.

It was a few days before the fair that Jemima went to find Flora, and being told that she was still in her chamber, laboured up the stairs to the West Bedroom, wondering how Flora could bear to be indoors on such a heavenly day. Jemima had been up since six in order to hear first Mass and take breakfast with Allen before he rode away to York for a meeting of the Turnpike Trust, which was making a determined effort to improve all the local roads, not just the London road. Since he left, she had interviewed Mrs Mappin, labouring under the delusion that it was necessary to give the housekeeper orders about the monthly wash and the necessity of making enough candles for the dinner on midsummer night; had comforted Abram for the loss of his favourite cat, who had eaten too many black beetles and died of a ruptured stomach, and persuaded him that Mrs Mappin had certainly not fed the beetles to Malkin on the sly. She had spoken to the laundress about washing her lace, and to the sewing maids about getting Miss Flora's dress finished in time for her to try it on before the day. She had picked and arranged the flowers for the Lady chapel, taken a piece of bread out to Poppy in the home paddock so that she should not feel neglected, dealt with four callers, written a note to Lady Marjorie and sent it with a basket of early gooseberries over to Shawes, and requested Godden, the kennelman, to look out for a prettily-marked kitten for Abram, who was a man who needed something to love.

The baby stirred inside her as she walked along the passage towards the West Bedroom, and she paused for a moment to put her hand over her belly and feel, even through her clothes, a petulant kick. Another boy, she thought, for it was big and restless. She was surprised to hear Mary's voice coming from Flora's room, and went in prepared to send her away and scold her for troubling Flora, but found her intervention was not needed. Flora was lolling in her bed, with her tray of chocolate and wheaten bread – she claimed not to be able to eat dark bread since she had been in London – watching and advising while Mary, seated before the glass, and wearing a pair of Flora's earrings, attempted clumsily to paint her face with Flora's paints.

'Like this?' she was saying.

'Yes, that would be well for Court, but at a private ball, you know, it would be quite out of place,' Flora replied.

'Tell me again what happens when you are presented,' Mary said, and then turned with a petulant frown as she saw her mother's image in the mirror. 'I wasn't troubling her, Mama,' she forestalled Jemima quickly. 'Flora said she was glad of the company.' Jemima looked at Flora, who shrugged slightly, and smiled. 'Besides,' Mary went on importantly, 'I have to know how things are done, for when I'm presented I want everyone to notice me and think how well I do everything.'

'And what makes you think you'll be presented?' Jemima asked. Mary looked round-eyed.

'But of course I will be. Papa will arrange it. And then I shall live in London, like Flora, and never be in the country.'

'Don't you really mind her prattle?' Jemima said to Flora, resisting the temptation to argue with Mary, whose values seemed to Jemima to need some rearranging.

'She's company for me,' Flora said. 'What brings you up here at this time of day?'

'Edward brought me a newspaper from Sir John Anstey, with his compliments. It is a few days old, but he thought you would be interested in the news. The French fleet has come out of Toulon.' She held out the paper as she spoke, and Flora took it automatically, but her face was pale. Jemima hastened to reassure her. 'Oh, do not be alarmed, it is not bad news. Hardly news at all, really, but he thought you would be interested.'

'Was there a battle?' Flora managed to ask. Jemima helped her by opening it at the correct page.

'There, you see, there's the report. No, Estaing and the whole Toulon fleet slipped out and into the Atlantic, and Admiral Byron was detached with thirteen ships to follow – to America, as everyone supposes.'

'And *Isabella*?'

'No, I have looked at the list, and she was not amongst them. She must have remained with the Channel fleet.'

'Oh.' Flora pushed the paper away without interest, and Jemima sighed inwardly. Where, she wondered, was the young woman who had read every list of ships in the *Gazette* for the mere pleasure of repeating the names over to herself? Flora had been more of a naval wife before her marriage than after.

'Well, now I have interrupted you, can I not persuade you to get up and come out into the fresh air? It is a perfect day – a slight breeze – not too hot. Dinner will be late today, because Allen is in York, so I have ordered a little nuncheon for us to take in the rose garden. Won't you join us?'

By the time Flora was dressed and had made her way down to the rose garden the rest of the party was assembled in the shade of one of the high hedges, and she paused for a moment, thinking how attractive a party it looked. Jemima sat on a rug spread on the grass, looking, despite her bulk, cool and comfortable in a dress of applegreen linen, her dark hair, streaked with silver, drawn back into a bunch of loose curls under a *bergère* hat. She was standing baby Harry up in his froth of white petticoats, and he was refusing to take his weight on his own feet, and crowing with laughter and grabbing for her hat brim with his fat fists. Beside her, little Louisa sat, leaning against her casually, while she frowned in concentration over the attempt to make a daisy chain when she had not the least idea of how to marry one limp stem to another. Her legs stuck straight out from the hem of her petticoats in the way only a small child's can, and from her dark curly head and her air of belonging one might easily have thought she was Jemima's baby, rather than Flora's.

Father Ramsay sat on the marble bench with James lolling on his shoulder from behind – something no other boy in the history of the world would have been able to do to Father Ramsay – both watching Edward, suddenly very grown up, carving the cold roast duck. Edward had brought the younger John Anstey and he was sitting on the other side of the cloth, next to Mary, holding out a plate to Edward for the first carving, which was evidently destined to become Mary's portion against all other claims. At a little distance Rachel and Alison and Esther and Flora's maid Joan sat with their own feast, keeping an eye on the party, ready to take the babies if they became a nuisance or run messages if required.

It was a pleasant, peaceful, domestic scene, and for a moment Flora felt oddly lonely, for it did not need her, there seemed no place for her there, not even as mother of Louisa. She wished suddenly that she could be back in London with her *friends* – only that was impossible, in her condition. She wished she was not pregnant; and she was within a whisker of wishing she was not married when Mary looked up and saw her, and invited her to sit beside her with a heroine-worshipping smile. Well, at least someone wanted her, Flora thought self-pityingly.

The talk, of course, was all about the fair.

'Mother, can I enter Sorrell in the pony race, or is she too big?' Edward asked.

'Oh no, Mama, don't let him,' Mary cried at once. 'You can't, Edward, it wouldn't be fair.'

'Why ever not?' Jemima asked in surprise.

'Because she wants John Anstey to win, that's why,' James put in quietly, but not so quietly it couldn't be heard. Poor Anstey went scarlet, and Mary glared furiously at James.

'Hold your tongue! You're such a child, what do you know about anything?'

'Mary, please,' Jemima protested, pulling her face back from Harry's groping hand, now sticky with food. 'I think Sorrell might be giving you an unfair advantage, Edward. It *is* only a pony race.' Edward smiled tolerantly.

'You won't believe what some people are entering, Mother. Down in the village they are almost drawing blood on the question of what defines a pony.'

'Well, never mind. It wouldn't seem right for Morlands to win all the prizes,' Jemima said peacefully. 'Can't you enter for something else?'

'Well, there's the sack race, I suppose,' Edward said. 'I can't see myself being much of a hand at catching the pig-in-a-lane, or the pudding-eating, and I know you wouldn't let me enter the wrestling or the cudgels.'

'The grinning match should suit you,' Mary said sulkily.

'I shall enter for everything,' James announced. 'And I shall certainly win the bull riding.'

'Only because you know the bull personally,' Edward said, grinning, 'I know where it is you've been going every morning, with a palmful of salt.'

'The cheese-rolling – that's a nice uncontentious competition,' Jemima said hastily.

'I don't see how you can enter for anything,' Mary said to James. 'You'll be playing in the cricket match.'

'Not all the time,' Edward pointed out, but James only looked serene, not even bothering to argue with Mary.

'Well, as the person in charge of the prizes, I can tell you that you wouldn't enjoy them if you did win, which you won't,' said Father Ramsay. The boys at once clamoured to know what the prizes were. 'Let me see,' he said, counting them off, 'there's a pound of tobacco, a round of beef, a truckle of cheese, a black piglet, a new hat—' The boys looked dismayed.

'I shouldn't mind the piglet,' James said at length. 'I could train it to follow me like a dog. It would be a splendid thing, to go around with a pig at your heels. And when it was grown, it would be big enough to fight all the other dogs, and I could teach it tricks, and it would be famous!'

'At all costs,' Jemima said to the priest, 'make sure James does not win the piglet.'

'And after all these games, what then?' Flora asked.

'Dinner in the house, for us and a few guests, and then a ball at Shawes, and fireworks on the lake to finish up. I wish the long gallery was big enough for us to have the ball here,' Jemima added with a sigh. 'That's the trouble with living in a moated house – there's no room to expand. Allen and I have talked about filling in the moat, but somehow I just couldn't bear the idea of losing the swans. So we must make do. It's only for very big balls, after all, that we feel the lack.'

'I suppose everyone will be there,' Flora said. 'It does seem hard that everything happens when I am in this condition and unable to join in. There was that ball at the Assembly Rooms last week, too.'

'At least you can go and watch,' Mary said peevishly. 'I am not even allowed to go, though Mary Loveday will be going, and I'm much taller than her.'

'You are too young,' Jemima said, repressing a smile. 'Mary Loveday is sixteen. It has nothing to do with height.'

'No one would know I'm too young,' Mary began, but Father Ramsay silenced her with a look, and John Anstey tried to comfort her.

'I'm sure you will be much missed,' he said. 'I'm sure I shall have no pleasure in the ball, if you are not there.'

'Well then, why do you not refuse to go?' Mary asked, rather too much to the point.

Edward grinned and said, 'Don't worry, Mary, I'll make sure he doesn't dance with Mary Loveday in your absence.'

'I'm sure it is a matter of indifference to *me*,' Mary said, tossing her head. 'He may dance with anyone he pleases. Tom Loveday said he will refuse to go to the ball at all if I do not go, and Horatio Morland said he would much sooner sit and talk to me than dance with a princess of England. But men are all so fickle, I do not pay any heed to anything they say.'

John Anstey's attempted defence was drowned in the laughter of Jemima, and Edward's comment of 'Well, if you have learnt *that*, Mary, you have learnt all that is necessary.' But Flora felt a strange sort of sympathy with Mary. The dancing part of a young woman's life was all too short. She remembered when she had been fourteen how she had been wild for balls, and at fifteen, wild for marriage. She had fallen in love with Thomas, as she now realized, not because of anything in his character, but because she wanted to be in love, had rushed through their marriage because she was desperate to be married. How she wished, now, that Charles had not come home that Christmas, that she had had time to be young and attractive before becoming a wife and mother. Here she was, swollen up like a woolsack, with all the pain and inconvenience of childbirth before her, and over there was little Louisa, to whom she felt no attachment at all. For the moment, in her self-pity, she forgot the pleasant two years she had had in London.

It was such a lovely day that even when they had finished eating they sat on in the shade of the scented Edward and John and Mary disappeared on some business of their own; Father Ramsay fell asleep, and James took the opportunity to slip away; the babies dozed on the rug beside Jemima, while she talked to Alison about the rearrangement of the nursery to accommodate the two new occupants. They were still there when Allen returned home from the city and came to find them.

'What a pleasant picture you all make,' he said, appearing in the gap in the hedge. 'I wish I could have a portrait made of you, just as you are.'

Jemima greeted him. 'You are early – I am glad. I was afraid once you got talking you would be tempted to linger and take dinner with the other trustees.'

'I have hurried back with some good news for you,' he replied. 'I hope it will please Edward, too, and Flora. John Carr tells me that he has some guests arriving today, to stay for a week or two – Lord Meldon, and Lord Calder. Naturally I begged him to bring them to our midsummer festivities, and especially to the dinner and ball. Carr said that Lord Calder especially asked to be remembered to you, my dear, and Edward, and that both young men will do themselves the honour of calling tomorrow, if you permit. Naturally, I assumed that you would.'

'How lovely,' Jemima said. 'I shall be very glad to see them – and Flora, you will be happy to meet your old friends, I know.'

But Flora stood up, almost in tears. 'Oh sir, how could you! How can I meet anyone in this condition? I should be shamed – I cannot receive them, I really cannot. To have the people I have known in London staring at me – and as for the ball, I certainly cannot go if they will be there! This is an end of it for me.'

She ran away towards the house as rapidly as her bulk would allow, leaving Jemima and Allen in a distressed silence.

'Oh dear,' Allen said at last. 'I am afraid I have – but I did not think – my dear, can you understand her distress? I thought she was missing her friends.'

'I seem to know Flora as little as any of my children,' Jemima said sadly.

In her own room, Flora stood at the window, staring out at nothing, her hands held against the hard bulk of her swollen abdomen, forced most unwillingly to come to grips with her feelings. I care nothing about Thomas, she thought. I wish I had never married him. I shall not be sorry if I never see him again. No, that's not true. I am fond of him, for he is a good and kind man. But I don't miss him, I don't want to be with him.

That was the first stage of self-knowledge; the second was harder still. She had to ask herself why she was so upset at the thought of the young lords seeing her in this condition when they had known when she left London that she was with child. I have missed him, she thought. I have been looking forward to going back to London after I am delivered, so that I can see him again. I do not want him to see me large with another man's child. I do not want him to know, more than he does already, that I am another man's wife.

Perhaps if Thomas had not been a sailor things might have been different. She had spent so little time with him that she had never got to know him, in the way she had Lord Meldon. She might have enjoyed his company as much, cared as much for his opinions, missed him in his absences as much, had they been shorter and less frequent. But as things were, there was no use in denying it to herself any longer. And she did not want Charles to see her like this, in case the sight of her pregnancy turned him against her and made him decide he did not want to see her again.

The young men called as promised the next day, and were received kindly by all, but Flora would not come down, and for the length of time they were in the country she remained in retirement, resisting all persuasion to join in any of the entertainments, and venturing out of her room only when she was assured that none but the family was present. Jemima observed it all with her private thoughts

214

kept private, and did not urge Flora to join them, thinking that if she had discovered in herself a preference for the young men's company, she had better not be in their presence more than necessary.

Edward's delight was a pleasure to see in his friend Chetwyn's arrival. He had finished at Eton, and in the autumn was to go to Christ Church, much in advance of his age, for he was so forward in his studies. Jemima had some doubts as to whether it was wise for such a young man to be exposed to the influences of Oxford, and was glad when Chetwyn reassured her.

'I greatly regret that I shall not be at the university myself,' he said, 'but as you know, my father's place at Wolvercote is less than three miles from the House. I shall be very often there, and I will undertake to guard over your son like a mother hen and keep him from harm, and if you will only charge me to, I shall take upon myself also the delightful task of reporting to you that he is not ruining his health or plotting to elope with the Master's daughter.'

'You are very kind, sir,' Jemima said. 'I shall part with him with an easier mind, knowing he is well cared for.'

'And I can help you further in telling you what he will need to take with him, to make him good and popular; and I shall bring him home to you at the end of each term, with a full report on his progress.'

The festivities went off excellently well, and the dinner and ball were both successful occasions, except as far as Mary was concerned, for all three of her beaux not only attended the ball, but danced as often as they could, which provided her with most unwelcome confirmation of the fickleness of men, and made her determined to punish them when laggard time at last released her from the confines of the schoolroom.

On the second day following, Calder and Meldon left York, calling at Morland Place on their way to make their adieux, still without having the pleasure of seeing Flora's face. When they had gone, Edward went up to her room and tapped on the door. At his second knock, a listless voice bid him come in. Flora was sitting by the window, her elbow on the windowsill and her chin in her hand, and she did not move or look up as he came in.

'They've gone,' Edward said at last. 'Back to London for a few weeks, and then to Oxfordshire. You're safe to come down now, if you want.'

She looked at him resentfully. 'Have you come to torment me?'

Edward looked at her steadily. 'No, to bring you a letter – from Lord Meldon.' Flora started at the name, and then flushed angrily.

'Do you mock me? Why should Lord Meldon write to me? And if he did, why should he send the letter by you?'

'It's all right, Cousin,' Edward said kindly. 'Charles has no secrets from Chetwyn, and Chetwyn has none from me. It was the only way to get a letter to you without anyone knowing.'

'Do you know what's in the letter?' Flora asked in a small voice. Edward continued to look at her with that steady kindness, as if he were twenty-six rather than sixteen.

'I am on your side,' he said. 'You do not need to pretend with me. And, indeed, I pity you, with all my heart. Your secret is safe with me.'

Flora stared at him consideringly, and then said, 'Give me the letter.'

The letter was brief. 'I hardly know what to understand from your refusal to see me, but even at the risk of rebuff, I must tell you that I have missed your presence all this year more than I could have anticipated. I have had no pleasure in anything but the anticipation of your rejoining our circle in the autumn. There is so much more I should wish to say to you, but I dare not commit it to paper. I beg you not to be so cruel as to remain in Yorkshire a day longer than necessary, but to return as soon as possible to London, and to one who wishes to be, your most humble and faithful servant, C.M.'

Tears rose to her eyes, and for a moment the page grew blurred, and she had to bite her lip to stop it trembling. She looked up at last to meet Edward's eye.

'I admit nothing,' she said. 'I have done nothing.'

'It's all right,' he said again. 'I know everything, Chetwyn has told me everything.' She looked at him searchingly. 'I will help you,' he added gently.

'It's not my fault,' she said, pleading for understanding.

'I know,' Edward said. 'I know.'

CHAPTER ELEVEN

It had never been Henri Maria Fitzjames Stuart's way to think ahead, or to anticipate the consequences of his actions. Luck, charm or his title had generally been enough to get him out of trouble, and he had come to think upon nothing in his life as a permanent state. So it had been when he took Madeleine from her home: he had never considered that she would be in his life, his responsibility for ever, and that the deception he had used to get her in the first place would be impossible to keep up. Nor had he wondered what her feelings would be, or whether he would care what she felt.

The baby changed things, and for all his sophistication, Henri was in a curious way unworldly enough not to have realized that it must do so. The baby was born in the August of 1777, and the heat and humidity of the Paris summer had made things very uncomfortable for Madeleine. Henri had been forced to engage a woman to look after her and keep house, and her presence and Madeleine's growing bulk made 'home' so much less attractive to him that he was hardly ever there, inventing various excuses and commissions to absent himself. All this Madeleine bore with great restraint, only once complaining that as he had taken her from her family, he might at least bear her company from time to time.

'Madame,' he had said shortly, 'you know very well that I must be a good deal at Court.'

'Yes,' she had replied. 'I know why you go there.' She had said no more, leaving Henri to feel at first that he had won an easy victory, and later that it had been too easy.

He was away when the baby was born, and received a frosty glare from the woman servant when he arrived on the baby's second day of life, with no knowledge that she existed.

'We sent for you, sir, but no one knew where you were. In fact, we could not find anyone who knew you,' she said coldly. In the background a steady wailing competed for his attention, so that he did not notice her insolence.

'The baby's born? Is he all right? How is Madame?' he asked with a sudden access of enthusiasm, and without waiting for a reply, pushed passed her into the bedroom. Madeleine was propped up on her pillows, with the baby in her arms, and she smiled at him so radiantly that he approached her with an answering smile of tenderness and affection.

'We have a daughter, Henri,' she said, 'a beautiful daughter.'

'A daughter,' he said, a little blankly, never having given a thought that it might not be a boy. Then he rallied himself. 'And you, Madame? Are you well? It was not too difficult a birth? I am sorry I could not be here.' He was wondering how to explain his absence, but Madeleine did not seem interested. She drew the shawl back from the baby's face so that he could see her.

'Isn't she beautiful, Henri? The most beautiful baby in the world.'

Henri peered at the wrinkled little thing, and racked his brains for something to say. 'She's very small,' he said at last, lamely.

'She'll grow,' Madeleine said, smiling.

'And very red?' he hazarded.

'That will pass, too. In a few days she will be as pale as a pearl. What shall we call her? Have you any ideas? Should we call her after you, do you think? Or after one of your patrons?'

'Henriette?' Henri mused. 'It is a pleasant name, I suppose. Or perhaps you would like her named after you?'

'No,' Madeleine said at once, and firmly. 'It will be better for her if she has your name – it will make you fonder of her.'

219

'My dear Madeleine, why should you think—'

'I know you wanted a son, Henri, and I am sorry not to have done better. But we will do better next time, and I promise you she will be very pretty, and everything you could desire in a daughter,' Madeleine said, and Henri felt at once touched and ashamed, and took her free hand and pressed his lips to it.

'I am not at all disappointed, my dearest. I am only glad that you are well, and I would not exchange her for fifty sons.'

'Then we shall call her Henriette-Louise, if it pleases you?'

'Certainly, certainly,' Henri said.

The baby began to wail again, and Madeleine, seeing him flinch, said, 'I had better feed her, Henri. She is hungry, that's all.'

'Well, there doesn't seem much I can do,' Henri said awkwardly. 'Perhaps—' He took a step towards the door. 'Perhaps I had better arrange to sleep with a friend for a few nights, so as not to disturb you.'

'Very well,' Madeleine said patiently. 'But Henri – I should be grateful if you would leave a direction where you may be found, in case anything should happen.'

'Of course,' he said awkwardly. 'I'll come and see you again tomorrow.'

He left with the woman servant the only name and address it was possible to give – Duncan's name, and the address of the house in the Rue de St Rustique – and made his escape. For the first few weeks he visited Madeleine every day, and as she had promised the baby soon became much more agreeable looking. But she insisted on feeding it herself, which shocked and disgusted Henri, and the little *apartement* was so filled with the baby's presence, the sound and smell of her, the preoccupation with her, and the talk of her, that his visits were a penance to him, and consenquently short. Besides, a baby so young was of no interest to him in itself, and Madeleine's bed was forbidden to him, and his visits began to be less frequent.

When Henriette-Louise was six weeks old, and Madeleine was out of bed, and the woman servant had been replaced by a girl-of-all-work, Madeleine greeted him one day with the alarming words, 'Henri, we must talk seriously. Please will you come and sit down.'

'But of course, Madame,' Henri said with a sinking heart, having a strong feeling that he was about to be rebuked for neglecting her. His chin took on a defiant jut. If she was going to make things difficult for him, he would have to do something about getting rid of her, he thought.

'Henri,' she began, gazing at him with her clear grey, disconcertingly penetrating eyes, 'it is time that we were honest with each other. For two years now I have lived with you as Madame Ecosse, and while I was without other responsibilities it did not matter. But now we have a child to think of. Henri, has it never occurred to you that I know who you are?'

Henri felt himself growing hot, and he had nothing to say. He could only shake his head in mute dread and embarrassment. Madeleine nodded.

'Yes, I know that you are the Comte de Strathord, and I know why you have to be away from me so much. It must have been very difficult for you, these two years, keeping me a secret from your friends, from all the people who know you as a member of the nobility, finding a way to fulfil your duties at Court without acknowledging it to me. It makes me wonder why you chose to make your life so difficult. Why did you not confide in me, so that I could help you? Why did you choose to make a deception on both fronts?'

'Why, I – because – I thought you would object. I thought you would go back to your father, if you knew the truth,' Henri stumbled inadequately.

'But why should I object to being the wife of a nobleman, instead of the wife of a gentleman?' she asked. Her gaze prevented him from withdrawing his, and yet was so kind and understanding that for a moment he trembled on the brink of telling her everything, as at a confessional, and having done. But he could not find the words and in the silence the moment passed.

'Well, now you know,' he said, perhaps a little ungraciously, 'what do you want to do?'

At last the pellucid eyes dropped, and in the relief he felt at being released there was the strangest hint of disappointment. She studied her hands for a moment, and then said briskly, 'I have been very much alone recently, and I have had time to think. I want to move away from here, Henri. I should like us to have an *apartement* on the left bank, near to my parents. I know that you will have to spend a lot of time away from us, and therefore I should like to have the support of my family to comfort me in the times when you are absent. My parents would be glad to receive me back into the family, especially now there is a grandchild, and then I should not be so lonely. Will you agree to this?'

'But – your father – if he knew—' Henri stammered.

'Oh, I shall not tell him, or my mother, that you are not Monsieur Ecosse. It is better that it remains our secret. I know you will come whenever you can, and when you do there is no need for you to have anything to do with my parents. Will you agree to this, Henri? I ask it as a favour.'

All the things he had loved her for became apparent again, and he felt ashamed that she should beg from him things so easy for him to grant. She asked so little, made matters so easy for him. If only she had been a little higher in rank, and he a little richer, he would have married her gladly.

'My grandmother would have approved of you,' he said suddenly, and took her hands in his. 'I have neglected you shamefully of late, Madeleine, but I shall make amends. You shall live anywhere you please, and you shall lack for nothing, you and the baby, if I can help it.'

So the move was made, to a tiny house on the Cour du Commerce, where a great many lawyers lived. Madeleine had two maids, one general servant and one to look after the baby, and soon settled in and made the place inimitably

222

her own. She made her peace with her parents, but Henri never asked her for the details of transaction, and true to her promise he was never asked to meet with them. But as autumn turned to winter he was often there, much more often than he had been at the house in the Rue des Martyrs, and he found again the peace and contentment he had had with her in the first year.

They also made a number of new friends. A pretty, intelligent, cheerful woman with a warm fireside and a well-stocked larder was a great attraction, and married and unmarried, the lawyers of the Cour du Commerce were eager for invitations to visit Monsieur and Madame Ecosse. There were plenty of evenings when Henri ate at his own hearth, with his child sleeping in the back room, and a lively discussion going on around him, in which his 'wife' took as much part as he did. He even came to take a certain amount of interest in his daughter as she grew bigger and better looking, and sometimes he and Madeleine would spend a quiet hour by the fireside discussing her future before going to bed, just like an ordinary couple.

But when spring came again, Henri grew restless. Henriette-Louise, as she grew, took up more of her mother's time; and Madeleine was pregnant again. At first it did not matter so much, but as she grew larger, and her bed was once again forbidden him, he began to turn to other pleasures, and to find his other life beckoning more strongly. The summer of '78 found him as little at home as the summer of '77.

Jemima stood by Flora's bed in the West Bedroom, one hand under her huge belly to support it a little, the other firmly clasped in Louisa's, and looked down at Flora with a mixture of pity and exasperation.

'He's a lovely baby, Flora,' she said coaxingly. 'Wouldn't you like to hold him for a moment?'

She gave a meaningful jerk of her head towards the new little nursery maid, a fourteen-year-old called Jenny, brought in to help Rachel now that Alison had been promoted to governess. Jenny took a hasty step forward and lifted up Flora's baby invitingly, and even, in her anxiety to help, gave him a little shake, as one might shake a rattle at a child, but Flora took no notice. Propped on her pillows, her hair tangled, her face pale, she continued to read – or, Jemima suspected, not to read – her novel. Little Louisa looked from her mother to Jemima and back, solemnly and silently as she did most things. She gripped Jemima's hand tightly, as if she feared to be snatched away. Alison had tried to tempt Flora from her bed with Louisa, and then had got very angry. Louisa, who was a timid child, easily startled, had cried, and Alison had smacked her. All the nursery staff were disappointed in Louisa, whose dark hair had lightened to an insignificant brown, and whose baby prettiness had turned out to be a false spring. Had she been a lively, spirited child, they would have forgiven her her plainness, but she was very reserved, cried easily, and was stupid at her lessons. Only when clutching Jemima's hand, or sitting on Allen's lap, and having nothing demanded of her was she happy.

Jemima freed her hand now to take the baby from Jenny. He was a bonny baby, big and well fleshed and placid, and Jemima held him to her for a moment and smiled down into his face, just for the pleasure of it. Then she sat on the edge of Flora's bed and offered her the child again.

'Flora, hold him for a moment,' she said, and Flora sighed, put her book down, and took the baby with a reluctance that almost amounted to aversion. 'See, he is lovely, isn't he?' Jemima coaxed. Flora looked at him blankly. 'Come, be a little enthusiastic,' she muttered. 'You look as though you were inspecting him for blight.'

It almost raised a smile from Flora. She actually met Jemima's eyes for a moment and said, 'I'm not very good with babies, that's all. Some people aren't, you know.'

'You don't have to be good with him. We have nursery maids for that. You only have to notice him a little. Come,

Flora, he's six weeks old, and you haven't even thought of a name for him yet.'

'How can I? Thomas is sure to want to name him, and I can't ask him, because he's in the West Indies,' Flora said sulkily. The *Isabella* had been sent on convoy with eighteen merchantmen to Port Royal in September to join Admiral Parker a month before Flora's baby had been born. Jemima was glad that Thomas would be near William again, but Flora had found nothing to be glad of, or sorry for, in the news that he had gone. Now, however, she was using his absence and distance as an excuse for a number of things, amongst them not naming the baby.

'You named Louisa when he was away,' Jemima pointed out. Flora shrugged.

'It's different with a girl. He's bound to want to name a boy himself.'

'Well, call him Thomas then,' Jemima said, and that at least caused a reaction.

'No!' Flora snapped, and then controlling herself she looked towards Jenny. 'What do you call him in the nursery!'

Jenny writhed with embarrassment at being addressed, and it took a nod from Jemima to get her to answer.

'Well, ma'am, Alison says all unnamed babies are called John.'

Flora nodded. 'That will do. Let him be John, then.' Her eyes gleamed a moment. 'It will be like naming him for his father, after all. He'll grow up a Jack, if it's in his blood.' She looked down at the baby with a small smile of secret malice, and then said loudly, 'Here, nurse, take him away from me. He grows heavy.'

Jemima dismissed Jenny with a nod, and she took baby Jack away, and Jemima also stood up, collecting Louisa's insistent hand on the way. 'Well, I must go. There are things for me to do. Flora, it is high time you were out of bed, you know. It is not good to stay too long abed after childbirth. I think you should come down tonight. Yes,' she forestalled Flora's sulky reply, 'I know you don't want to, but for once I shall insist. We're having the Hallowe'en feast tonight, and lots of games for the children, and some couples will come in for dancing, and I want you to be there. And Edward leaves tomorrow, and he'd be so disappointed if you didn't come. You know how fond he is of you.'

'Oh, very well,' Flora said wearily, but inwardly she felt a stirring of relief. Sulking was a self-perpetuating mood, for it became difficult to stop doing it without losing face, and she was growing bored with her self-imposed isolation. It was good to have an excuse to leave her bed and join in again. 'If you insist.'

Jemima stooped – not an easy thing to do in her condition – and kissed Flora's cheek. 'That's a good girl. And wear something pretty. Allen likes to have pretty women to look at, and he's only had me for weeks on end.'

Outside, Jemima found a servant to deliver Louisa back to the nursery, and went downstairs to find Allen. He was in the steward's room, poring over numerous sheets of paper that covered his table, and he looked up as Jemima came in and eased herself into a chair by the fireside.

'Well? Did you manage to rouse her?' he asked. Jemima leaned back to ease the crick in her back, and closed her eyes for a moment.

'Not really. She won't be interested in either of them. But I got her to give him a name at least.'

'Oh? What name?'

'Jack,' she said with a grimace, opening her eyes again. Allen's lips quirked in amused acknowledgement. 'And she has promised to come down tonight, for the feast.'

'Well, that's an improvement,' he said. 'And how are you feeling? You are not in pain, I hope?'

'No, just very uncomfortable. How is it, when one begins these things, that one never remembers what the end is like?'

Allen got up from his table and came over to her, kissed her, and put a hand behind her neck to rub it for her.

'Because when one begins, one has other things on one's mind,' he reminded her.

'Hmm,' she acknowledged. 'I think I'm getting too old for this sort of thing. I fear, my dearest, that this will have to be our last; unless you want to go out and get yourself another wife or two, of course, like a Turkish sultan.'

He straightened up, smiling broadly. 'Now really, Jemima, do you see me as a sultan?'

She was forced to laugh at the idea. 'Not really. What is it you are working on there?'

'Ah, yes, I'm glad you came in, because it is something I want to talk to you about.' He went back to his table, and she heaved herself out of the chair and went with him. 'Sit down in my chair, and I'll shew you,' he said. She took her place behind the table, and he spread the papers in front of her, and leaned over her shoulder while he explained.

'Enclosure?' she said. All the old prejudices she had heard voiced over the years echoed in the word. 'Is it really necessary?'

'It is essential,' Allen said firmly. 'It is impossible to bring about any real improvement while we keep on with the open-field system, and improvement there must be. Do you realize, we could increase our yield anything up to twenty times, and our rents too? The price corn is fetching, with the war on, and the growing demand for meat and milk and other foods in the towns make it essential to improve. There are so many things I want to try – crop cleaning, for instance. With the open-field system, it is merely wasted effort, but cleaning the crop can double or treble it.'

Jemima felt the claims were a little exaggerated, but she had to make allowances for enthusiasm. 'Very well – but won't it be difficult to bring about? Isn't an Act of Parliament necessary?'

'Yes, but that is not a problem. It is a formal matter, unless there are objections from interested parties, and with my contacts I should be able to get it put through without delay. The Government are all for enclosure, you know, so they would not put anything in the way of an Act.'

'But you said unless there are objections. How do other people feel about it? Won't they object?'

'All that's needed is the consent of two-thirds of the interested parties, but in fact I anticipate almost all of them will be in favour, once I've pointed out the benefits. I've been talking about it for years now, you know, at every tenants' meeting, and they've grown tolerably used to it. The benefits go to the tenants as well as to us. The only people who are likely to object are the cottagers with rights of commons, and grazing on the fallows.'

'And what happens to them?'

'We make them a payment in compensation for their loss of rights. In theory, they could go to law to object, but in practice of course they couldn't afford to. But if they did go to law, the law would simply allow them a payment in compensation, which is what we'll do anyway.'

'I see.' Jemima frowned, deep in thought. It was her duty, she felt, at this stage to voice any objections there might be on the part of her people, and she was trying to remember what she had read about enclosure from time to time. 'I seem to remember hearing it said that after enclosure there was less work to be done on the land, so that the labouring people lost their livelihood. I should not like that to happen to any of the people we employ.'

Allen stroked her head affectionately. 'That is an objection where land that was under the plough is enclosed for pasturage. That has happened in some places. But the sort of enclosure we are planning gives rise to more work, not less. At the moment, our labourers have nothing to do for long periods in between ploughing and sowing, and harvest and shearing. But once the land is enclosed there will be work all the year round, in tending the hedges and fences, digging and maintaining ditches for drainage, cleaning crops and so on. And with more stock being kept there will be more work tending them, too.'

'Then with all this extra work needed, which we will have to pay for, won't the profits be eaten up?'

'My darling, I don't think you have grasped the enormous increase that enclosure will bring. There are some initial expenses, such as the fencing of land not previously fenced; and then the rigs and baulks will have to be ploughed up, and the land levelled; and new drainage ditches will have to be dug, to take the place of the baulks. And the compensation payments, of course. But after that, it is all profit. No more wasteful fallow years – we grow clover or turnips in the fallow year, which gives us winter feed for our stock. More stock overwintering means more manure for fertilizing the land. Keeping the stock fenced at breeding time means we can begin to improve the animals by breeding only from the best and healthiest. Crops can be cleaned, without fear of another man's weeds spreading onto your own piece of land. And I've a mind to try drilling the seed, rather than sowing broadcast.'

'Now that is going too far,' Jemima smiled. 'What, you would scatter your seed one by one from a pepper-pot, like a courtier at a banquet? And waste all the land in between?'

'It is not like that at all, and you know it,' he retorted. 'Sowing in lines means you can get between to clean them.'

'Well, I'm not so sure cleaning crops is a good idea either.'

'If you had seen, as I have, the difference between wheat growing strongly in clean rows, and the feeble crops struggling for existence with weeds half-choking them, which is the norm, you would not hesitate.'

'I don't know,' Jemima said doubtfully. 'It has never been done that way. The old way has been good enough for our forefathers—'

Allen kissed the top of her head. 'That is exactly what the tenants have been saying every time I mention enclosure, but they're coming round to it, and so will you. It's the difference between making do, and doing one's best. Don't you want to be rich?'

She tilted her face up to him and laughed. 'No,' she said. He looked shocked.

'Heresy! Well, then, don't you want some improvements in the house? Don't you want more servants? Don't you want to build a new stable block at Twelvetrees?'

'Ah, now you are bribing me with things I can't resist,' she said, standing up. He helped her, and she turned to face him, suddenly serious. 'I know you wish to do the best for us and for the land, and that is good, and I will support you in it. But I don't want any of my people to suffer. Promise me that they won't.'

'Of course not,' he said firmly. 'As I said, enclosure is for everyone's benefit, not just ours. No one will suffer.'

'Good. Then what is the first stage?'

'A meeting of the tenants. I should like to have it here, because as you are the landowner I want you to be present. As I said, I have been talking about it to them for years, so none of the ideas will be new. The meeting will place the plan before them, and get their consent to draw up the proposal for the Act of Parliament.'

Jemima nodded. 'I see. And when?'

'As soon as possible. Let me see, not tomorrow or the day after – they are both holy days. The day after that, the day after All Souls, will that suit you?'

'Perfectly,' Jemima said. 'And now I think I had better go and see Abram about the feast tonight.'

'Surely he will have everything organized by now?' Allen said.

'Of course he will, but he loves me to ask him, so that he can tell me so,' she replied.

She crossed the staircase hall and the great hall, and was passing down the dark passage between the pantry and the buttery when a pain doubled her up, taking her breath away. For a moment she bent over, supporting herself with a hand on the wall, thinking only that it was too early, that she had not been prepared for it. The pain eased a little, and she straightened and tried to call out for help, but it gripped again, and her breath was expelled soundlessly.

The wall of the passage was cold and rough under her hand, and the darkness was swelling and receding in a way that made her feel dizzy. And then she heard Allen's voice.

'Jemima! Are you all right? What is it? Is it the baby?'

His hands were on her shoulders, he was turning her, taking her weight, and she gripped him by the arms, feeling, as the pain ebbed, the wetness on her inner thighs as the waters broke.

'Coming – very soon,' she gasped. 'Get me to bed.'

He got her arm over his shoulder, his other arm round her waist, and half-carried her back along the passage. When they reached the great hall, there was, thank God, a footman crossing it, whom Allen could send with a sharp order to fetch the women and get the bed prepared. 'How are you feeling?' he asked her anxiously.

'Better. Pain's easing for the moment,' she said. Then, something that had been puzzling her. 'Why were you there? Did you follow me?'

He was frowning with concentration as he helped her to the foot of the staircase.

'You cried out to me, so of course I ran to see what it was,' he said.

The stairs were ahead of her like a cliff to be scaled, and it was going to take all her concentration to get to the bedchamber without dropping the baby on the staircase, so she had no effort to waste in speech. But it was something she stored to talk about to him later, for she knew she had not made a sound as she stood there in the pantry passage.

Two hours later, Allen stood by her bed, holding her hand and gazing down at her with great love and not a little relief.

'How do you feel now?'

'Wonderful,' she said. 'That was the quickest delivery I ever heard of.'

'She was in a hurry to get here,' he smiled. 'If she goes

on in that way, she will end up as Secretary of State or First Lord of the Admiralty one day.'

'You talk such nonsense,' Jemima said contentedly. 'I think she looks like you, don't you think so?'

'She's lovely. What shall we call her?'

'I hadn't begun to think of names. I thought I had two weeks more at least.'

'I rather like the idea of Lucy,' Allen said. Jemima thought a moment, and then nodded.

'Lucy it shall be. I'm sorry about your enclosure meeting.'

'Oh, that doesn't matter. It can wait a few more weeks. I'm sorry about the Hallowe'en feast.'

'But you will go on with it all the same? I don't want Edward to be disappointed. And after my hard work to persuade Flora to come down—'

'Oh, we'll go on with it, as you insist, but I'm sorry you won't be there.'

'I shall probably be able to hear the fun, if you leave the long gallery doors open.'

He stooped to kiss her. 'I will. And I'll come in to see you every quarter of an hour.'

She kissed him back. 'I love you,' she said.

'I love you, too. I'll leave you to sleep now.'

'Yes. Don't forget to talk to Alison, though, about the wet nurse. I want her to come up here to the house. I don't want Lucy sent away to suck.'

Madeleine gave birth to a son in October 1778, and Henri, in an effort to make amends for last time, was in the house at the time she went into labour. He left for an hour or two to get something to eat when the midwife told him it would be a long job, and when he came back he found Madeleine's parents in the house. It was an embarrassing meeting with Monsieur Homard – Madame Homard was upstairs in the bedchamber. The old man grew scarlet in the face, hemmed a good deal, walked about the room with his hands behind his back, and then came up to Henri with the evident intention of tackling him man to man.

'Now, sir,' he began.

Henri interrupted him smoothly with a bow, and said, 'I am glad to give you meeting, sir. Our differences, I hope, are now at an end. You must forgive me for stealing your daughter away in the beginning, but it was my love for her that prompted it. And now we have given you a fine grandchild – two grandchildren very soon. Will you give me your hand, sir?'

Homard opened and shut his mouth once or twice as he tried to find the fault in Henri's reasoning. Then he coughed again, shook hands awkwardly, gave a little bow, and said, 'Well sir, well sir, I daresay you are right, sir. Ahem. A thirsty business this, don't you think? Women's business, eh? What do you say we slip out round the corner for a glass of brandy, until it's all over?'

Henri suppressed a smile of triumph and said, 'I think I had better stay, for she must be near her time now. But don't let me keep you.'

'Oh, no, no, no,' Homard said hastily, 'I'll stay, by all means. I only thought – we'll both stay, of course.'

But in the end he had to go to open his café, for the labour went on, hour after hour. Henri grew restless, then bored, then alarmed, and quite forgot supper. It was dark, and he had been sitting in the fireglow without noticing it for a long time, when Madame Homard came downstairs with a candle.

'Oh, it's you,' she said but was evidently too weary to feel much resentment.

'Your husband went away to his business. How is she? Is the baby born yet?'

'It's a boy child, but very weak. I do not know if it will live.'

That explained why he had not heard it cry. 'And Madeleine?' he asked.

'She has had a very hard time of it,' Madame Homard

answered. 'I have come down to get her some wine. Have you any in the house?'

'Yes – I'll get it at once. Can I go and see her?' Madame Homard looked doubtful, but having won over the father, Henri thought he knew how to fix the mother. 'I have been so worried about her,' he said. 'Let me take up the wine to her. I must see her, to ease my mind.'

'Very well,' she said at last, her expression not softening in the least. 'But you had better not stay long.'

Henri fetched the wine and climbed the stairs in the dark, and pushed open the bedroom door cautiously. The candlelight left dark shadowy places in the corners and on the sloping ceiling. The midwife was standing by the bed feeling Madeleine's pulse. The smell in the room was dreadful, like a butcher's shop, he thought, but there was, thank God, nothing bad to be seen. The bedsheets were clean, Madeleine had been tidied up, and there was a well-swaddled bundle in the little crib in the corner.

'I've brought the wine,' he said, almost in a whisper, and walked over to the bed. The midwife took the bottle and glass without comment, and Henri leaned over the bed, his face fixed in a tender smile. 'Madeleine,' he said.

But at once all his play-acting was stripped away from him when he saw how ill she really was. She opened her eyes and looked at him, but he could see she was too exhausted even to smile. Her skin had a cheesy pallor, her eyes seemed sunken in her face. He had never seen anyone look so utterly done in.

'Madeleine,' he said again, in quite a different voice.

'Henri,' she said, her lips hardly moving. 'I am so glad you came.'

'I have been below all the time. I have been so worried about you,' he said, and now that he really was worried, he felt it had been so all the time. 'Are you all right?'

'She has lost a lot of blood,' the midwife said. 'Here, Madame, you must have some wine. It will give you strength.'

'I'll do it,' he said, taking the glass from her. It took him a moment to work out how to lift her head and support it and tilt the glass, but he managed it neatly.

'Thank you,' she whispered as he eased her head onto the pillow again. 'I shall be better by and by, when I have slept.'

He took her hand and pressed it between his, and there was no answering pressure. It was limp and cold, like a corpse's.

'You must rest and get well, and not worry about anything,' he said.

'Have you seen the baby?' she said, trying to raise her head.

The midwife said sharply, 'Don't you move, Madame. You must not move. I'll bring the baby.'

Henri stared unwillingly at the tiny crumpled face revealed when the midwife drew back the shawl. It seemed hardly human. So much effort, for so little. But it was a boy, his son. He tried to feel pleased about it.

'A boy,' Madeleine said, echoing his thoughts.

'Yes,' he said, and roused himself to make an effort. 'He's very small.' Her lips twitched, acknowledging the reminder of the last time. 'And very red.'

'Give her some more wine,' the midwife ordered, taking the baby away again.

'Henri—' Madeleine said, when he laid her down again, 'the baby—'

'He's lovely, my darling,' Henri said dutifully.

'He must be christened,' she said.

She looked at him searchingly, and he understood what she was saying. That mute and wizened little creature, too weak even to cry, might not have the strength to cling to life. He must be christened as a matter of urgency, lest he die unbaptized and go into limbo for ever.

'I'll see to it,' he said.

'Now,' she said.

'Yes,' he said. 'I'll go at once.'

She closed her eyes with relief, and a tear – only one, all she had strength for – caught the light under her eyelashes.

'I'm sorry, Henri,' she whispered, and he pressed her hand tighter, not knowing what she was sorry for, too afraid to ask.

'Madeleine, I love you. Rest, my darling, get well,' he said, and it sounded like a plea.

The priest came and christened the baby that evening – Henri Jean Clement Maria. He did not move or cry when the water touched his face, and Henri, in giving him so many and such resounding names was acknowledging that they might be all the child would ever have of life. Madeleine seemed easier when it had been done, and sank into a deep sleep, which her mother said was the best healer. She remained in the house that night, and Henri made up a bed for her on the sofa downstairs. He sat in a chair by the bedside, dozing sometimes, waking with a start, wondering where he was. Early in the morning he woke, chilled to the bone, stiff and confused, to find Madame Homard beside him.

'Go and take my bed,' she said. 'I will watch with her until morning. You have done what you should.'

It was the kindest thing anyone had ever said to him.

In a day or two Madeleine seemed better. She was still very weak, and had little appetite, but she was cheerful and rational, and Henri, who sat beside her bed for most of each day, held her hand and talked to her and felt happier about her. The baby, on the other hand, had not improved. Madame Homard had decreed that Madeleine must not suckle it herself, for it would drain her strength, and she had taken it away and found a wet-nurse for it, but it fed poorly, and still slept too much and cried not enough. Madeleine, to Henri's surprise, did not object to it being taken away, and afterwards never asked after it. He thought sometimes that she had forgotten she had given birth at all, and though at first he was relieved that she was spared the distress he had expected for her, after a while he began to worry that it was not right.

She did not ask after Henriette-Louise, either. The child had been taken to a neighbour when her mother began

236

labour, and was still there, being cared for and fed. Henri asked Madeleine on the third day if she wished the little girl to be brought to her, but she only looked blank, and said no.

On the fifth day Madeleine was feverish and weak, and the midwife came back to examine her, shook her head and muttered, and gave her a dose. All day the fever mounted, but in the evening it went down again, and Henri, who had been alarmed, congratulated the midwife on her medicines.

'Don't you know, sir?' the midwife asked, though less sharply than she might have done five days ago, for she was impressed by his devotion. 'That's the way it goes – up and down.'

'The way what goes?' Henri asked, dry-mouthed.

'The childbed fever,' she said, shaking her head again in pity at his ignorance. 'It comes and goes, sometimes for weeks. Sometimes they cry out, delirious, and don't know where they are. Other times they are as rational as you or me.'

'And – in the end?' he hardly dared ask.

'Some survive, some don't,' she said abruptly. 'One can only pray. Madame is a good, strong, healthy lady. One must pray she fights it off.'

Henri went back into the room a little later, with a bowl of soup, sent over from the neighbour's house, and Madeleine, propped up on her pillows, met his eye, and gave a small, rueful smile.

'I'm quite hungry now, Henri,' she said. 'I will—'

'Yes, my darling?' he asked her, controlling his voice.

'I will try,' she said. He stared, wondering. 'Yes, I know. I have seen it before. I will try and live, Henri, for your sake, and the children. Give me the soup.'

'Oh Madeleine,' he said.

'No, hush, it's all right,' she said, and it did not seem odd that she should comfort him.

For a week she tried, and he watched helplessly as she struggled to win the battle with her sickness, losing a little ground every day. As the midwife had said, at times, when the fever was high, she raved in delirium, and he held her, trying to restrain her from wasting her strength in her wild struggles. Sometimes she would lie, half-conscious, tossing and muttering, unaware of him or her surroundings. But at other times she would wake, clear-eyed though weak, and would talk rationally to him, of the future, of being well, making plans for Henriette Louise. Of the boy baby she never spoke, and it was as well, for he gave up his unequal struggle on the sixth day and died as silently as he had been born.

On the fourteenth day she lay quietly, panting like a spent animal, holding his hand, her face flushed with fever, but her mind clear. Henri was talking to her, unaware of what he was saying, merely trying to keep her with him, awake and aware. Suddenly she gripped his hand tightly, as if a spasm of pain had seized her.

'What is it?' he asked anxiously.

'Henri,' she said, 'Henri,' and he saw that she was trying to make sure of his attention.

'Yes, I am here, I am listening.'

'Henri, you must get a priest. Bring me a priest. I want – him – to come while I still know it.'

'Oh, my darling—'

'It will not be long now. *Please*, Henri.'

Yes – yes – if it is what you want – but—'

'One more thing.' She still held his hand, so tightly that it hurt him, and he was amazed that she could have so much strength left. It was the mark of her determination.

'Anything. What is it?' She turned her head painfully to look at him, held him with her gaze.

'When he comes – please – will you ask him to marry us?'

He was utterly dumbfounded, and could find no words to answer her. She nodded slowly.

'Oh yes, I knew,' she said, with the faintest ghost of her old rueful smile. 'I knew your servant, you see. I had seen him waiting for you, outside the café.'

'But then, why did you—?' he asked in astonishment. She closed her eyes for a moment, and there was pain in her face.

'I wanted you too. I loved you, and I was weak. But now—' the eyes opened again, 'please, I beg you, let me die your true wife. I will not long be a burden to you. Please, for my sake, and the child's.'

He lifted her hand to his lips, and found himself in tears, all his strength gone out of him, all his duplicity and self-pride, everything that held him upright, so that he was as weak as a drowned puppy. He could not even say he was sorry, for the words would have been pitifully inadequate for everything he had done to her, and everything he felt now. He could only plead for her strength and comfort.

'Madeleine, don't leave me. Please don't leave me.'

'I'm sorry,' she said, and felt his tears on her hand as he clutched it to his face. 'I have nothing left.' She sighed, her strength ebbing. 'Don't let me die in sin,' she managed to say.

So it was in that tiny, dimly-lit room that Henri Maria Fitzjames Stuart, Earl of Strathord, finally took a wife. The priest who married them gave Madeleine the last rites, forgiving her her sins and annointing her with the holy oil. Everything was growing dim for her, an unpleasant reeling blackness coming and going in her consciousness, through which she could still feel Henri's hand clutching hers as if trying to anchor her to life, but she was too tired now, she no longer wanted to stay. She had done what she must – she could not now remember – but she knew it was all right. She had only to say goodbye now. Her lips moved, but she made no sound.

Henri leaned closer. 'What is it? I can't hear. Madeleine, what is it?' He pressed her hand, trying to urge her to speak, but she did not respond, only with a faint smile let the breath ease out of her.

CHAPTER TWELVE

He was lost, lost, utterly lost and deranged. He moved in a daze, and sometimes things impinged on him with the mad clarity of a dream, so that he seemed to be outside himself, watching himself moving in that dream. There were other people, too, coming and going inexplicably, as if emerging from a mist and disappearing again. Duncan was there, God knew how, arranging things, talking to him, though Henri could not understand the words. There was Madame Homard, looking horribly old and broken, as if some plug had been pulled inside her, and the life was draining out. There was Monsieur Homard, weeping like a child, and then rushing at Henri with his fists flailing absurdly, crying out and abusing him; and Henri could only stand and let him strike, not minding the blows, unable to tell him that he could not hear or feel him, until Duncan took him away.

There were the two old women who came to do things to Madeleine's body, and then for a moment Henri broke through the mist, and pushed them away, and tried to lift Madeleine in his arms to keep her from them. It was Duncan who restrained him, unclasped his hands, led him away and gave him brandy, talking, talking all the time but never saying anything. Neighbours came and went, and a priest, and an old priest who was Madeleine's godfather, whom Henri tried to thank, but without making any sense.

The strangeness lasted until the day of the funeral. Duncan must have arranged all that, too, for Henri knew nothing about it until he found himself inside the church with the coffin, black-palled and flower-decked, standing on a trestle before him. There was Duncan at his elbow, as always.

'What church is this?' he asked.

'St Germain-des-Pres,' Duncan told him, and Henri heard him, though for a moment, in his confusion, he thought of the Chateau of St Germain, and his grandmother, and he thought it was her funeral. Then he understood.

'Madeleine,' he cried out suddenly, and Duncan held his arm.

'Hush, the guests are arriving. Everything is all right.'

Henri tried to take hold of himself. The confusion had dispersed like mist, he knew everything, remembered everything, and the pain was terrible. Madeleine had removed the bulwark he had placed between himself and the chaos within him, and then had removed herself, leaving him alone with the knowledge of what he was. His grandmother had not needed to remind him of his shameful birth. All his life he had struggled against the knowledge that he was unlawfully got, that he had been his mother's shame and her death, his grandmother's burden, the family's dark secret, hurried away into obscurity; he was ignominy; he was an outcast. She had warned him again and again, thinking his fault was too much pride, not realizing that he had built up an edifice in which to live because the truth was too hard to bear. It had been a good façade, it had deceived everyone, even himself – everyone except Madeleine.

'Oh Madeleine,' he whispered. 'Don't leave me.' She had known what he was, always, all along, but knowing him, she had still loved him. Now she had left him. He turned his head sideways, to try to ease the pain in his throat, and saw to his amazement that two of the mourners filing in down the aisle were Meurice de Murphy, and Ismène. He fumbled for Duncan's arm.

'Duncan!'

'Yes, my lord,' he said gently. 'I thought you would need them. I told them everything.'

Everything? How could he face them if they knew everything? But they came towards him, and Ismène took the place beside him, and put her hand over his in a gesture of sympathy, and Meurice's face was grave and kindly.

'We have come to help you, Henri,' Ismène said. 'You should not be alone at such a time.'

'Ismène?'

'I wish I had known her,' she went on. 'She must have been a wonderful person.'

If he could cry, he thought, the pain might go away; but the tears would not come, not yet.

After the funeral Henri went back to the Rue St Anne, and there he stayed like a convalescent, crouching by the fire, eating and sleeping, while Ismène tended him. Meurice looked in from time to time, but he knew it was Ismène who could help his friend. He and Duncan did their part by arranging matters at the Cour du Commerce. It was not for another two days that Henri was able to cry. Duncan, who had been disposing of Madeleine's clothes, brought her few ornaments to ask Ismène what should be done with them. Ismène intercepted him at the door, but Henri, turning dully to see what was happening, caught sight of the things Duncan held in his hands, and at last the flood broke free.

Ismène sat on the floor in front of the fire, cradling him in her arms, while he wept and wept, rocking him and speaking vague words of comfort, knowing that this was good and right, and would ease him. Afterwards, when it was over, he told her everything, forgetting that she knew it already from Duncan; told her the story without shame or fear, remembering every detail of the four years in which he had known her. Then, for a while, he was silent.

'Poor Henri,' Ismène said at last, and freed herself to attend to the fire, rather than summon a maid to do it. It gave him time to compose himself and remove the outward signs of his weeping. Then she sat down again on the chaise, and he came to her knee as he had so often done, but this time not amorously.

'I loved her,' he said. 'I truly loved her.'

'No, my dear, I don't think so,' she said gently. 'Your need to be loved is so much greater than your need to love. You are not yet able to give love, and without giving it, you cannot receive it.'

'I loved her, and I loved Grandmother—' he began resentfully. She leaned forward.

'Don't you see how you wanted them to love you, how you plagued and tormented them, so that they could prove to you that they loved you in spite of everything, because only then would you know they had loved you enough? But it could never be enough.'

'I don't understand,' he said.

'No, I don't think you do, not yet. But you will. You are capable of loving. I will tell you this, Henri, though you will not believe it yet – that only when you love enough to give it without hope of receiving will you really know what love is. And you will *be* loved, too.'

The words comforted him by their intention, for he could not accept their sense. 'Ismène,' he said suddenly, 'do you love me?'

'I am your friend,' she said. 'Oh yes, I might once have loved you in that way, but fortunately for my peace of mind I was immune to it.'

'What made you immune? he asked, disappointed. She smiled at his transparency.

'My love for another man – a deep and strong love, which he returns.'

'Meurice?' he asked in astonishment.

'Oh Henri,' she laughed, 'of course Meurice. What a simpleton you are.'

'Oh,' he said in a small voice, and she knew it was necessary to change the subject, to salve his pride.

'And now,' she said, 'we must talk about something of great importance – your daughter, Henri. What is to become of her? What is her name, again?'

'Henriette-Louise,' he said, and frowned. 'Well, I suppose her grandparents will bring her up.'

'Is that what you want?'

'No,' he said at once, and then more emphatically, as he thought about it, 'No, not at all. She is—'

'All that is left of Madeleine?'

'Yes – and, after all, she is *mine*. I don't want her brought up as a café-owner's daughter.'

Ismène concealed a smile at the first revival of his pride.

'Very well, then, I have a proposition for you. Meurice and I have no children, and it has been a little of a disappointment to us, to have no little ones growing up around us. I have talked with him, and he agrees that if you wish we will have Henriette-Louise here, and give her a home while she is growing, but on certain conditions.'

'You want to adopt her?' Henri asked, not sure if he liked the idea.

'No, I did not say that. Meurice would be happy enough to adopt her, but I do not think it would be a good thing – for any of us. No, she shall be given a home, but on condition that you adopt her and legitimize her, and on the further condition that you behave as a father to her.'

'And what does that involve?' he asked, and she saw gladly how much more cheerful he looked already.

'You must visit her, interest yourself in her, see to her education; you must, when the time comes, provide her with a dowry and arrange a match for her. You must, above all, my dear Henri, become respectable, so that she shall not be ashamed of you.'

'I see,' he said, eyeing her thoughtfully as another question rose in his mind. 'And when you say respectable, does that mean—'

'That you and I are no longer to be lovers? Yes, it does.'

'But Ismène—'

'I am flattered that you protest. But come, you must

244

agree. You will like me much more as a friend, I promise, than you ever did as a mistress.'

'I'm not sure I believe you,' Henri growled. 'Well, if that is the way it must be—'

'It must. You know it must.'

'Then so be it.' He kissed her hand formally, and felt a lightening of his heart at the thought of the future. His daughter, to bring up and shape and watch grow, he thought, and to love – above all to love. And here would be a person who would belong to him entirely, and if he never gave her cause to do otherwise would she not love him, at last, as he wanted to be loved?

Captain Thomas Morland of the *Isabella* finally saw ship-to-ship action in December 1778 when the British took the island of St Lucia, and beat off the attack of the French fleet under Estaing. There were so many Caribbean islands that it was impossible to garrison them all, and several of them had already changed hands more than once, but St Lucia was close to the French headquarters of Martinique, and a good base from which to harass the French fleet, which was superior in numbers to the British.

In the autumn before and the winter afterwards there were inconclusive skirmishes around the islands, neither fleet taking any decisive action or causing any serious damage to the other. Thomas took some prizes – American merchantmen – and was at last able to reckon some prize money to his account; the weather in the Caribbean in winter was a great deal more pleasant than in most other places; and there was time ashore to enjoy the society of Kingston, Port Royal, and Spanish Town. As a handsome frigate captain in the prime of life he was much in demand whenever he did set foot on the shore, and he enjoyed the parties and dinners. He met the Admiral, Sir Peter Parker, at some of them, and was gratified by his friendliness. William was still serving as midshipman in his flagship and Thomas was able to exchange a few words with him once or twice when he came on shore. Thomas was also interested to meet the nephew that the Comptroller had mentioned to him, a young man of twenty called Nelson, who was first lieutenant of the flagship as a result of the most rapid of promotions. Thomas met him taking tea one day at the Governor's house, but didn't really like him. He thought him a little mad, and too pushing for one of his extreme youth and lowly rank.

In February 1779 letters which had been on their way for some time finally caught up with him in Port Royal, and he learnt of the birth of his son the previous September. For a while he contemplated the news in silence, torn painfully between pleasure at the thought that he had a son and heir to follow after him, and sadness at the thought that it might yet be years before he saw him. The war had been dragging on for four years already, and did not look any closer to being settled. Indeed, it looked very much as though Spain was about to enter the conflict in support of France, and in the defence of her Caribbean and mainland territories, and if she did, every ship of the Royal Navy would be needed to maintain Britain's mastery of the seas. Before he saw his home again the boy would be running around, talking, taking his first lessons perhaps. And if the endemic Spanish fever got to him first, he might never see his son at all.

In April the *Isabella* was involved in an unsuccessful attempt to retake Dominica from the French, and in June she saw action again when Estaing took Grenada, and received enough damage to necessitate docking at Kingston to refit. Thomas was in Kingston when the news arrived that Spain had indeed declared war on Britain. As it was no more than he expected, it was eclipsed in his mind by the surprise of the news that Suckling's nephew, Nelson, had been made post after only two years as a lieutenant.

'I suppose it's only what one expected while his uncle was Comptroller,' he muttered ungraciously to himself.

The new captain's new command, the *Hinchingbrooke*, was still at sea, and so he was given command of the shore batteries to defend the island against the expected invasion from Martinique. The idea that the whole of the island's defences were in the hands of such a young upstart annoyed Thomas, and he was extremely glad when the *Isabella* was warped out and he could get back to sea.

In September news came that there had been an attempted invasion of England by a joint French and Spanish force, which had only failed by good luck. The enemy fleet had delayed too long, allowing the Channel fleet which, taken unawares, had been stationed too far west, to scramble back onto station off Spithead. The enemy fleet had been forced to return to Brest, but the panic in England had been great and fierce criticism had been levelled at the Government for its lack of strategy.

Later that month the *Isabella*, along with the *Flame*, the *Daring* and the *Dover Castle*, was detached to the relief of New York, where General Clinton was hemmed in by Estaing and the French fleet. Thomas sailed with renewed hope of some decisive action whereby he might win glory and the chance of promotion, but as so often before in this war, he was disappointed. The French fleet caused disruption all along the coast but evaded direct action. Occasionally long-range shots were fired and minor damage done, but there was no confrontation, and in November the French ships stood out to sea. After pursuing them for some time, the British squadron realized they were heading home to France, and turned back to New York.

Thomas hoped they might then be sent back to the West Indies, for winter in the northern seas was bitter, but when he had revictualled he was ordered on blockade duty along the New Jersey and Delaware coast, the most monotonous and uncomfortable task he could have been given. He made the most of it by exercising his crew in the less frequently performed manoeuvres, and in checking and correcting the charts of his beat, which were at best inaccurate and at worst non-existent. Scurvy, the other great scourge of the navy, had made its appearance again, and one in five of the lower deck had it to some degree. Thomas shared the growing opinion that it was in great part due to the diet of salt meat, and during those dreary weeks of blockade, he enlivened the routine by landing small raiding parties here and there along the coast in search of fresh food. Fruit, of course, was impossible to come by, but they found potatoes and sometimes cabbage; they occasionally caught game; and Thomas, to the resentment of his men who hated experiment and change, tried the effect of fresh fish and sea kale in their diet.

The days began to lengthen again and the wind to lose its keenness, and one day the lookout's cry of 'Sail-ho! Sail on the port bow,' was followed by a cry of 'Deck there! It's a British ship, sir.' Thomas took his glass and watched as the ship came hull-up over the horizon. She hoisted her number, but Thomas did not need prompting to recognize the *Ariadne*. A moment later the signal midshipman reported, '*Ariadne*, 28, sir. Captain Hannibal Harvey.'

'Yes,' said Thomas, his eye still glued to the glass. She was still, to him, the most beautiful little ship in the world. A man always has a fondness for his first command, but *Ariadne* would have been beautiful to him if she had been his fiftieth.

'*Ariadne* signalling, sir,' the midshipman reported. '*Ariadne* to *Isabella*, have letters.'

'Make: "Am sending boat",' Thomas said. 'Mr Harris, clear away the jolly-boat. And I shall have a note to take to Captain Harvey.'

He hastened below to write: 'Dear Captain Harvey, if you can be tempted out of your ship, will you dine with me?' and five minutes later the jolly-boat was dancing away across the grey, heaving sea. In due course it returned, bringing a bag of letters, from which Thomas sorted out his own before turning it over to his first lieutenant for distribution, and a note of acceptance from

Captain Harvey. Thomas took his letters below and sent for his steward.

'Captain Harvey is coming to dinner. What can you give us?'

'Well, sir,' the steward said doubtfully, 'I don't think there's anything on board now but ration food.'

'No potatoes left?'

'No, sir. The last of 'em went rotten, sir. I think there might be a onion, sir, if the wardroom ain't 'ad it, sir.'

'Well, do what you can. And I'll have that last bottle of claret I've been saving,' Thomas added on an impulse. Wine shared was better than wine drunk alone, and who knew when he would next have company?

'Aye aye, sir,' said the steward, and left him to his letters. By the look of them they had been following him about for some time: the most recent, from Jemima, was dated November '79. He devoured it hungrily. Little Jack was taking his first steps, having discarded crawling almost as soon as he learnt it as being an unsuitable mode of progress for a lively young gentleman. Louisa was learning to ride, and Allen, bent on spoiling her, had insisted she had a proper habit, a miniature version of Jemima's. Harry and Lucy were thriving, Edward doing well at Christ Church and becoming a far more polished gentleman than Jemima would have supposed possible. Mary was dividing her attentions between John Anstey, Tom Loveday, and a new suitor, Patrick Hamilton, son of a rich clothier with a house on Lendal. James had given rise to a scandal by being discovered in the woods on Bachelor Hill with Maggie Henshaw, a well-grown village girl two years his senior. There had been uproar and counter-accusations, and it had been impossible to discover from either culprit how far things had gone; but the girl had not proved pregnant, and the clamour had died away.

Jemima's letters were always good to read, being full of chatter about the family and the animals and local matters, and it was only after he had finished it and laid it aside

249

that he realized it made no mention of Flora. And the only letter in the batch from Flora was dated September, and was a masterpiece in saying nothing. He put the letters down and stared out of the stern windows, and was still doing so when six bells struck and the bosun's calls began to twitter, announcing the arrival of Captain Harvey. Thomas hurried up on deck to meet him.

He was the same vigorous, handsome, smiling man that Thomas remembered, and they greeted each other with a degree of cordiality far greater than their brief acquaintance warranted. The steward had done wonders with the dinner considering his lack of materials: stewed pork with onions, beefsteak pie, pea soup, and a currant duff. The two captains ate with an appetite and drank the claret with an enthusiasm enormously increased by each other's company: the life of a ship captain was necessarily a lonely one.

Through the meal they talked, and Harvey gave Thomas all the news that he had missed being on blockade duty.

'Dalling's been making everyone's life hell in Jamaica,' he told Thomas. 'Parker can't stand him at any price. The Kingston ladies have to make sure if they invite Parker they don't invite the General. But he's ambitious, and pushing, and that's rare enough in this war. He mounted an attack on the mainland in January, up the St Juan River to try and secure Lake Nicaragua. The idea was to cross to the Pacific and thus cut off north from south. And who do you suppose was chosen to lead the expedition?'

'The senior captain on the station, I suppose,' Thomas hazarded. Harvey shook his head.

'Not a bit of it – it was that young spike Nelson! Made post but six months, and he's in charge of the whole landing party. That's a pushing young man, all right – a man after Dalling's heart, I should think.'

'He certainly seems to be getting on,' Thomas said, trying not to sound sour.

'Mad as a hatter, of course,' Harvey went on cheerfully. 'He was ordered to convey the troops to the mouth of the river, and that was all. But he went straight on up the river with the men, assaulted the Spanish batteries and laid siege to the forts.'

'It always seems to be that whenever there's action of any sort I am somewhere else,' Thomas mused. Harvey looked sympathetic.

'It's the fortune of war. But I don't think you would have wanted to be a part of that expedition. Heat, mosquitoes, leeches the size of hen's eggs, poisonous snakes – not to mention the fever. The Dons are hardened to it, of course, but it went through our men like a hot knife through butter. If they hadn't been recalled from the siege I dare say not one of them would have survived. On the *Hinchingbrooke*, for instance, they buried a hundred and fifty of their two hundred Jacks.'

'Not including Captain Nelson, I presume?'

Harvey grinned. 'He leads a charmed life. He's gone back to Port Royal, I understand, to await his new command – the *Janus*, when she comes in with Rodney.'

'Admiral Rodney? Is he coming out, then?'

'He's bringing out eight thousand men to reinforce the Caribbean. Stopped off to relieve Gibraltar on the way, in January, and should have arrived by now. There's another man with a charmed life. We ought to see some action with him.'

'Well, that is good news,' Thomas said. They were lingering now over the last of the wine, Thomas having no port left to offer, and the talk drifted to home matters and more general topics. Thomas was discovering that his estimation of Harvey on that one meeting had been correct – that he was, indeed, a man with whom he could be friendly. He was lively, intelligent, and well read, and Thomas felt a lack of reserve with him that rather surprised him.

'I read your *Gazette* letter, by the way, after the attack on Grenada, back in '79,' Harvey said suddenly. 'You have attracted some favourable notice in the Admiralty, judging from the gossip I heard.'

'Really?' Thomas said, a little embarrassed. Harvey smiled.

'The butchers' bill on St Juan will leave a few vacancies, sir, and I would be extremely surprised if there wasn't a sealed letter on its way to you.'

Thomas could only grunt noncommittally. *He* would be surprised, feeling isolated and forgotten as he did.

'Your name, of course, is kept before their lordships in London,' Harvey went on. His tone was one of a person making polite conversation, but Thomas thought there was some significance in his eye. 'I had the inestimable pleasure of meeting your wife last autumn at Court,' he said. Thomas started, and then recovered himself and tried to sound neutral.

'Did you? I hope she appeared well.'

'She seemed in excellent health and spirits, I'm happy to be able to report to you. And she sat at dinner between Lord Aylesbury and Lord Sandwich, which I'm sure she did out of her devotion to duty, for they are no company for a young lady at the moment, having nothing to talk about but provisioning and the Northern blockade. But she was making herself charming to them, and I'm sure towards the end of dinner Lord Sandwich actually made a remark about a play.'

Thomas allowed a smile to relax the frown between his brows, but he was sure there was some message for him here, if he could only discover it. But they were interrupted in their conversation by a messenger from the first lieutenant, to say that the wind was freshening, and Harvey stood up and made his apologies.

'I had better get back to my ship in that case, sir. Thank you for a most enjoyable dinner, and more than the dinner, for your inestimable company.'

'Thank *you*, Harvey,' Thomas said. 'On blockade duty such a diversion is doubly welcome.'

He escorted Harvey to the side, and they shook hands. The fortunes of war could mean that they might never meet again. Harvey gave him a keen look, and then reached inside his jacket.

'I forgot, sir – I meant to give you this. I'm sure you haven't seen a copy of the *Post* for some time. I thought it might interest you.'

'Thank you,' said Thomas.

The freshening of the wind necessitated shortening sail, and so it was not until much later that Thomas had a chance to peruse the newspaper Harvey left him. It was not a recent copy – it was not to be expected – but it was interesting all the same to see what preoccupied the people at home. He did not at first notice the item in the paragraph dedicated to society news, and when he did it took him a moment or two to understand it.

'At the Masquerade given at Carlisle House last Monday, the brilliant company was adorned by the presence of the dashing Mrs T.M. Her fashionable garb crowned with a headdress most wittily depicting a ship in full sail, Mrs T.M., wife of one of our gallant naval captains, led the dancing with the elegant Lord M. This correspondent understands that the couple were intending to leave the following day to go into Oxfordshire for the hunting. Mrs T.M. is known as a most excellent horsewoman, and it is expected that this year, as last, she will hunt Lord M.'s horses.'

Thomas sat for a long time staring at the page, conscious of a dull pain at the deepest levels of thought, while the surface of his mind said only there is nothing new here, nothing I did not know. It is all innuendo. Their relationship is quite innocent. But it was horrible to have such things suggested in public. Those who mattered would know who the 'gallant naval captain' was, and while they might claim to take no notice of gossip and common scandal, it would inevitably affect his standing. His hands gripped the newspaper until his knuckles were white, and the pages crumpled under them.

Did Harvey know? Was that why he had left the paper? And if he did know, was it done in kindness or spite? He could imagine Harvey saying, I thought you ought to know; but that could be said with concealed glee, as well as with serious kindness. But no: he remembered Harvey's face as he left to go over the side. That last searching glance was one of friendship.

A week later, in accordance with standing orders, *Isabella* put into New York again to revictual, and a sealed Admiralty letter was awaiting Thomas there. He was ordered to proceed at once to Port Royal, there to take command of the *Rochester*, 44, and to join Admiral Rodney's squadron. It was promotion, it was the removal to West Indian waters that he had wanted, and it was, if Rodney lived up to his reputation, a chance for action, and Thomas ought to have been delighted. But he realized that he did not know, he would never know, whether this promotion was due to his professional standing or Flora's activities in London.

Then he shook himself, and give a private, ironical smile. Why should he care? Patronage as well as ability had always been a requirement in the navy, and things were no different now. Probably dozens of officers had been promoted as a result of the heavy losses on St Juan. He had a job to do, and he would do it to the best of his ability, whatever the results. And at least it was better than the endless, tedious blockade duty.

In June 1780 London was convulsed by the bloodiest riots that had ever sullied her streets. Some minor easing of the laws proscribing Roman Catholics had been passed through Parliament, and Lord George Gordon, a Protestant fanatic, led a protest by the so-called 'Protestant Association' which in reality was nothing more than a mob driven to madness by hysterical oratory and unlimited gin. The houses and business premises of Roman Catholics – or sometimes of those merely thought to be sympathetic – were attacked and burnt down, and the magistrates were powerless to control matters.

The Government seemed unable to decide on any action, and members of the Cabinet cowered in their houses, but the King acted with resolution and courage, called out the Guards, and was prepared to lead them himself in his determination not to allow anarchy to prevail. But over three hundred people were killed before order was restored, and thousands of pounds' worth of damage was done. It was by mere good luck that Flora was not in London at the time, for she had been staying, as usual, in Chelmsford House. But Lady Chelmsford, being a little unwell as the result of a miscarriage, had decided to try Bath, and Flora had accompanied her. Lord Meldon had agreed to follow in a week rather than travel with them, for he and Flora were not unaware of the gossip which was being attached to them. The ladies took with them Chelmsford's elder daughter, Sophia, who at fifteen was wild for balls and entertainments. Horatio, now seventeen, was away at school, and the younger daughter, Amelia, who was five, remained at home with her governess.

When the news of the riots reached Bath, Flora was anxious, even agitated, about the safety of Lord Chelmsford and the younger child, but her anxiety was by no means shared by the child's mother. Lady Chelmsford only said placidly, 'To be sure, my dear, there would be no reason for them to attack Chelmsford House. *We* are not Catholics.'

Such unreasonable confidence was proved at last to have been perfectly justified after all, and Flora was able to return to the enjoyment of those pleasures Bath was renowned for. She had never been to Bath before, and everything interested her. She accompanied Lady Chelmsford to the baths themselves on the first morning, but never went again. The baths were attended very early in the morning; the approaches to them were dark, miserable, and not over-clean, the dressing rooms like dungeons; and the bathing clothes voluminous and unflattering. Thereafter Lady Chelmsford had to take her baths alone, Flora and young Sophia joining her afterwards in the Pump Room where she would drink her glass of water, and the three of them would walk about and hear the latest gossip.

After breakfast, and the morning service in the Abbey, they were free to enjoy themselves, walking, riding, driving, or shopping, until dinner at three. After tea the evenings were filled with card parties, the play, or the ball. To be sure, the round was no different from that of London, except in being more restricted, but Flora enjoyed the novelty; and there were pleasant drives and exploring parties to various beauty spots in the area. And with Lord Meldon there, she was perfectly happy.

It was he who brought to her the copy of the *Gazette* containing the reports of the battle between Rodney's fleet and the French off Martinique. He gave it to her one morning while they were strolling about the Pump Room, having left Lady Chelmsford and Sophia talking to some friends by the door. Silently he folded the paper and pointed out the paragraph.

'. . . . and I cannot end this report without mentioning in the strongest terms the exemplary conduct and courage of Captain Thomas Morland of the *Rochester* in leading the boarding of the *Artois*. Captain Morland received a slight wound, from which I am happy to report he is now recovering . . .'

Flora read the words over and over, and then looked up at Lord Meldon, and her lip began to tremble. Hastily he tucked her hand under his arm and walked with her along the edge of the room so that her face was turned away from the company, and their speech was covered by the music.

'Dear Flora, compose yourself,' he said gently. 'You see the Admiral says it is only a slight wound. He will be well by and by.'

She shook her head. 'That is not it,' she said, so low that he had to stoop to hear her. 'You know that is not what distresses me.'

He did not answer at once, but pressed her hand closer to his side, and their steps slowed. At last he said, 'Yes, I know.' Now they stopped altogether, and he said, 'I have to confess to you that when I first began taking notice of you I did it out of sheer mischief. Oh, I can't excuse myself – I was a peevish boy, I resented my father's happiness with my stepmother, I wanted to make trouble. But I was very soon caught in my own trap. My feelings for you, dearest Flora—'

'Oh, don't!' she whispered in belated alarm, but he went on.

'My feelings for you grew, first to a warm friendship and a lively interest – and then – oh Flora, you know, you must have known for a long time, that I love you.'

'Charles—' she began, and then realized that refutation was useless now. 'Yes, I know, and I should not have done what I did. As soon as I felt myself in danger from you, I should have quitted your company. And now it's too late. I love you too. Oh Charles, what shall we do?'

He could make no answer for the moment, except to press her hand.

'This report,' she said after a short silence, 'it brings it home to me. Oh Charles, I am a married woman. Thomas – I was so young when I married, hardly more than a child. He is older than me, I never really knew him. But when I saw he was wounded, I suddenly thought – what if he should hear? What if he should find out? It would wound him far more than anything the French can do.'

'But we have done nothing wrong,' Charles said urgently. 'You must keep reminding yourself, Flora, that we have done nothing wrong. We have been together in public, we have been as brother and sister. Gossip may surmise what it likes, but we know it is false.'

'*We don't!*' she cried. 'Whatever our actions have been, our feelings are wrong. Oh Charles, what can we do?'

There was a silence in which they looked at each other, and all the impossible possibilities passed through their minds and were dismissed. In the end he said sadly,

257

'Nothing. There is nothing we *can* do, except to be together.' He turned her, and they walked on, turning at the end of the room along the front of the orchestra.

'I'm so afraid he will be killed,' Flora whispered, 'and then I will never know if I wished for it or not.'

CHAPTER THIRTEEN

The Act of Parliament for the enclosure of the Morland lands went through in July 1781, just before the end of the session, but the fact had anticipated the Act, and already the three largest open fields had been ploughed and levelled. The levelling and laying-in of drains was an important part of enclosure, for under the strip system, cross-ploughing was impossible, and so the only method of draining had been the building up of the centre of the field into a crown. Over the years, moreover, the rigs and baulks changed levels drastically, so that the furrows were sometimes feet deep.

'It's a wonder to me,' Allen said to Jemima, 'that we ever grew anything at all under the old system. Now you will see the difference – a level field, well-drained, with a uniformity of soil and moisture, and nothing wasted in dividing up the holdings! Then imagine that field, well-manured from grazing our wintering cattle on a turnip crop, well bound together with a crop of good clover grass, sewn with row upon row of strong, clean corn.'

'My darling,' Jemima laughed, 'you do not have to convince *me*, remember.'

But there had been moments when she had had her doubts about the business, especially when, earlier that year, two of the smaller tenants had come to her seeking an interview.

'About this enclosure, mistress,' they said.

'Are you sure it is not Sir Allen you should be speaking to?' Jemima asked.

They looked embarrassed, and shifted their feet, and then one of them, a man called Fosdyck, said, 'Well, mistress, it's this way – the master's so set on it that he'd never listen to us. And we reckoned that, after all, it's you that's really the owner and if you said – if you made up your mind—'

'But what is it that troubles you? I understood that everything had been agreed, that you had all been advised of your allocations, and were contented.'

'T'isn't the allocation, mistress,' said the other, Master Black. 'Master explained all to us, and how if we put our strips together, and took a piece more for grazing rights, it would come to such and such an amount, and we couldn't say it weren't right—'

'The master wouldn't stint us wrong, we know that,' Fosdyck put in anxiously. 'But once we've got our allocation, what are we do to with it? We can't afford to plant hedges round it, nor to build fences.'

'Then there's drains to lay in, and a road to be built,' Black added. 'And my little bit is on the far side o' the beck, and I can't afford to build a bridge over it. How am I to get my ox and my plough over the beck?'

Jemima stared at them helplessly. 'Oh dear. I can't begin to answer your questions. But I will say this to you, I am sure Sir Allen has thought of all these things and will have some answer for you. And I will put your questions to him, on your behalf.'

But Allen had had no answer, in the sense of a solution. 'I'm afraid that it's true, that the smaller holdings will hardly be worth the expense of fencing,' he said, 'but what's to be done? The enclosure must go through, for the greater good, and if the allocations are fair, one has done all one can.'

'But what will happen to people like Black and Fosdyck?' Jemima asked. Allen shrugged.

'They will find a way round their problems, or they will sell their holdings. The latter is the most likely.'

'Sell to whom?' Jemima asked in a small voice. Allen tried not to look guilty.

'To me,' he said. 'I'm sorry, Jemima, it can't be helped. I'll give them a good price, and you know that the land will be better farmed by me than by them. And that will mean more meat and corn for everyone in the country.'

'But then what will happen to them?'

'They will find work – don't forget, there will be plenty to do in the new system, and I will employ them, if they ask me, and give them a fair wage.'

'I see,' Jemima said, and she had nothing more to say about it. She could see, she agreed with him, as to the necessity of it, but it saddened her all the same. She remembered when she had been a young girl and her father had taken her out to meet the tenants and labourers and outworkers, and had explained to her how their independence was precious to them. They liked to have their own little patch of land, however poor, and their own cow, however sway-backed, and to work in their own way and in their own time. It was inefficient, of course, led to poor husbandry, unequal work, sometimes destitution – but, as her father had said, 'A little freedom is as precious to a weaver as to any man.' She could see both sides of the problem, and it gave her pain.

But the worst thing was the loss of common rights to those cottagers who had them by right of tenancy of a certain dwelling. There was one old man called Horace Truman – Gaffer Truman, as he was known. He lived in a cottage on the edge of the common just beyond the Ten Thorns, and in that tiny, odiferous cottage he had raised fifteen children by a succession of three wives, and had outlived all of them. They had none of them ever been much above the level of starvation – and sometimes below it, when a pig died or a cow went dry. But he had survived, heating his hovel and cooking his food by the turf and firewood he collected on the commons, feeding his pigs with the acorns, his cow with the grazing and loppings, keeping a few chickens or a goose, doing the odd day's labour when he was badly off, and 'taking a holiday' – getting drunk – when things were going well.

And now he was a knotty old man – how old, nobody knew – gnarled and stunted with years of poverty, but upright still. He lived all alone now, and since he had never been out of his clothes since they were new, he smelled strong enough to make the eyes water, and the dirt had settled in the lines of his face like soil filling furrows. But he regarded Sir Allen that day with a bright and steady eye while the master explained to him, in person, what was happening in the matter of the enclosure.

Jemima, sitting her horse a little way off – upwind of him – saw the disbelief on his face, followed by the bewilderment. How could anyone take away his commons, that he had had all his life? he was asking. He had always, time out of mind, had the firewood and the grazing and acorns – and his father before him, that no one now alive could remember. Patiently, Allen explained it all again, but Jemima could see he did not understand, and that when he came to believe it was to happen, he could only think the master and mistress had betrayed him.

'But we'll give you compensation,' Allen said.

'Compensation?' Gaffer Truman didn't understand the word.

'Money – gold,' Allen said. 'Money to make up for losing the rights.'

And the old man again looked from Allen to Jemima, and said, 'But what use is money to me? I can't graze my cow and pigs on money.'

And when eventually they rode away, Jemima could not rid her mind of the memory of the last look he sent after them, bewildered and hurt.

Old Gaffer Truman could not adapt to the new life. He continued to exercise his rights until the common was fenced off, and then he broke through the fence and carried on as before until the plough was brought in, and the grazing ploughed up. Then from time to time he and his animals would be found trespassing on some other piece of grass, and he would be brought up before Allen, as Justice of the Peace, who would try again to explain to him. The compensation money had gone within a fortnight of payment on the longest and most glorious 'holiday' of

Truman's life, a debauch which would have killed a less hardened constitution.

'What am I to do with him?' Allen asked Jemima. 'He's drunk away the money, and he *won't* understand that he can't graze his animals where he likes.'

'He can't help it,' Jemima said, remembering the old man's words – 'what use is money to me?' Money was an alien substance to the cottager, who lived by what he grew and made himself, and who had rarely owned more than a couple of shillings at any one time, usually not more than a few pence. 'Can't you give him a little bit of land?' she begged.

'But he's had his compensation,' Allen pointed out.

'He doesn't understand money – land is what he knows. Just half an acre, Allen – it wouldn't be for long. He can't live for ever.'

'Don't be so sure,' Allen said, but in the end he agreed with her, and decided to offer the old man a corner of the West Field under the slope of Bachelor Hill, where he could gather firewood as well. He went in person to the rank cottage by the Ten Thorns to tell Truman of his decision, and found the old man looking a great deal older and more frail than he had remembered him. Truman listened in silence as Allen told him of his plan, and for a long time he did not answer, but looked away, past Allen, towards the land he had known all his life, but not as if he saw it. Some inner landscape filled his mind, some memory from his long, long life.

Then, 'Thankee, sir,' he said. 'You're right kindly, I'm sure, master. But I've never took charity from no man, not in all my life, and that's what it is, when all's said. No, master, if I can't have my bit o'grazing and such back, then I'll take no one else's land from him. I've lived free, and I'll die free, not beholden.'

'But what will you do, man?' Allen asked, exasperated. 'You can't go grazing your beasts wherever you please.'

'I knaw that, master,' he said. 'I've come to see that it's

263

stealing, and I'm no gypsy, and I won't do it namore. If I can't feed my beasts, I's'l sell 'em.'

'But then how will you live?' Allen asked. The old man continued to look past him with calm dignity.

'The Lord will provide, master, for me as for the sparrow.'

A few days later Allen heard that the old man had indeed sold his beasts, one gaunt cow, three wiry sows and a young litter, and half a dozen laying hens of dubious vintage. A few days after that Allen was riding past Ten Thorn Gap and decided to turn out of his way to see how the old man was faring, and found the cottage deserted. The hearth was cold, and though the few sticks of furniture were still there, there did not appear to be any personal belongings left – if, indeed, the old man had ever had any. Though he made inquiries, he could not find anyone who knew where Gaffer Truman had gone, and as far as he knew, no one ever saw him again.

William and Thomas were together again in the summer of 1781. Thomas, as a result of Rodney's report after the battle off Martinique, had been promoted in September 1780 to command of the *Daring*, 64, his first ship of the line, under Admiral Sir Samuel Hood. William at that time had been lying in hospital in Port Royal, recovering from the fever which had caused him to be left behind when Parker's flagship had returned to England, and on Thomas's request, William had been allowed to rejoin him.

He presented a very different aspect from the puny, seasick boy who had sailed from Spithead with him back in '75. At eighteen, William had reached a respectable five-foot-eight, had filled out with muscle. He had grown, Thomas thought, very handsome, his weather-browned face showing firmness and thoughtfulness, years of responsibility in his level gaze. His pale hair had never darkened, and he wore it in an old-fashioned pigtail almost a foot long. Thomas found him very able, well-versed in both the practical and theoretical aspects of his trade. It was a pity, he thought, that he was still a midshipman – but, besides ability, the requirements for lieutenancy were a minimum of six years at sea, and the attainment of the age of twenty.

'The moment you are old enough,' Thomas said, 'you must take your examination. There is no doubt in the world that you will pass it.'

In May of that year, General Cornwallis, who had been moderately successful in South Carolina and moderately unsuccessful in North Carolina, was ordered by the commander-in-chief Clinton to join up with the force under Patriot-turned-loyalist Benedict Arnold in Virginia. Virginia had remained largely in the hands of the Patriots since the beginning of the war, and General Cornwallis was eager to reverse this situation, but Clinton, growing more weary and discouraged with every year the war dragged on, was more interested in defence. He wanted a safe anchorage for the navy in Chesapeake Bay, and Cornwallis was ordered to fortify Yorktown for this purpose.

In this the close interdependence of the army and navy was exhibited, for while it was necessary to have a military base in Yorktown to make the Bay safe for ships, it was necessary to have the navy on hand in the Bay to make it possible to take and fortify Yorktown. And it was equally true for the French/American forces: they would have to march men into Virginia and request the French navy to sail into the Bay at the same time.

All these things were known in general terms but, as through the whole of the war, communication of detail was sadly lacking. Clinton's request for ships caused Admiral Hood to sail from the West Indies to New York with fourteen ships, *Daring* amongst them. They arrived in August to meet up with Admiral Graves and collect five more ships of the line in support. The 'all captains' flag was hung out in the *Royal Oak*, and Thomas called away his gig to go on board the flagship and receive information and orders.

'General Cornwallis had six thousand men at Yorktown,'

Admiral Graves told the assembled captains, 'but York-town, though it commands the Bay, will be hard to defend from the landward, and we know that Washington is marching towards Virginia with seven thousand men, so it is imperative that we sail at once to Chesapeake Bay to support Cornwallis.'

'And the French, sir? Do we know what ships they have in the area?' one of the captains asked.

'The Rhode Island fleet has left its base, and our observers think that they had siege equipment aboard, so it is logical to assume that they have gone to Chesapeake. I think we may expect them to be waiting for us. But we will be more ships than they.'

'And what of De Grasse and the rest of the French fleet, sir? Will they go to the aid of their companions?' asked another captain, Hammond of the *Achilles*. It was Admiral Hood who answered.

'Admiral Rodney assured us that De Grasse will not send more than a few ships to Chesapeake, if he sends any at all. The situation in the West Indies is far too delicate for the French to risk sending their whole fleet.'

A few more questions were asked and answered, and then Graves dismissed them.

'Thank you, gentlemen. We sail at first light.'

Thomas returned to his ship thoughtfully, his mind naturally turning to the question of Charles. What would happen to him, when Virginia was taken? Would he make any attempt to fight against the British? The family at home, as they revealed in their letters to Thomas, had begun to worry about Charles, for he no longer wrote to them, or replied to their letters, and though Jemima and Allen were supposing to themselves that the war had disrupted the already fragile postal services between England and Maryland, Thomas did not believe it. Charles had gone over to the other side; Flora was disporting herself publicly with another man. I was mistaken in that family, he thought bitterly. His best friend, and his wife – brother and sister both had proved false to him.

At first light on the following day the fleet sailed majestically out of New York harbour to take up their stations in rigid line-ahead, following the two flagships. *Royal Oak*, *London*, *Invincible*, *Monarch*, *Ajax*, *Achilles*, *Intrepid*; Thomas took station on *Intrepid*, and *Daring* filled her sails and ploughed along in the creamy wake directly astern. Behind him came *Minotaur*, *Montagu*, *Centaur*, *Vulture*, *Terrible* and the rest of them, making a line of ships, a death-dealing creature, five miles long. Two frigates, and the sloop *Ariadne*, held station out on the flank of the line, keeping watch on the horizons for the French.

At dawn on 5 September the lookouts sighted the outcrop of Cape Henry, the southerly point of the mouth of the Bay, and simultaneously came the cry of 'Sail ho!' Between the points of Cape Henry and the northern barrier, Cape Charles, lay the waiting French fleet.

'Get aloft with a glass, boy,' Thomas said tersely to William. 'Tell me what you see.'

William leapt for the ratlines, a telescope under his arm, while at the masthead the lookout was still counting.

'Thirteen, fourteen – twenty or more, sir. They're French all right, sir.'

A while later William's voice, adding more information. 'Twenty-four in all I count, sir.' Then, after a pause, in a different voice, 'Deck, there! Captain, sir, I think I know those ships. There's *Marseillaise*, sir, I'm sure of it, and *Languedoc*, and *Saint Esprit*. And – there's *Ville de Paris*, sir, Admiral De Grasse's flagship. It's the West India fleet, sir.'

So Admiral Rodney had miscalculated, Thomas thought. The West India fleet had come after all, and with them France's boldest and ablest sailor, De Grasse. Twenty-four French ships of the line not only outnumbered the English fleet, they very seriously outweighed her in firepower. Those big three-deckers carried forty guns a side, against the British seventy-fours. The *London* was the only British ship bigger, with ninety guns, while the monstrous *Ville de*

Paris carried one hundred and ten. As against that the coppered British ships were all more seaworthy and handier, and the British seaman was worth ten of his French opponent. But in a light wind, and with a moderate sea, these advantages would not count for much. Their only chance would be to trap the French fleet in the mouth of the Bay, with no room to manoeuvre, and batter them against the shores and shoals.

'Flagship's signalling, sir,' said the signals midshipman at his elbow. 'Flag to all ships, sir, prepare to tack.'

'Acknowledge,' Thomas said. 'Mr Wallis, prepare to go about.'

A few minutes later the signal came down, and Thomas tacked the *Daring* at the heels of the *Intrepid* before him, like every other ship in the fleet. Like a machine, the whole long line of ships came round in beautiful, rigid order, and headed for the mouth of the Bay and the waiting French. There was a movement at his elbow, and he glanced round to see William rejoining him.

'Flagship signalling, sir,' said the signals midshipman again, but this time there was a tremor in his voice which he endeavoured to control as he continued. 'Flag to all ships, clear for action, sir.'

'Acknowledge,' said Thomas. He met William's level gaze, and William gave a tiny smile, hardly more than a jerk of his lips, of excitement. Thomas noticed, as one notices tiny, irrelevant details at a moment of crisis, that William's eyebrows had been bleached white by the sun, like his hair.

'Drummer, beat to quarters,' Thomas said. 'Mr Wallis, we'll clear for action, if you please.'

Charles came in from the fields hot and uncomfortable and discontented. More and more as the years passed he wished Philippe had not died and left him the burden of his wealth. Charles was not Philippe; he was a botanist, not a farmer or a businessman. There was little he did not

268

know about the way flowers attracted the fertilizing insects with their colours and marks, or about their root systems, or the ingenious ways trees had of dispersing their seeds. But he did not know how to get the best out of his field hands, or how to drive a hard bargain with a Virginia merchant. He was not hard enough on his overseers, and they took advantage of him; he knew too little about business, and the tough Virginian buyers and sellers cheated him. The plantation was taking on a slipshod, half-neglected air, and he knew it, though he did not know how to prevent it.

When he got to the house, he found Eugenie in the drawing room, sitting for her portrait. It had been her own idea, for a cousin in Martinique had written that it was absolutely the thing to have one's portrait taken with one's children, and war or no war, Eugenie was not one to lag behind a fashion once she knew of it. The painter was a Frenchman from Paris, who claimed to have painted Queen Marie Antoinette herself. It was not clear why such an eminent man should have strayed so far from civilization; Charles suspected he had fled, like so many before him, to the West Indies to escape the consequences of some crime – debt, perhaps, or fraud, or a duel.

He paused in the doorway, however, to look at the scene for a moment, and to admit to himself that it was a pretty one, and that if the painter's skill captured it, it would be a lovely portrait. Eugenie had dressed all in white, white lace in tiers over white silk, her glossy black hair dressed high and topped with white flowers and plumes in the Parisian style. Little Charlotte, four years old now, was at her knee in a dress that was a miniature of her mother's, her dark ringlets falling over her shoulders, a pink sash round her middle making a splash of colour. Bendy, the spaniel, was on Eugenie's lap, his black patches and ginger eyebrows making a contrast with her snowy skirts, and beside her stood a diminutive Negro maid holding baby Philip, who at almost two years was too big and heavy for her, and was kicking her rhythmically through his flounced and lacy skirts in his endeavour to make her put him down.

At the sight of Charles, however, Philip's scowl of boredom changed to a smile of delight.

'Papa!' he cried, and wriggled so hard that the exhausted Negress was forced to put him down, at which he ran across the room and flung himself at Charles's dusty knees.

'My little man,' Charles cried, lifting the boy up. Thomas had been right in this, he thought, that the presence of his children growing up around him had been a great comfort, compensation in some measure for his loss of freedom and companionship. Philip adored him, and though little Charlotte was a capricious miss, and some-times dismissed him loftily and refused to smile for Papa, yet she would often creep onto his lap, and demand that he should come and tuck her up in bed, and tell her a story.

Philip's defection had spoiled the group, and the painter raised his hands in Gallic exasperation.

'*Monsieur, je vous en prie – Madame, je n'ai pas fini—!*'

But Eugenie looked round with a languid smile, and said, 'Ah, Charles. Yes, we have done enough for the morning. You may go, Monsieur du Barry. We shall sit again for you tomorrow.' The Frenchman, muttering in French too rapid for Charles to understand, began to pack away his gear, and Charles went across to kiss Eugenie's hand. She had grown lovelier over the years, and more gracious since the birth of her second son. She no longer chattered to him about fashions, and her silences were longer, and if he had still been in love with her he might have thought those silences were filled with profound thought. But though he cared for her, love had been too delicate a bubble to survive his loneliness and boredom and anxiety. He did not understand her, but no longer troubled himself to try. He was becoming a silent and morose man, and if he had thought about Eugenie, he might have wondered whether she was as disappointed in him as he in her.

'Well, madam,' he said now, by way of greeting.

'Well, sir,' she countered with a gracious smile. 'Do you not think the painting is coming along well?'

He went across to the easel to look at it. It would be an agreeable thing indeed when it was finished – if it were ever finished.

'It seems a pretty likeness, madam,' he said, 'but I think you should instruct your painter to hurry his work a little, lest the war interrupt it for good.'

'The war? Charles, what can you mean?' Eugenie said without the least change of tone. 'Mary, take Master Philip and Miss Charlotte back to the nursery, and send Sam with some wine for the master. He is very tired from his work.'

'The war, madam, is upon our doorstep,' Charles said with ironic patience. 'You cannot have failed to learn that the British are in Yorktown, that Washington has marched into Virginia with a large troop, or that the French navy has been achored in the Bay for days. At any moment the British navy will arrive, and we shall be convulsed with battle by land and sea.'

'Convulsed?' The word was extraordinary, pronounced in Eugenie's gentle drawl. 'You must not be so sensational, Charles. What can a battle by land or sea be to us?'

It was true, Charles thought, in the past year or two the war had passed out of their life to a great extent. With the theatre of war changing to the West Indies, York Plantation had ceased to be a staging post and hospital for the Patriots, and with his own manifest change of loyalties, the Virginia Patriots had left him alone. But ever since Cornwallis had marched into Virginia, he had known a crisis could not be postponed indefinitely. The painter bowed himself out, and they were alone.

'You do not think then, madam,' he said 'that we should pitch our weight into the scales? We should not aid the Cause? We should not do what we can to ensure our liberty and that of our children from the British yoke?'

'No, sir, of course not,' Eugenie said calmly, and it took

271

the wind out of his sails, so that for a moment he could not reply.

At last he said, 'You are monstrous calm about it, madam. Yet you welcomed the Patriots into our drawing room that first day like lifelong friends.'

'It was necessary,' she said, smoothing the creamy lace of her skirts. 'I did not wish to see you or my father shot, and my house burned down.'

So there at last was his answer. He stared at her. 'You do not care, then, who wins the war?'

'Why should women ever care about war?' she asked as if mildly surprised. 'Men make wars to amuse themselves. It is all waste, and women have to repair the damage. But you, Charles, why should you care? York is not your home, and you do not care about it.'

'I promised your father to protect it,' he said. She nodded.

'Yes, I suppose you did. Well, that is good.'

'And what do you think I should do about the conflict in Virginia, then?' he asked. She stood up, her every movement slow and graceful.

'Why, whatever is most convenient to you, sir,' she said easily, and with a bow of her head she left the room. Charles remained, thoroughly confused and taken aback by this extraordinary revelation. Eugenie's words had been spoken in a voice uniformly gentle and slow, yet their content had been as dark and sharp as West Indian spice. What other thoughts had she been concealing from him all their married life? When she was sitting embroidering, her face a mask of serenity, was she really watching him, criticizing inwardly? The servant, Sam, came in with the wine, and the news that a pinnace was coming towards the landing stage.

'It look to me like Mr Tomkin, sir,' he said. 'Shall I bring him in when he come?'

'Yes, of course, show him in,' Charles replied absently. He was brought abruptly back to earth, however, when

Tomkin, his nearest neighbour, burst into the room, wildly excited.

'The British have come, the navy – nineteen ships of the line, against the French twenty-four. There's going to be a battle, man! I'm going down to the headland to watch. Do you want to come with me?'

'Good God! Yes, yes, of course, I'll come right away. Sam—'

'Yes, master. I'll get your cloak.'

'And tell your mistress where I've gone – no time to speak to her myself.'

And minutes later they were running down to the landing stage where Tomkin's men were so eager to be off that Charles had to jump for it across a widening gap, landing clumsily upon a pile of weapons in the bottom of the boat.

'You never know if we might need 'em,' Tomkin said as Charles rubbed his bruises.

As soon as he saw the British fleet standing in towards him, De Grasse took the bold step, and one after another the French ships made a break for the open sea, where they would have a chance of fighting, rather than being forced aground. Thomas watched them with resignation: it was what was to be expected of an active commander-in-chief.

'They're coming out, sir,' Wallis reported belatedly.

'Yes,' said Thomas. It changed the odds, of course, giving the advantages back to the fleet with the greater firing power. But British Jacks were better than the Frogs, everyone knew that; and a French man-o'-war would only fire two broadsides at most to the three from a British first-rate.

'Flagship signalling, sir,' said the midshipman. 'All ships – wear ship, sir.'

Acknowledge.'

It was prudent to keep the weather gauge, of course.

Now the two fleets were in line of battle on converging courses that would meet at a point a mile or so ahead. Another signal from the flagship: 'Fire when your guns bear.'

Well, that was that. No need for any more commands. Each ship in turn would come within range of the enemy, each ship would engage one of the opposing ships, and would fight until one or other was disabled. Thomas found his palms damp, and rubbed them absently against his trousers. He need not chide himself for a coward – everyone found the waiting terrible, as the ships drew slowly, ever so slowly, towards each other. The eighth ship in line – that would be *Daring*'s target. Thomas could see her now. He had seen her before in the West Indies, often enough to recognize her without being able to see the name painted across her transom. It was the massive two-decker *Achille* – fortunate that the French spelled it without the 's'. Thomas could see her gunports were open, revealing a long, long line of guns, bared like teeth at her enemy; forty of them, and in such a moderate sea she would be able to use them all to good effect.

'Starboard a point,' he said quietly to the quartermaster, bringing the ship yet closer to the wind. She moved faster through the water than her enemy, thanks to her coppering; there might be a chance to intercept the *Achille* on her bow where some of her guns would not bear, rake her, and turn down her blind side before they had a chance to run out the portside guns. He glanced at William, and was proud of the boy, standing calmly, his fair brows drawn together against the sea dazzle, the blond curls blowing at his temples in the little wind, watching the machine of war approaching as if it were nothing more than a fishing vessel. And he glanced too at the lovely blue sea and the blue sky; it was a beautiful world, and they might both be leaving it soon.

The heavy rolling boom of guns echoed to him across the sea as the leading ships opened fire on each other, but Thomas did not heed it, concentrating as he was on the

Achille and the delicate question of how they would intercept each other. Closer and closer they came; close enough for a long shot? But no – that first broadside, delivered at leisure by unhurried gun captains, was too useful to give up. Closer yet. And now.

'Portside guns – fire.'

Almost before the command was spoken, the broadside roared out, and the *Daring* heeled to the recoil while the bitter smell of smoke drifted back to Thomas's nose. There were crashes from the *Achille*, and screams, and he saw splinters flying, and men going down. They were close enough now for him to see the captain of the Frenchman on his own quarterdeck, and to want, ridiculously, to wave to him. And another thing to notice – blue-coated snipers up in the rigging of the French ship. Then came the French broadside, deep orange flashes spouting from the mouths of her guns, followed a moment later by the flattened boom of the sound. A crash from the *Daring*'s side and a strange howling noise somewhere close behind him told him of the passage of two shots.

'Their guns won't bear, sir,' Mr Wallis said excitedly. 'Only half a dozen shots told.'

The thunder of *Daring*'s second broadside drowned anything further he might have to say.

'Hands to the braces,' Thomas shouted. 'Ready to go about.'

The *Daring* whirled round and ran down the port side of the *Achille*, delivering shot after shot into her blind hull. Not a gunport was open on that side, not a shot was returned, and the damage inflicted was enough, Thomas hoped, to level the odds. He tacked again, and came across her stern, battering it shapeless, but now the utmost of the advantage had been taken. Now he would have to bear the *Achille*'s fire in return. Her broadside came, ragged but terrible, shots crashing into the *Daring*, men screaming, men lying dead. One of the maindeck guns was blown off its carriage, and a man was trapped underneath it, shrieking wildly with the pain. Another broadside from *Daring*, another from *Achille*, and a high-pitched whistling made him duck as one of the stays parted and the severed end snapped through the air like a whip. A wild cry told him some wretch had not ducked quickly enough.

'They're aiming high, sir,' said Wallis, at his elbow. 'They're trying to—'

He stopped in mid-sentence, and Thomas turned to look at him. He was staring in what looked like surprise, straight ahead of him; then he crumpled gently to the deck, shot through the heart. Thomas had forgotten the French snipers in the crosstrees. William had crouched down to examine him, and Thomas snapped his fingers to two of the starboard-side guns crews, standing ready while their guns were not in use.

'You two men, take Mr Wallis below. Quartermaster, let her pay off a point. Mr Morland, my compliments to Mr Harris, and will he step up here in Mr Wallis's place.'

William dashed away on his errand. It was growing dark – or no, perhaps not. It was just the great pall of smoke drifting up and across them from the battling ships. The din was huge and continuous, so that it ceased to be a noise at all. Before and behind Thomas ships were engaged, firing broadsides into each other, dealing out death and destruction. He saw the *Minotaur* drift past him, her foremast down, severed six feet above the deck and trailing a mess of wreckage over the side, while men tried to clear it away with axes. Here came Harris, his face blackened with powder so that his teeth gleamed strangely white.

And then, chaos. Out of the pall of smoke on his disengaged side another broadside was delivered; one of the French ships from further back in the line had come up on the other side of him. A crash, a hideous groaning creak, and the mizzenmast swayed and then fell, bringing the main topmast with it. It was like the heavens falling in, noise, confusion, screaming. Thomas saw a man fall past him out of the rigging into the sea. And then as the mass of the wreckage turned the *Daring* as if she were on a pivot the *Achille* fired again, into *Daring*'s bow, aiming upwards. A shot from one of her maindeck guns came through the taffrail, spraying splinters outward in every direction, but Thomas had only time to receive a vague impression of something black flying at him, very fast. It struck him in the chest, killing him instantly, smashing his body backwards, taking one of the quartermasters and part of the wheel with it, and ended its flight by crashing into the raised poop.

William, about to step back onto the quarterdeck, saw it happen, and yet could not take it in. With her wheel gone and the mizzenmast trailing over the side, the *Daring* was out of control. Her bow collided with the *Achille*'s, snapping off both bowsprits, and she drifted on down to leeward, out of range of the guns, out of the battle and the bitter smoke, until, with the ceasing of her own guns' fire, it became quiet enough to hear the screams and groans of the wounded.

'Axemen, here! Mr Dunmow, fetch a party of axemen to cut away this rigging. Secure the guns. Mr MacArthur, get the carpenter up here as fast as you can, see what can be done about repairing this wheel. Mr Morland, take a party up the mainmast and clear away that fallen topmast.'

This was Mr Harris, taking command as was his duty, giving sharp orders for getting the ship under control again. William shook his head to clear it, and turned away automatically to obey, taking his eyes at last from the unrecognizable red mess under the poop at which he had been staring. Everything around him seemed clear but far away, as if seen through the wrong end of the telescope; a sense of unreality pervaded him, and it was better to allow it to have its way, to let himself think this was all a strange, mad, horrible dream. Later would be time enough for acknowledging reality.

All day the battle raged, and from the top of Cape Charles, Charles and his neighbour watched in fascinated horror. At sunset, when the sea and sky seemed dyed with blood, the firing grew scattered, and ceased, and the two battered fleets drew apart again, drifted slowly out of range, and hove to, to lick their wounds. Both fleets were badly mauled. No ship had sunk, no colour had struck, no side had won or lost. The two men returned to their pinnace in absolute silence, all their excitement gone. There seemed nothing to say. They got her under sail, and came around the point to see if there were any survivors to be picked up, for there had certainly been men in the water at various points of the battle. They found only one, a seaman who had managed to swim to the shore but had been unable to haul himself out of the water, for the shore was high and rocky. He was hanging wearily, almost unconscious with fatigue and cold, to a ledge just round the point.

It was impossible to get the pinnace close enough in to pick him up, and Charles in the end had to strip off his outer clothes and go in. It took some doing to prise the man away from his handhold, and swim him back to the pinnace, where ready hands hauled them both back on board and rubbed them down and hung coats about them. The rescued man relapsed into unconsciousness, and Charles, after swallowing a large amount of brandy, dozed fitfully under the thwarts as Tomkin sailed him homewards.

'Well, that's that,' he heard Tomkin say. 'The British won't try that again, and without the navy to back them up, the army won't have a hope of holding Yorktown. I reckon we might have seen the end of the war out there today.'

They might learn some more from the sailor they had picked up, Charles thought, if he ever regained consciousness. He wondered if Thomas had been out there today, if he had taken part in the battle, if he had been wounded. But he mustn't think of that. America was no longer a part of Britain, and he was no longer a part of the Morland Family. He must make up his mind to it, and make the best of the situation, and learn to stand alone, just as America would have to, from now on.

*

For three days the battered fleets lay within sight of each other while they cleared away wreckage, fitted jury-rigging, plugged shotholes, tended the wounded, and buried the dead. So many dead, a long, long line of them on every deck, to be sewed into the hammocks and slipped overboard. And on the fourth day sails appeared on the horizon and the Rhode Island fleet came into sight, arriving at last to reinforce the French. At the sight of the new ships, Graves gave the signal to withdraw. The French fleet retired into the shelter of the Bay to refit properly, and the British fleet limped away northwards to the safety of loyal New York harbour.

The *Daring* took her place in the line, carrying sail gingerly on a spare mainyard, fished to the stump of the mizzenmast, with Lieutenant Harris temporarily in command. In New York she was docked for repairs, but supplies were in such short order, and such high demand, that she was still far from refitted when the news arrived that on 19 October General Cornwallis, having suffered heavy losses in the siege of Yorktown, had been forced to surrender, four years after the surrender at Saratoga. Coming on top of the disaster of the naval battle, it seemed like the final blow. William, writing a difficult letter home, to tell of Thomas's death, added, 'We all feel that this must be the end. It is impossible to win a war under these conditions. Unless we make peace, there can only be further loss, and God knows we have lost enough.'

William felt his lip tremble as he wrote those words, and he laid down his pen for a moment, and put his face in his hands. He had been sleeping badly since the battle, for every time he closed his eyes the image was waiting there for him of Thomas, smashed to a red smear by the flying cannonball. If there was peace, he would probably be sent home again. He would like to see his home again. He thought of Morland Place, and could bring no image of it to his mind, but a general sense of greenness and quietness. He thought he would sleep better, with the silence of fields around him.

He picked up his pen again to write a little more, and to express his desire of going home, and seeing his mother and father again. Yet in the back of his mind, too deep to need acknowledging, was the awareness that when the green fields had healed him he would want to go back to sea again. He was a sailor, first, last, and always.

CHAPTER FOURTEEN

It was Jemima who met the stagecoach that brought Flora back from London at the beginning of November. It was a raw, dark day, drizzling rain, and clouds so low that they hung like wet rags about the tops of the tallest trees, and Jemima was glad to stay inside the Hare and Heather by the parlour fire until she heard the horn. Then she pulled her cloak about her and hurried outside to watch the six white horses approaching at a brisk trot. Childish though it was, she never quite lost the thrill of excitement at seeing the heavily-laden coach come into sight, hinting of travel and adventure and news from foreign parts. When she was a little child, her brothers had sometimes taken her down to the road to see the coach from London – though in those days the roads were so bad that the horses never went out of a walk. Well, now she was nearly fifty and had more grey hairs than she liked to count, and had seen all she wanted of foreign places, but still she clasped her hands inside her muff and felt her lips curve into a smile as the cumbersome, swaying vehicle drew into the inn yard.

It was a smile she banished hastily as Abel ran forward to let down the step, and helped out the small figure in heavy mourning. Flora seemed somehow frail in her burden of black, and she seemed to totter a little in the thick mizzle as Abel released her arm. Her maid Joan had scrambled out after her and was pointing out the boxes to the coachman as Jemima hastened forward to claim her.

'Flora, my dear child! My poor dear, you must be perished.'

She held out both hands and Flora's, in black kid, rested in them. Her veil was up, and Jemima observed the white, strained face and the blank stare of the eyes, and the back of her mind registered a small relief that Flora was so properly distressed at the news of her husband's death.

'Jemima – I didn't – I wondered if anyone would meet me,' Flora said vaguely. Jemima drew Flora's arm through hers and led her towards the waiting chaise to the side of the yard.

'But of course. Allen wanted to come, but he is suffering from really such a dreadful rheum that I had positively to forbid him to stir from the fire. So I came myself. Here is the carriage, waiting – we shall soon be home. My poor darling, you must have had a dreadful time of it. Such a long journey, too, by stagecoach! I really wonder that you did not come post. I am sure the Chelmsfords—'

'Yes,' Flora said abruptly. 'They offered to send me post but – I would not.'

Jemima drew breath to ask why, and then let it out again in silence. Flora would speak in her own time. She was obviously not inclined for speech now. Jemima settled her in the coach, saw that the boxes were being brought, and got in herself, with Joan following. In a few moments the coachman cracked his whip, the carriage lurched and then rolled smoothly forward as the two horses broke into a restrained trot. Flora gave a long, exhausted sigh and sank back into the corner of the seat.

'Oh, I am tired to death,' she said, and spoke no more on the journey home. Morland Place looked to Jemima extra-specially welcoming on such a grey, unpleasant day, with the beacon light in the barbican already lit and yellowly glowing, and a flag of smoke rising from the chimneys, promising glorious crackling fires, warmth and food and comfort. She leaned her face to the cold side-glass to watch it approaching, feeling her love for it swell inside her as it always did, even when she had been away only a few hours. It was home, with all that that lovely word implied, but more than that it was her kingdom, her heritage, her pride. She had served it and protected it and belonged to it for so many years, had so nearly lost it, and now was come to the golden harvest years when everything was being repaid. There was her husband, whom she loved, whose love and trust and confidence made them as close as two human souls can be, and her children growing up around her, and her happy household, and the estate growing fruitful and properous; it was hard to remember not to smile, sad to see the contrast between her own contented state and that of the poor bewildered creature beside her.

Oxhey opened the great door as soon as the carriage came into the yard, and Esther was waiting in the hall to help Joan take off the ladies' cloaks, and here was Allen, coming through from the drawing room to meet them, and gesturing back the others who were following, realizing that Flora would not want to have a crowd about her. Now here was something to give Jemima a twinge of anxiety, when she saw how white-faced her husband was, and heard how little voice he had left. His rheum had gone to his throat and chest, and he had lost his voice and gained an exhausting cough, and he should have been in bed these two days past, but he was always so stubborn about it, saying he had too much to do to lie abed.

'Flora, my dear,' he said – or rather croaked – 'welcome home. You know that you have our deepest sympathy.' He took her hands and kissed her on both cheeks, and continued, 'There is a good fire made up in the West Bedroom, and Joan shall take you up straight away, so that you can rest and compose yourself. Is there anything in your luggage you need immediately?'

'No – thank you. I have what I need in my bag,' Flora said with an obvious effort.

'Very well then. We shall see you at supper, I hope.'

He took Jemima's hand and pressed it warningly as Flora turned away, and when she had disappeared upstairs, he said, 'I thought she would not want to be amongst us at first. It must be a difficult moment for her, coming home.'

'I was going to take her to the fire to warm herself,' Jemima said, and he shook his head.

'Too many eyes upon her,' he replied, and broke into another bout of coughing, so that Jemima grew almost angry.

'You are very solicitous for others, and I wish you would do the same for yourself. Dearest, won't you *please* go to bed? Look how tired and pale you are. It distresses me to see it.'

He drew her hand through his arm and walked towards the drawing room. 'After supper, I will go. But I want to be here if Flora comes down. I'm well enough, my dear. You suffer more than I do from my symptoms.'

In the drawing room Mary, who had been the most eager to greet her cousin, pouted crossly at the news that Flora had gone to her room; James, who remembered her with affection always as his childhood protectress, merely shrugged and went back to his sketching, at which he was developing quite a talent. Edward was not yet home from Oxford, and Harry, Lucy and Jack were in the nursery, but Louisa had hoped to see her mother, and was waiting with a mixture of eagerness and apprehension that touched Jemima. She was in heavy mourning, of course, for her father, whom she did not remember at all, and Jemima thought it looked strange on a little girl of seven. She explained to her that her mother had gone to her room, and watched Louisa absorb it along with all the other disappointments of life with a childish philosophy. Then Allen resumed his seat by the fire, and having asked and received permission by the exchange of a glance, the little girl scrambled onto his lap and settled happily into her accustomed haven.

In her room, Flora submitted to the ministrations of Joan, and as soon as she reasonably could, dismissed her. Once alone she gave a sigh of relief, and walked over to the windowseat, and sat down to stare out at the grey world and think. Her impulse to come back to Morland Place had been an instinctive one of flight, but she was not sure, now that she was here, that it had been such a sensible thing. There was too much to remind her at Morland Place, too much to accuse her.

Here in this very room she had grown up; sitting on this windowseat and gazing out of this window she had spun her silly romantic dreams, had fixed upon Thomas as their object, persuaded herself that she was in love with him, longed so hard to marry him that she had carried the matter by her own will alone. Without her efforts would he ever have noticed her, beyond his pretty young cousin beginning to grow up? He had married her because *she* wanted it, and what had she done but bring him pain?

Oh, she could find excuses for herself. She could say that he had not been forced to marry her; that as he was considerably older than her, he ought to have been responsible for himself; that she was too young to know what she was about. She could cry out, passionately, inside herself that she had done no actual wrong, that she had committed no crime, that she had not been unfaithful to him, in the physical sense. But none of that was any good. Married to him, she had fallen in love with another man; she had been false to him in her heart and, worse, had never much cared about it, until the news of his death had brought it home to her.

Thomas, dead – killed by a cannonball in action. Thomas, kindly smiling Thomas, her childhood's hero, father of her children. And oh, her children! Here was fresh fuel for grief and guilt. She had been at Chelmsford House – where else? – when they brought the news. She remembered the quiet commotion of it, when no one could decide who should be the one actually to tell her. Then Charles had come to her, held her hands, looked so seriously and carefully into her face to prepare her – as if anything could be apt preparation for such news. And then, confusion, shock, bewilderment, and guilt. Charles, then and in later interviews, telling her that she must not blame herself, that there was nothing to feel guilty about; Charles, saddened by Thomas's death, yes, really saddened, and yet unable to hide his joy and hope that now they could really be together.

'Are you mad?' she had cried. 'How can I marry you? How can you even suggest it?'

'Oh, not now, this minute, of course,' Charles had said hastily. 'Of course there must be a proper period of mourning, but when that is over, I can claim you honestly and openly as I have always wanted to.'

And racked with guilt she had denied him, abused his callousness, and he had tried to persuade her.

'We have done nothing wrong. We have not contrived his death – not even wished it. Yes, I can truly say that, that I never wished him harm, and I know that you can say the same. But Fate has freed us, for each other. Why should we refuse what Fate offers us?'

'*Everyone* knows!' she had cried hysterically. 'If I marry you now, they will talk. They will always be whispering, staring at us and whispering. Oh, I have been so wrong! I cannot bear to think about it.'

And she remembered now also the last interview, when with the calmness of exhaustion and grief upon her she had told him in a voice that allowed no argument that she was going home to Morland Place.

'For how long?' he asked. 'You must not stay too long away.'

'I shall never come back,' she said. 'I shall never see you again.'

She held him with her eye, so that he should not plead with her, and in the end all he said was, 'But I love you.'

She fought against tears then. 'I love you, too. But I can never be with you again.'

So she had fled home, refusing even to allow them to send her post, for the greater scourging of her soul. The long, cold, uncomfortable journey had passed like a bad dream, and now here she was at Morland Place, in her own bedroom, where every evidence of kindness – the good fire waiting for her, the hot water ready in the silver ewer, Allen's understanding of her need to be alone,

Jemima's warm and sympathetic smile – reopened the wounds of guilt and injured self-esteem.

She did not go down to supper. Like an animal, she hid in her burrow. Alone, she went over and over the same train of thought, and wept until grief exhausted her, then slept, and woke to repeat the process. And every day, as the year shortened into darkness, her heart cried, senselessly, after Charles, longed for him as unheedingly as a dog whining at the door; and, like a dog, could not be comforted or explained to.

Edward came home for Christmas, and Jemima discovered all over again what a satisfactory young man he was making. At nineteen he had become steady, sensible, kindly, mature, a person she felt at once she could trust and confide in. He will be like his father, she thought, and there was great satisfaction in the idea.

Allen was still in bed, nursing his cough, but mending now, so Jemima had her son to herself the first evening, and they sat up late when the others had gone to bed, talking. It was natural for her to discuss Flora with him.

'She still keeps to her room, and when she does come out, she is so silent, and looks so pale and drawn,' she said. 'I must admit that at first I was a little relieved that she had such proper feelings, because, you know, I have had doubts once or twice whether it had been such a good idea for her to marry so young – but now, she looks so uncomfortable, I wish she could begin to get over it. Do you think you could persuade her to leave her room? You have probably seen more of her in the past few years than we have. She might regard you as less of a stranger.'

'I could try,' Edward said doubtfully. 'If she will see me tomorrow, I will do what I can – but she may not want to see me. I might remind her of too many things.' There was a silence, while Jemima wondered whether to ask him what things, and then he said, 'Has she had any letters, since she came back? Has she heard from Charles – Lord Meldon?'

A surge of relief came over Jemima that the subject had been broached. 'Oh Edward, what do you know about that – situation?'

Edward looked at her consideringly, his head cocked a little, and he looked so like his father for a moment that she wanted to hug him. 'Little enough, though perhaps more than you. It was never as bad as you have probably thought, Mother. There was talk – inevitably – but they behaved in public—' he hesitated, seeking the right words – 'not improperly, in the strict sense, though they displayed more intimacy than society allows between two people not married to each other. But it was more the intimacy of brother and sister. They were very close.'

'Were they lovers?'

'I think – not,' Edward said deliberately. 'Has she had letters from him?'

'She has had letters, but since I did not examine them before they went up, I cannot tell if they were from Lord Meldon,' Jemima said. Edward grinned suddenly.

'Mother, you are a truer gentleman than most of the gentlemen I know. Anyone else would at least have looked at the handwriting.' Jemima blushed at the compliment, and Edward went on, 'Well, I shall see if she will receive me tomorrow. She may be glad to talk to someone who knows a little of what was happening.'

'And talking of gentlemen,' Jemima said, 'what of your friend Chetwyn? We thought you would spend Christmas at Wolvercote again this year, and I was so pleased when I heard you were coming home.'

'Chetwyn is gone to Venice, for the carnival, as the start of his Grand Tour,' Edward said a little abruptly. 'He will be gone two years at least.'

'I see,' Jemima said. 'That will be pleasant for him. Will he—'

'Mother, I want to talk to you about Oxford,' Edward

288

interrupted her. 'I want to ask you if you would mind if I did not take my degree.'

'Well, I—'

'The fact is that I'd like to leave Christ Church. I'm not really learning anything there, and I feel it's a waste of my time and your money.'

'Taking the degree isn't of the first importance,' Jemima said cautiously, 'but it is meant to be of use to you, in making you the right sort of friends, and introducing you to society.'

Edward smiled ironically. 'I don't really have any close friends there, except Chetwyn. And besides, I can't believe that that sort of society is going to be much use to me in the future. My life lies here, Mother, at Morland Place, and I'd be far better employed learning about the estate and the business, and taking over from Papa. Now don't you think so?

'Are you unhappy at Oxford?' she asked, and he shrugged.

'No, not unhappy. I enjoy it really. But it is a waste of time, as far as I can see. I am the heir, Mother, and I should be here.'

'Well, my darling, I should love to have you here, of course, and I have no particular wish for you to finish your course at Oxford, if you don't want to be there. As long as you are sure—'

'Quite sure.'

'Then we shall ask your father tomorrow, and see what he says. There is certainly always more to do about the place than we can easily manage, and to tell the truth, I'd be glad to have you take some of the strain from him. He has not been well this winter, and though he keeps so hale and hearty as a rule, he is well past sixty, and I'm sure he made himself ill with doing too much. But for heaven's sake, don't press that as your reason for wanting to leave Oxford.'

'Trust me,' Edward smiled. 'No, I shall say the truth,

that I want to come home, and have nothing to keep me at Oxford now.'

'Won't you miss it at all?' she asked curiously. There was a shadow in his eyes for a moment as he answered.

'No, there is nothing there for me now.' But the shadow passed as quickly as it came, and she felt no invitation from him to pursue it. And he went on in a perfectly cheerful voice, 'Now what of Mary's affairs? Tell me the latest development. Is my friend Anstey still leading the field, or have the outsiders made ground?'

Jemima laughed. 'Whatever you do, don't speak in those terms when she's about, or there will be terrible storms. It's bad enough to have James teasing her, though I must say she's such a little popinjay I can hardly blame him. But he gets her into such a passion, and stays so cool and calm himself! That boy is so wicked.'

'He takes after you, Mama, it must be so,' Edward said.

'Now don't believe the stories your father tells about me,' she retorted. 'He only does it to tease.'

Mary's preference for her childhood knight, John Anstey, had grown so marked over the past year that Jemima was not at all surprised to receive an invitation to dinner with Sir John and Lady Anstey which pretty well necessitated a return invitation to dine and spend the day at Morland Place.

Sir John was in the coal way, a trade which had increased so enormously in the past twenty years that the Ansteys were rising rapidly in the world, and they were in the process of moving from their shabby old house on Skeldergate, handy for Queen's Staith where the coal barges unloaded, to a new house being built for them by John Carr on the Lendal, handy for the Assembly Rooms and the Mansion House.

Sir John had stood for Parliament, had been presented at Court, and knighted for his trouble, and was altogether a modern man and in a state of as much improvement as his fortune. Lady Anstey, on the other hand, was in the older style, a large, motherly woman, comfortably rather than fashionably dressed, who could neither read nor write, and had no conversation beyond her children and her servants. After the dinner in Skeldergate, when the ground was tested and the air snuffed by the Ansteys, a fine spell of weather persuaded Jemima to issue the return invitation without delay, and so at noon on the shortest day the massive Anstey coach rolled into the yard bearing Sir John and Lady Anstey, young John, and the next two eldest children, Alfred who was seventeen, and Augusta, who was sixteen.

The weather was fine enough and the ground dry enough for Jemima to suggest a walk in the gardens before dinner, and the four parents made a leisurely circuit or two while the young people were borne away by Edward and Mary for more vigorous exercise. The nursery maids followed at a distance with the youngest children, under Allen's instructions that they must have some fresh air every day unless it positively rained, while James, poised as always between the beginning and the end of the family, disappeared about his own mysterious business.

They dined at two, for they kept early hours except on special celebrations, and the Ansteys were used to it. Flora went so far as to appear for the meal, though she did not speak, and excused herself after desserts. After dinner, the whole party removed to the long gallery, and there remained pleasantly occupied until tea, the older people sitting about the fire and talking, the younger ones grouped about the harpsichord while Mary and Augusta played and sang, the little children playing quietly under Alison's eye.

Allen and Sir John discussed politics for a while, until the subject sank them quite naturally into silence, and Jemima, knowing what the next thing to be discussed would be, looked down the room to where Mary was seated at the harpsichord, accompanying herself in a pretty, old-fashioned song. It was a graceful performance, for Mary knew what she could do well, and polished her accomplishments to make the best of them, and did not attempt what she knew was beyond her.

But today she was looking more than usually pretty, in a dress of grey-blue that made her eyes look bluer. It had deep ruffles at neck, waist, and hem, and a deep square décolletage, filled in with a neckerchief of snowy muslin, against which her dark ringlets curled softly, making a picture both simple and effective. She really *was* pretty, Jemima thought with pleasure, and noticed that there was more colour than usual in her daughter's cheek, and that her eyes were very bright as she looked up for a moment at John Anstey, who was leaning on the harpsichord with eyes for nothing but Mary's face, and probably not hearing a word of the song she was singing.

'Well, Sir Allen, well ma'am,' Sir John said, and cleared his throat to indicate that their attention was required for what followed. 'A pretty picture we see yonder, don't you think? And I don't know where you'll find a prettier picture than Miss Mary, not if you search all England for a twelvemonth.'

Allen shot one quick, smiling glance at Jemima, and she replied for them both.

'Thank you, Sir John. She has grown exceedingly pretty of late, I must own.'

'Aye, and I'm not the only one to notice it,' he said, smiling and nodding. 'Though of course, my boy John has had the same idea in his head since the first time he came to Morland Place to visit. It's no secret, ma'am, that he has always had a tender spot for your daughter.'

'Indeed, sir,' Jemima replied, going along with the play, 'and his constancy does his heart credit, I'm sure.'

Sir John nodded again, looked from Jemima to Allen and back, and then got to the point as he was accustomed to do in business.

'Well then, ma'am, what d'ye say to a match between

'em? It's been in the wind this twelvemonth, and I don't suppose you'll be surprised to learn that my John has come to me and asked right out if I will speak to you and Sir Allen, and apply to make the business official. Now then, what d'ye say to't? I know Sir Allen well enough to know we sha'n't quarrel about terms. Everything open, and handsome, that's my way. I can't abide to be paltry, and secrecy serves no-one but the Dark Gentleman, I always say.'

'I agree with you entirely, Sir John,' Jemima said, suppressing her amusement, and giving Allen his cue in a glance. They had already discussed the matter of the match, well aware that it would be broached today.

'I have no objection to the match in principle,' Allen said, 'provided you are in agreement and the young people like it. We have known John for a very long time, and he is a good, steady young man, and I'm sure will do well. And as you say, I'm sure we shall not quarrel about terms.'

These of course were not the words Jemima and Allen had used when talking privately to each other about the matter. Jemima had said that the boy was steady, and would be good for Mary, if he could control her, and Allen had said that Sir John and Lady Anstey were not elegant people, and their company would add little to the enjoyment of family parties, but they were perfectly good, decent sorts, and one could not object to them, if it was what Mary wanted.

'Well then, sir,' Sir John prompted, while Lady Anstey beamed at what she thought was the conclusion of the matter.

'But I do feel,' Allen went on, 'that Mary is still a little young to be marrying – she is but seventeen.'

'Many's a lass marries younger than that,' Sir John put in. 'Sixteen or even fifteen is old enough. Marry 'em quick, before they get notions into their heads, that's my policy. Our Augusta is to be engaged next year, certain sure.'

'All the same, sir,' Allen said firmly, 'we are willing to agree to an engagement between them, and for the marriage to take place when Mary is eighteen.'

Sir John was not a moment in thinking about it. 'Right enough,' he said heartily, holding out his hand. 'So be it. Here's my hand on it, sir, and right gladly.'

Allen shook his hand, and said, 'We shall speak to Mary tonight, but I think we should say nothing now, lest we embarrass her in front of the other young people. May I ride into York tomorrow, sir, and discuss the settlement with you?'

'Certainly, certainly, whatever you say, Sir Allen. She's a right pretty little maid, is Miss Mary, and my John worships her, you can see that. It'll be a pretty match, and a credit to all, I'm sure of it.'

And looking at Mary's face as she sang to John Anstey, Jemima said, 'I am too, Sir John.'

That evening Jemima went in to the East Bedroom, which Mary shared with Louisa, to speak to her about the engagement. The East Bedroom was often called the Red Room, because the hangings were all of a heavy red damask. It was not a bedroom Jemima had ever liked much, finding it rather gloomy and sombre for her taste. In the early years of her marriage Uncle George had had it, and it seemed to her too masculine a room for two young girls. But Mary seemed to like it, relishing the space after sharing the nursery so long, and there was ample room for her to share with Louisa without minding, and for Lucy later to come in with them, if Flora was still using the West Room by the time Lucy grew too big for the nursery.

Louisa was already asleep, so Jemima could have privacy with Mary, and as she found her daughter brushing her hair before the glass, she stood behind her and took the brush from her hand, and took over the task. Mary submitted, gazing at her reflection with a half-smile on her lips, evidently deep in some daydream, as Jemima drew the brush through the long, soft curls and turned them round her fingers.

'You looked very pretty tonight, my dear,' she said at last. Mary did not answer, only intensified the little secret smile with which she regarded herself. Jemima watched her with some curiosity. She had never really felt close to Mary, never understood her, or had any very personal affection for her; but still it was gratifying to have raised something as attractive as Mary, and to have the means of making her happy now with the news.

'While you were playing the harpsichord, Sir John Anstey was saying something very particular to us,' Jemima went on. 'Would it surprise you to know what it was?'

She smiled at Mary's reflection in the mirror, and Mary's attention came back from some distance, and she met her eyes with an expression of inquiry.

'Sir John was telling us that young John has asked permission to apply formally for your hand in marriage.' Mary's expression did not at once show the pleasure Jemima expected – indeed, she looked surprised – and she went on, 'It was very proper of him to approach the matter in that way, though you may think it unromantic. But believe me, it shows him to be a very steady young man, with a proper regard for your comfort and propriety, and no doubt he will say all the right romantic things when he has permission to approach you.'

Mary jumped up so abruptly that the hairbrush was knocked from Jemima's hand and flew across the room to clatter against the foot of the bedstead.

'What? What is it you are saying, Mother?'

'Mary, my dear!' Jemima protested mildly. 'I am saying that John Anstey has asked for your hand in marriage, and your father and I have agreed that you may become engaged to him, and marry next year when you are eighteen.'

Mary's face slowly darkened with anger, to Jemima's astonishment.

'Without even asking me?' she cried in evident fury. 'You agreed to that without even asking me?'

The noises had woken Louisa, who raised herself sleepily on one elbow and said, 'What is it? What is wrong? Mama—?'

'Hush, Louisa, all's well. Go back to sleep, sweetheart,' Jemima said hastily, and went across the room to quiet her. When she returned she gestured Mary to be quiet and drew her aside to sit on the edge of the bed.

'Now then, Mary, please speak quietly, and tell me what is the matter. John did quite right to ask formal permission first, but I'm sure you and he had already come to an understanding—'

'Then you thought wrong!' Mary hissed angrily. Jemima coloured.

'You will not speak to me like that, Mary. I won't tolerate insolence.'

'What right had you to go engaging me to John Ansty?' Mary went on, too upset even to heed the rebuke. 'I don't want to marry him.'

'But – but we have all seen how fond you are of him. Of course, years ago, it was only a joke, but this last year, you have seemed to be growing in love with him. Surely we could not have been mistaken?'

Mary rubbed her face with her hands in what was for her a touchingly unstudied gesture, and she said more quietly, 'No – yes – oh, I don't know. I am fond of him, of course. I think perhaps I even love him. But I don't want to marry him. Please, Mother, don't make me marry him.'

Jemima was taken aback. 'Child, of course I wouldn't make you marry anyone against your will. God knows, I suffered enough myself from an arranged marriage. I should not have agreed to it at all, had I not thought – as your father did too – that you loved the boy. But you shall not marry against your will.'

'Promise me!'

'I promise, of course.' Jemima bit her lip. 'But tell me, child, what is it you object to?'

'Oh Mother, he's so *common!* I couldn't marry him – his father's a coal merchant. And his mother – I'd be ashamed to call her mother. I know John is a nice boy – I like him very much – and I know he's fond of me – but really, Mother, I'm not so desperate as to have to take him!'

Jemima now bit her lips, in an effort not to laugh, even though inside she was angry too. But she said, 'I can't understand you, Mary. Where could you get such ideas? The Ansteys are not elegant people, but they are good folk, and John is well educated, and will be rich—'

'He will be nobody! To think that I should be a mere Mrs Anstey!' and she made an indescribable sound of disgust. Jemima began to see the light.

'When you would sooner be Lady Something, I suppose, or the Countess of Somewhere?'

'Well, why not?' Mary said crossly. 'I am pretty enough, and I don't see why I should waste myself. Your mother was a duke's sister—'

'Mary, I'm ashamed of you,' Jemima said. 'I should have thought that you would have learnt better than that, even if only from the stories of my marriage to an earl. The ten years of my life when I was a Countess were utterly miserable. A title does not necessarily bring either happiness or respectability. A man's character is what is important, not his rank. I don't understand you—'

'No, why should you?' Mary said, colouring. 'You never cared for me, I know that well enough. One of your horses meant more to you than I ever did. It was Charlotte you loved. You took her about with you while you left me to the servants. Well, they've brought me up with a proper understanding of my expectations. I can easily get a lord, if I wait. I don't see why I should take any tradesman's son who asks for me.'

Jemima stood up, feeling brittle with anger, and sadness

that she had failed so badly with this daughter. 'That's enough,' she said quietly, but firmly. 'You are upset, and there is no point in discussing this matter further tonight. In the morning your father shall speak to you about John Anstey.'

'I shan't change my mind,' Mary said sulkily. 'And you promised—'

'No, I should not want to force you to marry against your will. If you are adamant, your father shall speak to Sir John at once. But I hope he may be able to improve your principles somewhat. And now, goodnight.'

Edward and Allen were together, discussing farming, when Jemima, looking as ruffled as a pecked hen, found them in the steward's room, and told them what had happened. Edward smiled a little, but Allen shook his head and looked grave.

'I'm sorry to hear it,' he said. 'I'll talk to her, and see if I can't make her see sense.'

'I doubt if you will, Father,' Edward said. 'Not until she's past twenty-five and beginning to worry about being a spinster. With every young lad in York chasing after her, she's bound to have a high idea of her own consequence.'

'But Edward,' Jemima protested, 'all that business about marrying a lord! Sure, we did not teach her such ideas!'

'Oh Mother, all girls think like that. It comes of reading novels, and chattering to servants. They vie with each other, you know, as to who will get the best husband, in worldly terms. It isn't to be wondered at.'

'But with my example before her,' Jemima said, reaching instinctively for Allen's hand. Edward looked fondly at them both.

'I wouldn't be surprised if you weren't the real cause, Mother. You are so entirely and obviously happy with my father that it must dishearten everyone else, knowing they have little chance of being as happy as that.'

'Nonsense!' Jemima said firmly.

'And besides, our family has done so much mingling with titled people – the Chelmsfords and the Aylesburys and Christmas at Castle Howard, and Papa coming and going at Court as if it were his own parlour – poor Mary must feel she ought to have her share of the glitter and excitement.'

'Oh dear,' Jemima sighed, 'put like that—' Allen pressed her hand.

'She'll grow out of it, I'm sure. She's very young – and I'm not so sorry, really, that she doesn't want to marry John Anstey, for she might grow bored with him in a year or two, and that would be disastrous. In a few years' time she'll know how to value him, and be grateful.'

'I hope you're right,' Jemima said.

Edward startled them both by saying, 'I think she has her eye on Horatio Morland – she flirts with him terribly when he's here. But she'll be disappointed if that's what she wants, for young Horace has as firm an idea of his merits as she has of hers, and it'll be a titled woman for him or nothing. He wouldn't have *her* upon a wager.'

'Edward, dear,' Jemima protested, 'where can you have learned such vulgar language?'

Edward grinned. 'At Oxford, Mama. I told you it wasn't good for me. Now ain't you glad I'm leaving?'

Mary and Flora between them had thrown so much gloom over the family that it was only natural that the Christmas celebrations should be rather more subdued than usual. The Chelmsfords, probably from delicacy, did not come into the country, and the Fussells were away, and the Ansteys were a little hurt, so the Morlands had the season to themselves. Despite Mary's sulks and Flora's abstracted unhappiness, Jemima could not help being happy. Allen was over his illness and Edward was home for good and proving such a companion that she wondered how she had managed without him. She hunted vigorously every day, with Allen and Edward and James competing to outride her and never succeeding, and spent the rest of the day indoors, enjoying the company of her second family, her little Harry and Lucy, and Louisa and Jack who seemed no less her own, since their mother had left them to her from birth.

Harry was out of petticoats now and having lessons with Father Ramsay, which he was eager each day to recount to her, partly, she was sure, to tease Jack, who longed to catch up with his cousin, even if it meant being parted from Jemima for several hours a day – for Jack was as devoted to her as Louisa was to Allen. As for Lucy, she was three years old, and as pretty and chubby and good-natured and adorable as any baby ever was, and lived to be cuddled, and showed no remarkable talent except for getting astonishingly dirty in an amazingly short time, if ever one took one's eyes from her.

On Twelfth Night Edward managed to persuade Flora to come down and join the feast, saying that it would be unlucky for anyone to absent themselves; and as, at Jemima's command, even the littlest children dined at the table, there were twelve of them ranged along the dining room, with Father Ramsay, and Alison at the end between Lucy and Jack to stop them falling off their chairs or sticking their fingers in the gravy.

It was, as Twelfth Night should be, a pleasant mixture of the Christian and the pagan, with Father Ramsay and Allen saying Grace and the prayers, and the others joining in with various toasts and the old good-luck charms. Abram himself carried in the boar's head, wreathed in bay and rosemary, and was toasted with a bumper before he withdrew, red-faced and backwards, as if from the presence of royalty, which was more or less how he thought of Jemima anyway. Jack, as the youngest gentleman present, proposed the toast to the King, in which Edward had carefully coached him, so that except for an unfortunate tendency to giggle, he acquitted himself magnificently, and then Edward, with perhaps a little more sadness in his voice than was usual, proposed the toast to Absent Friends.

And as they all resumed their seats, a half-heard commotion outside resolved itself into a loud knocking at the great door, which so startled them, coming at that precise moment, that Jemima bit her tongue, and Alison crossed herself twice in quick succession.

'Now who on earth could that be?' Allen said, staring round them all as if for suggestions.

'The unexpected guest,' Edward said. 'The angel unawares that we are always to be prepared for. Well, it must be lucky, on Twelfth Night, the night of prophecy.'

'Edward, I wish you hadn't said that. Suppose it was bad news,' Jemima said.

'No, it means we shall have lots of unexpected visitors all year, you'll see,' Edward said quickly, and they all fell silent to listen to the sound of Oxhey going to open the door. Footsteps crossed the hall, and Oxhey appeared doubtfully in the doorway, but was gently pushed aside by a travel-stained figure, rather wild in expression, at the sight of whom Flora turned first red then pale.

'Charles – Lord Meldon – what are you doing here?' Allen asked for them all.

'Sir, forgive me for bursting upon you with no warning,' he said, having difficulty in keeping his eyes on Allen, when they so wanted to be on Flora. 'I have just arrived in the country – I rode from Oxford. I could not wait any longer, so I came straight here—'

His words were distracted, and Jemima said, 'I hope it is not bad news? I hope no one is ill?'

'Oh, madam, no – I am sorry if I have startled you. It was wrong of me, I know, to come like this. You will think me so strange—' He bit his lip.

Allen tried gently to gain his attention. 'Well, since you are here, and no one is ill, won't you join our feast? We

301

are got, as you see, to the dessert, but you are most welcome to join us for it.'

Charles made an obvious effort to pull himself together. He drew himself up, his hands clenched on his hat before him to the detriment of the brim, and said, 'You are more kind than I deserve, sir, and since you are so kind, I would make bold to ask something. You will think it strange, I know – but really – sir, would you, of your kindness, allow me a moment's private conversation with Mrs Morland – with Flora?'

There was a brief silence as Allen and Jemima exchanged a look, and Flora's face went from white to red again, and she lowered her gaze to the tablecloth. Allen looked at her to try to gauge her desires in the matter, and Charles added, 'I beg you, sir. I assure you that I would not ask if it were not important.'

'My dear young man,' Allen said, 'it must be as Flora wishes. My dear?' He looked towards her, and after a moment's hesitation she stood up and walked out of the room, looking neither to left nor right, her head very erect, like a queen walking to the scaffold. Charles bowed slightly to the company, and followed her, closing the door behind him.

In the drawing room Flora turned to face him, her eyes dangerously bright, but her face betraying no sign of whether she were angry, pleased, or unhappy at the sight of him.

'Forgive me,' he said at once. 'I had to come. You don't know how unhappy I have been all these weeks. I held out as long as I could, since it was what you said you wanted. But then – we were at Wolvercote, and every room spoke of you. All through Christmas, I was haunted by you. I saw you everywhere, I heard your voice – Flora, my own dear Flora—'

'What do you want?' Her voice shook so much even in such a short sentence that she knew she would not be able to attempt anything longer.

'I came to see if you might change your mind,' he said

simply. 'I understand how you felt – it was a terrible shock to me, too, but there is nothing in the world we can do to make it different now. And what purpose would it serve for us both to go on being unhappy? It won't bring him back, or make up to him for anything.'

She made no answer. It was impossible. He came a step nearer.

'We were so happy together – we can be again. I love you so much – I'll wait for you as long as you like, but please say you will marry me. Please, Flora, let us be together. I will never love anyone but you.'

Her teeth were so tightly clenched that she could make no sound but a peculiar little whimper, but he took it for an answer, and took the last step towards her, and put his arms round her trembling body.

'What is it? What is it?' he whispered.

'People – will talk—' she managed to say.

'Let 'em,' he said fiercely, holding her closer. 'What can they say to hurt us? We know the truth. And if they don't like to have us around, we'll live in the country, and it will be their loss, not ours. We don't need 'em – as long as we have each other. Say you will – say you will.'

'Oh Charles,' she whimpered, and he felt her tears hot and then cold on his cheek. 'I've missed you so much.'

His relief at the words was such that he thought he might fall. He held her tightly, and closed his eyes for a moment, and she clung to him, all her resistance at an end.

'It will be all right, you'll see,' he said at last. 'I'll make it all right. I'll speak to Sir Allen and Lady Morland, and everyone else, and explain it all, and it will be all right. We'll be happy together, and people will understand then.' She was crying faster than ever, and pity came to reinforce his love. 'I know,' he said, 'I know. But it was none of it your fault. It wasn't anyone's fault.'

BOOK THREE

The Salamander

We've trod the maze of error round,
Long wandering the winding glade;
And now the torch of truth is found,
It only shows us where we strayed:
By long experience taught, we know –
Can rightly judge of friends and foes;
Can all the worth of these allow,
And all the faults discern in those.

George Crabbe: *Late Wisdom*

CHAPTER FIFTEEN

A full year of mourning was what Allen proposed, and a complete separation until the six months' deep mourning was finished. 'After that, an occasional visit here would probably do no harm.'

Flora, standing as close to Lord Meldon as she could get, as if she feared he might be snatched away from her, looked horrified. 'Must we wait so long?' she said. Allen gave her a grim sort of smile.

'My dear Flora, I am in no position to insist on anything. You are over the age of consent, and may do as you please. I can only recommend to you what I think would be in your best interests.'

'In point of law that may be true, sir,' Meldon said. 'But Flora regards you and Lady Morland in the light of parents, and she and her children have their home with you. That gives your recommendations a certain weight.'

'Very well – then look,' Allen said. 'There has been talk about you – whether warranted or unwarranted. If Flora receives you at all while in deep mourning, the scandal will not die—'

'But when that is over—' Flora began eagerly, and Allen checked her with a shake of his head.

'Lord Meldon is a public figure, and there is the more reason to be careful. A full year's mourning is the minimum for propriety. Remember your children, Flora, and think what people might say about *them*, too.'

'If you love each other, you should be willing to wait for each other,' Jemima said. Lord Meldon bowed his head.

'I have waited for many years without hope – a year with hope will soon pass.'

Flora sighed, but consented. 'But you will write to me, Charles? May he not?'

'Of course,' Allen said. 'And now, we had better make arrangements for your departure.'

'At once?' Flora asked in a small voice.

'At once,' Allen said.

When they were alone together, Jemima said to her husband, 'I think he really loves her. After all, he is an eligible young man, and could have anyone.'

'But you have doubts about Flora?'

Jemima shook her head. 'I don't know. She seems in earnest, but then so she did about poor Thomas.'

'She was very young then. And she has had a much longer acquaintance with Meldon – enough, surely, to know how she feels for him?'

'We can only hope so. Allen, do you think we could have managed things better? I have wondered often whether we ought to have kept a better guard over her.'

'We cannot blame ourselves,' he said comfortingly. 'We could not, in the last analysis, actually prevent anything she wanted to do. And if it had not been for the war, Thomas would have been at home more, and none of this would have happened.'

'Perhaps you're right,' Jemima said. 'She has not had such an easy time of it, after all, with her husband never home, and then her brother going.' She mused a little. 'I wonder what did happen to Charles? Do you suppose he is still alive somewhere?'

Allen shook his head. 'I think if he had been alive he would have found some way to let us know.'

'Then should there not be some process of law, to declare him dead?'

'Fortunately, that is Angus's problem, not ours. As Charles gave him power of attorney before he went away, Angus is head of the family in law as well as in fact. And, who knows, he might have some means of communication that we have not. It will all come out, anyway, when the war ends.'

'When!' Jemima sighed. 'And then we shall have William back, perhaps. I wonder if we shall recognize him'

Allen put his arms round her and kissed her brow. 'Are you hankering to have your children back, Lady Morland? Haven't you got enough to occupy you? You can always give *me* more of your time, if you have nothing better to do.'

Jemima smiled at the idea. 'Only give me the opportunity,' she said. And then, 'How curious!'

'What is, my love?'

'I have just thought – if Flora marries Lord Meldon, she will be Countess of Chelmsford one day.'

'A sea captain's widow, Countess of Chelmsford,' Allen smiled, 'I wonder what Annunciata would have thought of that.'

Flora and Lord Meldon were married in October 1782 in Westminster, and left at once for Europe for a protracted wedding tour, in the hope that the scandal which had revived on their marriage would die from lack of sustenance if they were out of sight for long enough. Mary, to her great delight, went with them as bridal companion, though Jemima had been unsure as to the wisdom of allowing it. But Allen said, 'It will take her down a little, to find she cannot queen it over the world as she does over Yorkshire.'

Jemima, once she had accepted Allen's opinion, was quite glad to have her gone, for she had been fretting and complaining all year, longing for change and excitement and some more public exposure than was possible at the York Assembly Rooms. Her rejection of John Anstey had made their social life a little strained, and when, emboldened by the notion that she preferred him, Tom Loveday had also put in an application for her hand, and had it rejected, Jemima had begun to wonder if they would have any friends left at the end of another year.

'I just hope she doesn't elope with some Italian prince,' she said to Allen when she agreed to the wedding trip.

'I'll have a word with Meldon to keep an eye on her. He's a sensible young man, and I think Mary will discover that she has more rivals in the world than her experience at home has led her to expect. She has been used to being the prettiest girl in the West Riding, but by the time she comes back, she may be grateful for a John Anstey, or even his younger brother.' And seeing Jemima's sceptical look, he added with a grin, 'Besides, if she does run off with an Italian prince, our problem will be solved once and for all, won't it?'

But concern for Flora or for Mary were soon driven from Jemima's head, for Allen was summoned to St James's, and returned with the news that he, too, was to be taken away from her: the King required his services at the peace talks in Versailles. The war had drifted on inconclusively since the surrender of Yorktown, achieving nothing for either side, except that Admiral Rodney had had some successes in the West Indies which had strengthened the British hand a little. But there was no longer any question but that the Americans must be given their independence, and the discussions that were taking place at Versailles were to arrange the terms of the independence, and to settle the interesting questions of territory.

'Canada, Florida, the West Indian islands, access to the Mississippi – these are all vitally important,' Allen was told by Lord Shelburne, who, after the resignation of Lord North and the unexpected death of Rockingham, had become the head of the Government. 'These are matters to be decided between us and France, though naturally the American commissioners will want to feel that *they* are deciding.'

Allen nodded. 'Of course, my lord.'

'And then, the independence itself – a new young country, with no experience of government, is going to need a lot of guidance. I have strong hopes that we may still retain a measure of control over the Americans – in foreign policy, for instance. And the terms on which we conduct trade with them will be crucial to our control of their foreign alliances, as you will readily understand.'

'Yes, my lord.'

'Well, the other commissioners fully understand their position. Your part will be to use your knowledge of the French Court and the French ministers to establish relations, and to give the commissioners an understanding of the best way to proceed, and of course to persuade where persuasion is possible. It's a matter of some delicacy, but His Majesty has every confidence in you, Sir Allen. You are acquainted with Vergennes, I understand?'

'Yes, my lord.'

'Well, I'll tell you something that he won't – the French are deep in debt over this war. Their man Necker raised the money for it by taking loans, instead of raising the taxes, and that means capital and interest repayments that will hobble the French for years to come. They'll be far more eager for peace than we will, so that they can retire and lick their wounds, which means we can make demands with a certain confidence. We might come out of this dreadful business more comfortably than we could have hoped.'

'I understand, my lord.'

'I'm sure you do. Subtlety, tact – keep the Frogs guessing. You know your way around Versailles – use that knowledge, and His Majesty will be suitably grateful.'

'Yes, my lord,' said Allen.

'I wish you did not have to go,' Jemima said as she helped with the hasty packing of Allen's trunk for the journey. 'A sea-crossing in the middle of winter—'

'Yes,' he stopped her. 'But since it must be, there's no use repining. And I dare say His Majesty will be suitably grateful.'

Jemima snorted derision. 'What can he give you? Another title?'

Allen grinned at her sturdy contempt for the treasures

of this world. 'He might make me a baronet. But of course, you've been a countess in your time, and it would be nothing to you. Still, Edward might like to have a title to inherit.'

'Edward has more sense,' Jemima said robustly. 'And how glad I am, now, that he decided to leave Oxford. He will be a comfort to me while you are away. Oh Allen—' Her lip trembled as her resolve gave way for a moment, and he hastened to hold her.

'Now, my love,' he said. 'It won't be for long. A few months at the most.'

'Promise you'll come back as soon as you can?'

'Of course I will, simpleton.' She laughed at the address and went back to her packing.

'And when you come back,' she said, 'we shall have to get down to doing something serious about the servant problem. You really can't go away again without a proper trained manservant.' Oxhey, the butler, had looked so alarmed at the prospect of the journey that Allen had excused him and was to take the young footman Peter to attend him, but he had no one to teach him his duties except his master.

'I don't intend to be going away much after this,' Allen said soothingly.

'All the same, you'll be the only man in Versailles who has to tie his own necktie,' she grumbled.

'It will give me a kind of distinction,' Allen smiled.

The preliminary articles of the peace were signed on 30 November 1782, but all through the Christmas celebrations the talks went on in the background to prepare the first definitive treaty for signature in January. Had he not been an early riser and accustomed to hard work, Allen might have found himself without any time to enjoy being back in France, but as it was, he was able to renew old acquaintance, hunt in the forests, enjoy social gatherings, and even visit Paris.

It was strange to be back in Versailles, and it wove its old familiar spell around him, despite the years gone past, and the change of monarch. There were the extraordinary contrasts which he had forgotten – the stiff, formal etiquette on the surface, and the licentiousness underneath; the gilded furniture, the mirrors and crystal chandeliers, the carpets and rich hangings of the public rooms, compared with the cramped and unsanitary accommodation which many of the inmates endured; the fabulous clothes and jewels, the powdered wigs and bare bosoms and splendour of Court gatherings, and the flea-ridden servants, the bedbugs and cockroaches, the stinking privies, and heaps of ordure in corners.

But it was all part of the teeming, exotic life of the richest Court in the world, and Allen loved it, though he knew that it could only be tolerable as a relish, not as a constancy. As a commissioner sent from the King of England, he was given much better quarters than he had ever had before, and two Versailles servants were sent to attend him in addition to his own man, who, to his embarrassed surprise, was allotted a servant of his own. 'That's the way it is here,' Allen told him soothingly. 'At Versailles even the servants have servants.' The King – Louis XVI – received him kindly, though vaguely, as he seemed to do everything. He had none of the majesty of his glittering predecessors, and in his plain brown coat and wig, with his pop-eyes and fat kindly face, he looked more like a country lawyer than a king.

But the little Austrian queen, Marie-Antoinette, made up for it. Tiny, dainty, pretty, and dressed always in exquisite, frilled, and glittering splendour, she dashed about like a dragonfly from one pleasure to the next, gracing every occasion she presided over, filling the rooms of the fairytale palace with laughter and chatter. She had provided the King with a son and a daughter, her other children having died in infancy, and they had now reached a *modus vivendi* by which they went their own ways, but met on terms of affectionate respect.

313

Allen renewed his acquaintance with the King's sister, Madame Elisabeth, who was proving a good companion for the Queen, and his mad old aunts, and many of the courtiers of the previous age who had survived into the new reign. But the happiest of his reunions were with officers of the Royal Ecossais with whom he had served in his years of exile. At the house of the Maréchal Macdonald, he met a handsome young colonel of the new generation, a Colonel de Murphy, who was very eager to make his acquaintance, and hastened to invite him to a supper party at his house on the Rue St Anne on the following day.

'I shall have one or two interesting people for you to meet,' de Murphy told him. 'The de Lameth brothers will be there, and the Comte de Mirabeau has promised to look in on his way from the Palais Royale, so I think you will not lack amusement. My wife is very interested in the new ideas, sir, of the *philosophes* – you have come across them, perhaps?'

'I believe I understand you, sir,' Allen said. 'I have read Newton's *Principia*, and some of the work of John Locke. But I must say that I am a plain man, and too busy about the affairs of my estate to have leisure for philosophy.'

He and the Colonel met each other's eye with perfect understanding, and Meurice gave a wry smile.

'And I, sir, am a plain soldier. But—' a very Gallic shrug. Women must have their little fancies, it said.

When Allen was shown in to the drawing room on the appointed day at the appointed hour, he found that there were several other officers of his acquaintance present, some young people he had seen about Versailles, and also someone he had been half expecting to meet round every corner since his arrival. A tall man, dark-haired, blue-eyed, with a very Morland cast of features, growing a little heavy about the middle now – he must be, Allen made a quick calculation, thirty-five or -six – came forward eagerly to claim his acquaintance and attention with a hearty shake of the hand and a smile that Allen found a little disturbing, because it reminded him of Jemima.

'You are acquainted with Monsieur le Comte de Strathord,' said Meurice de Murphy in a tone halfway between question and statement. Allen bowed assent.

'Not so well as I would like,' Henri said. 'Our acquaintance has been – shall we say – oblique. But I hope we will make up for it now, sir.'

'I knew your grandmother very well,' Allen said, rather bemused. Marie-Louise's child, he thought to himself; the Princess's baby, whom I brought here myself, before he was weaned, a little, mewling, orphaned scrap of an infant; now grown to this large and well-fed and – to judge from his clothes – wealthy man. The effects of the passage of time are always a little bewildering when one comes across them suddenly. During his last visit to Paris, when he had attended Aliena to discuss the matter of the pension with her, he had met the boy briefly when he had arrived home while Allen was still there. Aliena had introduced them, and they had shaken hands, and the boy had looked at him rather coldly and distantly. Otherwise he had seen him only in passing when they had happened to be at Court at the same time, and a bow or nod had sufficed. It was strange, therefore, to be claimed with such enthusiasm as an old friend. If challenged, Allen could not even have said whether the boy knew who he was, and why he had visited his grandmother.

'Grandmother spoke very highly of you,' Henri said, drawing Allen aside from the press of guests. 'I know she valued your friendship and your judgement, and I suspect she probably confided in you her disappointment in me.' Allen murmured something polite. Was this what was at the bottom? Did the man think Allen would recommend the pension to be stopped?

'Yes, yes, it is true. It is useless to deny it. I caused my dear grandmother much unhappiness, which grieves me now to think of it. But I loved her dearly, sir, and I beg you to believe it.'

'I have no reason to do otherwise,' Allen said cautiously.

'I'm sure you have every reason,' Henri replied, with that disturbing smile. 'I cannot doubt that Grandmother told you of my wicked ways, of how I gambled and drank and accumulated debts and generally attempted to ruin myself, and her with me. But I have been trying to make up for it in the past few years, and as I hope you may be able to discern from my appearance, I have found the means to keep myself respectably, and to provide for my child.'

'Your child?' Allen felt a twinge of dismay at the words. So there was a sprig, was there, of this renegade branch? He knew how Aliena had felt about it, how she had hoped the twist of the thread would end with her daughter, how distressed she had been when that daughter produced a bastard of her own. And if, now, this bastard had done likewise – for he spoke of keeping a child, but not a wife – the twist might never be unravelled. He pulled himself together. 'I was not aware, sir, that you were married.'

'My wife is dead,' he said bleakly. 'She died in childbirth of a son, who also died. My daughter is all I have. Would you do me the honour of coming upstairs now and seeing her?'

'Upstairs? And now?' Allen could not conceal his surprise.

'The de Murphys are my greatest friends, and since my wife died it has been most convenient for my daughter to live under their roof. They know that I mean to ask you, and have no objection to our leaving the company for a few minutes.'

There was nothing Allen could do, in that case, but bow his assent, though as he followed Henri from the room he was wondering why Henri wanted him to see the child, and coming up with no answer but the pension.

On the second floor at the back of the house, a suite of rooms had been put at the disposal of the little girl, and

Henri knocked on a door, listened, and led Allen into a very pretty sitting room all done out in blue and white, and far too formal an environment for the little girl who was led forward by a starched maid, and who dropped a very practised curtsey to the two visitors.

'Heloise, ma chère, viens ici. Je veux te presenter à Monsieur le Chevalier de Morland.' Henri held out his hand, and the little girl came and took it and looked up solemnly at Allen. She was five, going on six, a diminutive, self-possessed woman, for the more liberal attitudes to children had not yet reached France, dressed in a stiff-bodiced, wide-skirted, much ruffled version of a grown woman's dress. Her hair was dark, and curled and ringleted elaborately; her features were strongly marked, too much so for prettiness at this age, though Allen thought she would grown into her looks; most startling to him were the large, dark eyes, so dark they looked almost black, and oddly melancholy. He had seen those eyes before, in life, and in many and many a portrait. Here, five years old, brought up in obscurity, and destined, he hoped, to remain so, was perhaps the last small sprig of the Royal House of Stuart.

'Monsieur de Morland,' Henri was saying, translating the introduction into English, 'may I present to you my daughter Henrietta Louisa Stuart? Owing to the difficulties she had in pronouncing her own name when she first learned to talk, she has come to be known as Heloise.' The child curtseyed again, and continued to cling to her father's hand and to stare at Allen with those sad-monkey eyes. 'She does not yet speak very much English,' Henri had continued, 'though I am at pains to teach her, for I think it is an accomplishment that will be of use to her.'

'Languages are always useful, sir,' Allen said, wondering if they were coming to the nub of the matter.

'Certainly,' Henri assented, still in English, 'and I hope that when she is older, my daughter may be able to visit England – now, thank God, our two countries are at peace again.'

He sent the child back to her nurse, and turned away with Allen for privacy, relapsing into French as he sought to be eloquent.

'You have been patient, sir, and no doubt you have been wondering why I brought you here, what it is I want from you. Simply, it is this: I want a family. My grandmother isolated me from her own people, as if I were a disease that might infect them.' He shrugged. 'I understand her feelings, though I do not agree with them. But consider, sir, that innocent child you have just seen. Should she be punished for something not her fault, over which she had no control?'

'But how is she punished?' Allen asked.

'She suffers with me. I have no brothers or sisters, aunts or uncles, no cousins – at least, none that will own me. And so, neither has my daughter. That is a sad thing for a child – I know from my own experience how lonely a life she will lead.'

Henri turned his head to look at the child, and irresistibly Allen looked too. The little girl stood watching them with those sad Stuart eyes: great-grandchild of a King, grandchild of Marie-Louise, whom he had loved long ago. She looked very small and vulnerable, dwarfed by her elaborate clothes and the too-elegant room.

'And what is it you want me to do?' Allen asked at length.

'Make representation for me to the family; help me to be reconciled with them, so that, when she is a little older, my daughter may go to England and be received by them.'

'You don't know what you are asking,' Allen said. 'No-one knows of your existence, except for your grandmother's cousin, who pays your pension. It would involve explanations which would be painful, difficult, perhaps even destructive.'

'The story is an old one,' Henri said persuasively. 'There cannot be anyone alive now who would be directly affected by it.'

'There are many such,' Allen said shortly.

'Sir, I ask you to consider my request, to think about it, perhaps to discuss it with my benefactor. That's all. That would not be against your conscience, would it?'

'It would have to be discussed with Lord Chelmsford,' Allen said. 'But I cannot say—'

'Please, sir – just think about it. Now you have seen my child.'

'Very well,' Allen said at last. 'I will consider it. I cannot promise more.'

'Thank you, sir. Thank you.' He sounded genuinely grateful and relieved, and Allen began to think that perhaps he had misjudged the man, perhaps he really had turned over a new leaf. The idea was strengthened when they left to rejoin the party below and Henri turned back for one last look at the little girl, for the smile he exchanged with his daughter was one of real love.

The news of the January treaty was known in America in March 1783. Independence was granted to the thirteen United States; Canada was to remain British, Florida Spanish, the Mississippi was to be open to British and American ships and traders; the British army was to be evacuated with all convenient speed; the American army was to be paid and disbanded. Peace had come to America at last.

But there had been many who suffered: fishermen who could not ply their trade during the blockade had lost their livelihood; rising prices had afflicted those on salaries, and the poor who did not grow their own food; patriotic landowners who had supported the army had suffered, and the debilitating paper currency affected everyone. Only the merchants and financiers had done well out of the war, and in Maryland some merchants had done so suspiciously well that the Assembly ruled no merchant could represent the state in Congress.

And then there was the question of what to do about

those who had remained loyal to Britain through the war. A clause in the treaty provided that they should not be put to death, but otherwise they were at the mercy of the victors, and loss of all civil rights, confiscation of property, and summary banishment from their state was their lot. The Patriots regarded them with bitter hatred, and it was an uneasy time, when it was only natural that some came to feel the end had not been worth the gaining.

Charles's feelings about the end of the war were mainly relief that it was all over and that there would no longer be those terrible decisions to make, that tore him in two. He might even, he realized, renew contact with the family, now that England was no longer the enemy. He could write to Jemima, find out what had happened to Flora; contact Angus and perhaps even arrange for his portion of his father's estate to be realized and sent to him. Money – more especially gold – would be more than welcome at the moment, and if Angus had been doing well, which seemed likely, he might be only too glad to buy Charles out.

He thought of these things as he trudged along the riverbank in the heat of a June morning, with his gun under his arm, in case he spotted anything worth eating, and his gun dog at his heels. Everything looked very beautiful at this time of year, before the greens had burnt out to brown. The tall trees were deep in blue shadows, swaying gently against the copper-blue sky, and across the river there were perpetual scurryings and dartings, as life reached its crescendo. A heavy splash was probably an otter slipping away from the sound of his dog brushing the reeds; that small circle of spreading ripples would be a water rat. The river had a heavy, peppery smell which for him was the quintessence of summer, a smell of mallow and weed and rich mud – it must be that smell which intoxicated the ducks at this time of year. Here and there clouds of tiny insects jigged madly on the spot, and sapphire dragonflies quivered in the sunshine and joined their hinder ends delicately.

They had come through a bad time, he thought, but it was over, and now, as the river creatures stated and restated with the insistence of the stonechat's knock, it was the time for renewal. He would make it work, he decided. He would do better at managing the estate. That overseer, Benskin, he didn't trust him an inch. He would keep a firmer eye on Benskin, and if he had the opportunity, he would dismiss him, find someone better. There were plenty of poor men looking for work – a man who had lost his smallholding and had a family to feed might work harder and more honestly than that fat, arrogant bully, who had never known the touch of hunger in his life.

And he would do better at market, too, and not let those sly-eyed merchants cheat him, as he knew perfectly well they did, but somehow shrank from acknowledging. If Angus did sent him money, he could take in that low piece of ground at the northern end, and drain it and fence it. He might also rent a warehouse in St Mary's, so that he could keep his crop until he got a good price, rather than being rushed into a sale.

He would be kinder to Eugenie, too. She had had a miscarriage last year, and was feeling unwell, and had been hankering after a visit to her cousins in Martinique, which he had briskly told her was out of the question. Thinking about her, he realized that her life must be as lonely as his – more lonely, for women needed a female companion, to spend their long hours of idleness and solitude with. Perhaps there might be some little cousin in the West Indies who would like to come out and live with them, as Eugenie's companion, for a few years until Charlotte grew up. He would make inquiries, and try in the meanwhile to be a better companion to Eugenie himself. They had been married seven years, and it was time he settled down and made the best of things. Seven years! And in seven years more it would be time to think about young Philip's education. Should he send him to England for it? And when Philip was a little older still, and able to take charge, he, Charles, might be able to get away for a while, and go back home and visit—

He stopped himself abruptly, having been trapped into thoughts of England and home by allowing himself to wander. This was home, he told himself firmly. No looking back! No hankering! He gave himself a shake by way of rebuke and, calling the dog, turned away from the seductive river and headed back for the house. Perhaps he ought to allow Eugenie her visit. The largest of the boats would be adequate for a coastal run. He could take her along the coast as far as Savannah, and get her a passage from there – that would save money. That—

His train of thought was interrupted by a sharp barking from Sally, the gun dog, who raced forward towards the landing stage, drawing his attention to the masts of a pinnace tied up there. His stomach turned over in sickening recollection of the time the Virginia Patriots had made their first call, and his hand tightened on his gunstock. But no, he told himself, the war is over. He forced himself to breathe deeply until his heart stopped racing, and then turned to walk firmly and calmly up to the house.

The visitors were in the drawing room, sitting on the edge of their chairs as if they were not sure of their welcome, four men in the snuff-and-bottle colours of well-to-do but serious-minded citizens. Not Virginia men, anyway, he thought with relief – he recognized John Chase and Judge Morris, both prominent men of St Mary's City. As Charles came in they all stood, but before anyone could speak Eugenie came running to him – Eugenie, running! Her face was white and distressed, all trace of her languor gone and as he caught her in his arms he felt the premonition of something terrible.

'Oh, Charles, Charles, thank heaven you have come – these men – oh Charles—!' She clung to him with small, hooked hands like claws, while the four visitors stood up and regarded him solemnly – like executioners, he found himself thinking.

'Hush, Eugenie, it's all right,' he said vaguely, patting her shoulders with a useless gesture of comfort, more suited to a dog than a wife, while his mind raced over the possibilities of bad news and came up with no answers.

John Chase cleared his throat, frowned, and said, 'Mr Morland, I'm glad you have come back, sir. We were on the point of sending out for you. Sit down, sir, sit down.'

'Charles, they say that we must go,' Eugenie cried breathlessly, as he tried to ease her into a seat. She would not unhook her hands, and so he sat down with her, on the end of her sofa, still patting her foolishly.

'Go? What do you mean, go?'

'Allow me to explain, sir. Madam, please, calm yourself.'

'Calm? How can I be calm?' Eugenie cried shrilly, startling Charles, who had never heard any but a low, lilting voice from her.

'For God's sake, sir, explain!' Charles said angrily.

Chase hemmed again, and said, 'That is what I am endeavouring to do, sir. We have come – we four – as representatives of the Assembly of Maryland, to acquaint you with our decision concerning you, reached at the last session of the committee appointed to deal with Tories.'

'Tories?' Charles said, utterly astonished. 'Decision? What are you talking about?'

'You, sir, have been declared an undesirable person. Your activities during the war have been amply proved; you were undoubtedly associated with the British, passed on information to naval officers, and hampered the Cause in every way possible. Therefore we have declared all civil rights suspended, your property confiscated, and yourself and your family exiles. You are to leave here forthwith, never to return, on pain of imprisonment.' The tone of his voice suggested that he was disappointed not to be able to say on pain of death. But, Lord, these were civilized times!

Charles stared, dumbfounded, no longer ever noticing the pain in his arm from Eugenie's fingers. 'Hampered the cause? Are you mad? This house was all but taken over by the Patriot Party – it was camp, hospital, and staging post. What activities are you talking about? You have the wrong man, sir, the wrong man.'

'Not at all,' Judge Morris interposed sternly, lifting into a view a rolled document. 'It all came out in your trial.'

'My trial?'

'Your trial, sir, the day before yesterday.'

'You held a trial of me, *without my presence*?'

'Your presence was not necessary,' the Judge said implacably. 'There were ample witnesses to your villainy.'

'What witnesses?' Charles almost shrieked.

'The chief amongst them was a leading member of the Patriot Party, who himself witnessed your infamy. And your own overseer gave evidence against you, sir,' Chase said. 'Could anything be clearer?'

'No – it is becoming clear to me now,' Charles said slowly. 'This leading member of the Patriot Party – what is his name? Could it be Hampson?'

The four men exchanged significant glances. That he knew the name of the informer was clear proof to them of his guilt. 'It is,' said Chase, triumphantly.

'And of what, in particular, am I accused?' Charles asked with a terrible calm. The Judge unrolled the document with a grand gesture.

'Item: that you communicated by letter with the enemies of the American people, namely officers of the British navy. Item: that you did infamously and seditiously oppose and criticize the Declaration of Independence, and support the continuing tyranny of the British rule. Item: that you did refuse to make men and funds available to Congress for the furtherment of the war effort. Item—' here he paused and looked up, as one coming to the nub of the matter, 'that you did receive into your house a naval officer from the British ship of war *Ariadne*, and did in the presence of a witness give him certain information which led to the confiscation or destruction of a large

324

number of sailing vessels belonging to Patriotic Americans, and the destruction of large amounts of property, whose value is as yet unassessable.'

He rolled up the document again, and fixed Charles with a gimlet eye. 'Mr Hampson was able to give us full particulars of *that* little transaction. He was concealed in this very room, sir, and heard everything.'

'Ah, did he?' Charles said. 'And is that all?'

'All? Is it not enough?' Chase said indignantly.

'There is, in addition,' the Judge interposed, 'the matter of the British sailor you picked up after the battle in the mouth of the Bay, and failed to hand over to the authorities. No doubt you found means to return him safely to his friends – with useful information.'

'He was dying when I picked him up,' Charles said mildly. 'He died the following day. We buried him out there, in the family plot.' He gave a vague gesture towards the window. The whole business had taken on a quality of nightmare. He looked at the stern faces of his accusers, and knew without a doubt that anything he might say would be useless, or even be twisted about to make fresh accusation. He could almost hear the undercurrent of thought behind this ludicrous 'trial' – he, Charles, was an Englishman, and someone must be blamed. His wife, her father, were French by origin, and though the French had lately been their allies, they were not to be trusted, and would no doubt have turned the war to their own advantage had they been given the chance. And they were Papists into the bargain. Someone must pay. And speaking of pay – Benskin would not have done this without some advantage to himself. What could it be? And what was Hampson's benefit in this? He had the glimmer of an idea.

'Tell me, what do you intend to do with my estate when you have – confiscated it?' he asked, still with that deadly calm.

'It will be sold, and the money used to offset the war expenses,' Chase said.

'Yes, of course – someone must pay for the war. Sold by auction, I suppose?'

'Not necessary,' said the Judge. 'We have a purchaser already.'

Charles smiled, and at least John Chase had the grace to redden. 'The purchaser would be one Mr Hampson, I presume?' There was no need for anyone to answer him. Benskin's price would be a percentage, perhaps, or merely a rise in salary for continuing with the same job. York House was the best, the most beautiful house on the Bay, and it was natural enough that Hampson should have a hankering for it, as well as the good waterside property. He must have offered the Assembly a very good price for them to prefer his offer over that of a native Marylander.

The four men had risen, evidently feeling the matter was concluded.

'You will prepare yourselves at once to leave here, sir,' said John Chase sternly. 'You will be permitted to take a boat, your personal effects, and your personal servants. You have better make careful selection. We shall return tomorrow to take possession in the name of the Assembly.'

Eugenie began to weep hysterically. 'No, no, you shan't! We won't go, we won't go, I tell you! You can't turn us out of our own house, like dogs. We won't go!'

Chase kept his eyes from her, as if the sight embarrassed him, and addressed himself to Charles. 'We shall return tomorrow, sir, with a detachment of the militia, just in case you should think of making a foolish resistence.'

'But where can we go?' Eugenie cried. 'What can we do? If you send us away, how shall we live?'

'I am sure your British friends will help you,' the Judge said nastily. 'They would have rewarded you, had they won the war, so the least they can do is compensate you for your efforts on their behalf.'

Eugenie only wept louder. 'I don't know any British,' she sobbed. 'I don't know what you are talking about.'

John Chase, looking more embarrassed than ever, said, 'Most of the exiles are going north, to Canada. I believe there is a scheme by the British Government to award land in Canada to exiles in compensation. That would be your best bet.'

The Judge looked angry at this unwarranted softness. 'We leave you now, sir,' he said sharply. 'We shall return tomorrow. You had best be ready.'

For a long time after they had gone Charles sat still, holding his weeping wife in his arms, staring into space. He was utterly dazed. In a few minutes his life had been turned upside down, and everything still had the unreal air of a dream. He looked about the drawing room, remembering how strange its pirate's-hoard furnishings had seemed to him when first he saw them. They were all familiar to him now, as familiar as the lie of the whiskers on his own face when he shaved in the morning. Blindfold he could have walked about the room and never have bumped into anything. Over the chimneypiece was the new portrait of Eugenie and the children, smiling out serenely into an unchangeable world, flanked by the old and familiar likenesses of her mother and aunt. Outside the window the white roses burgeoned sweetly as they had done for a hundred and fifty years.

But tomorrow it would all be past for them. Tomorrow all these things would belong to another man. Tomorrow! They had only this one day to decide what to do, where to go, what to take with them. They must hurry, they must not waste time in useless grief. So he told himself, but he could not move. He held Eugenie, and waited for her tears to subside, for something to suggest itself.

Tomorrow they must leave – but the land would not know it, and the house would not care. They would go on just the same, as if he had never been. The crop would ripe and be harvested, the house would mellow a little and—

Then the idea came to him, not in a blinding flash, but creeping into his brain stealthily, like a dog inching towards the fire. The land – the house – it was a terrible idea, his brain wanted to reject it, and yet, and yet – it would be a revenge, would it not? it would be some small sweetener to the bitter days to come. But he must make haste – they must make their plans, and pack up, and be away before anyone came.

'Eugenie, Eugenie, sit up, dry your face. Here, take my handkerchief. That's right. There now, my love, listen to me, we must make plans.'

As patiently as he could, he jollied her along, until she had blown her nose and wiped her face and straightened her hair, and was attending to him.

'We have very little time, and we must not waste it. We must make a selection of what to take with us – clothes and household things, for us and for the children. And food, whatever we can take. We have to pack it all into the boat. We must find out which of the servants will come with us, and make sure they pack for themselves.'

'But Charles – where can we go?'

It seemed to Charles at that moment almost an irrelevance. He shrugged.

'*I* don't know. I suppose to Canada – there doesn't seem to be much choice. Or maybe to England? No, the boat wouldn't take us across the ocean. They say New York remained loyal – perhaps we can find out there whether there is any plan to compensate people like us.' She was staring at him like someone who has been hit fairly hard on the head, and he could see that it was beyond her to think about such things. All she wanted from him now was reassurance, and he gave it, feeling something growing inside him for her, a kind of warmth stemming from pity, for she, who had always been so complete and remote and untouched, needed him now. He would take care of her – he *would* take care of her.

'It will be all right, Eugenie. Everything will be all right. But we must not waste any time. I have a plan—'

'A plan?' Hope sprang to her eye.

'Not to save us – it will not help us. But it will confound *them* – our enemies.'

'Ah.' He saw her pull herself together with an immense

effort. 'Tell me what to do,' she said, with the nearest approach he had ever seen her make to briskness. He lifted her hand and kissed it, in grateful admiration.

'Yes,' he said. 'This is what we must do.'

All that day they scurried about, choosing and discarding and packing. Clothes, blankets, tools, cooking equipment, food and water – these were the essentials. They had room for so little, and there was so much they wanted, but Charles knew that if they took anything of real value they would be more likely to be pursued.

'We must take these,' Eugenie said at one time, coming to him with the crucifix from the altar in the chapel, and the other altar furnishings. He hesitated no more than a moment, and then packed them, hiding them as well as he could. Eugenie's jewels, too, they hid, dispersing them about the trunks so that if one was opened, others might escape.

The house slaves were grief-stricken, and many of them offered to come with them, and Charles was touched to the heart to find how loyal they were, and in particular how they loved the missus and the children.

'We can take only one or two of you,' he explained to Sam. 'There will be little enough room in the boat as it is – and we will be very poor after this, almost beggars. We will have to work like servants for our bread. It will mean hardship for anyone who comes with us.'

'I don't care, master,' Sam said, his eyes red-rimmed. 'I want to come all de same. You need me, master – I can sail de boat, and I'm strong, I can work, dig and plant, when you gets some mo' land. Let me come, master – I can't leave missus, not now.'

Charles accepted the offer gratefully, and with Sam's advice chose also Mary, who was good with the children, and Cloud, a half-Indian woman, and her husband Jacob, as being the strongest and hardiest of those who most wanted to come. When it was done, Charles dismissed all the other slaves and sent them over to the slave quarters with orders to stay there until their new master came to fetch them. He said goodbye to them all individually, thanking them for their loyalty, and they went away, many of them weeping, while Charles was already thinking about the next thing to be done.

'Thank God that traitor Benskin isn't here,' he said. 'He was probably shamed to show his face. Now, Sam, you and I had better see to the last part of the plan, while the other servants get the missus and children onto the boat.'

It was all done by an hour after sundown, and Charles sent the exhausted Eugenie and the servants and children to settle themselves in the boat.

'Have her ready to shove off at once, the moment Sam and I come back,' he told Jacob. Eugenie stretched out a hand to him.

'Please, Charles, be careful,' she said. He looked at her for a moment with compassion.

'You agree to this? I need your sanction. It is, after all, your home.'

'Yes,' she said steadily, holding his gaze. 'I agree. Better this way – better than letting—' Her voice failed her, and she swallowed and went on. 'Papa would have done the same. Do it, Charles, and let us be gone.'

He nodded gratefully, and he and Sam disappeared into the darkness. The preparations had all been made, and it would not take long. Eugenie settled the children and the women, while Jacob loosed the rope and sat ready to shove off as soon as the other two returned. Then they could only sit in silence, waiting. Sam would have further to run, Eugenie thought, for he was going round the fields. They had worked out the direction of the wind, and the corn and tobacco were dry and ripe from weeks of sunshine. Once it had taken, it would run with the wind all right. Charles, as was fitting, was dealing with the house – before her mental eye came the image of the drawing room, with all the furnishings and rugs heaped together in the centre, as they had left it. The other rooms were the same. She thought of the portraits over the chimneypiece, and wished they could have taken them, but paintings would be no use to them in their new life.

The grief she had been trying to ignore rose up for a moment irrepressibly, and she gave a half-stifled groan, and rocked herself, thinking of the lovely house, her home, the walks she knew so well, the hill with the tall trees, the family plot where her mother and all her forebears lay buried. 'Oh Papa,' she murmured. 'Forgive us. Oh Holy Mother, take care of us.'

The minutes passed slowly in the green silence of the dark river, where there was never quite nothing to be heard. The soft slap of water on the hull, the stealthy rustling of something moving through the rushes, the plop of a frog jumping into the water, the strange yarking cry of a night bird. Then Bendy stood up against her knees and gave a warning growl, and the night air stirred at the approach of something, and suddenly out of the darkness Sam and Charles appeared, running, panting, and jumped into the boat.

'Push off,' Charles said tersely to Jacob.

'Is it done?' Eugenie said, but she did not need to ask. She could smell it on them.

'It's done. Sam, take the tiller. We must put a distance between us and—' He did not finish the sentence; Eugenie drew in a sharp breath, and from behind her she heard Cloud whisper 'God a' mercy!' In the darkness where the house stood a golden flower had bloomed, like a lamp, but growing, burgeoning in the velvety night. For a few moments they were all transfixed, as if by some holy revelation. Then at a sharp word from Charles they pushed the little boat out onto the water and let the current take them down towards the Bay. Eugenie found her face was wet with tears, and yet she had no sensation of crying. It was like a new life, back there, the flower of flame that was blossoming, yet a malevolent life, that would eat up their past and cast them upon the world as naked as the newborn.

In the darkness, she felt her hand sought, and gave it into Charles's. His grasp was warm, and she returned its pressure.

'It's all right,' she said.

'Yes,' he whispered, and she had no idea which of them was comforting the other. The current slowed as it reached the Bay, but when they came round the break of the land, they picked up the breeze, and Sam and Jacob ran up the lugsail, and the boat bent to it and carried them down towards the sea.

CHAPTER SIXTEEN

'Well, my love, and what does Mary say of Naples?' Allen asked Jemima as they sat at breakfast one morning in September 1783. He had finished his own letters, and was denied his newspaper by Edward having picked it up a moment before and being now so deep in it that Allen didn't like to disturb him.

'What does Mary ever say of anywhere?' James drawled, leaning back in his chair and pulling a roll of bread to pieces. 'That the heat is insufferable, and the people abominable, or vice versa – that's what she said of Rome, wasn't it? Or perhaps she will say that they have made the most *charming* acquaintance and have been at the most *delicious* ball.' He gave such a languishing simper, and fluttered his eyelashes so girlishly, that Jemima had trouble not to laugh, which she didn't want to do because she was rather cross with James at the moment. 'With Mary, how well she likes a place depends on how many young men are in love with her.'

'Please sit up, and stop lolling. You will break the back of the chair,' Jemima said.

James straightened by an infinitesimal degree, and said, not at all disconcerted, 'So tell us, Mama, how has Naples answered?' He was so handsome that her heart was melted in spite of herself. He was not going to be tall, but his figure was graceful, and he held himself well, as small men often do. His dark hair had a slightly auburn burnish to it, which made his blue eyes look bluer. He was sensuous and lithe and lazy as a cat. He expected everyone to love him, and to dance attendance on him, and such was his beauty and charm that they usually did. At sixteen he had already, she feared, laid down the lines along which his life was to go, and she was angry with him at the moment because he would not decide on any career, but seemed to expect to go on living a life of sheer pleasure at Morland Place for ever. But when he smiled at her, she found her lips answering with a smile that was almost involuntary.

'She says the heat is terrible, but they have been invited to stay in a villa further up the coast, by someone who is a friend of Charles's cousins in Naples, and that they went to a ball last night where they met an Italian count who knows Charles's cousin Nicholaevna who is a Russian princess. And this count is to be a guest at the villa also.'

'Counts and princes – then Naples has her seal of approval, I take it,' James said, slipping a scrap of beef fat from his plate into the waiting mouth of Edward's hound, who swallowed it and then laid his massive head adoringly across James's thigh.

'No word of an elopement?' Allen asked innocently. 'There must be plenty of Scarlatti cousins who would take the problem off our hands.'

Jemima turned over the page and read on. 'There is a list of everyone she danced with at the ball,' she said, sighing as she worked through the names, 'but nothing to suggest she liked one more than another.'

'Mary is nothing if not generous – she likes to let everyone have a little of her,' James said.

'And that concludes the letter,' Jemima went on, reaching the foot of the page. 'James, please don't feed the dogs from the table – it gives them bad manners.'

'Sorry, Mama, I shouldn't have brought him in,' Edward said, trying, as usual, to intercept the rebuke. But James only lolled more and smiled more.

'Darling Mama, everything you say to me these days begins with the word "don't". It doesn't really suit you – gives you a cross little frown between your eyes. Don't you think, Father, that she ought to smile when she looks at me? Tell her now pretty she looks when she smiles.'

'Hush, you impudent boy,' Jemima said.

Allen grinned and said, 'I should think you would want to avoid drawing attention to yourself, Jamie, when at any moment your mother is going to ask you what you are intending to do today.'

James looked faintly put out, and Edward laid down the newspaper and stood up, stretching, and said, 'This is my moment for taking my leave. Shall I come to your rescue, brother, and say you are coming with me?'

'Why yes, of course,' James said hastily, standing up and shoving the freshly excited hound away. 'Don't you remember, Ned, that we agreed I should come with you today to – to – to do whatever it is you have to do.'

'We're going up to Popple Height to look at the tegs, don't you recollect?' Edward said grinning. 'You'll have to save your berating for this evening, Mama. Come, brother, look sharp.'

The two young men headed for the door, with the dog barking and bouncing between them, while Allen retrieved his newspaper and attempted to peruse it. He had no peace for it, for in the doorway James and Edward passed Alison, bringing the children down to see their parents before their day's work began. Louisa, suddenly growing tall at nine years old, but still solemn and shy, curtseyed to Jemima but headed straight for Allen, who put by his newspaper again with good grace to embrace her and coax her to talk to him. Harry and Jack vied with each other for Jemima's attention. At six and five years respectively, they had reached a noisy and boisterous age, and they competed in everything, in a cheerful and brotherly fashion. There was nothing between them for size or achievement, despite Harry's year's start over Jack. Lucy, had she been any other child, might have found herself swamped by them, but she shoved her way onto Jemima's lap with a determination to be cuddled that overcame any obstacles. She had already learnt how to queen it over the two boys, and despite their occasionally assumed air of male superiority, they rarely did anything without consulting their imperious young companion, who hugged and bullied them impartially, led them into mischief, and wept real tears when they were beaten for it.

335

The pleasant interlude lasted until Father Ramsay came into to collect his three charges, and Alison swept Louisa away to her sewing and music practice, but even then Allen had no leisure for the newspaper, because Mrs Mappin came in to ask Jemima about stores, and Oxhey followed her with a question for Allen about the brewing of October ale, and he and Jemima smiled at each other across the table with resignation. When these interruptions were over, and they were alone again for a while, Allen said, 'We really must get a steward, my love. These questions would have been referred to Clement in my youth—'

'Or to Pask in my day,' Jemima said. 'But do you really think—?'

'I do,' Allen anticipated her firmly. 'It's a matter of drawing all the threads together, you see, and of referring only those matters that need referring. So many of the things you are troubled with are not worthy of your attention. The servants often only need reassuring. A steward at the head of all the servants, outdoor and indoor, would make everything run more efficiently.'

'It sounds so – as though we were a great household,' Jemima demurred. He smiled.

'Call it by whatever name you like, the office is the same,' he said. 'The man who holds that office at Morland Place has always been called steward. And we are a great household.'

'Very well – have you anyone in mind?'

'I must look about for exactly the right man. It has been more years than anyone knows since we had to look, for it's been in the same family generation after generation.'

'Perhaps you might find some Clement cousin to take the post,' Jemima teased. 'But where would you put him when you found him? He'll hardly like to sleep in the attic with the other servants.'

'We'll have to do some altering, of course. It was time for it, anyway. And while we are talking about it, my love, I have another proposal to put to you, which will help matters. I'm talking of bells.'

'Bells,' Jemima looked blank.

'Bells,' he said firmly. 'It's very wasteful to have servants standing around at doors and in passages waiting to take messages, when they could be doing other things. And then when there isn't one handy, it is far from elegant to have to shout for someone.'

'Oh, elegant!' Jemima said, but he shook his head.

'If you don't mind not being elegant, think of the nuisance. Bells would solve all that.'

'Well, of course, I saw them in use when we stayed at Chelmsford House last year, but I never really understood how it worked,' Jemima said.

'It's very simple. There is a bell-rope in each room, and when you pull it, it pulls on a wire which runs through the house and in turn rings a bell. All the bells are fixed up in one place – a sort of servants' hall – and when they hear the bell, they see which room it was rung from, and someone goes and answers it. That means they can be getting on with other work, instead of standing attendance at the doors.'

'And when they hear the bell, they have to come all the way up to, say, the long gallery, to find out what was wanted, and then go away and do it,' Jemima said sarcastically. 'It sounds very efficient.'

'They get to know, of course, that certain summonses mean certain things – when you want the candles lit, for instance, or when you want wine brought. That comes with habit.'

Jemima looked restless. 'It sounds dreadful – to think I would have to wait while some slow-footed man traversed the house twice just to bring me something! I'd sooner go and fetch it myself.'

'Well, no doubt you will,' Allen smiled. 'There will be nothing to stop you. But one day when you get old and stiff, you'll find the bells save you a great deal of trouble.'

'You are determined upon it, then?'

'No, of course not – not without your consent,' he said,

raising his eyebrows at the idea. She relented at once and reached across the table for his hand.

'You always know best, my darling, and if you say the bells are best, the bells it shall be. I shall just have to get used to it. But where are all these busy servants to gather while they wait for their summonses? In the kitchen?'

'There'll have to be a reorganization of the offices,' Allen said, his face lighting with enthusiasm, for if there was one thing he relished more than another it was anything to do with architecture and the designing of houses. 'I've had some ideas for that. The pantry, you know, is hardly used, and if we knocked that into the kitchen and divided the kitchen off at the end, we could make a very good servants' hall. Then the buttery could become the butler's room, and all the store houses along that wing could be rearranged – wait, I've got some drawings in the steward's room that will explain it all. Would you like to see them? My arrangement would mean that all the new pantries could be reached without going out of doors, and if we put in a new chimney between the bakehouse and brewhouse, then we'd have room for a laundry too. And—'

'Yes,' said Jemima gently, 'by all means let us go and see your plans.' It would take a deal of getting used to, she thought, to ring a bell and wait for someone to come, like an invalid, not even knowing whether the summons had been heard, instead of shouting and hearing an answer at once; but other people had got used to it, and if Allen thought that their dignity would be better served by the new method, she would go along with it – with the private reservation that if no one was looking, she would probably just go and do whatever it was herself.

With poring over the plans together, and all the other things they had to do in the morning, Allen did not get a chance to read the newspaper, and it was therefore Edward who brought up the piece of news from it that would probably most have interested him. They were seated at dinner when Edward said, 'By the way, Father, did you see the paragraph about the West India squadron? Another seven ships came in from the West Indies, all to be paid off – and *Daring* was amongst them.'

'*Daring?* Does that mean William will come home?' Jemima asked, looking from her son to her husband.

'Unless he gets another commission,' Allen said. 'But the fleet is shrinking all the time – those ships being paid off are mostly being laid up, for now the war is over there's no need of 'em. So many of the officers will find themselves beached.'

'The senior officers, and those with influence at Court, will probably get commissions,' Edward said. 'I don't know whether anyone will speak for William. Sir Peter Parker might, perhaps – but he comes from a large family, and he will have nephews and second cousins, no doubt, all eager for places. I fear William may find himself on half pay for a long time.'

'You speak as though that were a tragedy,' Jemima said. 'Surely, if it means he can come home – after all, the war *is* over, and if it hadn't been for the war, he would never have gone to sea.'

'Mother dear, I don't think William will agree with you,' Edward smiled. 'The sea is his chosen career.'

'Was,' Jemima corrected stubbornly. 'And if he can't get on in it, he'll have to come home and do something else.'

'You are very illogical, Mother,' James said with a sigh. 'Here you are rating me every day because I haven't gone out and found myself a career, and pining for William to stop having one. And here's Ned, eating his head off at home, and you've no word to say against him. Why didn't you get yourself ordained when you took the notion, Ned? You'd have made a jolly churchman, 'pon my oath.'

'I pretty soon got rid of the notion again,' Edward said. 'As soon as I realized how much there is to do here at home.'

James opened his eyes wide in affected innocence. 'Is there a great deal to do at home? Why then, I had better tell Mother that I will stay at home after all, instead of studying for the bar, as I planned.'

Jemima could only laugh at the idea of James studying for anything. 'You'll see the bar from the other side one day,' she warned him genially. 'You'll be hanged sooner or later, I've always said so.'

James grinned, and ran a finger round inside his cravat. 'I've never liked anything tight about my throat, Mama. Dash it, you make me nervous, talking about it. I think I'll go up and see old Father Ramsay, and get myself absolution while I can.' And he stood up, bowed, and strolled gracefully away.

Jemima watched him go with affectionate exasperation, and Edward said, 'The oddest of all the odd things about my brother is the hours and hours he spends with Father Ramsay. What can they have to talk about, do you think?'

'Father Ramsay is very fond of him,' Allen said. 'He always was, though I confess it puzzles me.'

'It puzzles me, too, when I think of how savagely the reverend father used to beat William and me,' Edward said. 'Perhaps he really does confess his sins and ask for absolution. That would account for the length of time it takes – James's sins would fill a couple of hours in the recital.'

'I don't believe it for a moment,' Jemima said. 'I think he simply practises on Father Ramsay. If he can charm him, he can charm anyone.'

A few days later a letter came from William to say he was coming home. It gave no detail, except that he had been paid off at Portsmouth and would make his way home by stage, but that he would stop in London for a day or two on his way, to call at the Admiralty, so they had no idea when to expect him.

Allen lost no time in putting his plans for the kitchen and offices in hand, and it was only when work began that Jemima appreciated the extent of the disruption it was going to cause. Installing the bells was the simplest part of the matter, though it involved taking down panelling, cutting holes through walls and floors, chipping out channels in plaster and laying what seemed like miles of wires in unlikely places. The rebuilding and redesigning of the kitchen wing was a far bigger task, and would involve months of tearing down and building up, of brick dust and plaster dust and saw dust, of rubble underfoot, workmen in the way, meals delayed or missing altogether, cold food and sulks from the kitchen.

The servants, who loved a disaster and an excuse for complaint, approached the whole matter with lugubrious relish, and took such a perverse delight in telling Jemima that any order she might give was impossible to carry out because of the building that she finally gave up on the whole business, and absented herself from the house as much as possible, spending her time with the horses. The grooms at Twelvetrees would find her something to eat during the day, and she returned home to whatever scran had been assembled for the family with the serenity of one who has nothing to hope or fear from developments. The closest Allen got to acknowledging that he wished he had left the business to the next generation to effect was to say to her one night as they climbed between their gritty sheets, 'If I had only been able to arrange it, it would have been a good thing for us to go away for a holiday while the building was going on.'

Fortunately the weather had stayed fine, and so Jemima was quite happy to be out of doors all day. One day she was lungeing a young colt in the home paddock when she saw a stranger watching her from the rails. She had been so absorbed in her task that she had not seen him approach, and now she squinted against the sun trying to see who it was. He was standing full in the sun's eye, and all she could see was that he was tall, and had white hair, though his body was not an old man's. She checked the colt, brought him in to her, petted him, and then in courtesy led the horse over to the stranger to see what he wanted.

He stood quite still, waiting for her, and it was only when she moved into the shadow of a tree that she was able to see him properly.

For a long time she stood looking at him over the fence, while the colt nodded his head and shifted his feet, so that the sound of his bit chinking and his hooves rustling the grass became the accompaniment to that moment which she always remembered. A tall young man, it was, with a face very brown from sun and salt wind; a firm face, used to command; pale bright eyes, with the long steady gaze of one used to watching a more distant horizon than any he now saw; strong shoulders and hands; and fair hair, burnt white by the sun, drawn back into a long pigtail that hung forward over one shoulder, and breaking into soft wisps about the brows.

She knew, of course, who he was, but that was all: she didn't recognize him in any other way. There was nothing in this young man of the frail little boy she had parted with so reluctantly, with such fear for his life. He was big and strong – he looked stronger and older than Edward by far, though he was a year younger. The colt tugged at her restraining hand, and she let him put his head down to graze, and reached out very tentatively to touch the long silver-blond plait, as if she thought it might not be real.

'I heard that sailors tarred them,' she said. It was heavier than it looked, and felt rougher. She looked up shyly into his eyes. 'William,' she said.

'I left my dunnage at the inn, and walked,' he said, and it struck her with a terrible pang that she did not know his voice. Had she expected him to speak in a child's treble? No, not quite – yet she would not have known him for her son if she had heard and not seen him. It was the resonant voice one might have expected from a more barrel-like chest than his, though of course he had got the trick of pitching it to carry, as an actor does. Where the knowledge of his life should be in her mind, there was a blank. He had walked decks, looked out upon strange places, done things and seen sights, and she knew nothing of them at all. He was a stranger in more than looks: his life had gone so far apart from hers that he was truly a different person, someone she had never met before. She wanted to cry, and she wanted to touch him, and she could do neither, for they were both inappropriate.

'Everything's changed,' he said suddenly, his voice rising a little as if in protest. 'I would not have known where I was – fields – the strips gone – fences and roads where they didn't use to be. And a bridge over the beck where Charlotte and I used to catch guppies.'

I understand, she wanted to say. You have come home a stranger to yourself. I am as little your mother as you are my son, and we are both bereft. She touched the pigtail again, and then let her hand rest – very lightly, in case it offended – on his shoulder.

'It is the enclosure,' she said. 'It didn't occur to me how different it would look to—' she almost said 'a stranger' – 'someone coming back,' she finished.

'Everything's different. The trees are bigger, but the house looks smaller. And you—'

'I know,' she said quickly. 'I didn't recognize you, either.' She searched for something to say to reach him, or comfort him, and could find nothing. In the end she said, 'The swans are still there, on the moat.'

'Oh Mother,' he said, and began to laugh. He wasn't laughing at her – it was just his way of not crying, and in a minute she laughed too, for the same reason.

The household greeted William boisterously, or heartily, or tearfully, according to individual character, and there were endless exclamations of how he had changed and grown and become a man, but no one else, she thought, felt the strangeness as she had. Even for her, of course, it soon wore off, and the tall blond sailor took the place in her heart and thoughts labelled for 'her son William'; yet even so, through the evening, she found from time to time that she and William would steal glances at each other like shy young lovers, hopeful, but unsure.

Abram, who had been sulking quite frightfully since the beginning of the building works, refusing either to cook himself or to let anyone else do it for him, pronouncing, like one affirming an Article of Faith, that no food fit to be eaten could be prepared under such conditions – burst into almost simultaneous tears and smiles and rushed off to prepare a supper worthy of such an occasion. Allen gave the cellar keys to Oxhey with directions as to which bottles to open, and while they waited for the feast to appear, the family gathered in the drawing room to hear all William's news.

The first thing he wanted to tell them was that he had been made lieutenant. By the favour of the new captain of the *Daring*, he had sat for his examination in Kingston as soon as he attained the age of twenty, and, as Thomas had predicted long ago, passed it with the highest marks of the batch of candidates. A lucky combination of events – the fourth lieutenant of the *Daring* dying of the fever at a time when the Admiral was on hand to make the appointment – had led to his being given a commission just before his ship was recalled to England to be paid off.

'For you know, as soon as we knew the peace was signed we knew that the navy would be reduced. If I hadn't been made then, there would have been no chance at all of it. At least now, if I ever do get another ship, I shall go in as lieutenant.'

'You think it unlikely, do you?' Allen asked. William shook his head.

'They were saying in Portsmouth that four in five ships are to be laid up. I went to the Admiralty as soon as I could get to London, but so did everyone else, of course. Now they can pick and choose, it will be the fellows with rich patrons who get the commissions. But I'll keep trying – you never know, we might go to war with someone else by and by. And at least I'll get a lieutenant's half pay.'

'You want to go back to sea, then?' Allen asked the

question, for Jemima's sake rather than because he doubted it.

'Oh yes,' William said. It was not much, but the way he said it was all.

Other things he had to tell were not so cheerful. They naturally wished to understand the circumstances of Thomas's death, and he recounted the matter and the rest of the battle in Chesapeake Bay; which naturally led Allen to ask if he had heard any news of Charles.

'We thought he must be dead, since we have heard nothing for so long. Did you happen to find anything out?'

William stared. 'Don't you know? I made sure you must have heard by now, from them or from Angus.'

'They are alive then?'

'Oh yes,' William said. 'I came across them in New York. There's an agency there set up to deal with the exiles—'

'Exiles!' Jemima and Allen exclaimed at once.

'—to succour them, and send them on to the new settlements. There was talk of a settlement in Australia for them, but nothing has come of it so far. Most of them are sent to Canada, and given land, and some compensation – money to help them set up. A few come back to England, but it isn't encouraged.'

'Good God! I had not thought of anything like this,' Allen said. 'Exiled, indeed! For remaining loyal to Britain, I suppose?'

William, who had heard the whole story from Charles – his relief at meeting someone he knew had made him more than usually voluble – wondered how much of it to tell Allen, and decided in the end to keep his peace. 'That's right. It happened all over the country. The agency reckons there have been about fifty thousand so far, and more to come. It will change the structure of their society in the new United States, but I don't suppose they care about that.'

'And Charles has chosen to go to Canada?' Jemima asked.

'Yes. It seems that the compensation in land if they go to Canada is very generous, and he did not think they would settle happily in England now. He has written to Angus to ask him if he will find a way to release his share of their father's fortune to him – I thought Angus would have written to you by now, but perhaps the letter is on its way. They need almost everything – he and Eugenie and the children were banished with nothing but their clothes, and Eugenie is with child again.'

'A sad business,' Jemima said. 'It will be hard for them to start again with nothing, though Charles is used to living rough, from his expeditions. But from what he told us of his wife, I don't suppose she can ever have known hardship.'

'She's much stronger than she appears,' William said with a certain respect. 'She has pirate blood, and I suppose it will out.'

'Pirate blood? What can you mean?'

But at that moment Oxhey came in to announce that supper was ready, and the subject was abandoned for the moment. Conversation was lively through the meal. Father Ramsay joined them at table, and was eager to examine his old charge and determine how far his influence had shaped the young man; everyone, but Edward and James in particular, was anxious to hear William's adventures and stories of the battles he had been in; and William was determined to have all the details of the changes that had taken place in his absence. One thing Jemima discovered about her son was that shipboard life had given him a capacity for liquor which, though he seemed able to carry it like a gentleman, reminded her uneasily of her first husband. She had never liked to see wine quaffed like ale; and when the port was brought, William asked apologetically if there was any brandy.

'I know there won't be any rum,' he added, trying to make a joke of it, but his words reminded Jemima that on shipboard the daily rum ration, which was all that made life tolerable for the tars, was served even to the midshipmen hardly out of boyhood. Well, it was his first day home, and no doubt he would drop the habit once he had settled in. For the moment she let it pass without fuss, and caught Allen's eye to nod consent to the notion. Father Ramsay greeted the brandy with more cheerfulness than he ever greeted the port, for he had been brought up in Scotland, where it was almost as common as their own *usquebaugh*, and drank along with William, which took the edge off the situation.

They were so deep in conversation that it was only Oxhey ringing the bell that reminded them it was time for night prayers and bed, and they all went to the chapel, where Father Ramsay offered a special prayer of thanks for William's safe return. Jemima, who had William kneeling beside her, touched his hand at that moment and smiled at him, and when he smiled back at her he was a stranger again, and it made her shiver.

When prayers were over, Father Ramsay called William to him to say goodnight before he went up to bed by his own stairs from the vestry. Jemima walked out with Allen but lingered in the hall for the same reason. But when William came out, he was with Edward, the latter's arm draped about his shoulders, and Edward said, 'We're going to sit up and talk for a while, Mother. The fire's still good in the drawing room.'

'I'm sure William must be tired,' Jemima reminded him. William gave again his stranger's smile. He was taller and heavier than Edward, and it looked strange for him to have Edward's arm about him protectively like that.

'Oh no, ma'am, I'm not tired at all. I couldn't sleep now, if I tried.'

'I suppose you're used to sleeping in four-hour stretches,' Allen said pleasantly. 'Come, my love, let's leave the young people to it. You and I know where we belong.'

'Very well,' Jemima consented, but a little uneasily, though she did not know why. 'Goodnight, my sons. God bless you. James—?'

'I think I'll stay up a while too,' James said with superb

347

nonchalance, but with a pleading look in his eyes that begged her not to shame him in front of his big brothers, so she merely nodded and turned away with Allen.

'They'll want to hear the bloody details that he doesn't like to tell you,' Allen said to her when they were out of earshot. 'And perhaps they also suspect that William knows a little more about the ladies of Kingston than he's admitted to us.'

Jemima gave him a tired smile, and leaned against him a little. 'I doubt if there can be anything he can tell James on *that* subject, after that business with Maggie Henshaw.'

William did not come down to Mass the next morning, but Jemima thought he was probably tired after all, and did not send for him. He came in while they were breakfasting, looking fresh and trim, and she felt a thrill of pride in him, that he had grown so fine and handsome.

'I was thinking, William,' she said, 'that you might like to ride over the estate today, and see some of the changes for yourself. I've got a very nice young horse up that you could have.'

'Lord, ma'am, I haven't been on a horse in eight years,' William said with a faint tinge of dismay in his voice. 'You know, the last time I rode, it was on old Dove – is he still alive? Dear, stout old fellow!'

'Yes, he's still alive, though we don't work him much any more. He potters about in the home paddock, and sometimes carries a load for someone, but he's – well, he's older than you, I know, but I can't quite recall how old,' Jemima said, completely diverted.

'I was thinking of walking up to Bachelor Hill this morning with a gun – the rabbits are becoming a nuisance,' Edward said. 'Would you like to come, and stretch your legs?'

'Yes, indeed, what a good idea,' William said.

'You get a good view from the hill, too, of the new enclosures,' Edward added as a sop to Jemima, who knew herself ousted, and just for a moment was hurt. But of course, a young man wanted the company of other young men, not his elderly mother. She pushed down her unreasonable feelings, and forced herself to smile.

Allen, who always knew exactly what was going on in her mind, rewarded her efforts and said, 'I have to go in to York today, my love. Shall we take the carriage? If you can find something to amuse you while I attend to business, we could have dinner together at the King's Arms, and then take a stroll along the riverbank. I dare say you should like to eat something without brick dust seasoning?'

She smiled her gratitude at him. It was a scheme to delight her, to spend most of a day with him, and eat out. 'I haven't been into the city in an age,' she said happily. 'And there are dozens of calls I ought to make. I never seem to have the leisure for formal calls, and one ought not to neglect them.'

'Well, Mama, if you are dining out, shall not we take our dinner at the Hare and Heather, or somewhere, so that the kitchen need only provide a nursery dinner?' Edward suggested. 'Then the workmen can get on with the kitchen wall today.'

'Yes, certainly. I'll tell Mrs Mappin to tell Abram,' Jemima said, automatically getting to her feet to go and call for a servant.

Allen caught her hand as she passed and said, 'When this work is all finished, you will only need to reach for a bell-rope to do that.'

Jemima smiled down at him. 'Somehow I can't imagine I'll ever get used to it.'

That day's outing to York was doubly welcome, for autumn was always the busiest time of the year, and it was the only time she and Allen had alone together for weeks. After the first day, Jemima also rather lost sight of William, for she was too busy to notice very much what anyone else was doing. When she saw him, he seemed happy enough, and did not evince any need for her attention, and so she simply smiled and passed him by. The only thing that worried her was that he had only once come to Mass in the Chapel, although when the whole family went into the city on Sunday morning for the weekly service he accompanied them. But she assumed – perhaps because it was convenient to assume – that Father Ramsay would tackle him about it, and that it would right itself in the end.

At Michaelmas they gave a ball at Morland Place, and with three handsome and unmarried young Morland men at home, there was an eagerness on the part of mamas with unmarried daughters for invitations, which caused Jemima to be troubled by a great many formal callers, just at a time when she had no leisure to be polite. The ball could not, in any case, as she found herself explaining again and again to successive callers, be very grand, nor could there be the usual dinner beforehand, on account of the disruption caused by the building works, but there would be a buffet supper, and everyone assured her that an invitation of any sort to Morland Place was an honour, dear Lady Morland, even if it was only to take tea.

The Ansteys had successfully married off their eldest, Augusta, but they had two more daughters 'out' – Celia who was eighteen and Margaret, seventeen – for whom they were anxious to find matches. The Fussells had Amelia, seventeen, and Caroline, sixteen, amongst their brood, and then there was Tom Loveday's younger sister, Mary, who since she was not *very* handsome, and rather too clever, was Celia Anstey's *particular* friend.

It amused Jemima enormously on the evening of the ball to see the different attitudes of the young belles to her three sons. Edward, though he had beautiful manners, had been to Oxford, was really quite handsome, and was the close friend of an earl's son, was the least pursued of the three, for he had been at home too long to be a novelty. All the young ladies were at one in agreeing that he was incomparably the best match – he was, after all, the eldest son – and that his air and countenance were the best of any young man in or near York; but their eyes were always sliding off after the other two.

William was the prize that night, naturally so, on account of his only just having arrived. He was a naval officer, which was exciting, and he had been in the war, which was thrilling, and he had a long pigtail of silvery-blond hair, which set them all wriggling. On the other hand, Jemima gathered as she drifted about the room overhearing whispers, his very weather-tanned skin told against him, and the young women allowed, with some puzzlement amongst themselves, that there was something just a little cold and frightening about him. They were not sure what it was, for he smiled a great deal, danced every dance, and said all the right things, and paid very graceful compliments. All the same, they murmured, all the same . . .

Jemima thought she understood. He was too much a man for them: he had sailed the seas, faced danger, seen death close to, while they had never been further from their homes than an hour in the carriage could take them. His mind, like his body, was grown-up, and strong, and toughened to life, and it frightened them. She also noticed, again with faint unease, how much he drank that evening, although never once appearing to be the worse for it. That was part of his adulthood that would alarm these soft and silly girls.

And then there was James, handsome, smiling, wicked James. She noticed that at his approach the girls giggled madly, and clustered together, rather like, she caught herself thinking, a group of mares when Artembares was turned into their field. He was the best known to them of the Morland brothers; he said outrageous things, danced divinely, was incomparably the handsomest; and despite being only sixteen, he seemed to be able to have any of them he wanted, just for the asking. But he danced with each of them in turn, quite impartially, leaving them at the end of their pair flushed and flustered, while he remained smilingly cool. A piece of caution, Jemima thought, that sat strangely on such a young man's shoulders.

But towards the end of the evening she happened to see him dancing again with Mary Loveday, with whom, she now realized, he had danced more often than any of the others, and his demeanour was quite different. Mary Loveday was more than three years older than him, besides having a reputation for cleverness, and as they danced together, James's expression was pleasant and serious, and they seemed to converse on quite a different level from the normal light chatter and laughing repartee of the ballroom.

She was still watching them when Edward came up beside her. They exchanged a smile of greeting, and watched together in silence for a while.

'Not dancing, my love?' she said after a moment.

'I slipped out of the room just before this pair began,' Edward said with a wry smile. 'Not very gallant behaviour, I admit, but I have done my duty tonight with good grace, and felt I deserved a rest.'

'What, does dancing tire you? At your age I could have danced all night, every night.'

'It doesn't tire me, it bores me,' Edward said. 'No doubt you had an object in dancing – and perhaps young men were interesting to talk to. But to spend half an hour with any of those little gigglers, Mama, is a penance to me. Why must they breed girls so silly?'

'Speak low, my darling,' Jemima said, amused, 'or you will call down the wrath of the whole of York on your head. Not like silly girls? That is purest heresy.'

'I don't much like girls at all,' Edward said, and immediately wished he had not, but his mother did not seem to notice it. She was still watching James and his partner.

Presently she said with a nod in their direction, 'There is one girl who isn't silly – or at least, so reputation has it. Could you not like her?'

'I do like Mary Loveday very much,' Edward said. 'She talks rather like you, Mama, only softer.'

352

He hoped she would not ask the next most obvious question for a mother, and was relieved when she said, 'I'm surprised that James danced with her so often tonight.'

'James has always liked women older than himself,' he said cautiously. 'Besides, he probably knows he will not have the opportunity to dance with her after tonight.'

'Why is that?' Jemima asked.

'He has probably heard that she is to become engaged tomorrow to John Skelwith.'

Jemima's attention was successfully seized by this.

'John Skelwith? You can't mean the builder, who lives in Stonegate? But he must be twenty – no, thirty years older than her! I swear he's fifty if he's a day, and – well, one should not judge people by their appearance, but really, it seems a horrible thing to wed a young girl to a little, crooked man like that.'

Edward shrugged. 'He's very rich, and the Lovedays aren't. It's a good match for Mary, though I dare say if she had been handsome, they might not have closed with him so readily. But she's nearly twenty, and difficult—'

'She's a perfectly nice-looking, well-behaved girl,' Jemima said indignantly. 'A good match, you call it! What does she think of it herself?'

'I hardly know, Mama,' Edward said. 'Her parents have not your liberal views, and I dare say they have not asked her opinion. But don't you think she looks happy enough? For Mary, that is – she never smiles as the other girls do, without cause.'

Jemima looked at him carefully for a moment, and then said, 'You say you like her very much,' she said diffidently. 'Would it not be possible—'

'No, Mama,' he said firmly. 'I have no intention of marrying Mary Loveday, or anyone.'

'At present, you mean,' Jemima said, and he let it pass. 'But you must think about it soon, Edward. I know it is not urgent for a man as for a woman, but don't forget you are the heir, and you must get an heir yourself, and it does not always come so easily as you might think. The sooner you begin, the better.'

Now it really was necessary to distract her. 'I'm glad you brought up the subject of James,' Edward said desperately, 'because I'm a little worried about him.'

'Worried about James – whatever for?'

Yes, that had done it. 'Since William came home he has been copying his habits somewhat.'

'He could not do better, surely. William is so neat and tidy, and—'

'Mama, perhaps you have not noticed how much William drinks? It does not matter so much for him, because he is used to it, and in any case, he has had a life of responsibility.'

'Yes, I have noticed, but he never seems the worse for it, so I have let it pass,' Jemima said.

'But it is not the same with James. He is not such a steady character. He has wild enthusiasms over things. Too much wine is not good for him.'

'Not good for anyone, my love, but I cannot say that I have seen anything of it in James. After all, when can he have access to wine? Only at dinner, and he is under our eyes then.'

'You did not know, then, that William and James have been sitting up late at night, talking and drinking? I joined them for the first few nights, but it doesn't suit my digestion, and I soon left off. I thought James would too, but he admires William so. He has been drunk to bed many a night, and it worries me.'

Jemima frowned. 'That is bad,' she said. 'That must stop. Where do they get the wine from?'

'Oxhey gives it to them. He says he has no orders to deny William what he wants.'

'I'll speak to him, and to William. William can have what he wants, but he must not lead James into bad habits. Thank you for warning me, Edward.' She patted his hand. 'It will be a passing thing with James, I'm sure. He has his father's example before him. Once he gets used to William's being home he will leave off. And I've never seen him look ill in the morning, so he can't be drinking very much, even now.'

Edward said no more, though he was not so sanguine as his mother. He had seen James very drunk, and knew that at sixteen one could drink a great deal and still rise fresh from one's bed in the morning. But he did not want to make too much of it, and it had served in any case to turn his mother's mind from the question of his marrying. One day they would have to understand and accept it, but he hoped the knowledge would come upon them slowly, given time, and that he would never have to explain who it was he had given his heart to, long ago.

CHAPTER SEVENTEEN

The summer of 1785 brought the return to England of Lord and Lady Meldon from their honeymoon tour, and pausing only to pay respects to Lord and Lady Chelmsford, they came at once to Yorkshire, to bring Mary home, and to spend the summer themselves at Morland Place, while they decided where they would live.

'If you will have us, that is?' Charles added, but with a smile that suggested he did not doubt they would be welcome.

Seeing how happy Flora was, and how well he had looked after Mary, Jemima was ready to forgive him the past, and said warmly, 'Of course you must stay, as long as you want. It will be lovely for the children to have the chance to get to know you, and for Mary to have you here. And in August, you know, Allen has his seventieth birthday, and we are planning a big celebration for it, so you should be here for that.'

The reunion of Flora's children with their mother and stepfather was not an immediate success. Louisa was nearing eleven, still as quiet and shy as ever, deeply attached to Allen and quietly so to Jemima, and had neither the high spirits nor the beauty to make much impression on Flora. Charles tried to be kind to her, but she shrank back from him as from her mother. Her great fear was that they would take her away from Morland Place, which had always been her home, and from Allen and Jemima, who had brought her up from infancy and were her parents in everything but name. Had she been of the temperament to own it, frankly and openly, there would have been no problem, for Flora was as little inclined for her daughter's company as Louisa was for her mother's; but Louisa rarely spoke, and never about herself.

Little Jack was more of a success, for at almost seven years old he was handsome and lively and bold-tempered. He did not remember his father at all, and hardly remembered his mother, and like Louisa he regarded Morland Place as his home, but he was glad of the distinction that having a returning mother gave him over Harry, and was quite willing to play up to them, for the sake of the limelight. He showed off his accomplishments to his stepfather, claimed his mother's embraces, demanded to know what they had brought him back from Abroad, and where they would live, and whether they would send him to school and buy him a horse of his own. But it was all superficial, and once his point had been made to his playmate, he returned happily to his normal daily pursuits, and completely forgot Flora and Charles's existence.

Jemima was delighted with the improvement in Mary. She had gone away pretty, but she came back quite beautiful, her figure more womanly and graceful, though perhaps a trifle thinner; her face fined into true, classical beauty, the sort of beauty that made a room go quiet for a moment when she entered it. But more than in her looks, Jemima found her improved in her character and manners. She seemed much more grown-up and sensible, had lost her tendency to languish and giggle, and had quite outgrown her petulance and her inclination to think herself hard done by. Moreover, the travelling and the experience of society in foreign places had informed her mind and her taste, and Allen remarked agreeably to his wife that it was now actually possible to have a conversation with Mary.

The greatest improvement of all, as far as Jemima could see, was that, though she would soon be twenty-one, she did not seem at all anxious about marriage, and behaved herself in company with grace, neither seeking nor rejecting male attentions. She asked after her old friends, was glad to hear of Augusta Anstey's good fortune and noncommittal about Mary Loveday's but evinced no triumph that John Anstey and Tom Loveday were both unwed. Jemima wondered whether she would welcome a renewal of John

Anstey's attentions, but since Mary had apparently learned discretion, she did not like to broach the subject.

On the third day after their arrival, Flora and William walked apart from the rest of them when the family were taking their exercise in the gardens. Jemima and Allen exchanged a glance, and Allen prohibited Jack, who was still in his showing-off phase, from following, to allow them privacy. She would want to know about Thomas, Jemima thought, and it was now far enough in the past for both of them to be spoken of. Then there was also the fate of her brother Charles to be recounted. They were gone a very long time, walking at a distance from the party, up and down the pleached walk of the rose garden, and when they returned, Flora looked a little pale, and had her handkerchief screwed up in her hand. She wrote to her brother Angus that night, and a fortnight later received a reply from him, as a result of which she announced one day at dinner that she and her husband proposed travelling into Scotland to visit Angus.

'Oh, I thought we were to have the pleasure of your company all summer,' Jemima said. 'I know a number of people will be very disappointed. You cannot imagine the balls and dinners that are in the planning for Lord and Lady Meldon. You are quite a celebrity you know, Flora.'

'I shan't disappoint them, ma'am,' Flora said, smiling at the idea. 'We shall be gone, I suppose, a month, first and last. We shall be back at the latest by the end of July, and we shall certainly not leave you until September. Not for anything would I miss Allen's birthday feast. But there are certain matters of business—'

'My dear, you don't have to excuse yourself to me. It's perfectly proper and natural that you should want to visit your brother. I was being selfish, that's all.'

Mary did not go with Flora to Scotland, but she seemed contented enough at home. She renewed her acquaintance with William, though they had surprisingly little to say to each other, in spite of their being both so widely travelled. But it may have been because William was growing more morose as the months passed, for he continued to apply for a commission, without success. The only time she struck any warmth in their conversation was when she suggested that Lord Meldon might be able to use his influence on William's behalf.

'Do you think he would? Does he know anyone in the Admiralty?' William asked eagerly, but Mary could give him no definite encouragement. 'I'll ask him as soon as they come back from Scotland,' William decided.

'At the end of the summer they will certainly go to London,' Mary said, 'and it might serve if you went with them. I suppose we shall make our home in London – I cannot imagine that Lady Meldon will be happy to rusticate in the country – and then you know we shall be often at Court. Something will be done, I'm sure.'

'We? Do you intend to go with them, then?' William asked. Mary raised an eyebrow.

'It is not discussed, but I'm sure Lady Meldon cannot want it otherwise. We have been together for some time, now, and I know she is fond of me. And I do not want to leave her.'

'But won't you miss home?' William asked curiously. Mary shrugged.

'It is well enough for a holiday, but one meets no one here. Once one has been at Court, the simple life of the country has little charm.'

'That is how *I* feel about the sea,' William said, 'but I'm surprised anyone can feel it about the town.'

And each looked at the other with a certain pity, wondering how they could be so unsophisticated. There was no likelihood of a deep friendship between William and Mary.

For the rest, Mary occupied herself happily enough, taking her walk in the garden or orchard, riding when the weather was fine, visiting and being visited by her old friends. Shawes was at a convenient distance either for a walk or a ride, and she was often there at the invitation of Amelia and Caroline Fussell, who could never have enough of Mary's recollections of the courts of Europe, even if her mention of the various counts and princes she had danced with galled them. And when she could have the carriage, she liked to go into York, and see her friends there, take tea, wander around the shops with them and sigh for the shops of the metropolis, attend a play or concert with them.

Her dealings with the Anstey family were bound to be a little delicate, but she had the fortune to meet Augusta Anstey – now Augusta Keating – in a milliner's in Stonegate one day. Mrs Keating, eager to show her card with her married name, especially to one who had always been more handsome than she but was not yet married, made the first move of reconciliation, which Mary met gracefully. The following day Mary called to leave her card with Mrs Keating, and as luck would have it she called at a moment when John Anstey had just arrived, bringing his sister Celia to visit Augusta. There was a moment's embarrassment, and a moment's stiffness; but Celia, who had heard nothing talked of amongst *her* friends for weeks but Mary Morland's clothes and Mary Morland's hairstyles and Mary Morland's experiences abroad, longed to be reconciled; and John Anstey, besides being a genuinely kind-hearted man, was still in love with her. Mary's cosmopolitan polish smoothed the way, and they soon thawed, and then warmed, and by the end of the twenty minutes there might never have been any cause for coldness between them. When Mary took her leave, John Anstey's eyes followed her as wistfully as they had done since she was twelve years old.

At John's request, Sir John and Lady Anstey invited Mary to take tea at the new and elegant house on the Lendal, and though they, mo e than their children, resented the slight she had put upon them in refusing their son, and were reluctant to receive her at all, Mary's good manners and her sincere praise of their new house won them over. They were sorry to see all the symptoms in John of being as much in love as ever; but hoped that, as

360

Mary was still unwed herself, they might come to an understanding in time. Young Alfred, the second son, who was normally considered quite a rip, and who had been boasting privately to his sisters that he might cut old John out, was reduced to a most abnormal silence by Mary's beauty and manner, and on that first visit found his tongue only once, to ask her, stammering, if she would take another dish of tea.

James came scurrying into the hall one day in July when Mary was standing there drawing on her gloves.

'Are you going out?' he asked her. It was an unecessary question, quite apart from the gloves, for Mary was in a walking-dress of some elegance, dark yellow silk with a mustard-coloured frill at waist and hem, the deep, square neckline filled in with a lawn so fine it was almost transparent. Over it she wore a sleeveless green silk pelisse puffed out at the back and drawn up into three swags by three seams in black piping and three large jet buttons, and fastened in front by emerald-green ribbon. The same ribbon trimmed her spotless lawn cuffs. Her hair was dressed into a thick plait which was turned up and pinned behind, while her side hair was puffed out into a series of fat curls, and the whole was crowned with a neat black hat, tilted forward at an impudent angle by the thickness of hair, and decorated with ruched green bands and bows, three white ostrich feathers, elegantly curled, and a glossy black cock's feather, jauntily erect.

'I'm going in to York, to visit Celia Anstey – why?' Mary said. James waved a hand.

'All that, for Celia Anstey? Curled hair, curled feathers and all, for Celia Anstey?'

'Celia is a very sweet girl, and I dote on her,' Mary said. 'What do you want, you impudent boy?'

'You'll have the coach out, then? Let me ride in with you. I think you need an escort, sister dear.' He offered his arm to her with a mocking bow, but though she frowned at him, she accepted it. James always looked well, and it was pleasant to have a man beside one when riding in a coach.

'What do you want in York?' Mary asked. 'I hope you are not going to spend the day soaking in some tavern, or in that dreadful club? You know that drinking too much will ruin your complexion.'

'Oh, don't begin that old song again,' James said, leading her out into the courtyard. 'You don't sing it to brother William, I notice.'

'William doesn't drink as much as you,' Mary said.

'He does indeed – he drinks twice as much as me,' James said indignantly, and Mary paused, knowing it was true. But she was wary of William.

'Well, he's older. Besides, he hasn't any complexion to ruin. And he doesn't smoke cigars, which I know you do, because I've smelt them on you at night when you come upstairs. *And* he doesn't gamble.'

'Gambling is bad for the complexion too, is it?' James asked a little peevishly as they settled themselves in the coach. 'Anyway, who told you I gambled?'

She gave a sigh of exasperation. 'Oh Jamie, it's common knowledge. All the girls talk about it, and John Anstey eats at the Maccabbees Club sometimes, and he's seen you there.'

'Oh, all the girls talk about me, do they?' he said with a grimace. Mary looked at him sternly.

'I don't know how much you are losing, but I'm sure it is more than your allowance – isn't it?' James did not answer. 'What are you going to do, when you run out of credit? They'll go to Papa, and then it will be all up with you.'

'I'll do what I've always done – borrow from someone.'

'But that's even worse. You must have debts all over the place. What when they want their money back?'

'I'll borrow from someone else to pay them, of course. Really Mary, don't preach. I wouldn't have asked you to let me ride with you if I'd known you were going to dig into my little pleasures like this.'

'James, they aren't so little any more, and I'm worried about you,' Mary said. 'You're getting a bad reputation in York and it can be only a matter of time before it gets back to Mother or Father.'

'Mother and Father are too innocent ever to suspect anything, and I can manage Father Ramsay, as I always have. You needn't worry about me. Though I suspect it's *your* reputation you are fearful for. You don't want to be known to be my sister, the sister of a confirmed rake,' James said languidly.

'Don't put on that air with me,' Mary said crossly. 'Save it for your lady friends. And if you think Mother and Father wouldn't mind about all this, you are very much mistaken. For heaven's sake, James, have a little sense!'

'Oh don't worry, Polly, it won't get as far as Father. If I get into the soup, brother Ned will fish me out again. He's done it before. Marvellous economical old boy, is Ned. Never spends his 'lowance, puts it by for an emergency. Always good for a guinea or two at a rub, brother Ned.'

'Well, if he's fool enough to give it to you, I'll say no more. But you'd better keep out of trouble for the next few weeks, while he's away.'

'He won't be away long,' James said confidently.

'Why should you think that? He's gone to visit his friend Chetwyn, and he hasn't seen him for two years or more. He won't hurry back.'

'He won't stay long this time, because Chetwyn's Papa, the old Earl, is ill, and they won't want him hanging around the house making a noise. Ten to one he'll bring Chetwyn back here with him. And then there'll be two of them with spare guineas.'

Mary sighed, but left it at that, seeing that there was no future in arguing with him. There was some truth in the idea that she was concerned for herself, for most of her friends had been in love with James at some time, and all of them had been flirted with by him, and it did make things uncomfortable when his name came up in conversation; especially with Celia Anstey who, whatever she said, was still very much under James's spell, which made her petulant on the subject.

'So where is it you are going in York? You didn't tell me,' Mary said, to change the subject.

'Oh – I'm going to visit – another of your admirers,' James said with a certain awkwardness that Mary did not quite understand.

'Who can you mean?'

'Tom Loveday,' James said with a grin. 'Poor Tom, how he talks of you, sighs over you – quite touching to see it.'

'Be quiet, you impudent creature. And how long have you been friendly with Tom Loveday?'

'Ever since you came home, and he thought cultivating my friendship might bring him in your way,' James said with a grin. Mary drew her dignity on.

'We had better change the subject, or we shall certainly quarrel. Talk about something else, pray.'

They went into the city through the Micklegate, and crossed the river, but as they were about to turn the corner into Spurriergate, James rapped on the roof and said to Mary, 'You had better let me out here.'

'But Tom Loveday lives in Coney Street, doesn't he? We go right past the door – we can drop you there.'

'Ah, no, I forgot to say that I want to see my hatter first – a matter of some urgency. That's in Jubbergate, you know. I can slip through the lanes from here.'

Mary fixed him with a stern glance. 'You are not going to the club, are you?'

'Certainly not.'

'Nor an inn somewhere? Do you swear you are not going to do something more to disgrace us all?'

'Mary, dear, I swear I am not going to drink or gamble, now or at any time today. Now will you let me out, before we have a dozen angry carters around our ears?'

'Oh, very well.'

She let him out, and watched him walk quickly away down one of the alleys that formed a maze amongst the mean dwellings on either side of Peter Lane and Feasegate, and then knocked on the roof, and the carriage moved on. They passed, as she had said, right by the Loveday house, an old and shabby building on Coney Street, the more unhappy-looking by contrast with the smart new house of the Ansteys further along on the Lendal. She suspected James of having a kind heart underneath his air of indifference, and it occurred to her that he might have preferred to arrive at Tom Loveday's on foot, rather than emphasize, by coming in a coach, the Lovedays' poverty, which meant they could not afford a coach of their own.

At the Anstey house she was warmly received by the younger Ansteys, Sir John and Lady Anstey and John all being out. Her hat, as she had anticipated, caused great enthusiasm.

'Mary, darling, what a *love* of a hat! What a perfect *darling* of a hat!'

'And what a cunning way you have done your hair! I simply adore the plait – did you copy it from your brother, Mary dear?' This from Celia, who had been rather sour since her younger sister Margaret had become engaged to Edgar Somers, while she, who had now reached the dangerous age of twenty, had never even been offered for.

'She knew how much *you* admired it, dear sister,' Margaret retorted, willing to take revenge for the small needlings she had had to endure recently. But Mary had not come to cause quarrels.

'Try it on, Celia, do. I'm sure it will suit you better than me,' she said, reaching for the pins of her hat.

'I heard that hairstyles were coming down this year,' Margaret said with interest, 'but I see no sign of it happening. I wonder the Court ladies can bear it. It must be so uncomfortable.'

'Oh it is – but terribly amusing. Did I tell you of how Lady Meldon dressed her hair for the Royal Birthday ball in Naples?'

365

The time passed happily, and tea was brought in, and Mary told them of Flora's last letter, in which she described the multitude of delicious cakes and biscuits and pastries the Scots were accustomed to serve with tea. 'It is quite a meal with them,' Mary was saying, when a servant came in and spoke in a low voice to Celia, who coloured and said, 'Yes, of course, how stupid you are. Show him up at once.' The servant bowed and departed, and Celia said, trying for unconcern, 'Your brother James, Mary, is below asking for you. I did not know he was in town today.'

'He came in with me, but I dropped him off. I expect he only wants to know what time I shall be going home.'

'Well, he shall take a dish of tea, at least,' Margaret said, sliding her eyes at her elder sister.

Benjamin, the next youngest, cried, 'I must go and tell Alfred that James Morland is here. He will not like to miss him. What a capital fellow your brother is, Miss Morland.' And he jumped up and dashed away. The servant re-entered with James, and Celia, inquiring graciously and with perfect self-control if he would like tea, sent the servant for fresh china and hot water, and invited James to sit down.

'Upon my word, Miss Anstey, I did not intend to intrude upon you,' James said, sitting beside Celia readily and smiling his most charming smile. 'I only asked your servant to inquire at what time I should come for my sister, but—'

'Please don't apologize, Mr Morland. Your presence is very welcome – to all of us. What brought you to York today?' Celia said. 'We don't often have the pleasure of seeing you.'

'If I had known, ma'am, that I was to have the pleasure of taking tea with you, and Miss Margaret and Miss Elizabeth,' with a bow to each of the Anstey sisters, 'I should not have wasted my time elsewhere, and would have been on your doorstep the sooner.'

Mary watched all this, marvelling at his performance, and seeing how it had its effect on each of them, making Celia a little more at her ease, Margaret a little less loftily detached, and Elizabeth, who was not yet seventeen, a great deal more tongue-tied, pink, and admiring.

'But where *have* you been, Mr. Moreland?' Celia persisted, for something to say.

'Oh, I have been to call on my old friend, Tom Loveday,' James said easily. Celia looked puzzled.

'But Mr Loveday is not at home. He has gone to Harrogate these three days since, to visit his aunt who is sick.'

Mary, lifting her gaze from her teacup to her brother's face at that moment, thought he looked disconcerted for the fraction of a second, but his answer was pat.

'Oh, yes, certainly – so I discovered when I went to call. That was why I spoke of wasting my time.'

'I wonder you did not know of it,' Margaret said. 'I wonder Mr Loveday's sister did not tell you of it.'

'How might she do that, ma'am?' James asked. 'I have not had the pleasure of seeing Mrs Skelwith since—'

'Oh but Mr Somers – my fiancé, you know – told me that he had seen you talking to Mrs Skelwith on the corner of Petergate the day before yesterday, but as he was in a hurry he did not stop to speak to you,' Margaret hurried on, eager to bring in a mention of Mr Somers. James bowed his acknowledgement with perfect aplomb.

'Ah yes, I had forgot – I did happen to meet with Mrs Skelwith, quite by chance, as she was returning from somewhere or other – but it was nothing of a meeting. We barely spoke three words, you know, for we were both in a hurry. I am not surprised she did not mention her brother, for there was no time.'

The door opened at that interesting moment to admit John Anstey, just returned, closely followed by the servant with the tea things.

'Ah, here you all are! I'm glad to find the party not broken up. Miss Morland, your servant. Pour me some tea, Celia, there's a dear. What a dashed fast walker you are, James! I saw you in Stonegate, just ahead of me, and called out to you, but you did not hear me, and dashed off so fast I could not have caught you without running. But I guessed you were coming here – I knew Miss Morland was to visit today.'

'There, you see, Miss Anstey,' James said, smiling at Celia, 'you see how I rushed to get here, even though I had no hope of being invited to take tea.'

'What nonsense you talk, Mr Morland,' Celia said. 'May I refill your cup?'

'Thank you, ma'am – oh, and here are Alfred and Benjamin. Capital, capital. Do you know, it occurs to me that we have enough now for a round game. What do you say? Miss Anstey, would you care for a hand or two of something? Speculation, perhaps?'

Everyone was happy at the idea of a card game, and the gathering became quite boisterous, with James at the heart of everything, laughing and teasing and carrying everyone along with his spirits. When he and Mary were in the coach afterwards to go home, however, his spirits seemed to desert him suddenly, and he leaned back in the coach – almost slouched in his corner – and thrust his hands in his pockets, and sighed. Mary glanced at him, and saw how unhappy he looked, and was silent for a moment, wondering whether to broach the subject. Eventually she said gently, 'You did not come into the city to see Tom Loveday, then?' James did not answer. 'What was it, Jamie? What were you doing in Stonegate?'

'My bootmaker lives there, Mary, besides a number of shops—'

'And the Maccabbees Club,' she said quietly. He coloured.

'I was not at the club. I told you I was not going to drink or gamble. Do you doubt my word?'

'No,' she said. 'But as you will not tell me what you were doing, I must suppose it is something you would not like the family to hear about.'

'Suppose what you wish,' he snapped, and they were both silent. But he did look unhappy, and Mary felt a little sorry for him. Whatever it was he was up to, it evidently did not answer.

'James, do be careful, won't you?' she said, and he looked up, and sighed, and nodded.

'Yes,' he said. 'I have to be.'

It seemed to Mary an odd thing for him to say, but he volunteered nothing more, and they passed the rest of the journey in silence, he brooding, she wondering what fresh trouble he had got himself into now.

CHAPTER EIGHTEEN

Lord and Lady Meldon returned from their visit to Scotland at the beginning of August, bringing with them, to everyone's astonishment, Flora's brother Charles.

'Angus told me in his letter that Charles was coming to Scotland,' Flora explained. 'That's why I decided to go up for a visit. I didn't say anything, because I was so afraid he would not come after all. Right until the moment he walked in through the door, I was sure something would prevent him.'

She smiled affectionately at her brother, and he responded with a quirk of his lips, though Jemima thought he looked too astonished to find himself here to have much pleasure in it. He was very changed, she thought, much weatherbeaten, and looking older, and tired, with deep lines around his mouth that spoke of hardship and grief.

'We heard from William of your dreadful misfortune, Charles, and were so grieved for you,' she said. 'I hope your wife did not take ill from the experience?'

'She is well enough now, ma'am,' he said briefly, and his strange accent startled her. 'We did not know at the time she was with child. We have another son now, Louis.'

'How very dreadful for her! Poor creature! Did you not bring her with you, to England?'

'We couldn't have afforded it,' he said. 'I had to come, on business, to sort matters out with Angus. But I couldn't have gone away again without visiting you.'

'We are glad to see you,' Allen said warmly, 'and I hope now you are here you will stay for a good, long time. You intend to settle permanently in Canada, I gather?'

Charles nodded. 'And I must return as soon as possible. I take ship in ten days' time from Liverpool.'

'So soon?'

'My wife is alone with the children, apart from our servants. She is a brave woman, but things have not been easy, and the place where we live is—' he gave a curious grimace, 'not like this.'

'You are the best – the only – judge of your own necessity,' Allen said. 'You must let us know if there is anything in particular you wish to see or do while you are here, and we shall try to arrange it for you.'

Charles's face lit for the first time in a smile. 'I should like to see my American Garden,' he said. 'Does it flourish still?'

Jemima and Allen exchanged a smiling glance. 'It does indeed,' she answered. 'The eastern dogwood was beautiful this year, and the Chilean holly has grown enormously.'

'And while you're here,' Allen put in, 'you must come and look at my potatoes. I think I have created a new variety, and if it is successful, I shall call it the Morland, and make us both famous.'

Charles raised an eyebrow. 'I had almost forgotten the old scheme, that first sent me to Maryland.'

'If you're going to discuss potatoes, kindly go elsewhere and do it,' Jemima said. 'They have become an obsession with my husband – do you know, in his club in York they call him "Potato" Morland behind his back? And we have them at almost every meal—'

'That is a gross exaggeration!' Allen protested, but Jemima went on undeterred.

'—but it is all in vain, for he will never persuade Yorkshire people that potatoes are other than cattle feed.'

'Charles, I cannot let you listen to this. Come at once to the garden, and see how I have cared for your protégés,' Allen said.

Charles followed him out, but at the door he paused and turned, and said abruptly, 'I can't thank you enough for what you've done, for me and all my family. I had to come, to thank you.'

★

371

As James had predicted, Edward came back from Wolvercote bringing James Chetwyn with him, and Jemima greeted him happily, for he had always been a favourite of hers.

'I hope you will be able to stay for the birthday celebrations,' she said.

'I was hoping you would ask me,' Chetwyn said. 'Edward was for leaving me behind, but I swore to him that if he would only bring me along, you would be sure to make it all right. I had the De – *deuce* of a job persuading him,' he added, leaning forward and lowering his voice conspiratorially. 'He doesn't know about *us*, you see, dear Lady Morland.'

'What nonsense you talk,' Jemima smiled. Edward was standing at his friend's shoulder, and Jemima noticed how much happier he looked, and how much younger, than before he went to Wolvercote. He's been missing his friend, she thought, and was touched that they should have retained such love for each other since their school days. And it all began, she mused, when poor little Charlotte rescued Horatio Morland from his own folly at the hunt all those years ago; Edward's going to Eton had been a reward for Charlotte's courage – poor Charlotte, so long in her grave, quite forgotten, she suspected, by Edward, and even by William.

The question of William's future came up at dinner, when Allen asked Lord Meldon if he had decided where he and Flora were to live.

'We have almost decided on London, sir,' Meldon said with a glance at Flora. 'Although we both love the country, we are more used to the town, and at the moment it will suit me to be near Court. There are some handsome new houses being built to the north of the Oxford street, which would just suit us. Cavendish Square, for instance, is very pleasant.'

'The houses are so modern and airy,' Flora added enthusiastically. 'We visited in one of them, and quite fell in love with it. And many of our friends are moving in to the neighbourhood, so we should have plenty of society.'

'I imagine you will always have plenty of society, wherever you live,' Allen said. Out of the corner of his eye he could see Mary looking pleadingly at Flora, and when she at last, in desperation, gave a hem, he turned to her, feigning surprise. 'Why, Mary, that's a nasty cough you have. You must have been in a draught when you took tea at Shawes yesterday.'

But Flora had now picked up her cue, and came to Mary's rescue. 'I wanted to ask you – and you, ma'am – if you would be agreeable to Mary's accompanying me when we go back to London in the autumn. I have grown used to having her with me, and she is a most valuable companion.'

Jemima and Allen had been anticipating the request, and Allen had the answer ready. 'You have looked after her so well until now that we can only be grateful to you, as I'm sure Mary is, for offering her a more exciting home than we can.'

'But we should not like to lose her entirely,' Jemima added quickly. 'We wish to have her for holidays, good long ones. The town is not the best friend to anyone's health. And you will come and visit us too, I hope?'

Mary gave a fervent look of gratitude, and in her pleasure, generously brought up the subject of William.

'Charles, don't you think you might be able to do something for William? He is pining for the sea, poor creature, but without someone to speak for him at the Admiralty it seems they won't give him a ship. Couldn't you put in a word for him somewhere?'

'Of course,' Charles said good-naturedly, nodding across the table to William. 'I'm not sure how much influence I have, but my father will certainly speak for you, William, if I ask him. Why don't you come back to London with us in September, and we'll try what can be done? If Father presents you at Court, that will be a start.'

'Dear me, it looks as though all my little chicks will be

flying at once,' Jemima said with mock concern. 'And all in the same direction too.'

'Never mind, Mother, you still have me,' Edward said. 'I shan't desert the nest.' And he smiled across at Chetwyn, who winked in reply. 'And I've even brought you an honorary extra son, by way of replacement.'

'You're the only one of my children who's never caused me any concern,' Jemima said. 'You always did what you were supposed to, from childhood up.'

There was more company yet to come, for the week before the birthday, Lord and Lady Chelmsford came down to stay with the Fussells for a month, bringing the three children with them. The Fussells promptly gave a small dinner and a ball to which the Morlands, amongst others, were invited. The Fussells had five children, four of them girls, and the Morlands had not only three unmarried sons, but also the unwed Lord Calder staying with them, although, as Alison said to Jemima, 'They've had their eye on Lord Chelmsford's son Horatio for their Amelia ever since they first took the lease of Shawes. If Miss Mary don't want to be cut out, she'd better look sharp and fix him.'

Jemima rebuked her for speaking vulgarly, but afterwards applied to Edward, on whom she relied for information about the younger set, to know if Mary was still interested in Horatio Morland.

'I told you, Mama, that she had her heart set on being married into that family. The more so, now that Flora has married Lord Meldon.'

'Why so?' Jemima asked.

'Because she worships Flora, and would like to be her sister,' Edward said. 'But also, I suspect—' He hesitated. 'Has it occurred to you that Flora and Charles have been married three years, without sign of children?'

Jemima shrugged. 'It's early days yet,' she said, though her doubt showed in her voice, for Thomas had made Flora pregnant at once on both occasions he was on shore.

'Nevertheless, if they *should* fail of children, Horatio

would be the next Earl after Charles, and his wife would be Countess – or at least, her son would be Earl, one day, and I should be very surprised if the Fussells hadn't thought of that too. There have been a number of very expensive dressmakers coming and going at Shawes this past week.'

Jemima shook her head and sighed. 'The troubles that title has caused over the years,' she said. 'I should be very sorry if Mary ever came to have it, for it brought me no happiness.'

'Well, the present Lady Chelmsford is happy enough,' Edward pointed out, 'and Flora loves her Charles. I don't think you should condemn it from your own unhappiness, Mama. And I tell you what I shall do – I shall get Chetwyn to dance with Amelia Fussell all night, so as to give Mary a chance. How will that be?'

'Really, Edward—!'

'Why, Mama, it's a most generous offer, I'm sure,' Edward grinned. 'After all, I was planning to have him to myself all evening.'

It was only afterwards that Jemima thought there had been something odd about the last bit of that conversation, but she could not quite put her finger on it, and in any case, she was so busy preparing for the birthday that she had no time to brood over matters. But it came back to her at the ball at Shawes. Dinner had been very elegant, and afterwards the diners stood around in the drawing room chatting while they waited for the hour to arrive for the ball to begin. She was talking to Lord Chelmsford about horses when Allen strolled over to join them, and the Earl changed the subject.

'By the way,' he said, 'I've had a most odd letter from our young friend in Paris,' he said. 'The direction on the wrapper was most amusing – all it said was "To the Lord Chelmsford, London" – but of course it got to me all right.' Allen was giving Chelmsford significant looks, and even went so far as to hem, but the Earl was fumbling inside his coat for the letter, and did not notice. 'Deuce take it, I made sure I had it here somewhere – what? – no, that's not it. Well, no matter, I remember well enough what it said – said you'd spoken to our young cousin when you were there in '83, and undertaken to tax me about readmitting him to the family—'

He broke off at this point, at last seeing Allen's gestures. He raised his eyebrows politely, and Allen said, 'The matter has been a close secret, Charles. I'm afraid you may have—'

'What? Oh, Lord, you mean Jemima doesn't know? Dam'me – I beg your pardon, Jemima – I never thought – I assumed, as she was married to my brother—'

'I'm sorry to have overheard, even inadvertently, something I should not,' Jemima said quickly, trying to conceal that she was burning with curiosity. 'I shall take myself off at once, and give you privacy.'

Allen and Chelmsford exchanged looks, and Allen said, 'Well, I suppose it doesn't matter if Jemima knows it all, now she has heard that much.'

'Good heavens, no, you must not break a confidence for my sake,' Jemima said.

'It concerns a pensioner of mine,' Chelmsford said. 'Not to put too fine a point on it, he has a certain amount of Morland blood, albeit with a bend sinister in the way, Ma'am—'

'I shall leave you at once,' Jemima said, smiling firmly, and walked away, her thoughts racing, despite her determination not to be curious.

When she had gone, Chelmsford said, 'So what is all this, Allen? Why didn't you tell me about it?'

'He asked me to represent to you his wish of being taken back into the family, and I promised him I would think about it. I did think about it, long and seriously, but when I considered the inevitable repercussions, I decided it would be a most undesirable thing, and so I did not mention it to you. He has a child you see.'

'A child? A bastard?'

'Apparently not. He said his wife died. A girl child,

Charles, with Morland blood and Stuart eyes.' The two men regarded each other in grave silence for a moment.

'A most undesirable complication,' Chelmsford concluded.

'Precisely. And even if there were not a child, think of the explanations that would have to be made. You have seen already, in the last five minutes, how much trouble he could cause.'

'Damn it, Allen, I'm sorry about that. It never occurred to me—'

'It doesn't matter. There were reasons why I didn't tell Jemima about it. I suppose I will have to explain to her, but it won't be easy.'

'I'll write back to Henri and refuse, then. But has it occurred to you that there is no way in which we can prevent him from turning up on the doorstep one day, if the fancy takes him?'

'I think you have the means to put pressure to bear on him,' Allen said. 'You could make the pension conditional upon his maintaining secrecy.'

'Yes, that's true. Good idea. And I'll tell you what – I'll write and say that I shall continue to pay the pension to his daughter as long as he keeps mum. If he's a decent man, he won't want to jeopardize her future.'

When he rejoined Jemima, she smiled brightly at him and spoke pointedly of a neutral subject, and he lifted her hand and kissed it in token of thanks. He was afraid that if he told her the bare facts, she might guess the rest. Yet if he told her nothing, she might guess at worse things. He would have to think carefully what to say, and how to say it, and choose his moment.

Amelia Fussell and Horatio Morland opened the ball, to the chagrin of many of the young ladies present, who had hoped for the honour, but Jemima could not tell whether Mary minded, for she was at once approached by Tom Loveday, John Anstey, and James Chetwyn, and was too busy allocating them their time for her face to reveal anything to her mother. William presented himself with a bow to Caroline Fussell, and James claimed Celia Anstey's hand with a flourish. The other young people paired off, and the ball began. Mary had taken Tom Loveday for the two first, and Jemima was a little put out to see Chetwyn at once return to Edward's side, and the two of them plunge into deep conversation. She made her way quickly to them.

'Edward, why are you both standing here like this?' she asked in a voice low but urgent. 'Everyone will think you so rude. Look, there are young ladies with no partners. You, Edward, in particular – don't you see Miss Elizabeth Anstey sitting down? Go and ask her at once.'

'But Mama—'

'Don't you see, it looks as though you thought yourselves too good to dance with these girls. Would you insult the whole of York?'

'But I—'

'Not in the least, madam,' Chetwyn interrupted Edward firmly. 'Thank you for reminding us of our manners, when we had so lamentably forgot them. We shall pick two York roses this instant. Ned – you go that way, and I'll go this. Your servant, ma'am.'

He gave her a charming bow, gave Edward a firm shove in the small of the back towards the younger Miss Anstey, and walked off himself in the other direction, and a moment later led a blushing young lady into the set.

Relieved of her responsibility for a moment, Jemima was able to walk around, watch the dancing, talk to the other matrons, and remember, with a certain amount of wistfulness, her own dancing days. Edward danced the two first with Elizabeth Anstey, the two second with her sister Margaret, and the two third with Caroline Fussell. The two third were Mary's dances with Chetwyn, and at the end of them, Horatio Morland came up to claim her hand, and Jemima was so occupied in watching Mary and Horatio together, in order to determine if there was any truth in the talk, that she lost sight of Edward and Chetwyn. The two fifth Mary danced again with John Anstey, which was enough in any case to cause comment, but Jemima noticed, as must every gossip in the room, that Miss Morland's eyes and cheeks were bright, and that she had no lack of things to say to her partner. Jemima did not know whether to be pleased or worried. It would be good to think that Mary's genuine affection for John Anstey was stronger than her ambition for a title, and yet she had refused him before, and was, moreover, planning to go to London with Flora in a month's time, where she would be in Horatio's company and out of Anstey's sight.

It was when that pair ended that Jemima suddenly realized Edward and his friend were no longer in the ballroom, and a wave of anger rushed over her that Edward had ignored her stated wishes that he should dance. Chetwyn's rudeness was bad enough, and disappointed her, when she had thought so well of him, but Edward owed her a duty, and as unobtrusively as she could she slipped out of the ballroom to go in search of them. It was easy for her to move quickly and surely about the house which had once been hers, and she did not have far to look to find them. They were in the orangery, and as she came to the door, she saw them standing amongst some greenery, looking out of the window.

She had been about to call out to them, but something stopped her. They were not doing anything in particular, just standing side by side, looking out at the velvety night, not even talking. It was the way she and Allen sometimes stood, looking at the moon, or at the scenery, too close to need to speak, keeping pace with each other's thoughts with the ease of accustomed lovers. Edward had known Chetwyn since he was a young boy, and presumably they were close enough also not to need to talk. And yet—

While she hesitated, she heard one of them sigh – she could not tell which – and then Chetwyn laid his arm for a moment across Edward's shoulder, and Edward turned his head and smiled at his friend. Then something near her

379

rustled – the draught moving some leaves, perhaps – and Chetwyn removed his arm, and walked away, going towards the other door. At that moment Jemima walked forward, and Edward turned and saw her.

He waited for her apprehensively, while Chetwyn left them by the far door, and Jemima was never sure if he had seen her or not. Edward looked like a child expecting to be scolded for stealing apples, but she was no longer angry – there was instead a heaviness inside her, like the forerunner of sorrow. She stood for a while looking at him, wondering what to say. Should she berate him for leaving the dance? What was it that was cold and heavy in her breast? What was she afraid of? He looked so young, she thought. He had always looked younger than his age. And while she was still waiting for words to come to her, he said, 'Well, Mother, now you know.'

Know what? she wondered, but before she had time to say it, his mouth quivered, and his cheeks burned with a sudden flow of blood, and the understanding came to her with a great gush of shock, and fear, and, more than anything, grief. Grief for him, for Edward, her gentle son – no anger. She wondered why she had not known before, considering the ways of her first husband with his 'friends' – but even as she thought it, she knew that this could not be the same thing. Rupert's male friends were not like Chetwyn, and he had not behaved with them as she had seen Edward behave. That arm across the shoulder, and the smile, were loving and tender; she could not believe there was anything vicious there. And yet—

'For God's sake, say something!' Edward said desperately, his voice cracking. 'Shout at me, berate me, but don't – just – stand there.'

She let her breath out in a long sigh. 'Oh Edward,' she said, and the gentleness of her voice made him flinch. 'What can I say?'

He turned his head, a movement of pain, and she wanted to comfort him. How had he been tainted? Rupert was no kin to him. What had happened to him?

'How far—?' she began, asking a question she didn't want to know the answer to. 'I mean – you and – your friend – how far has it gone? Are you lovers?'

Edward looked at her puzzled. 'What do you mean?' he asked. 'How could we be lovers?' Her instant relief must have shown on her face, because suddenly he was scarlet, and a mixture of anger and shame made his eyes fill with tears. 'Oh!' he said. 'You mean—?' He shook his head, not in denial, but as one shakes away a troublesome insect. 'Of course not! How could you even think that we would—? How could you say such a thing?'

'I didn't say it, darling,' Jemima said. 'I didn't really think it – I only wanted to be sure.'

'Chetwyn and I are friends. He is my dearest, dearest friend. I love him.' Now his angry voice gentled, and he went on apologetically. 'That's why, you see, Mother – I'm sorry to disappoint you. But I can't find it in my heart to care about girls. I can't explain. I wanted to tell you, often and often, but I knew I could never make you understand.'

'I do understand,' she said.

'No, you don't. How could you?'

'It will change, Edward. Your feelings will change in time, and this love will become part of other loves you feel.' He shook his head, and she saw it was no use talking any more now. 'Go back to the ball now,' she said. 'And dance all the dances.'

He looked at her like something stricken. 'Are you ashamed of me, Mother?'

'No. No, of course not. You are my good, dear, gentle son, Ned. Nothing changes that. Now go back to the ball. Go on. I shall follow.'

Alone, she tried to compose herself. It is just a boyish fancy, she thought, nothing more. He will grow out of it. A young boy's hero-worship which somehow had not ceased when it should. In time it would assume its proper dimension in Edward's life. In a few years it would all be forgotten, and he'd be a husband and father like any other young man.

So she told herself, and with her mind she believed it. But as she turned back towards the ballroom, she felt for the first time the touch of age, and she climbed the stairs slowly, as though they wearied her.

'What's the matter?' Allen asked her as they got into bed.

'It's nothing,' she said vaguely, her mind still whirling so that she forgot for a moment that it was useless to say that.

'Jemima, my love,' he protested gently. She gave a small, troubled smile.

'I'm sorry. Yes, of course I am preoccupied.' In that moment she decided not to tell Allen what had passed between her and Edward that evening. If, as she hoped, he grew out of it, there was no need to worry Allen. If he did not, Allen would come to realize it in good time, and the knowledge, coming gradually, might be more palatable.

Allen, with his mind on his own problems, sighed and realized that there was no choosing the right time – it would have to be now.

'You are thinking about what Lord Chelmsford said,' he suggested. Jemima looked up at him quickly. She had entirely forgotten that episode, but now he had brought it up, it would do to explain her thoughtfulness.

'It is none of my business,' she said, avoiding a direct lie. Allen sat up and turned to face her.

'I have never kept anything from you, in all our lives together, but this was not my secret to tell.'

'Wasn't it?' Jemima mused. He looked at her carefully.

'What is it you are thinking?'

'I have tried not to think,' she said, 'but I suppose it would be natural to imagine – Charles said it concerned a Morland bastard, who lives in Paris—'

'And you thought it was mine?'

She reddened a little. 'Not exactly – but—'

'Very well. A natural assumption. And it answers a question I have been asking myself – whether to tell you more than you already know.'

'You said the secret was not yours to tell. I would not ask you to break a confidence.'

'No, I know that. But I don't want you to think worse than the truth. You remember Marie-Louise ran away to join the Young Chevalier in the '45 rebellion?'

'Of course. I went to say goodbye to her on the day before she left,' Jemima said. 'I gave her a locket to give to you.'

Allen nodded. 'And she died in Glasgow that winter.'

'Of a fever,' Jemima said, beginning to see where this led.

'Of the childbed fever,' Allen said steadily. Jemima made a small, soundless 'o' of understanding. The next question was trembling on her lips, but Allen continued without waiting for it.

'Her dying request was that the baby, a boy, should be taken to her mother, and those of us in the family who knew about it decided that was the best course anyway. Aliena was in a convent near Paris. I bought a house for her and the child with the compensation money the French Government paid me, and she gave up her vows and went to live there to bring up the child. Her brother Maurice, who was then the Earl of Chelmsford, paid her a pension, which has been continued by each Earl of Chelmsford since. On my trips to Paris I have sometimes transacted business on the Earl's behalf with Aliena and the boy. So now you know it all.'

The question was still there. 'Not quite all,' she said. 'Who was the father of the child?' He did not answer, wondering whether he could tell her, and she went on, 'Was it you?'

'No,' he said.

'I know that you loved her. You travelled with her for months. Tell me truly.'

'Truly, it was not me.'

'Then who?' There was a long, long silence. 'Who?'

'Your father.'

'*My father?*' He saw that the shock was all he had feared it would be; how much worse, if she learned about the child.

'I don't think he ever knew. I don't think anyone has known, except me and Aliena. But you see now why he has had to be kept away from the family, in exile, in secret.'

He saw her pull herself together. 'I am my father's heir, and in that sense, head of the family. It is right that I should know.' She gave a wavering smile. 'And to tell the truth, I am so glad it is not your bastard that I don't mind anything else very much.'

He took her in his arms, and drew her down under the covers, and settled her on his shoulder. 'I'm glad you know,' he said. 'I never liked having secrets from you.' In a few minutes he was asleep, but she lay awake for a long time, staring into the darkness and thinking.

CHAPTER NINETEEN

James Morland was reaching crisis point. He felt like a juggler who had added one more and one more egg to his act, and had come to the point where he could not stop juggling without breaking them all. His brother Edward knew some of it, but not even he knew it all, and he dared not approach him for more help. On the day after the ball at Shawes he took refuge in the Maccabbees Club, and there found Horatio Morland slumped by the fire that burned brightly, winter and summer, for it was a dark and chilly house. Horatio looked very much the worse for wear, and called James over in an expiring voice.

'Come and join me – boy, bring another pint of wine. Damnation, it's the last time I try to outdrink that brother of yours!'

'William?'

'Aye, that damned, pigtailed sponge of a man! Deuced if I could keep pace with him. Where it all goes, I don't know, for he wasn't even foxed when I crawled to bed. And you,' Horatio added, squinting up at James with sudden petulance, 'why do you look so damned jolly this morning?'

'I – jolly? I'm the most unhappy man in York,' James protested.

'You're young, that's what it is,' Horatio answered himself. 'When I was your age, I could rise from m'bed looking like that. For God's sake, sit down. You make me feel tired, looming over me like that. Boy, where's that wine?'

James looked about him nervously, but it was early yet, and there were few people in the club. At any moment, however, the more impatient of his creditors might enter, and there would be the Devil to pay. However, as Horatio was buying, and it was safe enough at present, he sat down, and took the glass that was proferred.

'Well, here's your health. And – and – what else shall we drink to?' Horatio said.

'To fortune,' James said gloomily. 'I wish to God I had one.'

'To larger allowances,' Horatio added fervently. 'My father is so deuced mean about it. If it weren't for the cards running my way last week—'

'They didn't run mine.'

'Confusion to unco-operative cards, and slow horses, and damned impatient creditors,' Horatio proposed, and they drank it deep, and refilled their glasses.

'And confusion to unmarried women and their ambitious mamas,' James suggested next.

'By God, I'll drink to that,' Horatio said. 'That ball last night – I felt like a sparrow in an alley full of cats. And the biggest jaws of all were Lady Fussell's. If she don't get me for one of her girls, she'll die in the attempt.' He drank the toast, and then eyed James with sympathy. 'Which one of 'em is it you want to avoid?'

'Miss Anstey,' James groaned. 'Celia. I suppose she's a nice enough girl really, but since her younger sister got betrothed, she's been after me like a bloodhound. She smiles, and talks, and laughs, and flirts, and holds on to my arm and – I can't get away from her.'

'You were being polite enough last night,' Horatio said without sympathy. 'It didn't look to *me* as if you minded her attentions. If you encourage 'em, you spoil it for the rest of us.'

'The trouble is, she knows an awful lot – too much – and if I don't keep her sweet, she'll ferret out the rest, and then it's all up with me.' He drained his glass absently, and Horatio filled it again. 'She saw me the day before yesterday in – a certain street, where I was visiting someone—'

'Someone you didn't want her to know about?'

'Of course. So I had to pretend I was coming to see her,

386

or she'd have found out one way or another where I was going. It's damnable.'

'Ah well, they can't come in here, to the good old Maccabbees, so let's forget 'em for a while. Drink up. Let's talk of something else. How's that horse of yours, that ginger devil? I wouldn't mind wagering that's the fastest horse in Yorkshire over the country.'

They talked and drank, and settled deeper into the chairs by the fire, and bit by bit they were joined by other like-minded young men, and the day passed in a haze of wine and fellowship. James had begun to feel safe, lulled into a false sense of security, out of which he was abruptly shaken by the arrival of a large and heavy young man, Dick Turner, a gentleman farmer and, as it happened, a man to whom James owed a debt of long standing.

'By God, Morland, if you've got the wherewithal to drink so deep, you've been lying to me. I'll have that twenty pound you've owed me since Easter, and I'll have it right now.'

'Now, Turner,' someone said, 'you can't call a gentleman a liar. 'Tisn't done.'

'Gentleman? Does a gentleman tell a gentleman he can't pay his debts, and then go squandering his all on claret?'

'*I've* been buying the wine,' Horatio said, but then, a demon of mischief waking in him, added, 'but a debt is an affair of honour, you're right in that. Morland, why don't you pay him?'

'He hasn't got twenty pound, that's why,' said another young man, swaying bibulously. 'He owes me more than that, since Michaelmas last. But dammit, I don't go about demanding it in that ferocious manner. Have a drink, Turner, and show your generous, manly heart.'

There was a surge of shouting as some advocated paying the debt and others claimed it was not gentlemanly to demand it, and the argument went on, growing more heated as the level in the bottles sank. Turner stood swaying belligerently on his massive legs, not entirely sure what he had last said, and James kept very quiet, drinking whenever his glass was filled and agreeing with everyone in turn. He had got to the point where he could not decide anything any more. From debt the conversation drifted naturally to horses, and then Horatio precipitated another argument by repeating his opinion that James's chestnut was the fastest horse in Yorkshire over the country.

At that point, young Lord Ashley, who was not as drunk as the rest of them, had his brilliant idea.

'Why don't we put it to the test? Turner here has a horse he boasts of. Why don't he and Morland race 'em together, point to point, and decide it? I tell you what, Morland, it could solve all your problems, too, for we'll take bets on it, and give you a purse if you win.'

'He won't win,' Turner said, 'so where's the point of it? His chestnut may be fast, but it hasn't the bone of my brown gelding, and bone counts across country. And a horse is only as good as his rider, and I'd undertake to beat that boy over any country you care to name.'

'Fair enough,' Lord Ashley shouted over the renewed babble of voices. 'You all heard what Turner said. If Morland beats him over country to be named by me, he'll cancel the debt, and pay him twenty guineas into the bargain.'

'And if I lose,' James mumured to Ashley under the cover of the shouting, 'I'll have to shoot myself.'

'You won't lose,' Ashley said. 'Turner's horse is a lumbering cart-nag, and you are twice the rider he is, and half as drunk. You'll win handsomely, and that'll be the answer to your problem. You can pay me back, too, from your winnings,' he added with a grin. 'Right,' he turned round and shouted to the gathering, 'let's see it done now. I say it shall be run from St Edward's Church on the south road to St Michael's at Acomb. That's about a mile and a half. Are we all agreed?'

There was a cheer raised by those who were not already using their voices to argue fiercely about odds and putting their money on their favourite.

★

It was around dinner time when James was brought home, carried by four rapidly sobering men, with another leading his limping horse behind him. He was carried up to a bedroom, and the apothecary sent for, and while Jemima hung over him and bathed his head, Allen drew out the story bit by bit from the young men. When he had dismissed them, he joined his wife by the miscreant's bedside.

'How is he?'

Alison, who was plying the cloth and the hartshorn, clucked and shook her head, and Jemima said in a low voice, 'He hasn't come to his senses yet. He has a wound on his head, but no other injuries as far as I can see.'

'He reeks of wine, sir, and that's a fact. Fell out of his saddle drunk, I wouldn't wonder,' Alison said. 'How a person's to know if he's knocked senseless or drunk senseless I'm sure I don't know.'

'What happened?' Jemima asked Allen. He turned her aside a little and spoke quietly, to keep it from Alison.

'Apparently they were all drinking in a club, and they made a wager about James's horse. There was a race between him and another young man, and James took a tumble over a hedge and they took him up senseless like that.' He glanced across at his son. 'I dare say the amount of wine he'd had affected his balance. The worst thing is that he's deep in debt all over town. One of those youngsters let it slip that he agreed to the race because it would clear some of his debts.'

'How can he owe money? What can he be spending it on?'

Allen grimaced. 'Drink. Cards. Clothes. I hope nothing worse. But you know how men gamble. Anything will do. Obviously he overspent his allowance and started borrowing to make it up. We'll have to have it out with him when he comes to himself, find out exactly what he owes and to whom, and pay it all off. We can't have this sort of thing. Reflects on us all.'

'When he comes to himself,' Jemima said, looking fearfully at his pale face. 'You mean *if* he does.'

Allen patted her hand. 'Hush, my dear. God keeps a special eye on rogues like James. He'll be all right.'

The apothecary, when he came, confirmed Allen's judgement, though less firmly. James had been lucky not to break any bones, but probably the drink had loosened him in his fall. The head wound was not deep, and the skull was intact, and provided he came to within the day, and was kept very quiet in bed for a week, he should be sound enough.

James woke up around dusk, groaned, was sick, complained of a splitting headache, and fell asleep again at once. The next morning he woke naturally, still had a headache, but had no memory of the fall, and only the vaguest memory of the race or the wager or the drinking that led up to it.

In the afternoon, Allen went in to speak to him.

'We know about your debts, child,' he said, and James had the grace to colour. 'Why did you let matters get to such a pitch? You should have come to me if you wanted money, not to strangers.'

'I didn't think you'd give it to me,' James muttered.

'Because you've wasted your allowance on drink and gambling?' Allen said. 'Well, I've no sympathy for that sort of thing, you're right there. But a debt is a matter of honour, and you implicate us all when you use your Morland name to borrow money.' He noted the pallor of his son's face, and said more kindly, 'I won't go on about it now, when you're feeling badly. But when you are well again, we will have to go over it, and you will have to tell me every penny you owe, so that it can all be paid back.'

It was not a prospect to please. Shame made James say sulkily, 'If you had given me a decent allowance in the first place—'

'I gave you what I thought you reasonably needed. I was not to know you had *un*reasonable demands too. But what hurts me most, James, is not that you are a drunkard and a gambler – though that is bad enough to have to acknowledge about one's son – but that you have been so secretive, that you have cared so little for us, for the family, as to bring us into disrepute through your actions.'

James turned his head away wearily, and Allen saw a tear shining in his eye, and knew he had said enough. He stood up.

'Rest now, and when you are well we will talk it all out, and see if we can't do better in the future. You have great abilities, my son, and it is a shame to abuse them so.'

He went away, and James closed his eyes and swallowed tears. Pain in his head, and shame in his heart, were yet eased by a relief that the juggling was over, the eggs had fallen and smashed, and that he no longer had to fear the worst. Provided, he thought wearily, the other matter did not come out – but there was no reason why it should. It was not connected in any way to debt or drink or the Maccabbees Club.

Celia Anstey presided over her tea kettle with more content than was usual. Her sister Augusta had come to tea, bringing with her Mrs Skelwith, the former Mary Loveday, who was looking pale and plain; and although her sister Margaret had her fiancé Edgar Somers with her, and was simpering over him abominably, Celia could comfort herself that James Morland was twice as clever as Edgar and ten times as handsome, and that he had danced with her more than with anyone else at the ball at Shawes. He seemed to have been expressing a definite preference, and she was just a little surprised that he had not come to call on her – using her brothers as an excuse of course – to follow up his advantage.

The doorbell below rang, and Celia noticed Mary Skelwith jump at the sound and turn her head irresistibly towards the door for a second before she recovered herself. She had exhibited the same restlessness once or twice before, and Celia leaned forward and said with honeyed concern in her voice, 'Why, Mary dear, you aren't looking so very well this afternoon.'

'I'm very well, Celia, thank you,' Mary said, composing herself with an effort.

'But you are pale, and seem so nervous, dear. What a shame your husband should be away at a time when you are not well. Sure, you must have been all alone last night?' She had brought up the subject of Mary's husband only because she thought Mary was ashamed of having had to marry such an old man as John Skelwith, but Mary looked if possible even paler, though two small spots of red appeared on her cheekbones.

'Of course I was alone,' she said sharply. 'But I am used to it. I am often alone.'

Celia raised an eyebrow. 'La, how strange you are! I didn't mean anything by it. Have some more tea, Mary dear.' The door opened, and Celia's maid came in, looking agitated.

'A letter for you, ma'am,' she said, and lingered after handing it over, making significant noddings of her head and rollings of her eyes.

'Very well. What is the matter, Jenkins? What is it you want?' Celia said impatiently, pausing in the opening of her letter.

'Oh ma'am, haven't you heard? Terrible news, ma'am,' the maid said with relish.

'What news? I haven't heard any news.'

'Mr James Morland, ma'am,' the maid nodded importantly. 'Had a fall from his horse, a bad one, and was taken up lifeless, ma'am.'

'What?' Celia cried out, but her attention was taken away at once by a strange moan from Mrs Skelwith, who half rose to her feet, and then sank back into her chair, deathly pale.

'Good God, she's fainted!' Mr Somers said, and while he and the other ladies crowded around her, patting her hands and fanning her face, Celia shook her unfortunate maid and scolded her, and then, seeing the letter she had been given was from Morland Place, hastily opened it.

Mrs Skelwith soon came to herself, and answered inquiries faintly with, 'I am quite well, quite well. Please, don't trouble yourselves.'

'Are you sure, Mary?' Augusta asked, and being in an interesting condition herself, her mind naturally ran that way. 'Perhaps you may be in the family way? Have you thought of it, dear?'

Before Mary could be obliged to answer, Celia, who had read her letter with some trepidation, said, 'It's all right. This is from Mary Morland, who explains it all. James had a fall and hit his head, but he is not seriously hurt, and will be quite well in a day or two. Jenkins, how could you be so stupid? Go away at once, and be more careful in future before you spread rumours.'

'That was how I heard it, ma'am,' Jenkins said stubbornly. 'I'm sure I can't help it if I'm told wrong.' She flounced out, and Celia turned to look at Mary with a sudden thoughtfulness, as several apparently unconnected threads came together in her mind.

'Are you all right, Mary?' she asked abruptly, and Mary met her gaze with her usual calm.

'Yes, of course. It was silly of me – but it is a little hot in here,' she said, and Celia let it pass.

The birthday celebrations were to spread over three days: on the first day a cricket match and horse races; on the second day a fair with all the usual competitions and quite a few new ones Jemima and Allen had thought up, finishing with fireworks and music; and on the third day a grand dinner and a ball.

In spite of his accident, and the unpleasant and embarrassing interview with his father that had followed his recovery, James had regained enough of his aplomb to ride his chestnut in one of the races and even to smile when he won a pipe of wine. In the evening there was a quiet family supper, from which he could not well absent himself. Everyone was there to wish Allen a happy birthday and drink his health, and offer their presents, but when they settled down afterwards to sit about the fire talking, James excused himself by saying he had a headache and was going to bed.

'Yes, you've had quite an energetic day, haven't you?' Allen said genially. 'You rode a good race, James.'

'I hope you have not been doing too much,' Jemima said with some concern. 'If you wake up with a headache tomorrow, you must tell me, and we'll have the apothecary over straight away.'

'I'll be all right, Mother,' James said, and kissed her, and went away, to prepare a bolster for his bed and slip out down the back stairs. He felt a little bad about it, especially since Mother and Father were being so kind, but he couldn't help it. He must see her, and tonight was his last chance, before her husband returned.

The next day was the fair, and long before dawn the stallholders were setting up, and the fires were being lit for the cook-pits. By midday it was in full swing, and the fields around the moated house were filled with people and noise and heat and smells and a hearty holiday mood. The games and competitions were under way, the jugglers and entertainers, the dancing bear and the dog that walked on its hind legs, the travelling musicians, the fire-eater, the Educated Horse, the gypsy who told fortunes, the Eastern Mystic who walked on nails, and the sword swallower were all giving their shows, and people were eating, gawping, playing, talking, gambling, dancing, and flirting, just as the fancy took them.

Celia Anstey, having shed her younger brothers at the cooked-meat stall, and her sisters at the gypsy's booth, wandered about in search of James, and finally found him, rather out of the throng, leaning against a tree and staring moodily at the bright scene before him. She went towards him eagerly, preparing to tease him a little and try to cheer his obvious sadness, when she suddenly saw what he was looking at, and stiffened. John Skelwith was standing at an ale stall nearby, talking to a group of his business acquaintances, with his wife on his arm. All Celia's hurt and jealousy rose up in her, and she walked over to James as stiff-legged as a threatened dog.

'Well,' she said, and James started and turned to look at her, and then turned his head away and settled moodily against his tree again. 'Well, that's put a stop to *your* little game, hasn't it?'

'I don't know what you're talking about,' James said wearily. 'Please, Miss Anstey, I don't want to be rude, but—'

'No, I'm sure you don't want to be rude to *me*,' she said pointedly. 'After all, you need someone to confide in, and there can't be many people left you can talk to. In fact, Mr Morland, it may well be that I'm your only friend.'

He pushed himself upright and turned on her irritably, like a bull goaded by flies. 'I have plenty of friends. I don't know what you're talking about, and I don't want to know. If you'll excuse me I'll—'

'Stay where you are,' she said sharply. 'I say you need someone to confide in – someone who knows about you and Mary Skelwith.'

He froze.

'Yes, that surprises you, doesn't it? You thought no-one knew. You thought you had been very clever.'

'There is nothing between Mrs Skelwith and me,' he said, and then, seeing it was no use to deny what she evidently knew, he gestured with his head towards the group he had been watching. 'Nothing, now. You see, he is back. It's all over, and if you were to speak of it to anyone, I would simply deny it, and then where would you be?'

'You think it's all over? You poor simpleton. Don't you know she's taken to fainting? Poor Mary, she turns pale and faints away, and I wonder what can cause that? I

395

don't suppose she's told *him* yet. He doesn't look as though she has, does he?'

James stared at the talking group for a long moment, and then turned to Celia, his face rigid with anguish. 'What do you want? he said in a low voice. Celia smiled, feeling her power over him at last, to make up for the years in which he had had power over her.

'Be nice to me, Mr Morland, that's all. You danced with me a good deal at Shawes, and if you dance with me tomorrow at the ball, people will think your attentions are growing very pointed. Well, you have to marry some time, don't you? No one would be at all surprised if you were to ask for my hand. I'm a good match, after all, and you're only third son. Though, of course, people will see that I'm fond of you, too. I shall be *very* nice to you, I think, if you are nice to me.'

She stepped closer, laying her hand on his arm and smiling up at him, and he looked down at her and saw the triumph in her smile and the apprehension in her eyes. He bared his teeth in what might charitably be called a grin.

'You're a fool,' he said contemptuously, and shook her hand off, and walked away. Rage and chagrin burned her cheeks.

'It's you that's the fool!' she shrieked after him. 'You'll see! You'll see!'

But he did not stop, or even turn.

For days no-one spoke of anything but the Skelwith Scandal, and even after the first excitement had died down, the subject was revived almost daily for weeks, told and retold, losing nothing in the telling. Deliciously it was chewed over, how skimble-shanked old John Skelwith was cuckolded within weeks of his marriage by that young spike James Morland, a mere boy; and how, when the old man found out the state of affairs, he had marched off on his own two bent legs, and broken in upon the

Morland family in the middle of their family dinner to celebrate Master Morland's birthday to demand recompense. And how the lady herself, following her husband in the chaise as soon as she could get the servants to turn it out, ran in, practically *en deshabille*, and clutched her husband's arm, sobbing, as if she thought he was going to strike someone.

York society was pretty uncharitable to the participants in the drama, finding their confusion and distress a matter for more mirth than sympathy, and Skelwith got shortest shrift of all, for it was generally agreed that when an ugly old man married a pretty young girl he must expect what he got, especially if he left her alone in the house for weeks at a time while he attended to business. Thus fame translated Mary at a stroke: she was a pretty young girl in this adventure, while at the time she married she was considered lucky to get Master Skelwith on account of being plain and twenty.

Celia Anstey was much ridiculed for her part in the episode, which was entirely contrary to her expectations. To hear herself derided as a cross old spinster, so eaten up with jealousy because her infatuation with the young man was not returned that she tried to stir up a duel in which he might be shot, mortified her so severely that for days she shut herself in her room, sobbing dismally.

'But what did you do it for, girl?' her father roared at her again and again. 'Did you want to make us a laughing stock?'

It only added to her shame when she heard him say to John, 'Now tha mayst be thankful that Mary Morland turned thee down. It wouldn't do to be mixed up with that family now,' and to see John's patient sorrow as he bore the sting. In the end Sir John solved the immediate problem by packing Celia, her mother and her unwed sisters off to Harrogate to take the waters and keep out of the way until the affair died down.

Various were the emotions of the Morland Family, immediately and afterwards, but amusement was not one

397

of them. It was they, of course, who witnessed the wounded husband's rage, so great that it transcended for a short while his undistinguished appearance, so that while he stood blazing in the doorway to the dining room there was nothing ludicrous about him, despite his bowed legs, despite the day-old traveller's stubble on his chin, and the large old-fashioned wig knocked askew on his head. It was they, too, who saw his young wife cling to his arm and beg his forgiveness, and saw him suddenly begin to weep.

The family dinner was broken up, the birthday ball cancelled at once, and on Allen, who should have been celebrating as the head of a happy, united and prosperous family, fell the burden of the interviews: with the miscreants, and with the outraged husband. The latter was the longest and most unpleasant, for while he sympathized entirely with Master Skelwith's anger, he had to try to soothe it, and to persuade him out of more violent and public expression of it. Skelwith was for casting Mary off, for calling James out, for horsewhipping him, for divorcing her, for having her whipped through the streets as a whore, for having them both put in the stocks in the Thursday Market, and finally for shooting him, her, and then himself to put an end to the unhappy business.

Allen wisely let him rage for a time, and then began gently to persuade him that a public casting-off of Mary would do no-one any good, and would only bring him public odium. It was a delicate point, for John Skelwith assumed that public opinion would be with him, while Allen, who knew the world pretty well, was already convinced that it would find the old man's plight laughable.

'Consider, sir, a divorce would need an Act of Parliament. It would be discussed in public places, written up in the newspapers. People would say – I'm truly sorry, but I'm afraid they would – that you weren't able to keep her, even for a few weeks.' Skelwith scowled, but Allen saw that he took the point. 'Consider again, the young woman is penitent, she has learned her lesson, is ready to make all amends that possibly can be made in such a sad case. Would it not be better to forgive her? You have the rest of your life to live with her. Would you throw away everything for one early mistake?'

'Mistake?' Skelwith said dangerously.

'Error. Crime. Sin. Call it what you will. She is young, sir, and high spirited, and I doubt she understood fully what she was about.' He was sure she *did*, but no matter. 'She has learned her lesson. Why not let it end there?'

'But the young man – he should not get off scot-free.'

'I think you can safely leave him to me, sir,' Allen said. Skelwith cocked his head on one side.

'Oh can I, sir? I don't think I can, sir. I think you will be lenient with him, your own son, sir. I want him horsewhipped. I want him—'

'Yes, I know. But who is to do it?' Allen said quietly. There was a brief silence, and then Allen said, 'I shall deal with him, sir, with all the severity the case deserves, I promise you. You have my word on that.'

When Skelwith finally departed, Allen leaned back in his chair and rubbed his eyes wearily. All the severity it deserves, he thought. 'God damn the boy,' he exploded aloud. 'Why couldn't he take his pleasures discreetly?'

Edward put his head around the door. 'Did you call, Father?'

'No. Yes – send James to me. Where is he?'

'He's in his room. I've been talking to him.'

'Is he penitent?' Allen asked, without much hope. Edward shook his head.

'Not a bit. He says that after the fuss you made over Maggie Henshaw, he gathered that if he had a mistress it would have to be a married one, and now he has done what you wanted you're upset about it.'

'Upset!'

'He said he didn't want to risk the brothel in Petergate, so what else could he do?' Edward shrugged. 'I suppose it's only what's done every day of the week in every town

399

in the country, Papa. Men will take mistresses, and women will be unfaithful.'

'But damn it, not a woman only just married! Why did he have to choose her, of all people?'

'Well, Papa,' Edward said gravely, 'I think, oddly enough, that he is in love with her.' He hesitated before asking, 'What did you agree with Skelwith?'

'I said I would give James the punishment the case deserved.'

'I see. Yes, that's very subtle. Well, I'll go and fetch the miscreant, shall I?'

'Yes, do, Ned. God knows what I can say to him. Where's your mother?'

'In the drawing room. She's taking it rather badly. When I've brought you James, I'll go and sit with her.'

Mary and William had taken themselves out of the way as soon as they could, and Edward found his mother alone, sitting staring at the fire. He sat on the arm of her chair and put his arm round her shoulders, and said, 'Don't take it to heart so, Mother. There's no harm done.'

'No harm done?' she said.

'No – believe me. Skelwith has been placated, James will be rebuked, and the gossips will have a wonderful time for a few days, and then it will all be forgotten. If the old fool hadn't made such a fuss, it would never have got this far in the first place.'

'You don't think he should have made a fuss?' Jemima said. 'Really, Ned, sometimes I just don't understand you. Not make a fuss when he finds his wife is having an affair with a boy several years younger than her, only weeks after their marriage?'

'Well, what did he expect? It isn't such an astonishing thing, now is it, Mother? It's been going on since the world began, and will go on for ever. Half the literature of the world is about old men being cheated by young wives And what harm is there, in the end? It will all blow over, you'll see.'

'But what about the sanctity of marriage?' Jemima cried. 'It is a holy sacrament.'

'There was never anything sacred about *that* marriage, nor about two-thirds of modern marriages, I should say. She wanted his money, he wanted her youth, so they made a bargain. It's business, Mother, not a sacrament.'

'Edward, don't talk like that, please. You have been brought up with better ideas, surely?'

'Things are changing, Mother. Ideas are changing. People today don't just accept everything they're told. Religion is being set aside, when it doesn't pay.'

'Edward!'

'Oh, don't worry, Mother, I'm still your dutiful son. That isn't *me* talking. I'm only telling you how people think. Things are changing, and you can't turn the tide back. People want to decide for themselves what's right and what's wrong, and what to do with their lives. They're not content to be told, and to ask no questions.'

'Very well, but we are talking of individuals, not these "people" with whose ideas you are so well acquainted. We are talking of young Mary Loveday ruined, John Skelwith deeply wounded and unhappy. And what about the child?'

'Ah, the child,' Edward said thoughtfully. 'Well, I suppose it will be all the same to the child, one way and another. It will be born in wedlock, and if it has some other man for a father, I don't suppose it will ever know. Such things happen all the time.'

'But not—' Jemima was about to say, but not in this family. And then she remembered the night of the ball at Shawes, and Allen's revelations about Marie-Louise's bastard child, who was, when all was said, her own brother. Her father, her dear, revered, beloved father, had sinned too. Edward was right. She burst abruptly into tears.

'Oh Mama, please don't cry!' Edward dropped to the floor in front of her, knelt at her knees and tried to take her in his arms, more distressed than he could have expected. 'Oh don't, don't. There's nothing here worth that. You've never cried, Mama, never.'

'I don't understand anything any more,' she whimpered through her tears and her hands. 'The whole world seems to have turned upside down. There's you – and James – and—'

'Oh dearest, darling Mama, please don't cry! I'm still here, still your same Edward, and I'll always be here, I'll never go away, never change. And James—'

'What will become of James?' she said miserably.

'James will survive,' Edward said firmly. 'He will always survive, even if the whole world goes up in flames. He is a salamander. Sooner weep for me than for James!' She fumbled for her handkerchief, and he drew his out and thrust it into her fingers, and she wiped her eyes and blew her nose and sat up, her old brisk self again.

'Oh dear,' she said. 'I'm better now. What a fool I've been. You must not tell your father what a fool I've been, Edward.' He was still kneeling before her, watching her face, and she thought how very young he looked, and she was glad in a secret and guilty way that he would stay hers, like that, and not marry away from her. She patted his cheek, and he smiled. 'Poor Allen! What a time he's having of it, and on his birthday, too, when everything was supposed to be so splendid for him.'

'Yes, poor Papa. We must try to make it up to him when the fuss dies down.'

Flora and Lord Meldon, who had once been the cause of tumult and scandal themselves, felt tenderly towards Allen and Jemima, and on the day after the news broke they came up with their scheme to ease matters for them. They proposed, when they left for London, to take with them not only Mary and William, but James too.

'I've spoken to my father about it,' Meldon said, 'and he's perfectly agreeable to have James stay at Chelmsford

House, and to present him at Court. He's sure he will be able to get James some appointment. The King likes well set up young men, and he will not forget what he owes to *you*, Sir Allen. As a gentleman of the bedchamber or something of the sort James will be in the way of making a career for himself, and the talk here will soon die down once he is out of sight.'

'And it will take him out of temptation's way, as far as Mrs Skelwith is concerned,' Jemima murmured approvingly, for from what she had seen and heard of James's attitude to the whole affair, she was not convinced he did not mean to take up again where he left off, only more discreetly.

Thus it was settled, and James, though not asked for his approval, was satisfied with the scheme. He was eager for new horizons and wider opportunities, and it would certainly be agreeable to be out of the way of his sniggering acquaintances and his scolding family for a while.

The last small incident happened on the day before the departure in the middle of September, when Mary had gone into York to make some last-minute purchases. She scorned the idea of hiding herself away and avoiding the Ansteys or Fussells or anyone else who might stare or laugh; but as she was walking along Pavement with her maid behind her, she almost bumped into a young man coming out of the hatter's shop, and when she saw that it was John Anstey, she almost wished she had stayed home.

There was a moment's awkward silence, and both of them turned a little red, and then John Anstey bowed abruptly, and Mary replied with a slight curtsey, and John said, 'Your servant, ma'am. I hope you are well?'

'Thank you, sir. I'm just – just doing some shopping, you see.' It was foolish of her to explain her presence, and the foolishness warmed John, and made him more confident.

'Miss Morland – I just wanted to say – I'm very sorry—'
'Sorry? For what?'

'For the unpleasantness. *You* know. For what Celia did. It was terrible, but she has been so miserable, if you saw her you would forgive her.'

'I'm not aware there is anything to forgive,' Mary said coolly. He looked at her sadly.

'I can understand your being angry. But really she has almost made herself ill, and my father has sent her and my sisters away to Harrogate until she's better.'

Mary felt she had been too cold, and tried to make amends.

'I am leaving too, Mr Anstey. Tomorrow. I go to London tomorrow.'

'Tomorrow? To London? And pray – pray, when do you return?'

'I don't know,' she said, and suddenly it seemed silly to be so stiff with the boy she had known since she was a child, her old friend and admirer, the first of her knights. She dropped all her formality and stiffness. 'I don't know if I'll ever come back, except for holidays, now and then. My life can't be here any more.'

'Can't it? Oh Mary, can't it?' He took her hands impulsively, affected by her change of mood, and she did not pull away. 'I'm independent now, and you are of age too. Our parents cannot oppose anything we want. Mary, couldn't you marry me? You know how I feel about you.'

'I know,' Mary said gently. 'I'm sorry, John. It wasn't my parents who opposed before, you know, it was me.'

'They told me that, but I didn't believe it, quite. You had looked at me – and said things – I believed you cared for me. I still believe it,' he said stubbornly, overcoming his shyness.

'I do care for you, John, but it's impossible. I can't live here, like this.' She freed a hand, to wave it at the city of York. 'There's a bigger world that I belong to. And especially now, after what's happened, I can't stay here.' She resumed her formality like a mantle, and gave a slight curtsy. 'Goodbye, Mr Anstey. I'm glad I had the chance to say goodbye to you before I leave.'

But for once John did not follow her example. He stood his ground, his face a little red, and his eyes defiant, and said, 'You'll come back, one day, when you've had enough of the wide world. And I'll be waiting for you. I'll wait for ever for you, if needs be. You'll come back to me one day.'

Mary stared at him for a moment, and bit her lip, and turned quickly away down the busy street.

CHAPTER TWENTY

Jemima opened Flora's letter and scanned it quickly, while Allen, lying on the sofa under a blanket, watched her face expectantly until it broke into a satisfied smile.

'It is done?' he said. 'William has a ship?'

'It is done. He is made first lieutenant into the *Albemarle*, 28, going out to the Leeward Islands.'

'First lieutenant in a small frigate will be the best possible start for him,' Allen said with satisfaction. 'And I imagine he is lucky to get the place.'

'Flora says her father-in-law had very little to do, now that Lord Howe is First Lord. She says that to the West India veterans the name of Morland is all.'

She read on. '*Albemarle* sails on the eighteenth, so he will be at sea at Christmas. What a shame! But I am so pleased for him. It was what he wanted.'

Allen smiled privately at this change in her attitude. 'And what of the others?'

'Not much. James is settled in, and gone down to Windsor for Christmas with the Court. Flora and Mary have been to a concert – Mary and Horatio danced together at Charlton House,' she turned the page, 'they are all going to Wolvercote for Christmas because Windsor is too Germanic and dull. And that's all.' She folded the page and looked up at him, smiling. 'It seems they are all well and happy, from the tone of the letter. Flora becomes a good correspondent.'

'Perhaps in time she will become a good mother, too,' Allen said. Jemima had grown so used to bringing up Louisa and Jack that she no longer thought of them as Flora's children, and for a moment she was confused.

'But she's not pregnant – oh, you mean Louisa?'

'And Jack; but Louisa mostly.'

'Well, it is a change for the better that she has Louisa at the boarding school in Chelsea, which is at least closer than Yorkshire. And she's taking her to Wolvercote for Christmas. I think now that Louisa is getting to an age where Flora can take an interest in her appearance and marriage prospects, she may become fonder of her. Flora never found anything interesting in babies, and who can blame her?'

'Hm. I hope it answers, because I miss my little girl very much. I have no one to warm my lap now.'

'Nonsense, you have Lucy. But I know what you mean,' she added, with half a sigh. 'It is very quiet with the children gone. I'm so glad now that we have our second family. Henry and Jack and Lucy will stop us growing dull.'

'And perhaps in time Edward will provide us with some grandchildren,' Allen said wryly.

'Edward hasn't time for girls, with all he does,' Jemima said defensively.

'I don't think he'd have any time for them even if he did have time for them,' he said. Jemima wondered how much he meant by that, and decided not to pursue it.

'I think he's a man who will fall in love late in life, and do it properly. For the moment I'm just grateful that he is so *un*-preoccupied, and hard-working, because otherwise you'd be doing it all, and the surgeon said you must rest, or you'd have another attack.'

'I know what he said, and he's a damn fool,' Allen said.

'He said it was brought on by the strain—'

'Of my birthday, yes. That is a nice irony, don't you think?'

'Oh, darling! I wish I could have kept all that from you,' Jemima said, taking his hand.

'Nonsense. We share things – everything. That's how we've always gone on. And as soon as I'm off this damned sofa—'

'You should be in bed by rights, and if I could have got you to stay there you wouldn't *be* on the sofa,' Jemima said sternly. 'And when you're well enough to get up, you and I are both going to retire from the business of running the Morland estate and the Morland family and, in your case, half of Yorkshire, and concentrate instead on the longest love-affair in history.'

He kissed her hand. 'You would really give up your horses for me? Now that's what I call real love.'

'Ah, well, I didn't say I'd give up the horses—' Jemima began, and he laughed. 'All right,' she said sheepishly, 'but horses will be part of our pleasure, and only the pleasant parts, I promise. The steward can govern all that as well, under Edward.'

'Yes, Edward's old enough now to take up the reins, and Godman is very experienced.'

'Hm. I just wish his name was Clement, though,' Jemima mused, looking into the fire, her hand still warm in her husband's. 'Do you think we can get him to change it?'

'Anything's possible,' Allen said. 'What time is it? Is it time for tea yet? I could relish a dish of tea – or two – and some hot, buttered teacakes.'

'You're master of the house, you shall have tea at any time you choose,' Jemima said, jumping up with an energy that belied her age and going briskly to the door. As her hand reached the doorknob, Allen called her back.

'Jemima!'

'Yes?' she turned inquiringly, and he smiled at her with affectionate amusement.

'Why don't you just ring the bell?'

In September 1787, on a beautiful, sunny autumn day when the leaves were just beginning to yellow, Henri Maria Fitzjames Stuart, Comte de Strathord, was riding in a closed carriage down the precipitous and fashionable Rue St Jacques. Beside him his little daughter sat very upright, as she had been taught, and in a pensive silence which allowed Henri to continue with his own thoughts. The Rue

St Jacques was the heart of the Quartier Ecossais, and it reminded him relentlessly of Madeleine. Here he had lived as Monsieur Ecosse, and woven his wicked plan around her. Here he had first loved her, and spent that long, lovely summer before their fraudulent marriage getting to know her, walking with her in the Jardins du Luxembourg.

Such a day as this, when the sunshine was that soft, deep yellow that only comes in autumn, when the warmth held a warning of cold to come, making it the more grateful, when the world was so beautiful and yet so poignant that one felt one must seize life and live it to the full, while there was time – on such a day Madeleine, loved and lost, seemed very close to him. And there was a great deal of her in Henriette-Louise – he thanked God for it. In her steady, sensible gaze, in her calm acceptance of whatever fate should mete out for her, and in her quick and lively humour, Henri found her mother over again. But in her looks there seemed nothing of him or Madeleine: Héloise was only herself – the last Stuart princess, as he had come to think of her.

She was not really pretty, he knew that. She had a breadth of face – presumably from her mother – which gave her too much bone, too many planes; for since the Queen was the style of beauty, what was required from a young woman was a little, pointed, kittenish face. Her large, dark, melancholy eyes, which might have come straight from a portrait of King Charles or any of his kin, were not an asset in a society which admired light eyes; and her nose was a trifle too long and her mouth a trifle too full for true beauty.

Yet altogether her face had such charm, and such sparkling vitality, that he could never look at her without thinking her beautiful, and he had observed her in enough company to know he was not the only one who thought so. When he took her riding in the Bois de Boulogne, in her emerald-green riding habit, with a feathered tricorne hat perched upon her glossy black ringlets, sidesaddle upon the white pony he hired for her, she attracted every eye, and strolling couples would stop to watch her go by. Old men would lift their hats to her, and smile, and dames would clasp their hands in enthusiasm at the pretty sight. And Héloise, who loved the whole world, would smile back, lighting her rather dark, sad face, and leaving a wistfulness behind her.

The years since Madeleine's death, the years in which he had devoted himself to her, had been happy and fruitful ones. He had worked hard, made himself such a reputation as a designer of interiors that what he did had transcended the barriers of prejudice and had come to be regarded more as an art-form than a trade, so that no one regarded him as ungentlemanly for earning his living by it. His fees were so enormous that no one was ever so indelicate as to ask what he would charge for transforming their house, and a bill would pass between Duncan and the customer's treasurer like a kind of immaculate conception. He had turned his hand recently to garden design and architecture also, and had travelled all over France, leaving his mark upon posterity.

All he did, he did for Héloise, to make her proud of him, and to provide her with the background of wealth that he felt she ought to have. Indulged and adored at every turn, she might have become insufferably spoilt; but Henri felt that Madeleine's spirit hovered around her child, guarding her from vanity and pride, and directing her energy towards love. For she did love; it was her driving force. From the moment she first opened her eyes, she smiled at every face that hung above her crib. From the moment she could walk, she used her mastery of her legs to take her running from one embrace to another. She brimmed over with love for her nurses, the servants, the dogs, the horses who drew her carriage, the sparrows outside the window, the beggars at the gate of the park. She wept over a pigeon with a trailing wing, and kept it in her bedroom and fed it bread and milk until it was well enough to be released. She would have hugged the beggar at the street corner, sores and all, had her nurse not restrained her, when he played a tune especially for her on his thin whistle-pipe. When she was five, she gave away her new shoes to a pauper child who ran beside her carriage with bare feet.

But most of all she loved Tante Ismène, and Uncle Meurice, and Papa; and Henri, swelling and burgeoning with her love like a plant watered after long drought, grew sleek and happy and kind. He had not entirely given up his old ways: a child's love, however, spiritually satisfying, did not fulfil his physical urges. He had mistresses, long-standing and casual, but he was circumspect about it, so that Héloise should not find out. He liked to drink and dance and play cards, and though he restrained himself to moderation on Héloise's account, sometimes he felt a need to break out that could not be denied.

On those occasions, he had two plans. The one was to tell his daughter that he would be away for a day or two, and to go off on a debauch at the house of one of his rich friends, drinking himself unconscious, gambling, making love, just as he pleased. At other times he would change his clothes for something simpler and return to his old haunts round the Cour du Commerce, where he resumed the identity of Monsieur Ecosse. He had made many friends amongst the lawyers and students there, and liked to drink and talk with them.

His chief friend there was a newcomer to Paris, a farmer's son from the Champenois called Danton, who had graduated in law and recently bought himself a practice and taken a wife. Danton's Gabrielle was just another such as Madeleine, which had been Henri's first attraction to Danton's house. There was always soup and bread and wine and a bright fire and a well-swept hearth at Danton's house, and a cheerful, friendly, sensible woman to greet his friends and make them comfortable.

Danton himself was an astonishing man, with a face so scarred and ugly that it by-passed the normal rules of beauty and had an attractiveness of its own. At two he had been gored in the face by a cow, trampled by a herd of pigs at five, disfigured by small pox when he was ten, and kicked in the face by a bull when he was fourteen. He was stockily-built, barrel-chested, short-necked, and large-headed, full of vitality, brilliant ideas, fervour, and untamed sexuality.

At Danton's house Henri met other lawyers, printers, unemployed actors, novelists and pamphleteers and poets and students, and here he was able to drink deep and listen to the conversation of this naturally rebellious group. The new philosophies took on a different slant when mouthed by these men rather than Ismène's polite and well-bred circle. Everything was ruthlessly criticized, and brisk and sometimes even sensible plans worked out for governing the country and, more particularly, Paris, when the time came. And they were sure the time would come. We cannot, they said, be satisfied for ever with muddle and incompetence, corruption and jobbery and the inequalities of wealth and poverty.

Though it was a release to become, for a little while, Monsieur Ecosse, Henri generally returned home after those debauches sobered and thoughtful. The time *was* coming, he thought, and if Paris went up in flames, he would have to learn to live in fire if he was not to perish. And he was determined not to perish: he had to survive, for Henriette-Louise's sake.

The carriage lurched on the uneven cobbles, breaking his train of thought and bringing him back to the present, and he found his daughter's eyes upon him, and smiled reassuringly at her.

'You were thinking very deeply, Papa,' she said.

'I was thinking about your mother,' he said, selecting one thing from the many. 'She would be so pleased that you are to go to school. You must be sure and work hard at your lessons, for she would want you to be an educated lady.'

'And you, Papa? What do you want me to be?'

'Clever, and beautiful, and happy,' he said, 'and since

you are already all three, you have only to be yourself to please me.'

'I hope I shall like it at the convent,' she said thoughtfully, and her eyes were a little apprehensive. 'You won't leave me there and never come back, will you, Papa? I shall see you?'

'Of course you shall, my love. I shall come every Saturday, and take you riding in the Bois de Boulogne, and every Sunday to Mass in the Church of the English Benedictines, and after Mass we shall go and walk in the Jardins du Luxembourg where I first fell in love with your mother.'

'I shall miss going with you to your work, Papa,' she said. Sometimes when Henri had a commission to work upon a chateau away from Paris he had taken Héloïse with him, and those trips had been amongst their happiest times together.

'Well, child, if I am to go anywhere interesting, I shall come and ask the Mother Superior to release you, and you shall come with me – how would that be?'

'Then I am content, Papa. Will there be other girls at the convent?'

'Girls and ladies, the daughters of rich men, and *Dames Pensionnaires*. You will make lots of friends from amongst the nobility, and that will be good, for you have been too much alone.'

'I never felt alone, Papa.'

'But you should have friends of your own age. I'm sure you will like it. Ah, and here we are.' Héloïse looked out of the carriage window with interest, and saw only a wall pierced with heavy closed doors, and a few small windows above.

'Where is it?' she asked in disappointment. 'I thought it would be a grand house.'

'It does not front the road – the courtyard is behind. You'll see.'

The carriage door was opened and they stepped down, and Henri took her hand and opened the heavy, nail-studded door of 171 Rue St Jacques, and it creaked and gave onto a dark, narrow passage. Héloise shivered a little, and thought that it was like a convent in a story after all, and that she didn't like it a bit. She held her father's hand very tightly, and he smiled down at her reassuringly. The passage was like a tunnel under the gatehouse, and at the other end it gave onto a square, sunny courtyard, with many-windowed buildings on either side, and before them was the frontage of the Convent of the Visitation itself.

It was a pleasant, handsome house, square and well-proportioned, with a curved flight of steps leading up to the great door which was open, and square, stone-silled windows, and, to Héloise's pleasure, an *oeuil-de-boeuf* window at the top under the peak of the roof.

'There, isn't that better?' Henri asked.

She smiled and said, 'Much better, Papa. It's a very pretty house.'

'And there's another courtyard behind, with flowers in tubs, and a little green space, and a beautiful old tree full of birds.'

A nun came hurrying out to meet them on the steps. 'Ah, welcome, welcome! Monsieur le Comte – and this is your daughter?'

'Lady Henriette-Louise Stuart,' Henri said.

'I am Sister Matthew,' the nun smiled down at Héloise. 'Why, goodness me, I should have known her at once for a Stuart – do you know, sir, she looks the very image of Princess Henrietta Anne of England – I have seen her portrait. We have many connections with the House of Stuart, you know, and only a few years ago we had the Lady Charlotte Stuart staying here – daughter of Prince Charles Edward, the Prince of Wales I believe his title is. She lived here for many years, and was always very comfortable. I'm sure you will be happy here too, my dear.'

Héloise curtseyed, and gave the nun the benefit of her smile, which made the good sister blink for a moment.

'Thank you, madame,' Henri said. 'Perhaps if we could see my daughter's apartment?'

'Yes, of course, please follow me. I have put her in the rooms overlooking the rear courtyard, as you requested.' An emphasis on the words and a sidelong glance indicated to Henri that a request of that nature would cost him dearly on the bill. Inside the great door, Héloise saw a passage leading right through the house to the sunshine of the rear courtyard, and she looked towards it longingly. But they were climbing the steep, handsome, curved staircase to the left, and from there traversed long corridors of shining floorboards, smelling of quietness and beeswax, a smell she always afterwards associated with convents. Then the sister opened a door and ushered them into what would be Héloise's rooms.

They were very small, as one would expect by the size and age of the building, and unexpectedly bare after the house on the Rue St Anne. There was a sittng room and a bedroom beyond; the floors were polished boards, but there was a good Turkey carpet in the middle of each room; the furniture was sparse, but elegant. Best of all, each had a window looking over the court, and the tree grew up right beside the bedroom window, so that Héloise could look out straight into the branches. The windows were open, and the warm, scented air streamed in from the sunny courtyard, and a collar-dove was cooing throatily somewhere in the branches of the tree.

'When you have a few of your own things about you, and some of your furniture sent over, I think you will find it comfortable enough,' Henri was saying, almost apologetically, but Héloise was gazing out of the window, and turned to them with an expression of delight.

'Oh, but it's *lovely*, Papa! The tree and the windows and – I like it very much! Thank you so much for putting me here, sister. You are very kind.'

Sister Matthew blinked nervously. 'I'm glad you like it, my child. I hope you will be happy with us.'

'I'm *sure* I will – don't you think so, Papa?'

She was so small, and so burning with life, that it filled him with a great pang almost like grief, and he couldn't speak for a moment; only felt in that moment that he would die to preserve her like this, innocent and happy.

Allen stood on the south side of Bachelor Hill and looked with content at the field before him. This had always been corn land, and over the years it had yielded less and less as the soil grew poorer. Now, thanks to the enclosure, he hoped to change things. The field was still hedged with hurdles, for the mixture of thorn and hazel and beech which he had had planted was still in its infancy, but within the fence was a fine sight, row upon row of sturdy young potato plants, of his own crossbreed, Morland. He had written a paper about them, and sent it to the Royal Society, and depending on the success of this crop, he might write and have published a pamphlet.

Two men and a woman were working their way along the rows, cleaning the crop, and as the nearest came within earshot he straightened up and called a greeting, to which Allen replied genially, 'It's a fine sight, isn't it, Tom?'

'Well, master, that's according,' Tom said cautiously. Resistance to Allen's 'new-fangled' ideas was strongest amongst the labourers, and he had yet to convince his tenants that there was any point in planting corn in rows, but in his own fields they had to follow his ideas.

'Now admit, Tom, that this was a poor field, and that these plants are doing better than the wheat did last year. And when the crop is gathered, I shall turn the young stirks in to graze on the green parts, and that will manure the field, and then you shall see next year what the soil will produce!'

'Well, I dare say,' Tom said, humouring Allen, and then added with a sly smile, 'but why take up the crop, Master Morland? Why not let the stirks eat it in the field?'

'Now you know perfectly well these potatoes are not cattle food,' Allen rose to the bait as always. 'They are

416

quite delicious, if you dress them properly. You must par-boil them, then slice 'em up with butter and sugar and mace and nutmeg, and bake 'em in a pastry case with a covering of thick custard, and that's a dish fit for the King himself.'

'God bless him,' Tom added fervently – the King's illness last winter, the winter of 1788/9, had revealed his great popularity with the ordinary people. 'Well, master, if you say so, it must be so. But I have heard that in Lancashire, where they have these new cotton factories, that they keep their Irish workers in great sheds like cattle, and feed 'em on potatoes.'

'Even if that were true,' Allen replied, 'it would only go to show how good and wholesome a food potatoes are.' Tom murmured agreement, but Allen could see that he thought it only proved that potatoes were fit for nothing but cattle and Irish peasants. He changed the subject. 'How is your wife, Tom? Better, I hope.'

'Main better, thank you, sir. Her La'ship was so kind as to send and inquire after her yesterday, and that cheered my missus so much that she's up and about again today.'

'Good, good. Then I hope to see you both at Church on Sunday,' Allen said, and turned away to complete his walk and return to the house. He was coming up for seventy-four, but he still kept remarkably fit and healthy, and he enjoyed a good long walk every day, though he didn't ride much any more, never having been a great horseman, and finding now that the hard saddle and the jolting hurt his bones. When he reached the house, the steward, Godman, came out of the barbican, which Allen and Jemima had had converted into a cottage for him, and said that there was a man waiting at the house to see him, with a complaint about a troublesome neighbour. Allen was no longer Justice of the Peace – he had asked permission to resign when he retired from actively running the estate four years ago – but the people had got so used to coming to him with their problems and requests that they still automatically came up to the house instead of going to the new man.

When he had dealt with the man and sent him away, Oxhey brought him a letter which had arrived in his absence, and he sat down on the windowseat of the drawing room to read it. It was from Mary, who in common with much of London society had gone to Weymouth in the wake of the Court. After the King's terrible illness during the winter – the doctors had called it 'flying gout', as they supposed the gouty humours in his feet had flown up and settled in his head, causing the madness – his recovery had been celebrated by a thanksgiving service in St Paul's Cathedral on St George's Day, after which the King and Queen and the Court had gone on the first extensive Royal Tour of the century. The King's popularity had been amply proved by the warm reception he received everywhere, and in Weymouth, a small fishing-town on the coast of Dorset, which was blessed with a wide bay of firm sand, he had settled down to bathe for his health, and, incidentally, to make Weymouth's fortune.

The rich and fashionable naturally followed the King's example, and Weymouth was *the* place to be that summer. Lord and Lady Chelmsford went there, taking Mary and Lord Chelmsford's half-sister, fourteen-year-old Amelia, with them: Allen's friend Charles, the fifth Earl, had died in 1788 at the age of sixty, and Flora was now Countess of Chelmsford. Mary's letter told of the delights of sea bathing, and how when the King went into the sea he was followed by a second bathing-machine containing a band playing 'God Save the King'.

'I imagine His Majesty must get very tired of that tune, for it is all we hear all day when the King is on the sands,' Mary said. 'There have been one or two little awkwardnesses, as one would expect from a remote and unsophisticated town. The Mayor of this place failed to kneel before the King, and when the equerry spoke sharply to him, he said that he could not kneel on account of having a wooden leg. The King passed it off very graciously. There is nothing much here in the way of a promenade, and no public rooms, but one or two country nobles have large

418

houses of decent sort which do very well instead, and since the Court was known to be coming, all sorts of new traders have moved in, so one can get what one wants in the shops. The worst inconvenience is the smell of paint everywhere, since every inn and ship is in a state of hasty redecoration.

'We are staying in the house of Lord John Courteney, which has a fine view over the bay and is very conveniently situated for the sands. Lady Chelmsford is much admired, and I must say I have never seen her in better looks. We have had some hunting over very pretty country, though rather too steep for good runs, and Colonel Mauleverer, a friend of Lord John's who is in the party, paid me a handsome compliment on my riding, and said that he had heard Yorkshire ladies combined grace with skill in the saddle, but was sure I must be outstanding even amongst them. It was all great nonsense, of course, but said in a very pleasant, gentlemanly manner, and so I did not object.

'We had a ball at Exeter House last night, at which the gentlemen of the militia were much in evidence, which was pleasant for the young ladies, as it meant there was no lack of partners. I danced a great deal, sometimes with Lord Chelmsford and with Lord John, but also with Colonel Mauleverer and some other gentlemen. We did not go to our beds until three o'clock this morning.

'After Weymouth, the Court is to go on to Exeter, and then to Plymouth for a naval review. I wonder if William will be there? Lady Chelmsford's naval friends tell me that *Albemarle* came in to Tor Bay last week, and that Tor Bay is not far from Plymouth. We do not go with the Court, being bound for Bath to meet up with the Dowager Countess, Lord Meldon, and Lord and Lady Carlton. Colonel Mauleverer says he will also be in Bath at the end of the week, so perhaps I may see him at the Lower Rooms on Friday.'

Allen read the letter through with amusement at the frequent mention of the Colonel's name. So he was the new beau, was he? Mary's letters – and Flora's too – gave a pretty clear view of the progress of Mary's affairs. There

419

was always someone, sometimes several at once, for Mary never lacked admirers, but they never lasted more than a few weeks. It would be all 'Captain So-and-so says' and 'Captain So-and-so thinks' for a month, and then his name would drop into oblivion, and the letters would be full of Sir What-you-may-call-him's opinions. But for all her enthusiasm, Mary was never touched by any deep emotion, and flitted, heart-whole and cheerful, like a butterfly from one flower to the next.

Sometimes, when she had nothing better to worry about, Jemima worried about Mary's having got to the age of twenty-five and being still unmarried, but Allen had a shrewd suspicion that Mary was simply enjoying herself too much to want to change her condition. She also had before her the example of what had happened to Flora when she married too young and too hastily, and perhaps she had taken that example too much to heart. And then there was the possibility, which Allen did not entirely discount, that she was really in love with John Anstey, though she would not marry him. Certainly there seemed to be something guarding her heart, for how ever many devoted beaux she had around her, she never seemed in any danger of falling in love with them.

Having finished the letter, Allen was about to turn to the newspapers when the door opened and Edward's dog preceded him in, and ran smiling up to Allen to press a cold nose into his hand. Edward said, 'Oh, Father, I'm glad you're back from your walk. There's something I wanted to talk to you about.' In his leather boots, stout breeches, and plain brown coat, with his hair tied behind with a bit of riband, Edward was the essence of a country squire, and made Allen, who sported a striped silk waistcoat and a wig, feel positively like a Macaroni by contrast. Edward dressed the same way for three-fourths of the year, and didn't seem to care what anyone thought of him, changing his style only when his friend Chetwyn came to stay. Edward was twenty-seven, and showed no signs of wanting to marry, and though Allen had suggested several possible matches for him recently, he had refused all of them. Twenty-seven was not so very old for a man, but Allen would have been happier if the next generation had been made a start upon, for he was over his three-score-and-ten, and none of his children had produced an heir yet.

Edward sat down on the windowseat next to him. 'It's about one of the farmers – the man Grimes. He's going deeper into debt all the time, and it can't go on any longer. You know he didn't plant the bottom field this year?'

'I know. What's to be done?'

'He's come to me offering to sell his land to us. If we buy it, we'll have the land almost clear to Acomb Wood, apart from those two ings at Otterwood Bank. The problem is that Mother isn't going to like it because Grimes says it's all on account of the enclosure that he's failed, and she worries so about that sort of thing.'

Allen sighed. 'I know, and there have been problems—' He thought of old Gaffer Truman; and there had been others. 'But I know Grimes. He's a diehard of the old school, and he *won't* improve, and you can't go on and on taking out of the land without putting back.'

'He says he couldn't afford to drain and fence—'

'He wouldn't grow the new crops, that's the long and short of it. He slaughters his cattle in the autumn because he can't feed them through the winter, so he has no winter manure – and they're a poor, scabby, sway-backed sort of kine in any case. He and his wife are thriftless and short-sighted – but still—'

'Yes – but still,' Edward gave a grim smile. 'Mother will say they are our responsibility.'

'We shall have to think something out. If we buy the land, we shall have to do something for Grimes and his family, or they'll spend the money and end up at the poorhouse – and then they'll be our responsibility in any case. Let me think about it, Ned, and we'll see what we can come up with.'

'Right. I thought I'd better see you alone first.' He

nodded towards the papers. 'Anything of interest in there? Anything more about this French business?'

'I haven't had time to read them yet. But the French business is most extraordinary, you know, Ned. For a monarchy so absolute to have ended so suddenly, completely, and bloodlessly is almost beyond belief.'

'We had to have years of civil war before our revolution was done,' Edward said. 'I suppose their King must be more reasonable than ours was.'

Allen shook his head doubtfully. What he knew of Louis XVI suggested that he was indifferent rather than reasonable, and yet could any King have laid down his power so easily? In the January of that year, after growing discontent amongst the French middle classes with the years of mismanagement, bungling and debt, there had been a call for an Estates-General, a meeting of all the representatives of the three estates, the first such to be held for nearly two hundred years. The three estates were the Lords, the Clergy, and the Commons, the latter being recruited from the class of wealthy merchants and lawyers, who had a great deal of the wealth of the country but none of the power. It was generally understood that a serious programme of reform, social, financial, and political, would be demanded by the third estate, while the fact that the King had consented to an Estates-General at all suggested that the reforms would be granted.

The Estates-General met in May, and there had been trouble at once over the voting procedure, for normally one vote was taken from each estate, and since the clergy always voted with the nobles, the vote of the third estate would be useless. Then there was a demand for all the estates to meet together, for normally certain matters were discussed only by the two upper estates, in conference with the King. The third estate claimed to be the only true representative of the people – or 'nation' as they called them – and awarded itself the title of National Assembly. In this it was supported by a number of liberal nobles and clergy who were also eager for reform: the tide of reformist zeal had reached its flood, Allen thought, and the *Philosophes*, such as he had met in France over the years, had sufficiently influenced general opinion that there could be no turning it back.

The King had ordered the estates to meet separately, as was the custom, and when the rebellious deputies had refused to leave the hall, he had sent soldiers to clear them out. But a combination of the unwillingness of the soldiers, the hostility of the crowd outside, and the determination of a group of reformist nobles who held the door had turned them back, upon which the King had reputedly said, 'Oh well, devil take it, let them stay.'

A few days later he had ordered the rest of the nobles and clergy to rejoin the third estate, and the self-constituted National Assembly had settled back to go about its work of reorganizing the structure of government.

'A revolution so complete, to take place in two months, without a single drop of blood being shed is most remarkable,' Allen said. 'I can only suppose it was because everyone wanted it, and no one opposed it.'

Edward grinned. 'Ah, but now the fun will begin! Everyone will have his own ideas of what's most important, and they will wrangle like dogs over their bones. Do you remember the Lighting Committee in York, how every man on it was convinced his own street corner was the most essential to be lit, and everyone had solid, unanswerable reasons for his opinion? If the French are like other men, there will be a great deal of wrangling, and very little doing, in this Assembly of theirs.'

'Ah well, men may be a deal worse employed than in arguing – at least that hurts no one. And the worst sort of men for arguing are those who have nothing better to do with their time. A man with a farm to run, a field to till, or a loom to serve is a great deal too busy to argue about politics. And talking of being busy, where *is* your mother?'

'Out in the home paddock with James, trying to get a saddle on Ptolemy,' Edward said. Allen started up in alarm, for Ptolemy was Jemima's new colt, and had steadfastly refused to be backed, bucking and rearing so furiously that Allen had been alarmed for her safety and had begged her to return it to the field – not being in a position to forbid her, as he would have liked, to have anything more to do with it. 'Oh, it's all right, Papa,' Edward hastened to reassure him. 'Jamie won't let her get too near. She was for backing the beast while you were out taking your walk, and Jamie said *he* would do any climbing aboard that was to be done. He'll manage things, don't worry.'

'I'm going to see, all the same,' Allen said determinedly, making for the door.

'I'll come with you,' Edward said. 'I must say, you know, James has changed very much since he went to Court. He's much kinder and more thoughtful now.'

'I think he has got the fret out of his feet,' Allen said, unconsciously using one of Jemima's horseman terms. 'And he was horrified by the way the King was treated during his illness. I think it woke him up to the value of a well-regulated and loving family, such as he came from. But do you think him changed in essentials?'

'Perhaps not,' Edward said. 'He's quieter, but he's still the James who lives for pleasure. Being at Court suits him, that's all – he can do what he wants, and not be different from anyone else. He said to me—' Edward grinned suddenly as he remembered it, 'he said to me, "Thank heaven I can live amongst people who don't make a terrible fuss about a little adultery." '

'Oh dear,' Allen said. 'Perhaps he was joking. Don't tell your mother he said that, for heaven's sake.'

Out in the home paddock they discovered that Jemima had Ptolemy on a lunge-rein, and that somehow the saddle had been got onto him. She herself was standing in the middle holding the rein while James, red with exertion, held the colt's head, and he was going round at an erratic trot into which he flung a wild backwards kick every four or five paces.

Allen started forward in exasperation that she should be

doing such a dangerous thing herself, and Ptolemy, seeing newcomers approaching, began to show off like a naughty child, reared up, breaking James's hold, and began to charge about the paddock, bucking in excitement. Everyone yelled at once, James had to dodge very sharply out of the way, and Edward scrambled over the fence to try to get to his mother, who instead of dropping the lunge-rein and making for safety, was hanging onto it and trying to control the creature. There was a moment of noise and confusion, and then Edward managed to get his hands on the rope, from which he could not detach Jemima, while James with a sort of despairing courage flung himself at Ptolemy's head as the colt pranced past and caught the headcollar. Ptolemy was very full of himself, but not stupid, and seeing himself heavily outnumbered he came to a halt and dropped his nose sweetly, though he eyed Jemima very wickedly as she came up, winding in the long rope.

'You disturbed him,' she complained to Edward and Allen. 'He was just beginning to settle down and go quite nicely, and you spoiled his concentration.'

'Oh Mother!' Edward laughed in exasperation, but Allen was crosser.

'It was very foolhardy of you – you might have been hurt. I've begged you not to have anything to do with that colt, Jemima, and as soon as my back is turned – it's most unfair of you, to take advantage of me like that.'

'Oh darling, I'm sorry,' she said contritely. 'I didn't mean to be deceiving you. But you're wrong about this fellow – he's a good colt really, just a little too vain and high spirited, not wicked. Now isn't that so, James?'

James leaned against the fence and drew out an exquisite handkerchief to mop his brow. 'If I had known what I was to be let in for, I'd have gone to Weymouth with the Court instead of coming home for a visit. You see what being a dutiful son gets you, Edward, by way of reward? I am exhausted, covered in dust, and all but trampled by this mad horse.'

'Oh Jamie,' said Jemima, 'you know that isn't true.'

'If you must have him broken,' Allen said, 'why don't you let someone else do it? There are plenty of grooms whose job it is to take these risks.'

'Because no one else understands him as I do. You'll be glad when he's winning races and earning you golden guineas, and then you'll thank me,' Jemima said stubbornly.

'I'd sooner have you in one piece,' Allen said, taking her hand. 'Please, promise me you won't do this sort of thing again. Have the grooms handle him, and just supervise matters yourself.'

'Yes, Mother, it isn't proper for a lady of your age and standing to be handling horses,' Edward said solemnly, and when she looked at him, about to protest, he winked at her, and she subsided.

'Oh, very well,' she grumbled. 'If you are determined to make me old before my time—' But she tucked her hand under Allen's arm comfortably, and allowed Edward to take Ptolemy from her as they walked back towards the house.

A groom came out and received the horse, and Edward and James walked ahead of their parents, James brushing himself down ostentatiously and saying, 'I shall be glad to get back to Court. The horses there generally keep at least two feet on the ground at the same time.'

'Have you decided when you are going back, Jamie?' Jemima asked. 'Not until the autumn, I hope?'

'Well, to tell the truth, Mama, I've been thinking of a change of direction. I've been considering the army, if Papa can stump up for a commission.'

'The army? That sounds rather energetic for an idle fellow like you,' Edward said.

'Oh, not really. It's a pleasant life, by all accounts, the army in time of peace. Lots of balls, and smart reviews, and marching about, and jolly red coats that the ladies love. Quite the life for me, I should think.'

'You are grown tired of Court?' Jemima asked. James met her eye seriously.

'There are things that go on that I can't like, Mama. You have always thought me a pretty hopeless rake, but compared with the Prince of Wales and his friends I'm an angel upon earth. And the King's getting old, and who knows, his illness may come back on him at any moment, and I don't want to witness again what I witnessed last winter. And if the King should die—' He shrugged, and Jemima was pleased at this evidence of a kind heart under James's appearance of idle sophistication.

'If it's what you want, James, then I don't see why it shouldn't be done,' Allen said. 'Better that you should have some occupation than live solely for pleasure – that only makes a man think ill of himself in the long run.'

'Must it be the army though?' Jemima said. 'Would you not like to go into the Church?'

'Oh Mother, really,' Edward exclaimed, while James grinned at the idea.

Jemima went on stubbornly, 'It's as gentlemanly a calling, and a great deal safer. And we'd have you at home more.'

'The army is safe enough in peacetime, Mama,' James said. 'I wouldn't be thinking of it at all if I thought I might have to do any fighting.'

They walked on companionably towards the house, and when they went into the yard they saw a strange horse there, tied to a ring and looking as though it had been ridden hard.

'A visitor?' Jemima said. 'Now who could that be?' The horse shifted its weight and sneezed, and taking a closer look at it, Jemima said, 'That's Sir John Anstey's gelding, surely?'

'Business then, for me,' Allen said. 'If it was social, he'd have come in the carriage, and brought the young people.'

'He's probably come to shoot me for not marrying any of his daughters yet,' James said languidly, but it was only a joke. All the unpleasantness had died down and been forgotten, and though Sir John was a little uneasy in

James's presence, his friendship with Jemima and Allen was restored to its old footing.

He was waiting in the hall for them when they went inside, and Oxhey came forward to announce him, but he did not wait upon formality.

'Ah, Sir Allen! Your servant, ma'am, young gentlemen. Sir Allen, have you heard the news from France?'

'What news?'

'Ah, you have not then. I thought perhaps you'd not have heard it yet.' He flourished a newspaper excitedly. 'It's in the paper, hot from London, and as soon as I read it I said to Lady Anstey, by God, madam, I said, I'll wager Sir Allen won't have heard this yet, and so I came straight over. I tell you, sir, it's a bad business, a bad business!'

'What is it, Sir John?' Allen said, beginning to feel apprehensive as he held his hand out for the proferred paper. Sir John looked round them solemnly, gathering his audience.

'Just three days since, sir, in Paris, a great mob of common people marched upon the castle – what's its damn name? – the Bastille, and stormed it, sir, and took it, against the King's soldiers, and cannon, and everything. They tore it down, and murdered everyone in it, and released all the prisoners, and marched off with them. It's a revolution, sir – and you mark me, it's only the beginning. Mob rule, anarchy, what you will! By God, sir, there'll be the devil to pay now! What do you think of that, sir?' he concluded triumphantly. Allen had the paper in his hands and was trying to read the account of the matter, but could not take it in, and when he lifted his eyes Sir John was still staring at him, a monument of disapproval and excitement at having been the one with the news. 'Well, sir? Eh?' Anstey prompted.

'Good God, sir,' was all Allen could say.

DYNASTY 1:
THE FOUNDING

Cynthia Harrod-Eagles

Triumphantly heralding the mighty Morland Dynasty
– an epic saga of one family's fortune and fate through
five hundred years of history. A story as absorbing and
richly diverse as the history of the English-speaking
people themselves.

THE FOUNDING

Power and prestige are the burning ambitions of
Edward Morland, rich sheep farmer and landowner.

He arranges a marriage. A marriage that will be the
first giant step in the founding of the Morland Dynasty.

A dynasty that will be forged by his son Robert, more
poet than soldier. And Eleanor, ward of the powerful
Beaufort family. Proud and aloof, and consumed by her
secret love for Richard, Duke of York.

And so with THE FOUNDING, The Morland
Dynasty begins – with a story of fierce hatred and war,
love and desire, running through the turbulent years of
the Wars of the Roses.

DYNASTY 2:
THE DARK ROSE
Cynthia Harrod-Eagles

The marriage of Eleanor Courteney and Robert
Morland heralded the founding of the great Morland
Dynasty. Now, Paul, their great grandson, is caught up
in the conflict of Kings and sees, within his family, a
bitter struggle bearing seeds of death and destruction.

And Nanette, his beloved niece, maid-in-waiting to the
tragic Anne Boleyn, is swept into the flamboyant
intrigues of life at court until, leaving heartbreak
behind, she is claimed by a passionate love.

A magnificent saga of revenge, glory and intrigue in
the turbulent years of the early Tudors as the Morlands
crest the waves of power.

DYNASTY 3:
THE PRINCELING

Cynthia Harrod-Eagles

The third volume in the magnificent Dynasty series.

Elizabeth I is now England's Queen and the Catholic Morlands are threatened by the upsurge of Protestantism. They must seek new spheres of influence if they are to restore the family fortunes.

John, heir to Morland Place, rides north to wed the daughter of Black Will Percy, a Borderland cattle lord. He learns through blood and battle how to win proud Mary's heart.

Lettice, his gentle sister, is married to the ruthless, ambitious Scottish baron, Lord Robert Hamilton, who teaches her the bitter lesson of survival in the bleak and treacherous court of Mary Queen of Scots.

Continuing the powerful story begun in THE FOUNDING and THE DARK ROSE, THE PRINCELING sees the Morlands fighting for their religion, their inheritance and their love.

The complete Dynasty Series by Cynthia Harrod-Eagles

1. The Founding	£5.99		12. The Victory	£5.99
2. The Dark Rose	£6.99		13. The Regency	£5.99
3. The Princeling	£5.99		14. The Campaigners	£5.99
4. The Oak Apple	£5.99		15. The Reckoning	£5.99
5. The Black Pearl	£6.99		16. The Devil's Horse	£5.99
6. The Long Shadow	£5.99		17. The Poison Tree	£5.99
7. The Chevalier	£5.99		18. The Abyss	£6.99
8. The Maiden	£5.99		19. The Hidden Shore	£6.99
9. The Flood-Tide	£5.99		20. The Winter Journey	£6.99
10. The Tangled Thread	£5.99		21. The Outcast	£6.99
11. The Emperor	£5.99		22. The Mirage	£6.99

The prices shown above are correct at time of going to press. However, the publishers reserve the right to increase prices on covers from those previously advertised without prior notice.

WARNER BOOKS   WARNER BOOKS
P.O. Box 121, Kettering, Northants NN14 4ZQ
Tel: 01832 737525, Fax: 01832 733076
Email: aspenhouse@FSBDial.co.uk

POST AND PACKING:
Payments can be made as follows: cheque, postal order (payable to Warner Books) or by credit cards. Do not send cash or currency.

All U.K. Orders	**FREE OF CHARGE**
E.E.C. & Overseas	25% of order value

Name (Block Letters) _____

Address_____

_____

Post/zip code:_____

☐ Please keep me in touch with future Warner publications

☐ I enclose my remittance £_____

☐ I wish to pay by Visa/Access/Mastercard/Eurocard

Card Expiry Date

_____